MY UNHOLY EVERYTHING

IMMORTAL HOLLYWOOD
BOOK THREE

STORMY O'HARA

AUTHOR'S NOTE

My Unholy Everything is the third and final book in the Immortal Hollywood series. It can be read as a stand-alone, but it does include some spoilers for the series, so if you haven't read the first two books and think you might want to, I recommend starting at the beginning. If you don't mind a few spoilers, then go ahead!

This book includes an FMC (female main character) who identifies as an open-minded, questioning and cursing Christian who struggles with some aspects of her faith, including purity culture. This book is not anti-Christian or pro-Christian in any way.

This is a spicy vampire romance and contains on the page sexual encounters between humans and vampires, vampires drinking human blood, humans drinking vampire blood, some mild violence, staking, shooting, crossbow usage, and a whole heap of cursing.

There is also mention of death of a parent, an abusive father, pregnancy, birth and PTSD.

These books are vampire lite, not too heavy or dark, but still may not be suitable for some readers.

Look after yourself and read with care.

To all the good girls with hidden desires, your secrets are safe with me...

PROLOGUE

pril

I'D HAD a crush on Finn Huxley my entire life. Growing up, he was the boy across the road who mowed our lawn and did odd jobs around the place for Mom when Dad was busy with preaching and tending to his flock. But it was the first day of ninth grade when I knew I was really in trouble. Finn had been away at baseball camp for the summer, and when he came back his shoulders were broader, his skin tanned, his curls of dark hair were longer and wilder, and there was a new kind of mischief in his dark green eyes.

I fell so hard that year, but I kept my feelings hidden. Finn was way out of my league. They called him Hardball Huxley. He hit home runs. He dated cheerleaders. He was popular and cool. But me? I was the preacher's daughter, the book-worm, the goody two shoes that people were only nice to so I would help them with their homework or let them cheat off my tests.

I didn't really have many friends, but I did have my mom.

But that year while I was drooling over Finn's tight t-shirts and baseball swing, my mom was getting sick.

It was Finn who found me screaming over her one morning when she wouldn't get up.

It was Finn who drove us to the hospital in Culpepper.

When my father gave the sermon, it was Finn who stood beside me at her funeral.

Finn became my rock, and I became something to him too.

One night, just before graduation, we were out hiding from our dads in a cornfield, and he kissed me. It was the most romantic moment of my life. My first kiss. With a guy I had crushed on for forever. A guy who had become sexier than the sin my father always warned me about.

But Finn had a reputation, and my father would never have allowed us to be together.

So we started sneaking around. We spent those last few weeks of school kissing in cornfields and just about any place we knew for sure we wouldn't get caught.

"Come to prom with me," he said one night while I was lying on the cool earth beside him, corn stalks rising high around us like an army protecting us and our love. We'd never said the words, but I knew what it was. This was *love*.

I'D BEEN DREAMING of prom all year. A little bit of magic in this ghost town. My heart beat wildly in my chest as I took one last look in the mirror. My long brown hair styled in waves, my eyes smoked out with grey shadow and my dress, oh my gosh, my *dress*! I bit my lip, smudging my pink lipstick. For the first time in my life, I felt truly sexy in the lilac and black floral satin dress that hugged my every curve. A flush hit my cheeks as I thought about what I was wearing underneath — lilac lace, just for him.

Finn had booked a room at the Lucky Motel, and it was going to be my first time.

My father would kill me if he even knew I was going to prom with Finn, but if he knew I was going to give Finn my virginity at the motel later, he would have Finn burned at a stake.

There was no way in heaven or hell my father would *ever* let me be with Finn.

But I decided that night to start living for me and not for my father's approval.

I packed my small purse with everything I needed for the evening — lipstick, lip-gloss, condoms, and then, because my dad would never let me go anywhere with Finn, I climbed out the window and walked to the crossroads where we had planned to meet.

I stood there in that beautiful dress, my heart pounding with anticipation of the most magical and perfect night of my life.

This is it. Prom. Finn. Losing my virginity.

My phone pinged, and I jumped. I opened my messages with shaking fingers.

I was so excited and nervous I felt like I was about to explode.

And then I saw the text message.

Finn wasn't coming.

CHAPTER ONE

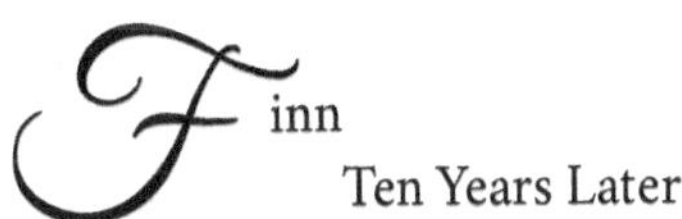

Finn
Ten Years Later

TEN TIPS for when you've just been turned

1. You will be hungry ALL THE TIME so drink when you can.

2. Don't go out thirsty. SERIOUSLY DO NOT DO THIS!

3. Listen to your maker. You'll feel like a teenager getting told off all the goddamn time, but they have the skills and knowledge that YOU need right now.

4. Tell your family you're going away for a while. You DO NOT want to be around people you love.

5. Faking your own death NOW can solve a lot of problems later.

6. Find at least five Donnas or Dons (human blood donors who dig the fangs) and claim them all. This will give you a reliable food source.

7. You are going to kill someone. Try not to judge yourself when you do. It's all just part of the journey!

8. Don't go out in the sun. You won't die, but you will get

*crispy. Try to get your hands on some "LIZARD JUICE".
TRUST US.*

*9. Garlic and holy water are no big deal but watch out for
SILVER!*

10. ENJOY your new-found strength and immortality!!
www.babyvampire.com

I THROW my arm around the pretty brunette's shoulder. Her short brown hair makes a curtain for her brown eyes and angular features. She looks nothing like April, but it's April that I'm thinking of as I pull this girl close and kiss her on the cheek.

She's not April, but she's warm, and she's willing, and right now that's enough.

I don't need to glamour her — she knows what I am. Most of the girls that hang out at Vincent's, the art deco vampire club in West Hollywood, know what we are, and that's exactly why she's here. They call these girls Donnas, as in *blood donors*. Girls who have a thing for vampires. I may be a rising star here in Hollywood, but she doesn't even care about that, she just wants The Bite, and I want to give it to her.

"Should we head out back?" I mumble into her hair.

I've only been a vampire for just over a year now, but my insatiable thirst for blood has barely dulled since the day I was made. Maverick, my maker, promised me it would get easier, but so far, it hasn't. Not for me. I'm yet to drain anyone to death, a rare feat for a "baby vampire" apparently, but I've come close too many times to count.

There's a constant burning in my throat, a thirst like nothing I ever experienced when I was human, and once I sink my teeth into a victim, all rational thought leaves my brain, all willpower leaves me. All I care about is *blood* and quenching this thirst that I know, no matter how many people I drink from, will never truly be satiated.

The longer it is between drinks, the worse it gets. It's only been a day since I last fed, but I am so thirsty right now I feel like my throat is going to catch fire and burn me alive from the inside out.

"Do you mind if I eat first?" she asks, voice raised over the big band playing a cover of a country song that was big last year when I was still human. She doesn't need to raise her voice, I can hear *everything.*

"You're hungry?"

She shrugs. "Yeah, and when I get bitten, it kind of makes me woozy." She blinks. "In the *best* way, if you know what I mean. But I don't want to pass out, so I think I should eat first."

"Sure, let's order you some food. What do you want?"

"I hate the food here," she complains.

Trust me to find the most high maintenance Donna in the club.

I run a hand over the dark stubble on my cheek. No matter how much I try, I can never get a clean shave now. A side-effect of being turned — my hair will never grow again, and when I do cut it, five minutes later it's back to how it was before. My body, although stronger and faster, is still the same as it was the day I was turned, no amount of pull-ups will change that. I'm glad I was working out before I was turned, but I sometimes wish it hadn't been nearly three days since I'd had a fucking shave.

I look around the club. I could let this one go, get another Donna, but there's something about her dark hair that reminds me of *her,* and how long can it really take for a human girl to eat a burrito?

"There's a burrito place down the block," I tell her.

"Do they have fries?"

"It's been a while since I've eaten fries," I tell her. "But I think so."

She hooks her arm into mine, and I let her drag me out through the club and onto the street. It's late, and the line to get in is long. Not everyone who comes here knows about vampires and Donnas, most people just come here for the music and the weird goth meets Gatsby vibe.

"Hey! There's that guy!" someone in the line calls out as we pass.

"Oh, shit! That's him from that movie with Maverick Stone!"

"What's his name again?"

"Hey! Hey you! Can I get a selfie?"

I ignore them all. They don't even know my fucking name, why would I give them a selfie? Who are they going to even tag?

But like I said, I'm just a *rising* star. I did a couple of terrible movies about ten years ago. When it looked like my career was going to dry up, I worked in sound production for a while, just to pay the bills. But I kept taking acting classes and going to auditions, and one day I landed a role in a Maverick Stone movie.

That movie, *Double Agency*, only came out last week, but as soon as that movie wrapped, I knew I had a window of opportunity, and so I grabbed it. I already have a rom com out on Flixie, two more movies coming out this year and three in post-production.

It helps that I don't need to sleep.

In a couple of months from now, everyone in this line *will* know my name.

We arrive at the burrito place, and when she orders, I hand over the cash. If I'm going to bite her, the least I can do is pay for her burrito.

She sits across from me and grins. "Thanks for doing

this," she says, unwrapping the paper on the burrito. "Most of you guys would say no, want to drink from me first and then get me a meal."

Why didn't I think of that?

Because somewhere deep down, you're still the same guy you were before.

I shut the voice down.

I'm not that guy. I'm not the kid from Lucky, Arizona. I'm not the boy next door. I'm not the baseball hero. I'm not the kid kissing his crush in a cornfield and then standing her up at prom.

I'm the guy who let her down, who broke her heart, and that was long before I was turned into this monster.

"I like your watch," she says, her eyes lighting up as she stares at my wrist. "Is that a Rolex?"

I look down at my brand new gold Rolex. It was a gift. Not really a gift, a marketing opportunity for them while I wear it at all my promotional appearances. It arrived at my house this morning with a note saying it was "from my publicist," whoever the hell that is.

But fuck it, who am I to say no to a free Rolex?

"Yeah," I tell her.

"So cool!"

"What's your name?" I ask when she's done scoffing down her burrito.

"May. Like the month."

Of course it fucking is. The universe just loves to rub my face in all my mistakes.

Sometimes I wonder what would have happened if I had just stayed that night. If I had taken April to prom.

I might never have made it to Hollywood. I might never have broken into movies.

I might never have become *this* fucking monster.

And sure, I might have ended up living in Lucky, Arizona for the rest of my life, but at least I'd still be human.

"Okay, let's go," she says, standing up and throwing her paper in the trash. She grabs a business card from the counter, and we walk out onto the street. "I collect them," she tells me, holding up the card with a nervous smile. "I don't know why. Memories, I guess." She flicks the card against her fingers. "Oh! Shit!"

It's the smallest amount of blood. Just a paper cut. But it's fresh, and I'm thirsty as fuck, and before I even know what I'm doing, I grab her in my arms and speed into the back alley down the side of the burrito place.

I shove her against a wall. My fangs burst out of my mouth, and she lets out a scream.

Ah fuck!

I pull back, realizing what I've done. "Sorry, May. I just — it was the—"

"The blood," she says with a smile, putting her bloody finger to my lip.

I lick the blood off, but it's not enough. It's like a grain of salt on your tongue when you haven't eaten in a week. My mouth waters, and I'm ravenous, and I can't stop. I groan and push my body into hers.

She grins and presents her throat to me. My fangs are suddenly so deep in her neck, and I'm drinking like the wild, crazed, insatiable monster that I have become.

But this time I don't have to worry about stopping myself.

It's the lights and the sirens that do it.

CHAPTER TWO

inn

GLAMOURING VS INFLUENCING: How to Do It Right

If you want to glamour someone, you have to look deep into their eyes and wait for their brain to turn malleable. You'll know when it happens because they'll kind of go weak and look at you like they'll do anything you want. Then, you can basically reprogram their brain with whatever thoughts and ideas you want. It's pretty cool.

Influencing is just a lighter version of glamouring. Instead of going deep into their eyes, you can just kind of set the intention that your words will influence everyone around you. Speak clearly, and you'll influence anyone who's close enough to hear you.

www.babyvampire.com

I DON'T HAVE much time, but I quickly stare into May's eyes. I don't feel her mind open to me, but I don't have time to wait.

"This was nothing. We were just making out. You're okay." I lick my finger and run my saliva over her neck to close up the wounds. But *the blood.*

There's so much fucking blood.

It's all over my face, my shirt, her neck. It's running down her cleavage and all over her dress. Hell, there's even blood on her legs.

Jesus, this looks fucking bad.

"Hands up!" one cop, a woman in her fifties, calls out to me.

"Drop your weapon!" yells the other, a younger guy who looks agitated.

I try to wipe as much of her blood off my mouth as I can, but now I wish I'd paid more attention when Maverick was teaching me how to drink clean.

"Step forward, slowly!" shouts the woman.

I try to consider my options here. I could run, scale the back wall and get the hell out of here, but leaving May here covered in blood? No, it's better to stay, glamour these two cops into believing some bullshit and make them let me go.

I step forward with my arms raised. I stare at the guy and tell him, "The girl was injured, I was helping." He narrows his eyes at me. He doesn't drop his gun.

Shit, why isn't my glamour working?

Suddenly, the woman is behind me, putting me in hand-cuffs. She doesn't make eye contact with me, but I try my influence instead. "The girl was in trouble, I came to her rescue," I tell her.

"I'm okay!" May yells out. "Everything is okay!"

And now we have an audience. *Great.* There are more people here than I can glamour, and with the cops not even listening to my influence, I have no idea how I'm going to get out of here.

The woman shoves me into the back of a police car and then tends to May.

I could break free of these handcuffs, I could rip the door off this car and run, but then what?

And judging by the group gathered around the back alley with their phones out pointed right at me, I think I may have well and truly fucked up this time.

CHAPTER THREE

pril

Dear Diary,

I fucking hate Finn Huxley. He stood me up on prom, and it was the worst night of my life. Not because there was anything wrong with prom, but because all I could think about was Finn. Him standing me up. The promise I made to myself that Finn would be my first.

But Finn wasn't there and so I gave my V card to someone else instead.

It was awkward and not very good, and I cried afterwards because it should have been Finn.

And I don't hate him. I don't hate him at all. Even though he stood me up. I love him, and I always will.

April xox

. . .

"WELL, I'll be! If it isn't Finn Huxley on the morning news!" Loretta throws a dish towel over her shoulder and leans on the counter to get a better look at the TV screen above the specials board.

Loretta has worked at Lucky's Diner for thirty years. She's a good thirty years older than me, her curly black hair already greying, but I still consider her one of my best friends.

I look up at the screen that plays the morning news while customers sit and eat breakfast on their way to wherever they are going next.

And there he is — Finn Huxley, covered in blood, being pushed into a police car.

I let out a gasp. "What happened?"

"Shhh!" Loretta shushes me, grabs the remote and turns up the sound.

"Finn Huxley, one of the actors in the new Maverick Stone movie, was arrested last night and is being held on a charge of assaulting a woman—"

"No," I whisper, shaking my head.

Finn Huxley may be a lot of things — asshole who stood me up for prom, dickhead who ghosted me, jerk who I promised my virginity to, but he's not this.

Is he?

"Well, I'm not surprised," says Clive, standing just a little too close behind me considering we broke up a year ago. "That guy was always bad news."

We watch the footage of Finn being led into a police station, and then they show some clips from his latest movie, which I will definitely not be watching.

Who wants to see a guy who broke their heart up on the big screen? Not me.

"This just in—" says the newsreader. "All charges have been dropped against Mr. Huxley."

New footage now appears of him walking out of the police station dressed in a clean black t-shirt that shows off his broad shoulders and muscular torso.

Jeez, he looks *jacked* compared to last time I saw him. He was always in good shape, but now he's almost bursting out of that shirt. His hair is a tangled mess of thick curls, and as his eyes flick to the camera, my lower belly flips.

"New information has come to light. Finn Huxley was not the perpetrator of this crime but merely attempting to help a woman who had been a victim of a violent crime."

I let out a breath I didn't even know I was holding as the woman on the TV shares statistics about the recent LA crime wave.

"I always knew he was a good kid," Loretta says. Her dark eyes meet mine, and she places a hand on my shoulder.

Sure, I dated her nephew for six years, but she knows I've always carried a torch for Finn Huxley.

We thought we were keeping our relationship, if you could even call it that, a secret. One month of secretly meeting in empty classrooms and cornfields, but apparently everyone in town knew.

"There's nothing good about him," Clive says, his own dark eyes flashing to mine, a deep flush appearing under the deep brown skin of his cheeks. "So, he didn't assault that woman. Big deal. Doesn't make him a hero."

It's been one year since Clive asked me to marry him, and one year since I said no. He still thinks I'll come around, that I just need time. But six years is a long time to date somebody without them asking for your hand in this town. For a while, I thought it was what I wanted. I thought we could have a life together, that we'd get married, have some kids, take over the diner one day. I thought maybe I could be content with that.

Because I did really like Clive. I still do. He's a good guy.

But when he finally got down on one knee, I realized it wasn't what I wanted at all. I didn't want to be with a man who took *six years* to ask me to marry him.

There are slim pickings in Lucky, Arizona, when it comes to men. But my whole life is here. My father, my friends, my job here at the diner, my part-time job at the library, the choir.

I have a full life. I really do.

The only thing missing in this Arizona town is *heat.*

But I have my own way of dealing with that. Instead of dating, I live vicariously through the romance serials I write on Scripty.

CHAPTER FOUR

inn

"We need to do something about your image." Brandon Curtis, a famous Hollywood producer with thick blonde hair perfectly styled like it's still the fifties, frowns at me over his large oak desk in his Hollywood Hills mansion.

"What's wrong with my image?"

Maverick Stone, my maker and massive pain in my ass, raises an eyebrow under the dirty blonde hair that's falling over his brow. "You're affecting the publicity of the movie."

A beautiful blonde woman in her early thirties looks up from her phone. "You have two more movies coming out this year, Finn," she tells me, like I don't already know that. "That's a lot of publicity. TV, radio, print interviews, online magazines, merch deals, travel—"

"I'm sorry, but who the hell are you?" I ask.

"I'm Natalie."

"Who?"

"Your publicist."

I glare at Brandon. "Publicist?"

"Natalie will help you get to your engagements, make sure you're where you need to be, and make sure you're wearing and saying the right thing."

"What's wrong with what I'm wearing?" I ask, looking down at the old baseball t-shirt I've paired with faded black jeans and an almost worn-out pair of Vans. No gold Rolex today. I couldn't get all of the blood out of the cracks.

"Do you even have to ask?" asks Maverick.

I raise an eyebrow at him. "Your t-shirt and check shirt combo is more lumberjack than movie star."

"This shirt is designer," he huffs.

"I can assure you," says Brandon, shutting us up, "Natalie is very discreet. She's fae. She understands the immortal lifestyle."

I raise an eyebrow at her. I've been told all about the fae and the uprising in the fifties that caused vampires and fae to kill each other. We're supposedly working together now as part of the New Order of Concordia. Maverick is the vampire member of the secret society that meets once a month to discuss vampire, fae, werewolf and witch business. But this is my first time meeting an actual fae.

"Thanks for the Rolex," I tell her. "But I don't need a publicist dictating my every move. Just give me a schedule, and I'll be where you want me, when you want me."

"Finn," Maverick uses that tone like he wants to kick my ass. "Yesterday you were meant to be at the radio station at nine to talk about *Double Agency*. Instead, me and Brandon were glamouring every cop in the LAPD to get you out of jail."

I can't deny it was bad.

"If I'd had time, I could have glamoured the cop and—"

"But you didn't have time, and you're still struggling with your glamouring," Maverick berates. "You fucked up."

"Again," Brandon sighs.

"We've been bailing you out for months," says Maverick. "And honestly? We're all getting sick of your shit."

"Maverick, take a breath," Brandon says. "He's still a kid."

"I'm nearly thirty," I tell him.

"In vampire terms, you're barely a toddler," Maverick says.

"Finn, you're a good kid," says Brandon, ignoring my almost thirty years on this planet, but I guess compared to him, I am a kid. He's got about three hundred years on me. "We all need something to take the edge off," he continues. "We're just asking you to be more discreet about it. For your image, for the studio, and for vampire kind."

"It won't happen again." There's no promise, no truth in my words. Because honestly, I have no idea how to control my fucking insatiable thirst.

Natalie turns her phone around. It's an image of me leaving Vincent's with a woman I don't even recognize on my arm.

"Do you even know who this is?" she asks me.

I shrug. "No fucking idea."

"This is Summer Sanders. She's an adult movie star. Not only that, but she only just got out of rehab for narcotics."

"Sex work is work," I tell her.

"I'm not denying that," Natalie says. "But in a couple of weeks we start promotion for *Jungle Story*, which is a *family* movie."

I let out a loud groan. "What's everyone's fucking problem? It's not a big deal! Maverick has had sex with half the women in this fucking city!"

Brandon's gaze turns steely. "When you're in my films, you represent me, the studio, your co-stars *and* the Fraternity. None of us wants to be associated with a vampire who can't keep his fangs in his mouth."

I glare back at him. I'm not even sure I want to be in the Fraternity of the Everlasting Rose anyway. It's full of stuffy old rich and influential vampires making back door deals while they participate in wild blood orgies. It's not my idea of a good time, and Maverick basically forced me to join, even though most of the members don't think I deserve to be in it. I know what they think when they look at me — I'm not rich, famous or vampire enough to be in their exclusive club.

"Look, man, I get it," Maverick says, trying to be the cool guy now. "You're a movie star, you want to have a good time, let off some steam, fuck numerous women. No one has a problem with that. But you've been taking it a little too far."

"The studio is starting to consider you a liability," Brandon says.

I throw my head back and laugh. "A liability? I'm making more movies than anyone! I'm raking in the money for you guys!"

"Not yet, you're not," says Brandon.

A thick silence descends in the room.

"I know it can take some time to adjust—" Maverick starts.

"Adjust?!" I smack a fist on the desk. "You turned me into a fucking *monster*!"

"The only thing worse than a baby vampire is an adolescent." Maverick sighs, rolling his eyes. "We've all been there, Finn. We know it's hard. But if you want to keep working in this industry, you need to toe the line."

"Are you kidding me? You have the worst reputation of any movie star *ever*! You still get any role you want!"

Okay. So maybe I am sounding just like a teenager now, even though I'm nearly thirty.

I'm never going to turn thirty.

The thought of it puts another piece of kindling on the fire that's already raging within me. "You're an asshole, and the studio keeps hiring you!" I fire at Maverick.

"When I'm an asshole, at least I'm acting *human*."

"Fuck you," I tell him, before folding my arms just like a petulant teenager.

"No one is expecting you to be a saint," Brandon says. "Go home with a different girl every night, but take them *home*. Don't drink from them in back alleys or public restrooms."

He's referring now to the woman I nearly drained in the restroom at the studio's Christmas party.

"May I remind you that while I may not be perfect, I have still never killed anyone—"

"Yet," Maverick adds, "and you're increasing your chances by acting like this."

"Glamour them before and after," Brandon says. "Make sure no one else is around. We can find you some Donnas to practice glamouring."

"You need to drink more blood bank blood," Maverick says. "You're too thirsty when you go out."

"Yeah, yeah, we've been through all this shit," I say.

"Then fucking act like you know this shit," Maverick broods. "These rules aren't there to stop you having fun, they exist to keep us all safe. If someone finds out what you are, we're all fucked."

"There's only a week left of *Double Agency* publicity," Natalie chimes in. "Then you have a week off before promotion starts for *Jungle Story*. Why don't you take these next two weeks to regroup?"

"Regroup?" I laugh. "I was tied up in a basement, almost drained to death by vampires who then turned me into one of them. Now I can't ever get rid of this *insatiable* fucking thirst, and you want me to *regroup*?"

Maverick shakes his head. "You make it sound like me

and Brandon were the ones who drained you. Meanwhile, you still practically live at Vincent's even though it was Vincent himself who *did* almost drain you to death!"

"He said he was sorry."

"Yeah, I'm sure now that you're becoming a big star and spend a fuck-ton of money at his club he is fucking *sorry!*" Maverick says.

"Hey, I'm not the one banned for life." I raise my hands in fake surrender.

"I wouldn't go in there if that asshole paid me."

"Alright, now," Brandon says. "Let's focus on the issue at hand here. I think Natalie's idea is good. Publicity for *Double Agency* is going well. Trix and Maverick can handle the last week without you."

"The public are loving Maverick and Trix," Natalie agrees, like I needed a reminder of how love-sick and pathetic those two are. "It will be no problem for them to go ahead with the final appearances without you."

"I want to do it! I can do it!" I whine, really sounding like a toddler now.

"It's non-negotiable," Brandon says. "You need the break. Get your head right."

"And if I don't?"

Brandon stares at me over the desk. "If you don't do what I'm asking you to do, you will no longer be welcome in the Fraternity. And you also won't be making any more movies."

Ah, fuck.

CHAPTER FIVE

inn

REGROUP.

The word feels like a sick joke.

I throw myself down on the couch in my Santa Monica beach house I bought when the paychecks started coming in. Glamouring the realtor also helped me get a great deal on the place. My house is all glass, a pretty wild choice for a vampire, but every window is tinted and has blackout blinds. But the best thing about it is that even when you're inside, you feel like you're outside. It's just past midday, the sun is high, there's not a cloud in the sky and the sound of young people laughing and enjoying the first days of spring rises from the beach below.

Vampires aren't supposed to be able to daywalk, but the sun serum I take every day means that even though I'm dead, I can still enjoy the beach on a sunny day.

Thank fuck.

I love this house, but two weeks of rattling around here won't help me *regroup.*

I sigh and make my way into my enormous bedroom with gigantic walk-in robe. I had this idea that once I started making bank, I'd fill it with designer suits and high-end sneakers, but I've been so busy I've hardly had a chance to shop, and the idea of an assistant buying my clothes? No thanks. Most of my clothes are the same staples I've been wearing for years—black jeans, t-shirts, skate shoes, a couple of leather jackets.

I grab a duffel bag and start throwing things in. It's warming up, but the nights are still cool. It takes me a second to remember I no longer feel the cold. But still, I throw in a couple of hoodies and some PJ pants along with a bunch of jeans and t-shirts. I grab my stuff from the bathroom, most of which I still use out of habit and yearning for my old human life over necessity. I think I'm the only vampire I know who flosses.

I glance at the gold Rolex on my bedside table, still encrusted with May's blood. It's a beautiful timepiece, but no one in Lucky will be impressed by it. *April* won't be impressed by it. I leave it where it is, throw the bag over my shoulder and then stand at the door, wondering if this is a really dumb decision. I should probably try to talk myself out of it before I fuck everything up even more.

The vampires who took me had been hiding out in an Airbnb just a few miles out of the town. The irony was that we were only there because of *me.*

I met this guy Aiden at Vincent's club. We got to talking at the bar and bonded over being from shitty small towns. I told him about Lucky, Arizona. I told him it was so quiet out there that it was the only place on earth you could get away with hiding a dead body.

He took me literally, and I nearly died in the basement of a house just a few miles from where I grew up.

But instead of dying down there, I was turned into *this.*

A few months later and I was back in LA, staying in Maverick's spare room in his Malibu mansion, trying to control my bloodlust and learn how to be a good vampire from *him.* Which was hilarious in itself.

One night I'd had enough of hiding out. Maverick was out for the night, staying with Trix at the hotel he'd put her in while I was staying with him, because who would want a baby vampire around their new human wife? I got in my car and I just started driving. I didn't even know I was driving to Lucky at first. Not until I realized I was on the I-40 and heading that way. Heading *home.*

But not home to see my dad, home to see *her.*

I parked out the front of Lucky's Diner, pulled my baseball cap low and hid in a booth up the back.

She didn't see me, but it was the first time I'd seen her in over ten years. There was this asshole customer who came in. Her boyfriend, Clive, gave the guy a free fucking pie and then I nearly drained him to death in the empty lot next to the diner.

I nearly killed him, and if I get too close to her, I could hurt her too. Worse.

Maverick's words from that night ring in my ear — *stay away from the girl.*

I shift the bag on my shoulder as I head out the door.

That night I didn't hurt her. I nearly killed a guy for making her feel like shit. But I had no intention of hurting *her.*

But what if I got close to her? What if I got her alone? What if I couldn't control my insatiable thirst around her? What if I took too much of her blood?

If I ever hurt her, I'd tell Maverick to stab me in the

fucking heart with a stake. He gave me this life, he could take it away.

I throw my bag in the back of my bright orange GT Ford Mustang, my dream car from when I was thirteen, and then I load up with four boxes of blood bank blood. It's not quite enough for two weeks, but it's a start. Once I know where I'm staying, I'll order some more from the supplier — some mystery person who smuggles blood out of blood banks, into wine bottles and into vampire hands. Whoever they are, I'm grateful. The blood bank blood doesn't do much for me, but without it I would have killed by now for sure.

I grab a stack of the little glass bottles of sun serum and fill my glove box with them. I'll need to order some when I get there, too. Some vampires don't take it, preferring instead to do things the "natural way," but there's nothing fucking natural about any of this. So if I can take the serum that's made from synthesized lizard blood and not have to completely give in to a life of darkness, I will.

I pull my baseball cap over my eyes, like the car isn't going to attract enough attention, and I hit the gas.

Fine, I'll go and *regroup*. I'll go back to the place where I was born and made. I'll find my dad and say what needs to be said. I'll find April, and I'll apologize for all the wrong I did to her all those years ago. I'll eat some of Loretta's waffles. I don't need to eat human food anymore, but there are some things I still crave, and waffles covered in half a bottle of syrup are one of them.

I'll play human for a couple of weeks. I'll be a big boy. I'll toe the line. And when I'm back, I'll be in control of my bloodlust and my destiny, and I'll become the biggest fucking star in Hollywood.

CHAPTER SIX

pril

THE LUCKY LIBRARY IS SMALL. *Very* small. It's about a quarter of the size of the diner, but we still manage to fit a lot of books into the space. There's a reading nook by the window that looks out onto Main Street and our romance section is the best within miles. I may have had quite a lot to do with that. Most of the people who come in are stay at home moms looking for a way to entertain their kids for a few hours or retirees looking for a good cozy mystery or thriller. But due to our extensive romance catalogue, we also get women coming in from nearby towns to pick up or drop off the latest Mindy Musgrave or Lana Laverne romance novel.

I only work a few hours a week here, but I cherish every moment. When it's quiet, I get to catch up on my reading or open my laptop and write.

And today, I'm writing.

I settle down behind the desk, take a sip of coffee from the pot I just brewed and open my project.

It's a second chance small town desert romance about a woman who works at a bar and a man who blows back into town after five years, only to discover that she's had his *baby*! It's dramatic, fun, and poignant in parts too. And judging by the two thousand people who've already read and liked the first few chapters on Scripty, the app where I upload my writing, I know I'm onto something. Maybe this will be the book that *finally* gets me some interest from an agent. I've been sending my writing to agents for years now, and I have over one hundred rejection letters so far.

But even if the agents don't like what I'm writing, the readers on Scripty do.

I get stuck into my story, and an hour later, a heavily pregnant woman walks into the library.

"Can I help you?" I ask her with a smile.

"Lana Laverne," she gasps, trying to catch her breath from walking the ten steps it takes from the street to the library.

"Are you okay?" I jump up and usher her to the couch in the reading nook.

"Sweet Lord, this is comfortable," she says, blowing her breath up into her dark bangs and sinking into the pink velvet couch I found in a yard sale.

"Can I get you anything? Water? Coffee? Epidural?"

She lets out a laugh. "All of the above? No, just water, and the new Lana Laverne. It said online that you have it."

"We do, you're in luck!" I grab the book off the new release table and hand it to her. "I'll be right back with your water."

I set her up so she's comfortable and leave her to read while I get back to my writing.

. . .

I'M DEEPLY immersed in the world of my story, and it takes me a second to realize she's standing above me. My eyes flick to the time on my laptop. Two hours have disappeared, but it felt like ten minutes.

"Have you read this?" she asks, holding up the book.

"I sure have."

"What did you think?"

"I loved it. I love all her books."

"What about this guy though?" She squints at the book cover. "Pursuing her even though she's dating someone else?"

"Kind of a red flag, I guess. But her relationship is on the rocks. She's not happy."

"How do you know when a guy is the one?"

I shrug. "Don't ask me. I dated a guy for six years while waiting for him to propose, and it was only when he eventually did, that I realized he wasn't the one."

She leans on the desk. "God, at least you *realized* before you married him." She looks down at her belly. "Or had his baby."

I have a sudden vision of myself heavily pregnant with Clive's child and wishing I'd never married him.

"I wish I could get those six years back and just spend them reading."

She lets out a howl of laughter and then clutches the desk as her face twists in discomfort. "I better let you get back to work," she says.

"Oh, I'm not really working, I'm writing."

Her eyes light up. "What are you writing?"

I squish my nose up, trying to decide if I should tell her.

"You're a romance writer," she says with a knowing grin.

"Trying to be. How did you know?"

"This pregnancy is making me a little bit psychic."

"Really?"

"Nah, you just have that look about you. Sexually frustrated. Getting off on creating fictional men who will ruin all real life men for all of us who are lucky enough to read what you're writing." She gives me a sad smile. "Also, I used to work in publishing. I can recognize a tortured creative a mile away."

Tortured? Well, she's not entirely wrong.

"Are you on Scripty?" I ask her.

"Oh god, I *live* for Scripty!"

"I'm on there. I'm Evie Everhart." I don't even realize she's going to be the only person who knows my secret until I say it.

Her mouth drops open. "Hold the phone! I *love* Evie Everhart!"

I can't help the massive grin that crosses my face. "Please don't tell anyone," I ask her. "No one around here knows it's me."

"Oh, girl, your secret is safe with me. But I have to ask you, what's going to happen with Rock? He's going to stick around when he finds out about the baby, right?"

"Well, no spoilers, but you know it's going to have a happy ever after."

"It's his baby, though, right? *Right!?*"

"You'll have to wait to find out," I tell her with a sneaky smile.

"I'm Katrina, by the way."

"April. So nice to meet you."

"Oh, no. The pleasure is *all* mine."

And then, a look of pure terror crosses her face as something splashes onto the floorboards below.

"WHO CAN I CALL?" I ask as they wheel her into the maternity ward.

There was no time to call an ambulance, so I helped Katrina lie down in the back of my old Toyota hatchback and spent the half hour drive to Culpepper telling her to breathe and praying I didn't have to deliver a baby by the side of the road.

"Call my mom?" she asks, handing me her phone.

"What about the father?" I ask her.

She shakes her head. "I don't even know who he is." She lets out a shriek. "Well, I know who he is, but not his name or his number."

Okay, this is a romance novel right here.

But I can't think about my next story right now. I have to call Katrina's mom.

"I'll wait out here," I tell her, as they wheel her into the delivery room.

"Oh, hell no. Girl, I need you with me!"

I let out a nervous laugh. "Me?"

She glares at me, and the doors close.

"You better be quick, April!" I hear her yell out.

I call her mom, who screams and tells me she'll be right here, and then I take a moment to breathe.

It's only then that I realize I'm in the hospital where my mom passed away. A wave of grief hits me, and tears burn at my eyes. I clutch the silver cross my mom bought me for my thirteenth birthday and silently ask her to be with me and Katrina.

And then I take a deep breath and go help deliver a baby.

I STAND BEHIND the glass and look at all the new babies. Katrina's mom showed up just in time, and because they only let one person stay with her, I was relieved from my duties. But I didn't go home. I just sat in the waiting room. The same waiting room I sat in with Finn so many times while my mom was sick.

And then I got to meet the baby. A little boy with a seriously powerful grip for such tiny fingers. Katrina and her mom were so grateful for my help, and I was so grateful I got to be a part of it.

But looking at the babies now, I just feel sad. Sad that it didn't work out between me and Clive. Sad that the only man I'd ever really loved left me and left town. Sad that I don't think I'll ever love anyone like that again.

Sad that my mom's no longer here.

It's late evening when I finally get back in the car and drive back to Lucky, tears in my eyes the whole way. I stop at the library to pick up my laptop, but instead of going home I shoot Dad a message to tell him I'm out with friends and stay in the library and write.

Time passes, and soon it's ten o'clock, and I know I should go home, but I'm too deep in the story. Too happy in my fantasy world where men chase the women they love, do anything for them, where they try to heal their own broken souls to be better men for the women they're falling in love with.

And then a text from Clive comes in.

CLIVE: WYD?

SERIOUSLY?

No. Nope. I can not become the What You Doing girl.

Well, maybe I could if the sex was any good. But it was always so mechanical, always missionary, and there was very little in the way of foreplay. The guy always just seemed to want to get in and get out, and my pleasure?

Well, it was nothing compared to the sex scene I'm about to write!

I ignore his text and go back into my fictional world of multiple orgasms and happy ever afters, and I stay there until it's after midnight, until the bar has closed and Main Street is empty, and then I go home to reality.

inn

HOUND of the Bakervilles *zero stars*

Worst movie ever made. Even two-year-olds hate this. No, really. My two-year-old literally said — DADDY TURN IT OFF!
@Filmmmbufff3456

WHEN I REACH the sign that welcomes me to Lucky, Arizona, something immediately restricts in my chest. I've been back exactly once since I left. The night I nearly killed that trucker.

When I found out the day of Prom that I got the role for *Hound of the Bakervilles,* I knew it was my one ticket out of this place. If I waited any longer, if I waited for a better role, or until after graduation, I knew I could miss my window. They say you get one chance in Hollywood, and if you don't take it, that's it.

So I had to take mine.

I made my video audition for the movie on a whim. I saw the buzz online around the studio's open audition and thought, why the fuck not? I'd been in some school plays and really enjoyed it, but it wasn't something I had really thought about doing as a job. Of course, I was going to be a professional baseball player.

I went down to the local animal shelter, and some friends from drama club helped me make my audition video in a pile of puppies who'd recently been abandoned. Not only did the video get me an in-person audition in LA, but it also got all those puppies adopted.

Dad hated everything about it, tried to stop me from going to the audition. Mom stood up to him for the first time in her life and drove me to the audition. In LA she was different. I knew it from the second she got out of the car and inhaled like it was her first time breathing air.

There were three reasons I didn't show up to prom that night, and needing to get to LA as soon as possible to start filming was just one of them.

Another reason was that I knew if I went to prom, if I held April in my arms while we slow danced in the gym, if we'd gone through with our plan to be each other's firsts at the motel outside of town after, I knew I wouldn't have been able to leave.

And maybe that would have been okay. Maybe a life with April in this town would have been better than being *this*.

But my soul called me to something else. If I stayed in Lucky and gave up my dreams, I knew that one day I'd resent her and resent this place, and I couldn't do that to either of us.

April was my first love. She was my only love. But I couldn't ruin her life by pretending that I didn't want *more*.

The third reason I wasn't there for her that night?

My asshole of a father. My ticket out of Lucky was my mom's too.

I grab my bag, one box of blood and shove open the door to my motel room.

I put the blood on the chipped and scratched dining table and drop my bag down on the bed. Fuck, I can't believe me and April were going to come here for our first time. Doing it in a cornfield would have been better.

The room looks like it hasn't been renovated since the seventies. The brown bedspread and retro desert paintings definitely have a kind of vintage charm, but the musty smell emanating from everywhere makes me want to gag.

I open the windows and shove another box of blood into the door to keep it open.

Then I crack open a bottle and drink.

Maverick and Brandon are thorns in my side, but they aren't wrong about everything. I need to get my bloodlust under control. Especially if I'm going to see April.

I down the bottle and grab another, texting the supplier with my address here and an order for four more boxes and a box of sun serum. That should keep me going until I've *regrouped*.

MAVERICK: Where are you? How's the regrouping going?

Finn: Sitting in a motel room in Arizona, drinking blood.

Maverick: Whose blood?

Finn: From the bank.

Maverick: Smart move. You will get used to it eventually. I promise. I'll get some more sent to you.

Finn: Already ordered.

Maverick: What are you going to do in Arizona? You're not going to Lucky, are you?

Finn: Just going to regroup. Not going to do anything stupid. Don't worry about me.

Maverick: Finn, you're my progeny. I'm always fucking worried about you.

I SHOVE my phone in my jeans pocket, down another bottle of blood and then grab my keys and drive to the bar.

CHAPTER EIGHT

Finn

THE BAR HASN'T CHANGED at all in the last ten years. Still the same old dive the block behind Main Street. The place looks like a shed, and it's only the neon Budweiser sign in the window that lets you know that it's even a bar and that it's open.

I was underage the last time I was here, but that never used to stop anyone serving me.

I slide into a seat at the bar and run a hand through my hair. I feel like a ghost of my own past sitting here again after all this time.

"Holy shit!" The bartender turns around and grins at me, his dark eyebrows shooting up. "If it isn't Hardball Huxley!"

I haven't heard that nickname since high school. It comes with both a warm and sinking feeling in my chest.

"Ed!" I give him a huge grin and lean over the bar to shake his hand.

"Nah, man. This needs a hug!" Ed comes round the side of the bar and pulls me into a hug. The guy is built like a truck, and the embrace is smothering but comforting. He's rounder in the middle and his hair is longer, but it still feels like no time has passed.

He pulls back and takes a look at me. "You look great, man! Such a heartthrob."

I roll my eyes.

"Botox? Expensive face creams? You don't have a wrinkle on you! I guess that's how it is when you're a big fucking star." He claps me on the back. "Good to see you, Hux. Now what are you drinking?"

He returns to the bar and grabs a bottle of cheap whiskey. "The usual?"

Something about him remembering my old usual gives me a warm fuzzy feeling I haven't felt in forever. I try to push it away. This isn't my life anymore. Time *has* passed. Cheap whiskey hasn't been my drink for years, and I can't pretend I'm the same guy I was.

"Give me the top shelf," I say.

He roars with laughter. "My bad! Forgot you had money now." He pours me two fingers of the best whiskey in the place and slides it over to me.

"Have one with me?"

He grins, filling a second glass and shooting it back before I've even sipped mine.

"Jesus, it's good to see you." He smacks his empty glass on the bar.

"Okay, fill me in," I say. "What's been happening with you for the last ten years?"

He shrugs. "Working here. Married Jemma, two kids, one more on the way."

I force a grin. Wife, kids, things I'll never fucking have

now. I dated Jenna for a while in high school. She was a great girl, but the spark just wasn't there between us. "Congrats, Ed!" I hold up my glass in a cheers. "You've been busy."

"So have you! Saw *Double Agency* in Culpepper last week. Man, you were amazing. Better than Maverick. You'll be starring in your own action franchise in no time!"

I'm about to tell him about all the other movies I've been working on, but I decide not to.

"When did you and Jemma get married?"

"You'd know if you came to the wedding."

I try to think back. "I don't remember being invited."

"Your dad said he'd tell you next time he talked to you."

"You know we don't talk."

He nods. "I should've thought of that, but I had no other way to reach you. Your old number stopped working. I wish you'd kept in touch, man."

I down the drink and wish I could feel the burn. "Yeah, me too."

He pours me another drink, and another, and eventually I think I might be feeling a little buzz.

A group of girls come in, all dressed in short shorts and cowboy boots and Ed lets out a whistle. "Sweet Jesus, if only I was single! You attached, man? Because if not—"

I kind of hate the way he's ogling these girls when he's got a pregnant wife at home, but the girls are hard to ignore, and I'm suddenly very thirsty for something that isn't whiskey.

I grab my drink and give Ed a wink as I saunter over to the girls. I have no plan. No idea how I'll drink from one of them without making a fucking mess of it, but my throat burns, and those girls are showing a lot of pulse points.

"Oh my god, you're that guy!" one of them squeals.

"What guy?" I ask with a grin.

"You're in that movie!" another one of them gushes.

They all look the same. Long blond hair, huge eyelashes. They're all pretty, but none of them are *her*.

"Nah, I'm not him," I tell them. "But I get that a lot."

"You look *just* like him!" one of them says, pushing her fingertips into my chest, her long nails practically stabbing me.

I shake my head and give her a grin. "I can pretend to be him, if you want."

She raises an eyebrow. "Wanna dance?"

"Sure."

Some nineties country song plays on the jukebox, and I place my hand on her lower back, leading her to the dance floor, which is really just a gap between some tables.

She throws her arms around my neck and looks up at me like I'm her knight in shining armor. If only she knew what I was thinking.

I'm not a knight here to save her, I'm the fucking villain about to drain her life force.

My fangs twitch at the closeness of her body, her warmth, the strong beat of her pulse.

I close my eyes and take a deep breath. I can't bite this woman here. This isn't Vincent's, and she's not a Donna. She's just a country girl out for a good time with her friends. If she wants anything from a guy in this bar, it is not the ecstasy of The Bite.

"You local?" I ask her, staring out at the game on a big screen behind us. But it's no use. I don't have to look at her neck to hear the gushing and pulsing of the blood.

She shakes her head. "We're from Phoenix."

"How the hell did you end up in Lucky?"

"We were on the way to Sedona, but our car broke down."

I narrow my eyes at her. "Lucky's a bit of a detour."

She clears her throat. "One of the girls wanted to see her grandma on the way."

"I see," I say, not buying her story at all.

"But we're the kind of girls who like to make the most out of shitty situations. And, who knows? Maybe this all happened for a reason? Maybe you and I were meant to meet?"

Okay, I met her ten seconds ago and she's already acting like we're fated lovers?

"Just to be clear, I'm not looking for anything beyond tonight," I tell her. "I don't do relationships."

She laughs. "Oh, me neither! Well, not anymore. I just came out of something big." She glances at her left hand on my shoulder, and as I look down, I can see the imprint of a ring.

"You're married?"

"No. I was engaged. He cheated. Honestly, I'm just looking for a rebound. I just want to forget. Just for tonight."

"Well, you might be in luck with that." I don't know what I'm saying. Why am I promising anything to this woman?

Of course I've had sex with Donnas since I was turned. It's one of the only things that's kept me going. Everything is heightened for vampires, and that includes how damn good sex feels.

But even meaningless sex only works for me now if I'm drinking their blood at the same time.

So far I've only done it with Donnas. Girls who are willing. Girls who *want* The Bite. Not random girls from bars who flirt with me but have no idea what the fuck they're getting into.

But I could do it. I could have meaningless sex with her, drink her blood and make her forget all about it afterwards.

But that's not who you are.

I shut off the annoying moral voice within.

She grins a too-white grin, and while she's not really my type at all, my fangs are getting itchy as fuck for blood.

"You okay?" she asks, batting her extra-large eyelashes at me.

"Wanna get out of here?" I ask.

"Definitely."

CHAPTER NINE

inn

I GET her back to my motel room and immediately crack open a bottle of blood. If I drink some of this before I drink from her, I'll stand a better chance of being able to stop when I should.

"Want a drink?" Obviously, I can't offer her the blood, but I can maybe grab her a beer from the office.

"I'm good." She throws her purse on a chair and takes a seat on the edge of the bed. "Do you want to kiss me?" She looks up at me with her heavily made-up eyes.

I take another gulp of blood and then sit next to her.

"Yeah, okay," I say, even though I don't want to kiss her. I just want to bite her fucking neck.

She gives me a nervous smile, and I take her face in my hands and kiss her. She tastes like vodka, chips and emptiness. She's here for the same reason I am. Just to make the pain go away for a little while.

I pull back and push her long blonde hair extensions from her shoulders. "I can make it go away," I whisper to her.

She bats her lashes. "What do you mean?"

"I have a… special ability."

"Oh?"

"I'm… I can…" I take another swig of blood from the bottle beside me while I get ready to glamour her into letting me drink from her.

A tear falls from her eye. "Whatever it is, I want it. I just want to feel better. Even if it's just for tonight." She puts a hand out like she thinks it's drugs.

"It goes in your neck," I tell her, running a hand down her throat.

Her eyes close. "Do it," she pleads.

I'm nervous. It's my first time doing this with a human who doesn't know what I am, but she's willing.

She wants drugs, not vampire fangs in her neck!

I ignore the inner voice, let my fangs burst from my mouth, and I bite.

She gasps at first, but as the sensation of pleasure hits her, her body relaxes, and I drink. The sensation is so damn fucking good. Better than sex. Better than anything I ever felt when I was human. Well, except for kissing April in the cornfield.

She moans and groans with ecstasy, and it only makes me want more of her blood.

Her heart rate lowers, and I know this is the point where I need to stop, the point that I sometimes ignore for way too long. But there's something about her, about being in this motel room, that brings me back to myself.

You've had enough.

I pull my fangs out and lick her neck, cleaning away the blood. I lick my finger and run it over her skin, closing the holes I made.

She lies down on the bed, and her eyes fly open. "Woah," she gasps.

I notice a trail of blood down the side of her shirt, but it doesn't look so bad. It could easily have been from a nosebleed.

I kiss her cheek. "Thank you," I whisper.

"No, thank you," she murmurs, staring up at the smoke-stained ceiling.

She stays there for a few minutes, and I think about what it would be like to fuck her. It could take even more of the edge off for both of us.

But no. I don't want that. Not here. Not in the motel where me and April were supposed to spend prom night.

She sits up and blinks at me. "You—you bit me."

I force my fangs to retract and then hold her head in my hands. I gaze into her eyes, and her mind opens easily for me.

"You came to my motel room. We fooled around a little but didn't have sex. You enjoyed yourself. You're getting over the guy. You know you deserve better. You are going to be happy again."

She nods, and a soft smile crosses her lips, and then she's asleep in my bed. Okay. I guess I'm on the couch tonight.

Fuck Maverick. There's nothing wrong with my glamouring.

But one thing Maverick didn't teach me during glamouring training is that you can use it for good as well as evil.

CHAPTER TEN

pril

Mom seems to be feeling better. Hopefully she's over whatever it was. She was in bed for days, and Dad was worse than usual.

Finn spoke to me again in class today. He asked me about the biology assignment. I wasn't paying any attention in class, though. I was too busy doodling "April Huxley" all over the inside back cover of my notebook, so I had no idea what the assignment was! He obviously only asked me because everyone thinks I'm smart. He must have thought I was so stupid when I said I didn't know.

When I close my eyes, all I see is Finn! His handsome face, his unruly dark curls, his green eyes that always seem to be hiding something. He has great hands too. Strong, sexy, big, but not weirdly big. When I think about his hands, all I can think about is him touching me with them!

Love, April, the idiot xox

. . .

"Hey Ed," I say, pouring him a coffee as he stares up at the morning news behind the diner counter.

"April, holy shit, you'll never believe who came into the bar last night."

"Language!" Loretta calls out from the kitchen.

"That woman has hearing like a hawk!" Ed laughs.

I lean over the counter. "Okay, I'm intrigued. Who came into the bar?"

"I'll give you a clue, and you have to guess."

"Can't you just tell me?"

"Nah, this is more fun."

"I have other customers."

He just shrugs, and I move about the busy diner filling coffee cups, taking orders and placing down plates of the best pancakes and waffles this side of the state line.

"You could use some help in here," Ed says.

"Usually I have some, but Clive had to drive out to Culpepper to get some syrup. We're nearly out. He should be back soon though."

"First clue — brown hair."

"Well, that really narrows it down."

"Okay, how about curly brown hair that's always a fucking mess."

An image of Finn hits the back of my eyes. But what would Finn be doing here? He hasn't been back in over ten years.

"Just tell me, Ed."

"Second clue — Hollywood."

I stare at him for a few seconds, and my face must give me away because he does a slow nod.

"Finn. Huxley."

Just the sound of his name lights a fire in my lower belly.

"April!" Loretta appears next to me and grabs the

coffeepot out of my hand. It takes me a second to realize I've poured half the pot on the linoleum.

"Finn's back," I tell her, every nerve in my body firing and freaking out.

She looks up at me. "Oh, honey."

Then Clive bursts through the back door. "Got the syrup!" he exclaims.

I look at him, standing there grinning with a huge plastic bottle of syrup in one hand and a box in the other.

"I have to go," I say.

"Go where?" Clive asks.

"I think I left the iron on."

Loretta looks my uniform up and down, it's very clear I didn't iron it this morning.

"I'll just be ten minutes."

She knows exactly what I'm doing. Where I'm going. A wave of guilt washes over me, but I'm used to guilt. I'm a preacher's daughter. So I push the feeling down into that place within me where all the rest of my guilt lives, and I throw my apron on the counter.

"Ten minutes!" I call back as I rush out of the diner.

CHAPTER ELEVEN

pril

I GET in my car and take a breath.

What the hell am I doing?

It's been *ten fucking years* and I'm *still* jumping at the chance to see Finn.

I start the car with shaking hands and drive through town towards his house. I'm on the dirt drive to his dad's house when I realize there's no way Finn would just show up on his dad's doorstep after all this time.

Finn never had a good relationship with his father. But if he's not here to make amends with his father, why *is* he here after all this time?

I look up at his old house, so full of old memories. The only car here is his dad's old truck.

Finn's not here, and if he's not staying at his old house, there's only one other place he'll be.

I hit the gas and spin the car around, spitting up a circle

of dust, and then I head out towards the highway. My heart beating faster and faster the closer I get to the motel.

I haven't seen him in *ten years*. What am I going to do? Just go knock on his door? What am I going to say?

Hi, Finn. I haven't seen you for ten years, but you broke my fucking heart, you asshole!? Why didn't you take me with you? Why didn't you at least fucking call me?

Maybe I won't say anything. Maybe I'll just fall into his arms, and he'll throw me on the bed, and we can just pretend the last ten years never happened, catching up right where we left off.

As soon as I see the orange Mustang parked outside, I know it's his. My heart races so fast I think it's about to take off and fly out of my body. Finn always had a thing for those kinds of cars. He said when he was rich and famous, he'd buy twenty of them.

I let out a breathy laugh.

Holy shit, he did it.

Finn did everything he said he was going to do. He went to LA, he followed his dreams. He got out. He made it. He bought his dream car.

A tear falls down my cheek. I'm happy for him, really truly happy, I'm also so sad. I'm sad that I didn't follow him out there, that I didn't ask him if that was something he even wanted. I'm sad that he didn't ask me to come with him.

I'm sad that I never found *my thing* and followed my own dreams.

I'm sad that I'm still here in Lucky, working at the diner. No life, no man, no future.

I sit there for longer than ten minutes, reliving the past, battling with my past. The decisions I made, the decisions Finn made.

In the end, I decide I don't want to see him again. I'm too scared that my feelings will still be there. I'm scared that when he opens that door, I'll fall right back in love with him again. And what good would that do? It's not like he would still want to be with me after all this time. He's a big movie star now, and I'm still just the girl next door. Literally. I've never even moved out into my own place. I still live in the same house I grew up in, cooking and cleaning for my dad, still living under his roof and his rules.

But what scares me even more is that I'll see him and feel nothing. That it will all be gone. That what I thought was the love of my life was just puppy love. Just a teenage infatuation fueled by hormones. That this feeling I've been carrying around all this time will turn to dust and part of me just isn't ready to let that go. Because if I didn't love Finn and I didn't love Clive, what does that mean? That I'm incapable of love?

I can't let it happen. Finn still gives me hope. That's what I've been carrying around all this time. *Hope.* Hope that one day I can have that again, what I had with Finn. That I can feel that way again someday. The way I felt about Finn gives me hope that one day I'll find something better than Wednesday night missionary position with the guy I work with, who still couldn't commit to me even after six years.

I flip down the visor and check my makeup. I wipe away the mascara under my eyes and blink at myself.

I can't let him see me like this anyway. Not in the same diner uniform I've been wearing for the last ten years. Same boring hairstyle, same make-up. Same old April.

I put my foot on the clutch, about to drive away, when the door to his room opens. Out walks a gorgeous blonde woman in cowboy boots and the shortest jean shorts I've ever seen. She has a serene smile on her face, like she's just had the best sex of her life.

She probably has.

I hit the gas and get the hell out of there.

CHAPTER TWELVE

inn

I DON'T LEAVE the motel room all day. There's something about Lucky in the daylight that has me on edge. Like even with the sun serum, if I go outside, I'll fucking burn.

There are things I need to say to my dad. Air to clear. But not today.

I want to see April like I want air, but what am I meant to do? Walk into the diner in the middle of the lunch rush? No, I need to orchestrate something that feels more... fuck, I don't know.

I sit in my room and drink. Now that I know more blood is on the way, I'm not worried about exhausting my supply, and I end up getting a blood high that makes me feel stupid and ravenous. By four in the afternoon, I have the munchies like nothing I've experienced in my whole life. I want to go to the diner. Order a whole pie and five plates of waffles. But

I can not let April see me like this. High off human blood. *Fuck.*

I drive down to the bar. Driving with a blood high conveniently only makes you even better at driving. Seriously.

"Well, if it isn't the hardball hero back for more!" Ed laughs as I take my usual seat at the bar. He grabs the whiskey bottle from last night and places two glasses in front of me.

"What I really want is some food," I tell him, pushing the bottle away.

He narrows his eyes at me. "You high?"

I just laugh. "Yeah."

"Dude, I love you, but promise me you won't drive high."

He had zero problem with me driving back to the motel after I'd had half a bottle of whiskey last night, but okay.

"It's not that kind of high," I say, giving him a wink.

All this blood has made me too fucking bold.

He shakes his head but gives me a look like if he wasn't at work and didn't have two and a half kids at home, he might ask me what it was and if he could have some.

"If you want good food, you won't get it here. You might want to try the diner."

"I can't go down there," I tell him.

He just raises an eyebrow and passes me a sticky menu, which I'm pretty sure hasn't changed since I used to come here and get drunk with the team after a big game. It even has new prices written over the old ones in marker.

No one in town cared we were here underage. The high school baseball and football games were the only things that kept this town entertained. We were treated like Major League players, like gods. We loved it, lapped it up, got wildly drunk on the tabs of old guys who played before us and wanted to relive their glory days for a couple of hours.

Ed gives me a look. "Are you doing okay, Hux?" he asks, leaning over the bar.

"Loaded fries, two burgers, onion rings, another loaded fries and a sundae," I tell him.

"That's gonna be a lot of food."

"Good. Can I get a bag of pretzels while I wait?" I ask, nodding to the bags behind the bar.

"Those bags have been there for about five years."

"Don't care."

"Jesus, you are high." Ed laughs and passes me two bags of pretzels.

I eat them in minutes, and when Ed brings my food out, I demolish it in no time.

"Dude, how?" Ed laughs when he takes the plastic plates and empty sundae dish away.

But now that the blood high has worn off, I'm thirsty for blood again.

Will this cycle ever fucking end?

I try to think of Maverick and Brandon. Maverick has been a vampire for nearly a hundred years. Brandon is much older, but they both seem to live normal lives. As normal as immortals in Hollywood can, I guess. They show up for work, they make great movies, hell, Maverick even has a human *wife*!

Neither of them attack women in back alleys. Somehow, they got their bloodlust under control. So there must be a way for me not to be consumed by this fucking *thirst* every moment of my immortal life too.

"Want anything else?" Ed asks.

"Nah. I think I'm going to go back to the motel, sleep it off."

"Good idea. Hey, come to the game tomorrow after church? You can meet the kids and see the wife. Jenna would love to catch up with you after all this time."

All those words are foreign to me now — church, kids, wife, the game.

"Yeah, sure," I say, with absolutely zero intention of being there.

"Starts at three-thirty. You know where."

I give him a nod and start moving through the bar. But it's busier now, filled with vaguely familiar locals and strangers getting drunk and passing through on their way to somewhere better.

The scent of warm bodies and the pain in my throat makes me want to go on a rampage, and for a split second I see myself doing it. One by one, I rip into everyone's throats, taking all the blood I need and want, leaving carnage in my wake.

A horror story that I'm very capable of writing.

I squeeze my eyes shut, pushing the vision away.

That's not who I am.

I take a breath and then step outside into the night. I'll go home. Drink more blood bank blood. Try to sleep or at least close my eyes and rest.

"Hey."

I turn and see one of the girls who was part of the group from last night. She's blonde, tall, and wearing those cowboy boots and shorts they were all wearing before.

"Hey." I give her a little wave and then turn towards my car.

"I was hoping you'd be here," she calls out to me.

I turn back to her. "Me?"

"Yeah. I was just standing out here, trying to get the courage to go in and talk to you."

"How'd you know I was here?"

She nods toward my car. "That's yours, right? Ford Mustang? GT Fastback?"

"You know cars?"

"I like fast cars," she shrugs.

"Me too."

"I can see that." She takes a step towards me and gives me a flirtatious look. "Danni told me she had a really great time with you last night, and I was wondering if you and I could —" She bites her lip, and I'm too fucking thirsty to resist.

"Get in," I tell her, unlocking the car.

She slides in, and the swooshing sound of her raised pulse makes my fangs itch.

I drive fast.

It's not like I *want* to be this guy. I can see that it looks bad. Picking up a different girl every night. Biting random women just to keep the monster inside me from ripping out the throats of everyone in the bar.

But here's the thing — I know deep within my soul, if I even still have a soul, that if I don't do this, if I don't feed from humans when the blood bank blood loses its appeal, that I *could* go on a rampage. I could kill everyone in that bar if I let it get out of control. That is what I'm capable of now.

And so, feeding off a few innocents for the greater good is really my *duty*. And it feels so damn good for the girls I do it with.

At least, that's what I try to tell myself as I unlock my motel room door and guide her inside.

"What's your name?" I ask. At least I'm asking for her fucking name this time.

"Deena."

"Are you sure about this, Deena?" I ask her.

She nods and sits on the edge of the bed. "She said you'd make me feel really good. That'd I'd forget everything, and I'd just be... okay for a little while."

I run a hand over the stubble on my cheek. "It's not what you think," I tell her. "It's not sex. It's not drugs."

"I don't care what it is. I just really want you to do it." She reaches towards me and grabs my hand, pulling me down to sit on the bed next to her.

"Okay. Close your eyes," I tell her.

I don't bother with foreplay, with kisses, with kind words. She wants The Bite, even if she doesn't know that's what it is, and I want her blood.

She closes her eyes, and my fangs are in her neck, splitting skin, giving her the venom that makes her eyes roll back in her head as she moans in pleasure from it.

I take my fill of her, sucking her blood, satiating myself until the burning in my throat dulls. And then, as I always fucking do, I keep going, trying to get *more*. More of what, I don't even know. It's like being on the edge of orgasm, it feels so damn good, but you're not quite there.

That's what it's like every time I drink, but I never fucking *get there.*

I feel her heart rate start to slow, and I quickly pull my fangs out, licking the blood from her neck and the drips that made it into her cleavage.

I blink at her as she slumps onto the bed. It's the first time I've stopped in plenty of time.

I lick my finger and run it over her neck to close the wounds. A little blood has dropped onto her white top, but it's nothing like the night in the alley. It's not even as bad as the blood on Danni's shirt from last night.

Shit. I might actually be getting better at this.

She looks up at me. "That was… fucking *exquisite.*"

I give her a soft smile. "I'm glad you liked it."

"Are you going to fuck me now?" She starts unbuttoning her shirt, her big brown eyes full of desire for me.

I should want this. Before I came back to Lucky, sucking and fucking went hand in hand. But not here. Not in this motel. Not in this town.

I look into her eyes, and her mind goes pliable. "You

won't remember any of this," I tell her. "But you'll know that you had a good time, that you were safe with me. You'll stop picking up random guys in bars and know you're worthy of something much more meaningful."

She nods.

"You think Finn Huxley is the best actor in the world. You tell all your friends to see his movies, and you write five-star reviews for him on all the movie sites."

"Oh god," she says. "I *love* Finn Huxley. His movies are incredible! Have you seen them?!"

I laugh.

Okay, so I managed not to almost drain her to death, but I guess I'm still a long way from saintly.

CHAPTER THIRTEEN

inn

CHRISTIAN VAMPIRES & Vampires in Churches

The myth about vampires not being able to enter churches is just that—a myth. Why would an all-loving and all-powerful God want any of his creations to be cut off from his love?

We are not demons. Holy water doesn't burn us, and Jesus's love still welcomes us over the threshold into any church.

If you'd like to learn more about how to keep your faith after being turned, you are warmly welcome at our Sunday services in Las Vegas.

www.christianvampireslasvegas.com

SUNDAY MORNING and the last place I expect to be is parking my Mustang next to an old truck in the dusty lot by the church.

Lucky Christian Fellowship is a non-denominational

church that aims to serve the spiritual needs of the entire town and the people who live on the farms and ranches between here and Culpepper.

Growing up, Mom dragged me to church every week. Dad never came except at Christmas and Easter. I used to sneak in all kinds of shit to avoid having to pay attention — comic books, a portable radio stuffed down my shirt, earphones hidden behind tuffs of my wild hair.

But whenever the choir got up to sing, I'd pay attention. That was when April, along with a bunch of middle-aged women, would get up on the raised platform in the corner up front and sing for us while we meditated on "God's good grace" or whatever.

I was meditating on God's good grace alright, the good grace he had to create such a beautiful creature as April Abernathy.

I feel like a fucking fool. I'm a movie star. I'm a vampire. Why the fuck am I going to *church*?

But it's the same reason I went back then that's brought me here today. I can't wait any longer. I need to see her.

I wait until my watch reads 9:59 and then I get out of the car and walk into the warm spring morning towards the church. It still looks like something out of the Wild West. Built at least a hundred years ago, its weatherboard walls are only a little more faded than I remember. The central spire still stands with the cross on top, and a little wooden walkway guides me inside as a piece of tumbleweed crosses my path.

I'm about to slip in between the double wooden doors when the door swings open, welcoming me in.

Minister Abernathy gives me a stern look.

"You coming in, Finn?" he asks, like I was just here last week, not ten years ago.

I nod, and he gestures for me to enter.

I slide into the back row, instantly remembering how uncomfortable these wooden benches are. Minister Abernathy strolls down the aisle in the same brown Sunday suit he was wearing last time I was here. He still looks the same, too. Less hair, more wrinkles, but he still has that "stay the fuck away from my daughter" look in his eye as he glances back towards me.

He stands at the front of the tiny chapel and starts the service with a prayer and a welcome, and then Clive, fucking *Clive, April's* Clive, gets up on the little stage at the side and plays guitar while we all sing a hymn.

I don't sing. I just stand there looking for *her.*

I think I spot her brown hair through a gap in the crowd. Okay, crowd is an overstatement. There's only about twenty people here. Most I still recognize. They all look a little older than I remember, but there are many familiar backs of heads in front of me.

I keep staring at the girl I think is her, the girl I *know* is her, all throughout the song while my heart beats double time in my chest.

She's right there. Just feet away from me.

A bad vision suddenly drops into my mind to torment me. Visions of ripping the throats out of the congregation, leaving death and destruction in my wake just to get to her, just to hold her in my arms. Just to drink from *her.*

Okay, it's one thing to imagine doing that in a bar, but in a church?!

I look behind me. I should go. I should get out of here. I can't hurt these innocent people. I can't hurt *her.*

You had a whole bottle of blood before you came here. You drank from Deena last night and Danni the night before. You are fine.

I run a hand through the back of my hair and try to breathe.

You're not going to go into a rage and kill everyone.

I take a deep breath and take my seat as the song ends.

I spend the next half hour staring at the back of her head, ignoring the sermon like I always did. Maybe if I had paid more attention in church all those years ago, I wouldn't have become *this*.

As soon as the service ends, I'll go. I've seen enough. I know she's here. She's still here. She's fine. She's living her life. She's okay. It's enough. It's all I need. I saw her again. I got what I needed. I'll just go and pretend I was never here.

And then it happens.

"And now I'd like to invite you to take some time to meditate on God's good grace," Minister Abernathy says, and everyone stands.

Three older women step up to the stage, and then the back of the head I've been staring at this whole time moves. She stands, and my heart skips a beat as she walks down the aisle and towards the stage.

She's wearing a yellow sundress, and the way the light through the windows hits her hair makes her look like an angel, like sunshine personified. She turns around and smiles at the other women in the choir, and my heart catches fire.

Clive plays a few chords, and then they start singing.

April's beautiful face changes into something so holy, like it always does when she sings in church. She closes her eyes, and I can tell she's tapping into something powerful. God's good grace, I guess. I wouldn't know. I never found it.

A year ago in the diner she looked beautiful, even in her uniform, even pouring coffee and wiping sweat from her brow, but here in her element, she's even more incredible to behold.

My feelings for her haven't changed. If anything, I only want her more than I ever have.

A different vision appears in my mind now. Everyone is

gone. It's just me and her here. She's singing but doesn't know I'm watching her, she's too caught up in God's good grace. I stand up and I walk down the aisle towards her. Her eyes fly open. She's surprised to see me, and then she smiles.

"Finn!"

"Yes, baby. It's me. I'm back."

I grab her by the waist and pull her close, kissing her hard and fast. She kisses me back with a passion I haven't felt since high school.

I grab her by the ass, and her legs wrap around me. I carry her to the altar, throwing the candles and Bible to the floor. I rip off her panties, shoving her skirt up around her waist, and I lie her down on the altar. She begs me for it, and all I can do is fucking comply.

Suddenly I realize I'm the only one still standing.

And that's when she sees me. Our eyes lock, and everyone else disappears. The last ten years disappear. It's just the two of us, in the dark of night in the middle of a cornfield, sharing our secrets, our kisses and our hearts.

The other women take their seats, and after a moment of hesitation, April turns and takes her seat in the front row.

It's only when Minister Abernathy gives me a look that I quickly sit.

I spend the rest of the service replaying that moment, that look between us.

I want to believe that she was thinking the same thing I was thinking. That she still wants me like I want her. But ten years is like an ocean between us. She's with Clive and I'm—

Well, I died over a year ago in the basement of a ranch house not far from here, and then I was re-born as this unholy abomination.

I somehow find a little humanity still within me and decide that the right thing to do is to leave it to her. Let her come to me if she wants to. She knows I'm here. She knows

I'll be at the motel. If she wants to see me, she knows how to find me.

But when the service ends, I don't leave. I can't get my legs to do it. So I stay in my seat and watch as she runs out through the door in the back.

She doesn't want to see me.

Okay. This is fine. I can live with this.

But I still don't move. I sit and watch everyone make their way through the back door that leads out to the cemetery and a small courtyard area with benches where everyone used to sit and chat after church.

But I don't follow them.

Minister Abernathy is the last to leave, but before he does, he gives me a look and starts walking towards me.

I think he's going to invite me to come out back for a coffee and a cookie, or maybe even tell me to get the hell out of his town.

But that's not what he does.

"Finley," he says, using my full name. "Good to see you in church."

"Thanks for having me," I say, like I'm fourteen again.

He places a hand on my shoulder. "You're always welcome at church, son."

I don't know why that makes me want to burst into fucking tears.

"I saw you there, and I thought maybe you'd convinced your dad to come back."

I doubted my dad would be here, but I didn't even look for him. I was too busy staring at the back of April's head and fantasizing about fucking her over the altar.

"Come back?" I ask.

"He had been coming every week for a while there."

"He was?" That's hard to imagine.

He nods. "Haven't seen him for a year or so now, but you

tell him he's always welcome." He gives my shoulder a squeeze, and I nod up at him. "You take your time in here, son. Sometimes I like to just come and sit here. Get my mind and my soul right."

I just give him a nod.

"Good to see you, Finley."

I nod again, and he disappears down the aisle and through the door at the back.

And I sit and wonder what it would even take to get my soul right.

CHAPTER FOURTEEN

pril

I MAY NOT BELIEVE in God in exactly the same way my father does, but I believe in *something*. I have to. Because when I'm singing in the choir, our voices raised into the spire of the chapel roof, something else takes me over. I'm no longer myself, I'm just a conduit for something bigger than me, something more beautiful and more powerful than I alone could ever be. It's like it's not even me singing, but something else that has taken me over, something *good*.

It's the same feeling I get when I'm deep in flow with my writing. It's otherworldly, magical, mystical. Something *more*. Something *else*.

The song ends, the veil comes down, and I'm just April Abernathy again. But when I look out at the congregation, the same twenty people who come each week, I see *him*.

I stare at him for too long, and Loretta has to nudge me off the stage and back into my seat.

Finn's back.

It's all I can think of for the rest of the service, and suddenly I hear my father reminding everyone to come to bible study on Tuesday, even though we all know only the same three people will attend — my father, me, Loretta and Clive.

At the end of the service, it's my job to make tea and coffee and pass out the cookies, and today I can't get out of the chapel fast enough. I leap up and rush through the door at the back of the chapel and then run into the tiny back kitchen.

I close the door behind me and try to catch my breath.

Finn's back.

Someone tries to open the kitchen door, and it sends me flying onto my hands and knees.

"Honey?" Loretta looks down at me on the ground. "What on earth is going on?"

I stand up and brush myself down. "I thought I saw—"

"Finn Huxley," she says with a knowing nod.

I start frantically grabbing cups and pouring coffee from the warmer.

"Let me help." Loretta grabs a tray and starts placing cups onto it.

"Why is he here?" I ask her, like she has any idea.

"Seeing his father, I suppose."

I shake my head. While his mom was always supportive of his dreams, he couldn't wait to get away from his dad. Nothing Finn ever did was good enough for his father. Even with nearly straight A's, his grades were never good enough. When the baseball team lost a game, it was always somehow Finn's fault. Finn's dad lived in a world where if you weren't the best, you were worthless. Rich, coming from a guy who basically lives as a hermit and buys everything with coupons.

But Finn's older now. He's found success in his own right,

maybe he wants to throw it in his father's face. Or maybe he wants to make peace.

But the way he looked at me just then… Could he be—?

He's not here for you. And even if he is, he's ten years too late!

"Honey, that's enough coffee." Loretta gives me a look. "I'll take these out. You get the cookies."

I try to take deep breaths but practically hyperventilate instead.

Finn's back.

But when I walk out the back of the chapel into the garden courtyard, he's nowhere to be seen.

I pass out coffee and cookies and smile graciously like I always do, having the same conversations I have with the parishioners every week. The weather, the strange people who passed through the diner, the diner menu, people asking me when Clive and I are going to tie the knot. The whole town is still in denial about our breakup.

I try to convince myself I love it here. That I'm happy here. I try to tell myself I don't need anything else. I remind myself that my father needs me. That after losing my mom there's no way he could lose me too. This is where I was born, and it's where I'm supposed to live my whole life.

I have my creative outlets, my writing, my singing.

I have more than most people, and I'm grateful for it all.

But every day, the desperate teenager inside of me gets louder. The part of me that would have done anything just to get out of here. The part of me that nearly bought a bus ticket to LA, willing to forgive Finn everything just to be in his arms again. The girl inside me who just wanted to be with the guy she'd fallen so hard for and stick by him while he followed his dreams, and maybe find her own in the process. Every day I get closer to thirty, that girl gets harder and harder to ignore.

"Let me give you a hand with the dishes," my dad says once everyone else has finally left.

"You go home and rest," I tell him with a smile.

He never expects me to take up his offer. It's just what he says when he's ready to go home.

"Are you sure?"

"Of course."

"Thank you for all your help today, April."

It's a script we repeat every Sunday. The same words he used to say to my mom every week when she was here and she would look after the drinks and the cookies.

Another reason I can't leave. I took my mom's place in so many ways when she died. If I left, who would pour the coffee? Who would lock up the church?

"Happy to do it," I tell him.

He gives me a nod and leaves me to finish cleaning up.

When I'm done, I walk into the little cemetery out the back of the chapel. I do this every Sunday. Once everyone is gone, I sit here for a little while and talk to Mom.

Maybe that's why Dad always lets me lock up. Maybe he knows this is what I do.

"I saw him today," I tell her. "Finn." Like she doesn't know who I'm talking about. Like I haven't mentioned him a million times. Mom is the only person who still knows *every-thing*. "Seeing him was like—" I let out a breath.

What was it like?

"It was like the last ten years just disappeared." I tidy up her flowers as I talk. "He's been on the TV. They thought he had hurt someone, but he didn't. It was all a crazy misunder-standing. But you know, Clive is still convinced he's some kind of bad guy." I sit back on my heels and look at her gravestone. "Seeing him today just made me—"

It made me realize my feelings for him never went away?

But both me and Mom already know that.

I sit for a little while longer, telling her more about Finn's movie, which I still haven't been able to bring myself to see. I tell her about the annoying old women still asking me about Clive, and I complain about Dad being even more distant than usual.

"I always roll my eyes at everyone in town for having the same conversations after church every Sunday, but then I come here and tell you the same things I tell you every week," I say with a sad laugh. "Is this going to be my life, Mom? Every week exactly the same?"

I take a breath and stand up, placing a hand on her headstone.

"Maybe I should just marry Clive and give in to my fate, huh?"

A breeze picks up, and I feel like I can hear her voice telling me to follow my heart. It's what she always used to tell me when I didn't know what to do.

Follow your heart.

"But follow it where, Mom?" I ask her with a whisper.

I kiss my fingers, then touch her headstone, and then I walk back into the chapel kitchen to put the dry dishes away.

I lock the back door and then head into the main chapel to lock the front doors.

My heart leaps into my throat.

Finn Huxley is sitting in the back row of the chapel, eyes on me like I just walked down the stairs in my prom dress.

"Finn?" I practically gasp.

He doesn't say anything, and for a second, I think he might be a figment of my imagination.

But no. Not even my imagination could come up with how good he looks in a black button-up shirt, hair a tangled mess, eyes smoldering like he is thinking some very un-godly thoughts in this place.

"What are you doing here?" I ask, freezing in place just in front of the altar.

"I just needed to commune with God," he says with a smirk.

Oh, god, that fucking smirk!

I take a few steps towards him. "I thought you didn't believe in God?"

"Honestly? I don't know what I believe in anymore."

My feet move towards him all on their own. "Seeing you here, Finn. It's like—"

"Like the last ten years never happened?" He blinks and takes me in. Those deep forest green eyes transporting me back to a night in a cornfield where we kissed until curfew.

But there's something else in his eyes now. Something older and darker. Something heavier than what he was already carrying before. And of course there is. He's no longer the Finn I once knew. He's big city now. Finn is a *movie star.*

I don't even know this man.

At least, that's what my rational mind tries to tell me. The way my heart pounds in my chest, and the way my boots keep walking towards him tell a different story.

CHAPTER FIFTEEN

inn

APRIL LOOKS like a dream walking down the aisle towards me. Her thin yellow sundress strains over her breasts, and when the light hits from behind, I catch a hint of white lace panties underneath.

Dear god.

I swallow as I take her in, this dream that I'm not even worthy of closing my eyes for.

Her heart rate is high, but I don't know what it means. Could I still affect her in the same way after all this time?

She takes another step towards me, and I can see it in the depths of her deep blue eyes. The same eyes I used to stare into for hours as we just held hands and talked.

She still wants me.

God only knows why. The way I treated her. The way I just *left.* I never even fucking *called.*

"Ah—April," I practically stutter. "I came here to say I'm sorry."

She throws back her head and laughs, showing me her delicious and delicate throat. Of course I want to sink my teeth into it. Of course I want to drink her sweet, thick, warm blood. I have no doubt she'd be the best I've ever tasted. But in this moment, right here, right now, with her just feet away from me, her blood isn't what I want. All I want is to fucking hold her.

It's the first time since I was turned that blood hasn't been the first and only thing I've wanted.

"Finn, you had ten years to apologize," she sighs. "Why now?"

"I'm trying to get my shit together. Trying to make amends for my past or whatever." I run a hand through my hair. "And part of that past is you."

She frowns down at me now. "So, after all this time, you're only here to clear your conscience." She places her hand on the back of the seat in front of me and twists her lips. Without even thinking, I put my fingers on hers.

She looks down at my hand on hers but doesn't pull away.

"You were my biggest mistake," I tell her.

She pulls her hand back and folds her arms over her chest. "Well, thanks for coming all this way to clarify that."

"*Leaving* was my biggest mistake."

She blinks down at me like she's been waiting ten years to hear this but now the words mean nothing.

"How I did it was—" I shake my head. "I was young and stupid, and I should have stayed. I should have explained. I should have told you in person." I run a hand over the back of my neck. "I should have at least fucking *called*."

She drops her arms to her sides and looks defeated. "It's okay."

"What? You forgive me just like that?"

"I was mad at you," she says.

I slide over and tap the wooden seat next to me, terrified that she won't sit. But she does, and her scent of apples, cinnamon, coffee and wildflowers is intoxicating. She's so beautiful. Even *more* beautiful than I remembered. More freckles dust her nose and cheeks, and her blue eyes still blaze with a passion most people in this town probably still don't know she has. My eyes land on the small mole on her bottom lip that still begs to be kissed after all this time.

She stares up at the cross over the altar while she talks. "You ditched me on prom night. That's something I'll never get over. But I understand why you did it. It was just one night that we'd all hyped up to be this huge, big deal, but you were thinking about your future. Your forever. Your big dream was about to come true. You know I would never have wanted to stand in the way of that. If you had shown up at prom and I'd found out later that you'd chosen me, chosen that one night over your entire career and all your dreams, I would have been so pissed at you." She takes a deep breath. "And so yeah, seventeen-year-old April will always be pretty mad at you for what you did. You broke her heart." Her voice catches, and I know she's not as okay as she's pretending to be. "But this April? She's happy for you."

She turns to me now, and she's so damn pretty I don't know how I'm going to keep my fangs in my fucking mouth.

"I'm glad you followed your dreams," she says with a nod. "I really am."

"I tried to text you that one time," I say. It sounds pathetic. I tried to text *one time.* "You never wrote back." Again, I feel like such a dick bringing that up. I deserted her on prom night. I left town. And all I did was send a text two months later asking how she was.

She shakes her head. "What was the point? You were

going to be in a movie, and I was going to be stuck in Lucky for the rest of my life. It was never going to work between us. What was the point of replying? By then I was all cried out. I just wanted to move on. Try to forget about you, let you forget about me."

"I could never forget about you, April." I reach out and take a tendril of her chestnut brown hair. My fingers run over her warm cheek as I tuck the hair behind her ear.

Her eyes glisten and widen.

Okay, I shouldn't have done that.

"Sorry. I shouldn't have—" I pull my hand back like I've touched fire and rub my hand over my jeans. "It's just this is so—"

"Yeah," she says.

"Ten years later, and I still think about you all the fucking time."

She lets out a half laugh, half whimper.

My hand tentatively moves to cup her face, and when she leans into me instead of away, I rub my thumb on her cheek, more deliberately this time. "Do you ever think about me?" I almost whisper.

Her eyes flutter closed. "All the fucking time."

My lips are on hers before I can stop myself, before I remember I'm no longer a seventeen-year-old boy with a debilitating crush on the girl next door, before I remember I'm a fucking vampire with insatiable thirst who's come close to killing too many fucking times.

But none of that matters right now. All that matters is her sweet warm mouth on mine. One taste of her takes me right back to that night in the cornfield when things got extra heated. We nearly made love for the first time, but instead promised ourselves to each other after prom. That was my decision, not hers. She was willing to give it up right there on the dirt. It was me who wanted it to be special. Candles, music, rose petals. The whole damn thing.

I kiss her gently, willing my fangs to behave, but she's the one who's hungry. She kisses me like I'm her savior, like I'm her oxygen. Her tongue sweeps over my lips as she gasps, hot and heavy as she presses her perfect breasts into my chest.

Okay, this was not what I was expecting.

My hands wrap around her waist, and I pull her onto my lap so she's straddling me, and holy fuck, she looks like an angel as she bites her lip and catches her breath.

I run my hands over her shoulders, avoiding the silver cross at her neck, and up into her hair, removing her hair tie and letting her hair cascade over her shoulders.

"We shouldn't be doing this," she whispers, leaning in to kiss me again.

I don't know if it's because this is her father's church, or because of Clive, or because we haven't seen each other for ten years and no matter how much she's okay with it, I know I broke her fucking heart. But right now, I don't care why she thinks we shouldn't be doing this, I just know that we both want to.

Our mouths smash together again, and my hands run over her back, her shoulders, down her arms and up over the perfect rise of her breasts. Her hands are all over me too, my shoulders, my chest, and then she's tugging the hair at the back of my head as she presses her body hard into mine.

"Finn," she gasps into my mouth.

"I want to make you come."

She lets out a howl of nervous laughter and pulls away slightly.

"What's so funny?" I ask, toying with one of her dress straps, pulling it down and then placing a kiss on her bare shoulder.

She lets out a little moan. "Finn. I've never—"

"Never what? Come in a church before?"

She shakes her head and presses her lips into a line. "Finn, I've never... *come.*"

My eyes widen as I take her in. This goddess of a woman straddling me in the back row of the church. I trace lazy circles with my thumb over her freckled shoulder. "Clive doesn't make you come?" I ask, kissing her shoulder again, this time lingering.

Great, now I'm thinking about fucking Clive!

"No."

"But you've made yourself come, right?"

A slow smirk crosses her face, and then she whispers into my neck, "Sometimes when I make myself come, I think about you."

Holy fuck.

"When I make myself come, I *always* think of you," I tell her.

Her pulse rockets and her breath hitches.

"But no one else has had the pleasure?" I ask, still nibbling the warm freckled skin of her shoulder.

"No."

"I didn't know what the hell I was doing back then, but I know what to do now," I tell her.

I look up, and some of the heat has gone from her eyes. Of course, telling her how experienced I am was not that smart. Now she's probably thinking about that fucking news article with me and Summer Sanders.

"Okay," she says, and I can't believe my fucking luck.

"April, you are so beautiful," I murmur as I place gentle slow kisses down over her cleavage and across the top of her breasts.

This doesn't look like regrouping!

She lets out a low moan, and I ignore the voice, licking and sucking my way around her dress straps.

Her back arches, and my hands move to her breasts, her nipples hardening through her dress and her bra. I give them both a little squeeze, and she gasps.

"Baby, I'm going to make you come so good, so hard."

"Quit talking about it, and just fucking do it," she demands.

CHAPTER SIXTEEN

pril

I DON'T HAVE to ask him twice. He moves his hands over my breasts, runs them over my waist and then they're on my bare thighs, lifting the hem of my sundress.

Oh god. Am I really going to do this?!

But I'm already doing it. It's already happening, and I have absolutely no way of stopping it now.

This is Finn. My first love. My only love. And he's here with hunger in his eyes and fire in his touch.

"Is this okay?" he asks, as his hands slide up under my dress.

I huff out a laugh as I'm transported to ten years ago, him asking me if I'm okay, testing the waters, always stopping before we went too far.

But ten years ago, I was just a girl. Inexperienced. Okay, so I'm still kind of inexperienced, but I'm a woman now, and right now I can't think of one good reason to stop him from at least trying to make me come. I don't know if I can come with a guy, but Clive didn't even really try in all those years we were together, and here's Finn, here for five minutes willing to give it a shot.

"Yeah, it's okay," I tell him, smiling at him as I wind my fingers through his dark, disheveled and oh so familiar soft hair.

His fingers slide my panties to the side, and at first, I'm a little embarrassed at him finding me like this — I'm so wet and hot and wanting! But when he feels my wetness, he just lets out a heavy groan, his eyes practically roll into his head, and I know I have nothing at all to be embarrassed or worried about.

I never did with Finn. At least, not until he left.

Don't think about that now!

He slides his thumb up and down over my clit, and I grab onto his shoulders. "It feels so good," I whisper into his messy dark curls that smell the same as they always did — clean, woodsy, with a hint of gasoline. "But I don't know that I can come like this," I add.

"What do you need me to do?"

"What if someone comes in? I haven't even locked up yet and we're in *church*!"

"And I'm worshipping the goddess," he says, moving his thumb in circles now. "Tell me what you like."

I'm losing my inhibitions in a major way right now, but I can't tell him what I really want. I can't tell him I want him to throw me over the altar and fuck me like I've never been fucked before. I can't tell him that all those times I've been with Clive I was thinking about him.

I forget about Clive, and I forget about the unlocked door, and I give myself full permission to be here now with Finn's fingers on me. "Harder," I tell him. "More."

He presses his thumb harder onto my tight bud, and my entire body does an involuntary shake. It feels fucking *divine.*

"I can be a patient man," he says. "I don't care if we have to sit here until next Sunday's service, I *will* make you come. I'll do whatever you need me to do."

His words are like liquid fire, heating my core. He's a *man* now, not the boy I was with so many years ago... I throw my arms around him and press myself harder into his hand, his body, my face in his hair.

His circles speed up, and I can feel it happening. I can feel the climax building. I didn't know my body could do this with someone else!

My body starts to shudder as he continues making circles in my panties with one hand, and with the other, he rips down one side of my dress and shoves my bra down, exposing my breast. He groans my name, and when his tongue flicks my nipple, I am fucking *done.*

My back arches and my eyes fly open, anchoring on the highest point of the church ceiling.

Oh god, I'm coming in church!

The wave of pleasure hits like nothing I've ever been able to do to myself. I gasp and pant and grab and beg him, for what, I don't even know! I just want this feeling to never end, this climax, this pleasure, this bliss, this heaven, this perfect moment with Finn, the love of my life.

I collapse down onto him, his hand still in my panties, his mouth still on my breast.

I think I just had the holiest experience I've ever had in this place.

"What just happened?" I ask.

"You just met god," he says with a smirk.

CHAPTER SEVENTEEN

Finn

APRIL PULLS up her bra and dress strap, and I very reluctantly pull my hand out of her panties.

Fucking hell, that was amazing. The way she came around me, the way she held me like I was the only thing keeping her tethered to this plane of existence.

"Just to be clear," I start, placing her dress down back over her thighs, "While that was truly wonderful, it's not why I came to church today." I slide my hands up to her waist. "But don't get me wrong, I'm not complaining." I give her a hesitant smile, unsure of what she's going to do next, of what this all means to her.

She shakes her head, and I can tell that she's starting to come to her senses. It's time for her to go back to Clive, and for me to go back to wandering in the shadows trying not to kill people.

Then I realize that all that time, while I was focusing on

April's pleasure, I had stopped focusing on my own. I just wanted to make *her* feel good. For a few minutes, I'd almost forgotten about my insatiable bloodlust.

How?

"I need to go," she says. "Before my father wonders where I am."

"You still live with your dad?"

She nods. "Things haven't changed much for me. Not like they have for you." She slides off my lap, and while my fingers twitch to hold her here, to stop her, I don't. She brushes down her dress. "I'm sure you've done that with a hundred women in the last ten years."

I don't tell her that a hundred would be a gross underestimation. I also don't tell her that what we just did was more meaningful to me than all of my other sexual encounters put together.

"That was fun," she says. She reaches for her hair band that I threw onto the floor and ties her hair back. "But we both know what it was."

"Oh? And what's that?"

"A little walk down memory lane?" She shrugs, like her whole world didn't just shift on its axis like mine did.

"I'll be in town for a few weeks," I tell her. "If you want to finish what we just started."

"I don't think so."

Wow, okay. That fucking hurts.

She walks towards the doors. I stand and follow her. "Well, if you change your mind, I'm around for more of — that." I gesture towards the pews and send up a little prayer to the gods of this place for some more of this please, please, *please.*

She leans against the door. "It was great to see you, Finn. But I have a life to get back to. I can't play pretend with you for the next two weeks. I have a job, responsibilities, commitments. I have a life."

"I'm not asking you for your whole life." I lean into her, planting a gentle kiss on her forehead. "Maybe just a couple of evenings?"

Her brows knit. "No. I can't."

"How about just one evening?" I ask.

Her eyes are suddenly everywhere but on me. She stares down at her hands. "I'm happy for you, Finn. For all your success, everything you've achieved in your life. And this was... honestly? This was really special to me. But it was just... it was what it was."

"Which was what?"

"A hookup with an ex."

Her words sting. "It was so much more than that, and you know it."

She opens the door and gestures for me to leave, still not looking me in the eye. "Whatever it was, it's over now. I have to get back to my life now, Finn."

I take a hesitant step out of the church. She steps out behind me, closing and locking the door behind us like she's locking the door on what just happened in there.

And she should. She should move on. What do I expect showing up ten years after I stood her up at prom? What can I even give her now? I'm not even *alive.*

"You're right," I tell her. "A lot has changed."

"That's the thing," she says with a sad laugh. "For me, nothing has changed."

I can see the ache in her blue eyes, and I want to kiss it away. I want to give her so many orgasms that she walks around all day floating above the clouds where the rain can't get her.

Taking her head in my hands, I kiss her mouth once more. Softer, gentler this time.

A tear falls from her eye, and I quickly wipe it away.

"I'll always be here for you," I tell her.

She shakes her head. "You can't just turn up after radio silence for ten years, finger me in a church and then tell me you'll always be here for me. It doesn't work like that."

"April, I *want* to be here for you. I know I wasn't before, but I want—"

"What you say you want and what you do aren't always the same thing."

She gets up on her tiptoes and kisses me on the cheek. "It was good to see you." She steps back, putting what feels like rivers and oceans between us. "Please don't tell anyone about this."

"Never."

"I guess I might see you around until you leave."

"Yeah."

"Don't expect anything from me. I can't do this again."

But it sounds like she's telling herself, not me.

I reach out to grab her hand, but she steps back and shakes her head. Another tear falls from her eye before she turns towards an old beat-up Toyota hatchback.

Then I stand outside the church and watch her drive back towards her life that doesn't include me.

CHAPTER EIGHTEEN

pril

Dear Diary,

*Lucky High got into the finals! It was *the* event of the school year and I loved every second of it. Of course, I spent the whole time staring at Finn, who looked amazing in his tight pants and baseball shirt that I just wanted to rip right off him! Watching him swing that bat made me feel so good in what I'm pretty sure is definitely the "wrong" way.*

Sometimes I worry about my sexual feelings. Am I too sexual?! I mean, I probably shouldn't get that excited just watching him hold the bat like that... the way his fingers wrapped around it... the way he swung it with his whole body, putting all his strength into it... the way he smacked the ball out of the park. The way he slammed the bat down on the ground and ran. The way he slid into home base. JESUS SAVE ME.

At one point I thought he looked up at me in the stands, but then I realized I was standing right behind Jemma. He must have been looking at her. I mean, why wouldn't he? She is his girlfriend, and she is beautiful. She's so popular. Long blonde hair, cheerleader body, and she was wearing a MID-RIFT! My dad would never let me out of the house like that! Not that it matters. I would never have the confidence to wear something like that, anyway!

April xox

"WHAT KEPT YOU?" Dad calls from his recliner in the lounge room, where he likes to sit and read the Bible on a Sunday afternoon.

I'm still reeling from my encounter with Finn as I hang my keys by the door.

I can't lie to my dad. "I ran into Finn."

He puts the Bible down and looks at me over his wire-rimmed glasses. "Finn's back."

"He's not back," I say. "Just passing through."

His steely gaze doesn't move from my face, and I wonder if he knows. Can he see the fire in my belly? The desire in my heart? Can he see that my whole head is full of Finn? Can he somehow tell what we just did in the back row of his church?

My whole body heats and I know I need to get out from under his gaze. "Sandwich?" I ask him.

"Thank you, April."

We eat salad sandwiches out on the porch in silence. Neither of us mentioning Finn again.

I don't know what my dad knows about me and Finn. I don't know if he knows we were sneaking around. I don't know if he knows I was lying to him when I said I was working on a science project late at school, or when I said I was at the library or at Katie's house studying.

I had no problem lying to my dad then. I would have done anything just to spend time with Finn. But when Finn left, the guilt kicked in. All the lies caught up with me, and I felt terrible. I decided I didn't want to lie and hide anymore. But I didn't need to, because Finn was gone and my life got so boring that I had nothing to lie about, anyway.

"How are things with Clive?" Dad asks, pushing his plate into the center of the weathered table between us.

I shake my head. "We're not getting back together. Things with Clive are done."

"He's still a good match for you."

Here we go.

"But Dad, I don't love him."

"Love takes time. If you have affection and care for each other, it will become love."

"We dated for six years."

"An engagement could change things. If you'd just say yes. I know he'd still accept, as long as you apologized to him for taking so long."

I push my plate away. "He had *six years* to ask me."

"Perhaps he just wasn't ready. You're both older now. Ready to settle down."

The idea of getting married and starting a family when I still haven't even *lived* yet sounds like hell. I see my life with Clive flash before my eyes — our wedding at Dad's church, everyone we know hugging us and wishing us well. A honeymoon in the next town, where we start trying for our first baby. Buying a house of our own that looks exactly like the one I've lived in my whole life.

That is not the life I want. But if I stay here, what else is there for me?

"I need to get ready for the game." I stand and take the empty plates. "Can I get you anything else?"

"I'll sit here a little longer, I think. Enjoy the game."

Dad never comes to the games because he believes Sunday is God's day, not a day to play sports. But it's the only time that everyone in the town can get together. It would be great for the community if he would come, but I've asked him too many times to bother again now.

I change into a pair of gym shorts and my Lucky Strikes baseball t-shirt, and head down to the field, looking forward to having something to take my mind off the events from this morning.

CHAPTER NINETEEN

inn

LATER THAT AFTERNOON, I get in my car and drive down to the baseball field. I can't sit around my room obsessing about what just happened between me and April. I can't drink myself into another blood high. I need to get out. I need something to do.

You're hoping she'll be there.

I get out of the car and walk towards the old baseball diamond. I take in the wooden bleachers, the cornfields out at the edge of the field, and memories of so many nights spent out here playing ball, drinking, acting like a fool, hit me all at once and it's almost too much. I nearly turn and go back to the car.

"Finn Huxley!" Jemma's voice calls out. I turn and give her a wave. She's still got that blonde cheerleader thing going on, but she really is heavily pregnant, and two little kids are hanging off her. She throws her arms around me, but I don't really know how to hug her when she's so huge.

"Jemma. So good to see you," I tell her.

She grins at me. "These are the kids. Joe and Jimmy."

"Hey kids," I say to them with a smile.

Joe starts screaming, and Jimmy hides in his mom's dress. They're clearly terrified of me. Kid's intuition?

"Jeez, sorry. They're usually better with strangers than this. What's wrong with you two?" she berates them.

"All good. I'm pretty terrifying these days," I shrug.

She rolls her eyes. "You? Terrifying?"

When me and Jemma were dating, we nearly did the deed, but I freaked out. She was more experienced than me, but I just wasn't ready. Couldn't go through with it. She was so cool about it. Looking at her now with these kids hanging all over her feels like a weird alternate universe. Jemma, the coolest girl in school, pregnant with Ed's kid. Ed was cool enough in school. He was still a jock, but everyone thought me and Jemma were perfect together. There were even whispers that the two of us were going to be crowned prom king and queen.

But I wasn't even there, and I still have no idea if we won.

Jemma wrestles the kids onto the bleachers, and I take a seat behind them. Joe looks back at me for a second and then quickly grabs onto Jemma again.

"If I'm freaking them out, I can go sit somewhere else," I tell her. There's only a handful of people in the stands and plenty of other space for me to sit.

The girls from the bar arrive, and both Deena and Danni give me a wave. I wave back politely and then pull my base-ball cap down over my face, hoping they won't come over here and try to talk. Thankfully, they take their seats down at the front. I guess they're just looking for something to do in this ghost of a town too.

"No, it's fine," says Jemma, wrangling Joe. They'll calm down once the game starts."

Ed and a couple of other guys I used to play with stroll onto the field and start warming up. It's strange seeing them here like this. They all look a little older, but they're still out here throwing balls and swinging bats. Some of them still look fit, like Ed, but most of them don't. There's a lot of Dad bods out there, and it makes me feel… old?

But while these guys are going to continue to age, every year a little less hair and a bit more flab out on the field, I'm going to stay this way forever.

The other team from Culpepper steps onto the field and starts hurling good-natured abuse at our team. They clearly play each other often. Well, it's not like there are that many teams around here.

And then she steps onto the field, and I can't believe my eyes.

April Abernathy is dressed in gym shorts, a baseball cap and a tight white t-shirt that reads *Lucky Strikes Baseball* on the back.

"Wait, April is playing?"

I don't realize I've said it out loud until Jemma replies. "Yeah, she's been playing with the team for the last few years. Clive got her into it."

Fucking Clive.

April was one of those girls in high school who would do anything to avoid gym. She had no hand-eye coordination. She was always picked last for a team, and for good reason. She sucked.

But now, here she is, carrying a baseball bat and looking hot as hell.

"Fuck me," I whisper to myself as she puts her bat down and shoves a glove onto her hand.

Ed calls her over to run some warm-up drills. He throws

the ball to her, and she misses the catch, having to scramble for the ball on the ground.

I let out a chuckle. Okay, so she looks hot, but she's clearly still not great at the game.

"Sorry!" she calls out to Ed.

"All good! Pass to me!" he calls back.

She throws the ball back, and it curves towards the other team, who all laugh at her.

Fucking bastards. I'll rip their throats out after this.

Ed jogs over to retrieve the ball and tells the other team to fuck off.

"Sorry!" she calls out to Ed again.

A dumb smile hits my lips. She looks so damn cute out there, trying her hardest, but still failing miserably. Damn, I'm so glad I left my room and came out to see this.

The game begins, and April slides onto the bench where I guess they keep her until they get desperate.

I clap and cheer for our team while they give it a damn good try. Some of the guys I used to play with are still decent, but nothing like they were. The other team, full of middle-aged men who I'm pretty sure are at least half-drunk, are still killing us.

It's our turn to bat, and Ed steps up to the plate. He takes an okay swing and gets to first base.

Clive is up next. He looks back at April, giving her a smile, and I want to punch it right off his face.

Clive.

Jesus. We were friends once. I know it's not his fault I'm still obsessed with April, but the idea of him making a play for my girl after I left still stings.

Now you're making a play for his girl.

Yeah, okay. So walking into town after ten years and bringing his girl to orgasm in her father's church may not have been the most loyal thing I could do. He's been here the whole time, and I just walk into town and take what I want. I take his girl. Kiss her. Rub her clit until she's screaming my name in God's house, while he's… what? Waiting for her at home?

The guilt hits hard. It's worse than how I felt almost killing that trucker who was an asshole to her in the diner.

Clive was my friend, and I did *that* with his girl.

But it wasn't all me. She wanted it as much as I did. But still. Shit. I should never have done that. I should never have put myself in the situation of being her temptation.

I watch the game, feeling like an absolute piece of shit, cheering for Clive like this will somehow make up for what I've done.

Our team starts doing a little better, until Andy, one of the best players on our team at Lucky High, steps up. He swings and then screams out in pain, clutching his shoulder.

Ed rushes over to see what's going on, and after a quick talk, Andy sits on the bench and April is called up to bat.

Ed hands her the bat, and even from here I can tell she's nervous as hell. She looks over at the stands and catches my eye. Her eyes go wide. She didn't even know I was here until now.

"Go, April!" Jemma calls out. "You've got this, girl!"

Everyone in the bleachers starts chanting her name.

"Come on, April!" I shout, my voice carrying across the field.

She's not holding the bat right, and she swings way too late. She strikes out once, twice, and then on her third try, hits the ball so gently that it rolls along the dirt.

"Run!" Ed shouts out, and she does.

And holy fuck, when she *runs* in those damn shorts. *Fuck.* And the way her breasts jiggle in that tight t-shirt, I feel like I'm back in high school, getting all hot and horny just from the sight of her.

She makes it to first base, grinning and jumping up and down and *oh god*, when she *jumps*. She claps her hands in glee like it's the first time she's ever got that far. Maybe it is.

The next player strikes out, and then another player starts running to first, but ends up hobbling off the field.

These guys are so not what they used to be.

"We win!" calls out one of the guys from Culpepper. "You don't have enough players left to keep playing!"

Ed glares at him. "We can play one down!"

"Not in the rules! We win!"

There's a long conversation between Ed and the other captain, and before I fully think it through, I'm down on the field.

"I'll play," I tell him.

A grin lights up his face, and he places a hand on my shoulder. "The Hardball Hero is back!" he calls out.

A couple of minutes later, I have a bat in my hand for the first time in years, while the crowd roars, "Hardball Huxley, Hardball Huxley!" over and over.

I feel like I'm back in high school, everyone screaming my name and I'm about to bat for the championship.

My eyes find April still on first base.

Playing baseball with April and my old friends was not on my Lucky, Arizona bingo card, but here we are.

It's only when the ball flies towards me in slow motion that I remember what I am now. I'm not Hardball Huxley, I'm not the star of the baseball team, I'm a fucking vampire who could knock this ball into the next state.

I try to ease back, try to soften the blow, try to remember what it was like to have regular human strength, but I still knock it out of the park. I throw the bat to the ground and jog to first base, where April is standing there staring at me, lips slightly parted, cheeks flushed. I want to run straight to her, take her in my arms, kiss those warm lips of hers.

"April," I tell her as I get closer. "You've got to run, baby."

She shakes her head like she's coming to her senses, and then she's running ahead of me around the bases while I stare at her perfect rear end in those shorts.

We both make it home, I give her a high five, and then Clive is up to bat.

I slide in next to her on the bench while her boyfriend glares at me. "I didn't know you could play," I say.

She raises an eyebrow. "I can't, really."

"You did good out there. But if you ever want some pointers, just ask."

"It's hard to ask someone who's not here. If I need some pointers, I'll just ask Clive."

The sound of his name on her lips makes the guilt rise in my throat.

"About earlier," I begin, my mouth near her ear, voice low. "I never should have—"

"I don't know what you're talking about," she says, giving me a hard glare.

She's gone cold on me. This is not the April I was giving a religious experience to earlier today.

But I get it. That was a moment out of time. Now we're back in the real world.

Clive strikes out, and our team goes into the field.

"You wanna pitch?" Ed asks.

I shake my head. "I'm out of practice."

"Nah, you're not. You're better than you ever were."

It's clear I'm not getting out of this. I take the ball and try really hard to slow down my pitches to human speed, but it's tough. The first two team members strike out. I pull back even more, slowing everything down, and the next guy gets to first base.

But we still end up winning by a landslide.

CHAPTER TWENTY

pril

Dear Diary,

Finn came over and fixed a faucet today. Water was spraying everywhere. Mom's in hospital again, and Dad was out, and I didn't know what to do. I ran out into the front yard drenched, hoping to find some help. Finn was over in his yard throwing baseballs at an old scarecrow. He looked over at me and then asked if I was okay. I told him, "No! My faucet is broken!" He said, "I can fix it." He was so confident. It was so sexy! He threw a baseball, smacking the scarecrow right in the face, and then he walked over and into my house.

Finn Hardball Huxley was actually standing in my kitchen. Can you believe it?!

His wet t-shirt will forever be imprinted into my brain!!!

Oh yeah, and he fixed the faucet.

April xox

· · ·

I ORDER a Coke from the bar and then go sit with the team. The only seat available is next to Clive, right across from Finn. I take the seat and look down into my Coke for a second while I try to calm my nerves.

Seeing Finn out on the field today was such a blast from the past. What we did in the church this morning was a throwback, but we did something new, something we'd never done before. Seeing him play baseball was like going back in time. He's bigger and stronger than I remember. More filled out, more muscular, faster too. But the way he gripped that bat, the way he threw that ball — my inner teenager was totally losing it.

Only this time now I know how he feels about me. Or felt about me.

It's in the past.

Finn isn't sticking around. What more would he want with me than a fumble in the old church?

But there was nothing about what we did in the church that felt like a fumble.

I look up, and he's staring straight at me. The smoldering look in his eye tells me he's thinking about the church too.

I turn to Clive. "Good game, huh?"

"Would have been better if you'd learn to hit the ball," he says with a laugh.

You did good out there.

Finn's kind words earlier were in total opposition to Clive's.

"But at least we had Finn to come and save the day!" He gives Finn a too-forced smile.

I never told Clive the details about me and Finn. But he knew Finn had asked me to prom and then stood me up that night.

Finn shrugs. "I was just trying to help out some old friends."

Clive raises an eyebrow at him. "You still consider us friends?"

"Yeah, of course."

"Even after all this time?"

"Yeah."

"Even now that you're a too good for us hotshot living the Hollywood dream out in LA?"

Finn looks down at his beer and then, when his eyes hit Clive's again, his gaze is… *threatening.*

Finn always had this way of being the boy next door who would come over and fix your faucet one minute, the next he could glance at you with this look in his eye. Like he was capable of anything.

And that's exactly how he's looking at Clive right now. Like he could kill him with a look.

Finn throws back his beer and smacks the empty on the table. His eyes find mine for just a moment, and he flashes me a dark look that's all smoke and fire. The heat in his eyes tells me he's not finished with me, that what we did in the church really was just an appetizer.

My heart hammers in my chest as I think about what he could do to me, what I *want* him to do to me.

"It's been great catching up with you all," he says. "But I guess I should head back."

"Head back where?" Ed asks. "To go sit in your motel all on your lonesome?"

A vision of that woman leaving his motel room hits me like a punch to the gut. Maybe he won't be alone.

Finn glances at Clive. "I've got work to do. I have some scripts to go through. Need to decide what movie I'm going to take on next."

"Oh, Finn!" Jemma gushes, trying to keep her two cute but crazy kids under control. "Don't go! Tell us more about movie star life!"

"It's not as glamorous as it looks," Finn says.

Jemma laughs. "Oh, I bet it is. I bet it's incredible. So exciting. What was it like working with Maverick Stone?"

Ed rolls his eyes. "She's always had a big crush on him."

"Well, who doesn't?" she laughs. "Maverick Stone is my free pass, isn't that right, Ed?"

Ed just rolls his eyes while Jemma goes on and on. Finn grins over at her in a way that makes my stomach twist.

I was always jealous of Jemma. She was the girl every guy wanted in high school, and Finn was the one who got her. They dated for a good few months. I think they were even still dating when my mom died and Finn started spending more time with me.

Even when me and Finn got together, I was still terrified of Jemma stealing him away from me again.

And now she's here, eight months pregnant and looking at Finn like he hung the fucking moon.

Ed doesn't seem to care. He's just listening to her going on and on about movies and taking a trip to LA someday. He's over it. He's moved on. He knows Finn is going to leave again, go back to his life and he'll get his wife back.

It's so easy for him. It's so easy for all of them. Finn will leave, and it will just be a minor blip to them. That time that Finn Huxley, the kid who grew up here and then made it big in Hollywood, was passing through for a couple of days.

But for me, it won't be that easy.

I'll never be able to forget this.

I'll never move on.

Clive turns to me and waves his empty beer. "Can you get me another drink, babe?"

Usually, I'd put him in his place, tell him to get his own damn beer, but right now I'm thankful for the excuse to get away. I grab his bottle and my almost finished Coke and head to the bar.

And that's when I see her. The girl I saw leaving Finn's motel room, her eyes on Finn like she's replaying whatever sexual encounter they had together. A ball of lead drops in my stomach as I take my spot next to her at the bar. She's gorgeous, blonde, tall, with legs for days.

"That's Finn Huxley," she tells me, like I wasn't just sitting there talking to him.

"Yeah, I know."

"God, he's sexy."

Something else I already know.

"I'm so *drawn* to him," she says. "I have this feeling like we're just *meant* to be. Does that make sense? I mean, I hardly know him. I'm just passing through town, and I've only been with him once, but it was like nothing else I've ever experienced in my life. Hopefully he's up for it again tonight."

I nearly smash Clive's empty bottle on the bar.

"I must sound kind of crazy," she laughs.

"No, not really." I tell her, shooting a quick look at him over my shoulder. "There is something about Finn Huxley that makes you feel like that."

She raises a perfectly sculpted eyebrow at me.

"But the thing about Finn Huxley is that he'll make you feel like you're the only woman in the entire world, give you the best orgasm of your life, the *only* orgasm of your life and then break your fucking heart. Again."

"Oh, I'm so sorry. I didn't know—"

I shake my head. "How could you have known?"

I throw back the rest of my Coke, slam my glass on the bar and leave.

CHAPTER TWENTY-ONE

Finn

Dear Mr. Huxley,

We do sincerely apologize, but we are currently experiencing supply chain issues, and we are unable to fulfil your order at this time. Please accept this complimentary box of Sybline to keep you going until these issues have been resolved.

Sincerely,

Celestial Beverages

Sybline?! What the fuck is Sybline?

I grab a bottle out of the box and crack it open.

Jesus, it smells like *wine*!

I take a sip, and it's revolting.

I don't know what else to do, so I call Maverick.

"How's the regrouping going?" he asks as soon as he answers.

"What the fuck is Sybline?"

"Oh, shit, not you too."

"What's going on? What is this shit?"

He pauses for a moment. "There's an issue with the blood supply."

"Yeah, I got the memo."

"My contacts assured me it would be resolved soon, so don't go on a panic kill or anything."

"I hadn't thought of panicking or killing until you said that."

"I know the synthetic blood tastes like shit, but it will satiate you."

"It tastes like *wine.* I didn't even like wine when I was human, and now it tastes even worse!"

"How much blood do you have left?"

"Two bottles."

"That's not enough."

I kick off my shoes and throw myself down on the bed. "I drank from a couple of humans."

"Yeah? Drain anybody yet?"

"Jesus, no! Just two women I picked up at a bar."

"That's my boy! A threesome!"

"No, on different nights."

"Oh, well. Still. Good effort. And hey, at least you didn't kill them."

"Jesus, Maverick!"

"Did you get the bites a little cleaner? Did you stop as soon as their pulses slowed?"

"Yeah. Mostly. I think I'm getting better."

"You might think you're getting better, but if your supply gets low, your murderous instincts *will* start taking over."

I think of the vision I had the other night of killing everyone in the bar.

He's right. I think I am doing well, but if I have to rely solely on drinking from humans, it could be another story.

"Okay, here's what you do," Maverick tells me. "Force down a bottle of that Sybline. Find a human to drink from, and then get your ass back to LA."

"What? No."

"No?"

"No. I need this. I need to—" Fuck, what do I need to do? "Tie up some loose ends."

"When your thirst becomes insatiable — and it will — you won't be capable of tying up loose ends."

"I'm better. I can handle this." I don't know if it's true, but I *want* it to be true, and that has to count for something, right?

"Finn, just last week you bit that woman in the alley because you couldn't control your thirst. That doesn't just go away after two clean drinks. You will take two steps forward, one step back. That's just how it works."

"I'm not ready to leave, and you can't make me."

"I can make you. You already have an ultimatum from the studio."

"Yeah. I know. But I really think being here is good for me right now. I think you were right. I needed to get out of LA. If I come back now… I'm not ready."

He lets out a deep sigh. "Okay. Drink the Sybline. Find someone to drink from. Get some rest and then call me in the morning with an update on how you're feeling."

"Yeah, okay. I can do that."

"Then, if you're still doing okay, you can tie up your *loose ends*. Quickly. Don't fuck around. Get it done and get back here."

We hang up, and I take another gulp of the synthetic blood. It is truly disgusting, but I really don't want to go on a rampage, so I keep drinking until the bottle is empty.

I really don't want to go back to the bar again after drinking there this afternoon. But I saw the girls I already drank from there earlier and it would be easier to get one of them back to my room again than trying with someone else.

I haven't been gone that long, but I don't expect to see half of the team still out drinking. Clive, Ed, Jemma and a couple of the other guys are still here. Ed's kids must have been picked up and taken home by someone else. I saw April leave after talking to Danni at the bar. She didn't come back with Clive's drink, she just left. Clive only noticed she was gone when he realized he still didn't have a drink. Asshole.

I give them a small wave and head straight to my new favorite seat at the bar hoping Deena or Danni will magically appear.

Fucking Clive slides in next to me, and Ed appears behind the bar, placing down a bottle of whiskey in front of me.

"Sorry, you already drank all the good stuff," he says with a laugh.

"This is fine," I tell him.

Clive gives Ed a look, and Ed nods, disappearing back to where Jemma and the other guys are still drinking.

I throw back a shot and then pour myself another.

"Leave her the fuck alone," Clive tells me straight out.

"What?"

"April. I saw how she was looking at you."

I turn to him, intrigued now. "Yeah? How was she looking at me?"

"Don't be a dick. You know how she looked at you."

Yeah, I did. But I didn't know everyone else noticed it too.

"What's it to you?" I ask. "I didn't see a ring on her finger."

Thank fuck.

"You piece of shit," he says through his teeth. "You can't just come back here, turn everyone's lives upside down and then let us all eat your fucking dust."

I shoot back another whiskey. "I'm not here to cause trouble."

"You broke her heart once. And I've spent *years* healing it. I've been here for her *all* this time." His hand curls into a fist on the bar. "She's with me now. Get the fuck over it. And get out of my town."

"I can get out of your town, Clive. But I'll be everywhere." I turn to glare at him now. "I'll be on every TV, on every movie poster. Every time you take her to the drive-in it'll be my face she sees on the big screen, and when she sees me up there, all she'll be able to think about is the way she felt when she was falling apart on my—"

"You fucker!" Suddenly he's on me, grabbing me by the neck of my t-shirt, pulling me off my chair, and glaring at me like he's about to throw me into the bar.

I glare back at him for a second, and then I just laugh. Clive can't take me, he can't do shit to me.

Except take my girl.

"Hey! Break it up!" Ed appears and tries to pull us apart, but he doesn't need to. I shove Clive off me so hard he falls against the wall at the other end of the bar.

"He's going after April!" Clive spits, wiping some blood from his forehead. He must have hit his head on the bar on the way down—

Blood, fuck!

My thirst kicks in, and I fist my hands.

You're okay. You won't kill him. Not right now, anyway.

"Clive," Ed starts. "April dumped you *one year ago*. You've gotta let it go and move on."

One year ago?

"Wait, you're not with April?" I ask.

Clive glares up at me. "You thought I was with her and still looked at her like that? You piece of fucking shit—"

He scrambles to his feet and then launches himself at me again, but Ed holds him back.

"Why the fuck are you acting like you own her?" I ask.

"Yeah, he does that," Ed says. "It's gotta stop," he tells Clive. "She's not with you. She's allowed to fool around with Finn. She can do what she wants. You don't have a claim on her, man."

They're not together.

Okay, at least now I can stop feeling like shit for taking his girl and start feeling shit about the fact that April just didn't want to see me again.

"Let's get you some air," Ed says, dragging Clive out of the bar while guilt leaves my body, making me feel so much lighter now that I know I wasn't creeping on his girl.

There's still no sign of either Danni or Deena, and so I join Jemma and the other guys from the team.

"What the hell just happened between you and Clive?" Jemma asks, her eyes wide.

"He thought I was creeping on April."

"Well, he does kind of have a claim on her," Jemma says.

"She dumped him," I say.

"We're all kind of rooting for them to get back together," she says with a shrug. "He's good for her. Steady. Stable. He's a nice guy. They belong together."

She doesn't say it, but what she means is that Clive is all the things I'm not.

I might be a movie star, a big deal in Hollywood, but I'm still not fucking good enough for these people.

Suddenly all Jemma's interest in me and my movies is gone. I was just a little entertainment for her afternoon. A story to tell for years to come.

The truth is, she has no real interest in *me*.

"I gotta get home to the kids," she says, giving me a look

like she feels so sorry for me that I don't have what she has. "It's way past their bedtime."

"Yeah. Sure," I tell her. "It was great catching up with you."

"Yeah. You too, Finn." She puts a hand on my shoulder, and I give her my other hand to help her get up.

The guys who are left start talking about their rivalry with Culpepper, and I end up on the edges of the conversation. After a little while, I tell them I'm going to get another drink and then I take a seat up at the bar, drowning my sorrows in cheap whiskey like an old man drinking alone and trying to avoid his own pathetic existence.

At least, that's how it feels until Deena appears, sliding into the seat next to me.

"Did you miss me?" she asks.

I throw back the whiskey in my glass. "Like you wouldn't believe."

She grins at me. "Really?"

"Want to come back to my room?" I ask.

She nods and grabs her purse. "Like you wouldn't believe," she says.

CHAPTER TWENTY-TWO

pril

The Fallen Star *by Evie Everhart*

It's been ten years since I've seen him, but he's never been far from my mind.

I could never forget how he made me feel that summer I was his.

He walks into the church like a fallen angel. Tight black jeans hang off his hips, a dark grey t-shirt that fits like a second skin stretches over his chest, and he carries a leather jacket over his shoulder. The guy oozes cool. But there is nothing cool about the heat in his eyes that tells me he wants to pick up right where we left off that last night he was here.

I gave him my virginity, and I gave him my heart, and the next morning he left to follow his dreams while I stayed behind to be the dutiful good girl.

But the only good girl I ever wanted to be was his.

. . .

I SLIDE a plate of waffles towards Ed, who's sitting at the counter staring at the TV screen, and then place a fruit plate in front of a glamorous blonde woman a few seats down. She's clearly passing through on her way to anywhere but here. I walk around the diner with the pot, refilling cups on autopilot.

Is this going to be my life forever? Filling the same cups over and over until I die?

It's a depressing thought.

But at least I have a shift at the library tomorrow, and I have an idea for my first full-length novel. I bite my lip as I think about what I started writing last night.

Finn Huxley fan fiction.

My writing has always been a little on the steamy side, but this story feels like it's going to be even hotter.

Ever since he gave me that orgasm in church, I feel like something that's been asleep for a long time has woken up inside of me. I would probably feel stupid about it if I didn't feel so goddamned sexually awakened.

And it was only his thumb!

"When is he leaving town?" Clive asks Ed as they both stare at the TV screen.

"I don't know, man. Just let it go," Ed mumbles through a mouth full of waffles.

"I won't let it go until he's out of our lives for good."

"He's not here for April. He told me," Ed says.

I look over at him. "I'm right here."

"Sorry, April," says Ed. "But just to put everyone's minds at ease, he took that girl back to his room again last night. I think they're together or something."

"What girl?" I demand.

But I already know what girl, and my face blazes with heat as I glare at Ed, giving Clive all the evidence he needed that I still have feelings for Finn.

"Just some blonde at the bar. Her truck broke down Friday. She and her friends have been staying at the motel with Finn."

With Finn?!

"How does it take three days to fix a truck?" I huff.

Clive's eyes narrow at me. "April, I don't like the way you've been acting since he came back into town."

"No," I say, walking behind the counter and smacking the coffee pot back in the machine. "I've had enough of this shit."

"Language!" Loretta's voice calls out from somewhere in the back.

"You can't just act like you fucking own me, Clive! We. Are. Not. Together! Get it into your stupid head! We are done! We were done over a year ago!"

Clive's mouth drops open and, right on cue, Finn walks into the diner. Black jeans slung low on his hips, white t-shirt hugging in all the right places. He holds my gaze while he slides off his leather jacket and takes a seat in a booth by the window like I wrote the scene myself.

"He's not welcome here," Clive says through a clenched jaw.

"Clive, oh my god, just stop!" I tell him.

"Clive!" Loretta calls. "Get back here now!"

I give Clive a look like I hope he's happy now he's upset his aunt.

"And if I hear one more curse word from your mouth, April, I swear to God I will—!"

I grab the coffeepot and walk towards Finn, my heart thumping like a wild bird in a cage. His dark hair falls into his eyes, and he looks like the best kind of trouble sitting there staring at the menu, pretending like he didn't hear all of that.

Take me away from here, I want to tell him. *Let me be yours again.*

But he doesn't want me to be his. He wants to fuck some blonde woman from the bar. In the motel where we were supposed to do it for our first time.

A dagger pushes into my lower belly as I think of him with his thumb on *her* clit.

"Coffee?" I ask, holding the pot up, a smile plastered on my face.

"Uh, sure. Thanks."

I pour his cup.

"Anything else?"

"Yeah. Can we... talk?"

"Talk?"

"Somewhere else."

"I'm working."

"When do you get off?"

I get off every time I think of you.

"Not until four."

He sighs. "Shit. I'll be gone by then."

Okay, now that dagger is in my heart.

He looks up at me, eyebrows tight together. "I don't want to. I just — I have to go."

"I thought you were here for a few weeks?"

"There's been a change of plan."

"Well, I guess at least you're telling me to my face this time." I let out a strangled laugh.

"April, please. Can we just—"

"What? What is there to say? You came, you saw, you left. Or should I say, *I* came, you saw, you left?"

"Jesus. Please don't do this, you know what that was—"

"The best fucking five minutes of my life?"

I feel a traitorous tear burn in my eye. But no way am I crying in front of Finn.

"No, I get it." I say, blinking away the tear. "You have a life to get back to. You have movies to make. You have hot blondes to fuck."

"Language!" Loretta calls out.

It's only then that I realize everyone in the diner is staring at us.

"What?" Finn asks. "What blondes?"

"Goodbye, Finn. Forever!"

It's dramatic, but I don't regret it. I turn on my heel and rush through the diner, into the kitchen and out the back door. I lean against the wall, take a deep breath and try to steady myself.

But Finn is leaving. *Again.* And after all this time, it's like the hole in my heart that was never healed in the first place just rips wide open again.

inn

"Okay, who was *that*?" Natalie slides into my booth and looks at me with wide eyes.

"What are you doing here?"

She purses her lips like I shouldn't be surprised.

"Maverick sent you."

She nods. "He was worried about your… situation. He thought it might be best to have your publicist close by. You know, just in case."

"In case you have to cover up a murder?"

Her lips purse again, but she doesn't say no. Of course Natalie is more than just a regular Hollywood publicist.

"I'm fine. Really. Everything is under control. But I've decided to drive back today, anyway."

Not my decision at all, but when I talked to Maverick this morning and told him I was fine, he said that he and

Brandon had decided the best thing was for me to come back to LA, lie low at my place with as much blood bank blood as I needed.

House arrest, basically.

And when I tried to argue about it, Maverick said it was "non-negotiable."

"I brought you some supplies to at least get you back safely," Natalie tells me.

"Thought there was a supply issue?"

"There is, but Maverick had some spare. He was worried about you."

"I'm fucking fine! Jesus!"

"You're not fine, Finn. You're starring in some kind of teen drama out here with that woman who was just screaming at you." She looks out the back of the diner in search of April. "What did you do to her? Why is she so pissed?"

"She's not going to go to the press, if that's what you're worried about."

Her eyes widen. "I'm not worried. I actually think this is kind of juicy."

I shake my head. "My personal life will never be part of your publicity plan."

She gives me one of those fake Hollywood smiles. "Do me a favor and don't leave town. Not yet."

"But Maverick and Brandon said I had to go."

"I'll talk to them."

"Why?" My eyes narrow at her. "What are you going to do?"

"Something that could completely flip the script." I can tell she's trying to frown at me, but the Botox won't let her. "Get rid of any Donnas you have in your room," she says.

"I don't have any Donnas in my—"

Oh, fucking hell.

"Jesus. They were Donnas?!"

She just laughs. "Of course they were. Do you think we'd let you come up here all alone with no food source?"

I GET BACK to my motel room and Deena is still asleep in my bed. I slept on the couch after she passed out. Not from me taking too much of her blood, but from her draining the mini bar while she just talked at me. It was nice actually, to hear about someone else's problems for a change.

"Deena," I say, giving her leg a shake. "Or should I say, *Donna?*"

Her eyes flash open. "Huh?"

I glamoured her afterwards, so she probably doesn't remember that I bit her. But she knows what I am. And she'll know why she was asked to come to Lucky, Arizona.

"Oh, you found out."

"What's with the secrecy?" I ask, folding my arms. "Why pretend to be a bunch of girls with a broken-down truck?"

"It's what Maverick wanted us to do. He claimed us, so we're his, actually."

"Fucking Maverick!"

"He was just worried about you. He sent us here because he wanted you to practice."

"Jesus!"

"I'm sorry," she says, grabbing her shorts and pulling them on. "I didn't want to lie to you. I actually really liked you. Did we—" She looks down as she zips up her shorts.

"No. And I'd never glamour that out of anyone. If we'd had sex, I would have let you remember. Only assholes glamour girls into forgetting who they've slept with."

She shrugs. "Sometimes it's better to forget." She suddenly looks so sad, and I feel bad for her.

"If you think that, why do you do it?" I ask.

"For The Bite," she shrugs. "It feels so good, even if it's just for a little while. It's worth whatever else happens."

That's when I realize the truth about the Donnas. These girls are just addicts. They're so addicted to our blood they'll do anything to get it.

And we just use them.

I used her, but I can tell she's been with a lot of guys who have used her worse than I have. The thought makes me feel sick to my stomach.

I shake my head. "Maybe you should get some help."

She laughs. "Oh yeah, vampire blood rehab. Let me know when that's a thing!"

"I'm serious. Don't you want to get off it?"

"Why would I want to do that? The Bite is the only good thing in my life."

It might not be the right thing to do, but I grab her by the shoulders and look into her eyes until I feel her mind open. "You're no longer addicted to The Bite. You don't want it anymore. You take back your power and take back your life. You can do anything you want. You follow your dreams, and you make amazing things happen in your life."

She nods dumbly. "Yeah. I don't. I do. I am," she says robotically.

I break eye contact. She shakes her head and then looks back at me with a weird look on her face.

"Are you okay?" I ask her.

"Yeah. I just had this crazy idea suddenly."

"You did?"

"Yeah. I think I'm going to open my own diner! I always wanted to do that, but suddenly… I feel like I can now."

I let out a laugh. "You should definitely do it." I grab a napkin from the mini-bar and write my number on it. "Call me when it's up and running. I'll be there."

She takes the napkin and then wraps her arms around me in a tight hug. "I don't know what you just did," she says into my hair. "But it felt like… some kind of magic."

I give her a kiss on the cheek, and she leaves, wandering off back to her own room.

CHAPTER TWENTY-FOUR

pril

"Honey, it's all gonna be okay." Loretta wraps me in her arms and rubs a hand over my back. "You got over him once, you'll get over him again."

I pull back and shake my head at her. "I never got over him the first time, Loretta. That's the whole problem."

"You have to try and let him go. And he's gone now, he's leaving Lucky. Out of sight, out of mind."

"Wait. He already left?"

"Yeah, honey. He's gone. Gone back to LA"

I press my lips together and nod at her. "Good. That's good. We can all just go back to normal around here."

My heart aches as I think about what "normal" is around here.

Finn came here to tell me he was leaving. He wasn't here to ask me to come with him.

"Honey? You okay?"

I give her a nod and fix my apron. "I'll be fine," I tell her.

Then I walk back into the diner, grab the coffeepot and turn back onto autopilot.

The fancy blonde woman who's been sitting at the counter with her fruit plate gives me a curious look while I refill her coffee. "You're April, right?"

"I'm sorry, do I know you?"

"No. But I know you." She gives me a perfect Hollywood smile. "I'm Finn's publicist."

"Oh. Okay. Honestly, I don't really know what that is."

"Have a coffee with me and I'll explain it to you."

"I can't. I'm working."

She takes a glance at the emptying diner. "I'm sure your boss could give you five minutes."

I glance over the counter at Loretta. "Fine with me, honey."

"Natalie," the woman says, holding a hand out for me to shake. Her grip is warm and strong, and I instantly both dislike her immensely and really want to hear what she has to say.

She nods towards a booth in the back. "For a little more privacy."

I take a seat, and two seconds later, Loretta is standing over us, pouring me a cup of coffee.

"Can I get you anything else?" Loretta asks.

"No, thank you," says Natalie.

Loretta gives me a look like she can't wait to hear all about this later and wanders off to clear tables from the breakfast rush.

"I can see you're a busy woman," Natalie says, "so I'll get straight to it. I want you to date Finn."

A loud laugh attacks my throat. "*What?*"

"Just for publicity."

"I'm sorry, but *what*?!"

"He was your high school sweetheart, am I right?"

"Hardly," I scoff.

"You have a history. And you have chemistry."

I shift in my seat. "So?"

"I want you and Finn to *date*," she makes air quotes around the word, "for the next two months while he's promoting his new movie. It's a family film, and his reputation hasn't been very family-friendly of late. If we can change the narrative and have him dating his high school sweetheart, we can show the world that Finn Huxley is just a small town boy with a big heart. It could help the movie and his career in a very positive way."

I just stare at her. I'm not really sure what to say or what to think.

Fake dating Finn?!

"Your first date will be this afternoon and into this evening. You and Finn will wander around Lucky together while I take a bunch of photos I can sell to the paps."

"Paps?

"Paparazzi. Tomorrow, you and Finn will leave Lucky and head back to LA. We'll put you up in a hotel near Finn's place in Santa Monica. It'll be more family friendly if you're not staying at his place, of course. I'll set up dates for you in all the right places in LA. Your relationship will go viral. Everyone will forget about Finn being arrested and his connection with that adult film star."

"Adult film star?"

She ignores my question, and I know I'm going to have to Google this later because what the hell?

"Two months. That's all I'm asking."

I shake my head. "Even if I wanted to go along with this, I have a job. I have two jobs, actually. I can't afford to just go stay in LA for two months."

"We have a generous publicity budget. The studio will pay for everything."

"Everything?"

"And you'd be paid for your time, of course."

"Wait a second. It sounds like you want to *pay* me to date Finn."

"That's exactly what I want."

"But it will be fake."

She gives me a look like she already knows nothing between me and Finn is fake.

"The three of us will sit down and have a meeting. Discuss how it will all work. Set the ground rules so there are no misunderstandings."

"I can't just leave my dad and my job," I say.

"I've already found someone who can cover your shifts for the next few months."

"What? Who?"

"A lovely girl called Deena. She's new in town and looking for work."

"You already asked Loretta about this?"

"Yes." She takes a sip of her coffee. "Perhaps it would help if you knew how much we were going to pay you." She writes a number on a napkin and slides it over to me like we're in some mafia movie.

I turn the napkin over. "Holy shit!"

"Language!" Loretta yells.

"Ten thousand dollars?" I exclaim. "You want to pay me ten thousand dollars to fake date Finn for two months?"

"That's a crumb," she says, shaking the napkin and returning it to me.

"Fuck me!" I throw my hands over my mouth.

"A hundred thousand dollars. Two months of dating Finn. All expenses paid. What do you say?"

My head starts bobbing up and down. I mean, how could I say no to *a hundred thousand dollars*?!

"There's just one caveat. You'll need to sign this." She slides over a document. "A non-disclosure agreement. It's very important that you don't tell anyone about this arrangement. If you do, the contract will be void."

"And I'll lose the money."

"Exactly."

"So, what am I supposed to tell everyone?"

"Tell them what the entire world is about to think. That you're in love with Finn."

CHAPTER TWENTY-FIVE

inn

"You asked her to do *what*?!"

Natalie shoves a copy of the signed NDA at me as she enters my motel room.

"You have to admit," she says, sliding a chair out from the table and making herself comfortable. *Too* comfortable. "It is genius."

"How the hell is this genius? You can't just use people like this!"

"She signed it."

"Because you offered her an amount of money that would take her years to earn! You didn't give her a choice!"

My heart would be racing if it still beat. This whole thing is insane. I can't let Natalie do this. I can't let April pretend to be mine when all I want with all of my cold dead heart is for her to be mine.

April dating me for money isn't what I want. April getting

paid to pretend to be with me? Why the fuck can't this just be *real*? Why can't she come back to LA with me because *she wants to*?

Because you didn't even ask her, asshole. Just like last time.

I run a hand through my hair.

"Everyone always has a choice," Natalie says, flicking through the agreement.

"You forced this onto her. And you didn't even ask me first!"

"Finn, I don't need to ask you. I'm your publicist, and I don't work for you. I work for the studio, and they pay me good money because I know what's best for your career. I can make or break you. Don't forget that."

Wow. Okay.

"So, what? I'm just supposed to go along with it all? Pretend we're together?"

She looks at me like I'm stupid. "Yes. You are an actor, aren't you?"

"What about her? She's not an actor."

"No, but she's holding a torch for you, and that's even better. She won't have to act."

I sink into the chair across from her.

I won't have to act either.

I grab the NDA and flick through it. It's standard. Full of jargon. April's smart, she would have understood every line. She knew what she was signing. The basic gist of these things is that if you disclose any confidential information, you can be in some serious trouble. But Starlight Studios taking April to court is not something I can consider.

"You can't hold her to this."

"It's standard."

"She's not like us. She's a good person. She doesn't under-stand our world. This whole thing is a terrible idea."

There's a knock on my door, and while Natalie goes to

answer it, I roll up the document and shove it in my back pocket.

April walks in, still dressed in her cute diner uniform. Her hair is in tangles around her shoulders, and her eyes refuse to meet mine. Looks like she's regretting her decision to sign already.

"April, please sit." Natalie gestures to a chair.

"You don't have to do this," I tell her.

"It wasn't your idea?" April asks.

"No! It wasn't."

"How about I make some coffee?" Natalie suggests, making her way all of one foot towards the coffeemaker on the desk.

"It was all her idea," I say, gesturing towards Natalie, who I don't think has ever made her own coffee in her life.

April notices Natalie has no idea what she's doing and jumps up, taking the coffee filter off her and takes over. I watch her hands work, shoving in the filter, filling it with coffee, placing it in the machine, adding water. Why is this so fascinating? It's not like I've never seen someone make coffee before, but her movements are so comforting. Jesus, and this is exactly why I can't have her hanging around as my "fake girlfriend" because there's nothing fake about any of my feelings for her. If she comes to LA, if she's suddenly part of my life there, and then after two months she *leaves* — well, if I wasn't already dead, her leaving would kill me.

Leaving her the first time nearly killed me, but I would have suffocated here. Just like I can tell April is suffocating here too.

And then I realize — maybe this is *her* ticket out. Maybe she really wants this.

"There's only two cups," April says. "I'll go get another."

"I'm good," I say. "I don't really drink coffee."

"Since when?" she asks.

I shrug. "About a year ago. I lost the taste for it."

Natalie gives me a look.

"You used to be a total addict," April says. "You'd drink a whole pot when you came into the diner on weekends."

"I wasn't there for the coffee," I say, looking up at her in a way that's way too flirtatious for a fake relationship.

A light blush hits her chest, and I want nothing more than to touch her skin there, to slide her dress down her shoulders, to throw her on this bed that should have been *ours* that night.

I can feel Natalie grinning at us like the two of us are a publicist's dream.

"Wait, you had a coffee in the diner," April says.

"I like the smell of it," I say.

I like the smell of it?! Jesus.

"April, I need to ask you to delete your social media accounts for the duration of the contract," Natalie says, getting back to business.

"I don't really use social media," she says. "So that's no problem."

"Do you have any other kind of online presence? Anything that people could find?"

"Uh, like what?" April asks, leaning against the table while the coffee maker drips behind her.

"Websites, blogs, anything of that nature."

"Um. No." Her heart rate increases slightly when she answers, and I know she's lying. But Natalie has probably already done extensive research on her, she'll find all her accounts and shut them down herself if necessary.

"We also need to set some ground rules, get clear on the terms of the arrangement."

God, it all feels so *professional.*

April just nods.

"April, you'll be expected to be Finn's date for all publicity events relating to the movie over the period of the contract."

Wow, who knew a date could sound so clinical?

"At these events, you'll both be expected to act professionally. You will hold hands. Finn, your hand can touch her lower back, but no kissing or touching at these kinds of events."

April's eyes flit to the carpet, but Natalie keeps rattling on. "I'll be organizing casual dates for you too. This will all be done with publicity in mind. Hot restaurants, celebrity bars, I'll come up with some great photo opportunities. On these dates, you will act like two people in love. I want canoodling. Finn, you can put your arm around her as you walk, some kissing but without tongue—"

"Jesus, Natalie!" I say, rubbing a hand through my hair. "We know how to act!"

"Do you?" She gives me a look like she's remembering me in the back alley, or with the adult film star that I honestly thought was just a Donna. Turned out she was both. "Sometimes with these arrangements, lines get blurred."

April's eyes find mine for a brief moment, and then she turns her back to me and gets very interested in the coffee machine.

"You need to assume that you are never alone," Natalie says. "Someone is always watching, waiting for you to slip up. Even when you think you're alone outside Finn's apartment or on a secluded beach, there can always be someone listening or watching."

"My place isn't bugged," I tell her.

"No, but you have a *lot* of windows."

"They're tinted."

April pours the cups of coffee. She passes a cup to Natalie and then picks up her cup but stays in place, leaning on the desk.

"The three of us in this room are the only ones who can know about this arrangement," Natalie says.

"What about Brandon?" I ask.

She shakes her head. "The fewer people who know, the better."

"You don't trust Brandon?"

"Of course I trust him. That doesn't mean that he needs to know."

"Maverick?" I ask.

She shakes her head. "No."

"You want me to lie to my—" I'm about to say *maker* but then remember April is standing right there, drinking coffee in my motel room. "Good friend?" I finish. We're not even close to being friends most days, but I can't explain to April that Maverick is basically my vampire dad.

"It's not a lie. It's just withholding information." Natalie tidies up the papers in front of her, not realizing she doesn't have April's NDA, which is still in my pocket.

"He'll be pissed when he finds out," I say.

"He won't find out, because you won't tell him," she says with a smug smile. "All communication will go through me. We don't need anyone finding your text messages or over-hearing phone calls. I have you both in my phone under fake names. If you need to talk to each other, you message me, and I'll pass on your messages." She stands and gives us a look like she's not actually sure we can be trusted with all this. "At three this afternoon, you'll meet at the diner for coffee and pie. You'll have a picnic in the park for dinner, and then you have a date tonight at the drive-in. Change your clothes before you arrive at each location so we can make it look like you've been spending time together for weeks, not just one day."

"What do you want me to wear?" April asks.

"Nothing too slutty," Natalie says.

I can't imagine that April owns anything slutty, but I kind of wish she did.

"Tomorrow morning we'll drive back to LA," Natalie continues. "April, you can ride with me or drive your own car. We don't want anyone to see Finn dropping you at your hotel. We'll let the photos from Lucky start to circulate and then I'll orchestrate a first date for you in LA."

I run a hand over my cheek. "Yeah. Got it," I tell her, hating everything she's said since April arrived. No, I'm pretty sure I've hated everything Natalie has ever said.

Natalie looks over at April. "Do you understand, April?"

"Yes. I understand," she says.

"Finn, could you walk me to my car?" Natalie asks, like her car isn't just two seconds away.

"Sure." I give April a look and then walk Natalie out.

"You need to tell her."

"Tell her what?"

She rolls her eyes at me. "What you are."

"What?! No!"

"She needs to know the truth. She needs to know what she's really getting into here."

"No way!"

"You know, I'm pretty shrewd. I'll happily pay someone to play pretend. I'll clean up all kinds of messes for the vampire elite, but I'm not a monster. April will be putting herself in danger spending all this time with you. And if something happens to her—"

"We'll be in public! I'm not going to do anything to hurt her!"

Her mouth forms a hard red line. "You're still learning how to control yourself. She needs to know why the money is so good."

"It's danger money," I say, realizing it's not just a damn good wage.

"An arrangement like this is always dangerous enough without one party being a vampire."

"What if she freaks out and doesn't want to do it?"

"Then I'll offer her more money," she says, cracking a smile.

She gets in her car and drives off, and I turn back to my motel room.

Being in this motel with April, an NDA, a plan to fake-date the fuck out of my reputation and having to tell April I'm a member of the unholy undead was *so definitely* not on my bingo card.

CHAPTER TWENTY-SIX

pril

Finn closes the door behind him and leans against it. He looks up at me, and for just a split second it's prom night. Me and Finn. Alone in this motel room. The promise we made to each other hangs in the air. We're both nervous but excited, and I can't wait to have him throw me onto this bed and take my innocence.

But my innocence is already gone. And his *definitely* is.

I can see in his eyes that he has seen so much more than I ever have or ever will.

"You don't have to do this," he says. "If you need money, I can give you money."

I'm about to tell him it's not about that, but it is a life-changing amount of money, so it can't *not* be about that, but the money isn't the only reason I'm doing this.

Two months with Finn in LA? I would have done it for ten thousand. I would have done it for free.

The money is just a sweet bonus.

"You used to always talk about getting your ticket out," I say. "And this feels like mine."

"It's only two months."

"But with the money, I could get myself set up in LA. I could stay. If I wanted to. Or go somewhere else. I have a bit of money saved, but not much. Most of what I earned over the last few years went on paying Mom's hospital bills, but we managed to get them all paid off a couple years ago—"

"Oh, Jesus. April. I'm so sorry." Finn's dark brows knit under his tangle of hair. "If you need money, please just tell me."

"With Natalie's offer, I won't need anything from you. Or from my dad. Or from anyone."

He pushes himself off the door and steps towards me. "You're thinking about moving to LA?"

I shrug. "Maybe. I don't know. But I do know that I can't keep rotting away in Lucky."

"Why did you stay all this time? Was it just to help pay off your mom's debt?"

I shake my head. "No. There are other reasons. Dad, Clive, my friends, my work... my whole life is here."

"Then why would you even want to leave?"

I let out a laugh. "Dad, Clive, my friends, my work, my whole life is here." I bite my lip to stop it trembling as I tidy the coffee cups away. "You want the truth?" I ask, finally turning to face him.

"If we're going to do this, I think we should be honest with each other about everything." His lip twitches, and the movement makes me want to press my lips into that twitch until it relaxes.

"I never had the guts," I say. The simple truth. "Sometimes, no matter how much you want something, you need someone or something to give you a push."

"You make it sound like I'm about to push you off a cliff."

"You're just helping me jump." I clean out the coffee machine, throwing the filter and grounds into the trash.

"I need to tell you something about me," Finn says. "Before you do this."

I lean back on the desk and fold my arms. "Okay."

A tormented look crosses his face, and I'm not sure I want to hear it.

"Shit. You're married."

He shakes his head.

"In a relationship?"

He laughs. "No."

"Gay?"

He rolls his eyes. "Did I seem gay to you when I made you come in church?"

A fire lights in my belly and spreads through my body. "Not really."

He takes another step towards me. "What we did in church. We can't do it again."

"I know. I read romance novels, Finn. I know how fake dating works." I don't add that I also write romance novels and that I had a really successful serial a couple of years ago about a couple who fake dated.

"Please don't call it fake dating."

"Pretend dating? Making people think we're in love? What do you want to call it?"

"An arrangement."

"Well, I know how these *arrangements* work. I know it's not real. Is that what you're worried about? That I still have feelings for you, and I won't be able to separate them from the *arrangement*? Because if that's what you're worried about, don't. Just because you made me… *come*," I feel my face heat at the word, "it doesn't mean I have *feelings* for you. That was just us reliving our youth for eight seconds. Let's leave it in the past with everything else."

"It was a lot longer than eight seconds," he says with a dirty smirk.

"This could be a new start for me. I don't want to drag the past into it."

"Everyone is going to think it's real," he says. "Natalie didn't explain this to you, but you're going to become famous by association. People will know who you are. You can never tell anyone it wasn't real. Never. You'll always be the girl who dated Finn Huxley."

"I'm already that girl."

"Sure, but I wasn't a big deal back then."

"Finn, you were always a big deal. You were famous in this town long before you went to Hollywood. How different can it be?" I push off the desk. "I should get going if I need to look cute by three."

"You already look cute," he tells me.

I roll my eyes. "Save the flirting for when we're in public," I tell him.

"There's still something I need to tell you," he says. "Before you commit to this."

I shake my head. "Doesn't matter. I'm already committed."

I send Natalie a quick text asking for some money up front so I can buy some new clothes. She replies that my clothes, hair and make-up will all be included as expenses and that she'll have some clothes waiting for me at my hotel.

Okay, wow.

For now I guess I have to make do with what I have. I go through my wardrobe and start with a blue sundress covered in daisies. It's something I used to wear on dates with Clive. It's a little worn when you look closely, but in photos it should look okay. I also choose a pink dress with butterflies, and then jeans and a t-shirt for our date at the drive-in.

Our date at the drive-in. Something I wish could have been real when I was secretly dating Finn years ago.

First secret dating, now fake dating. Great.

I put my hair in a braid, put on a little eyeshadow, blush, mascara and lip-gloss and then pack my bag for the day. I slide my laptop into the bag as well just in case I have some time in between dates to do a little writing.

Then I take a deep breath and make my way downstairs, where my dad is sitting reading in his favorite chair.

My heart races as I prepare myself for this conversation. I can't tell him about the contract or the money. But I do need to tell him I'm going away for a while.

"Dad," I say, my voice wavering.

"Yes, April?" He looks at me over his glasses.

"Can we talk?"

He gestures to the couch, and I take a seat, smoothing down my dress as I do, making sure I'm sitting up straight.

"I'm going on a date with Finn." His eyes widen, but I don't wait for a response. If I do, I know I won't be able to say everything I need to. "And then I'm going to LA for a little while to spend some time with him."

Dad takes off his glasses and rubs the bridge of his nose. "Finn Huxley?" he asks, like there are any other Finns in this town.

"Yes. I know this is sudden. I know what you must be thinking of me—"

"I always knew you had some puppy love feelings for him. But April, this is madness."

I want to roll my eyes at his use of the term *puppy love.* My feelings were never puppy love.

"I know it sounds crazy, but we both care for each other deeply and I—"

"No, April. I will not allow you to see that boy." He puts his glasses back on and picks up his book. "I forbid it."

"Dad," I say, as years of anger and resentment rise in my chest. "I'm twenty-eight years old. You can't *forbid* me from seeing anybody."

He gives me a look like I've just broken his heart. It's the first time I think I've ever spoken back to him in my entire life.

I open my mouth and I'm about to do what I always do — tell him he's right and that I'll do whatever he expects of me. Because he's right. This *is* madness.

A hundred thousand dollars.

Two months with Finn.

My ticket out of here.

"He will break your heart," Dad says. "And you'll be back here in a couple of weeks crying on my shoulder. I'll be the one who has to pick up the pieces. And what about Clive? Have you even begun to consider how this will affect him?"

"I don't care about Clive," I say, standing up from the couch. "Everyone in this town wants me to be with him, but I don't love him. I love Finn!"

"April," my father warns. "If you walk out of this house!"

"What? What will you do?"

"If you run away to LA with that boy, you will not be welcome back in this house."

For years I have stayed. I have done what I was *supposed* to do instead of what *I* wanted, and all the bitter resentment I've been keeping hidden away inside boils up within me.

I have tried my best to be a good daughter, to make my father happy. I have done everything that has been expected. I stayed in this town long after I wanted to leave, I dated the boy my father wanted me to date, I went to church every week, I washed the dishes and cleaned the house. I helped my father pay off Mom's debts. I have given *years* of my life to this man. And now that I want to live my life on my own terms, do *one fucking thing* for myself, he's willing to close the door on me. Just like that.

He looks at me now like he's expecting me to say sorry, to say I'll stay. To agree with him. It's what I've always done, so why would this be any different?

But this time it is different.

"Dad," I say, a tear falling down my cheek. "This is something I just have to do. I have to go. It's time."

He just nods and looks down at his book. "Then I'll pray for your soul."

CHAPTER TWENTY-SEVEN

inn

APRIL WALKS INTO THE DINER, an absolute vision in a blue sundress, and a smile tugs at my lips.

April is *mine*.

For the next two months, she's with me. It may be make believe, but at least I'm the one who gets to make believe with her.

I just stare as she walks towards me, not really sure how I'm supposed to act now that we're officially faking it. Hug her? Kiss her on the cheek?

I can feel Natalie's eyes judging me from her seat at the counter while I try to get into character. If this was my first *real* date with April, what would I do?

I slide out of the booth that Natalie chose for us and take a step towards April.

We just stand there for a moment, both of us unsure of how to act, what to do.

April takes a step towards me, her eyes on the logo of my t-shirt, and I take it as permission to lean in. I place a hand on her back and lower my lips to her warm, freckled cheek. I kiss her cheek and immediately regret it. Now all I want to do is kiss her again, on the mouth this time, and then throw her down on the table of this booth.

How the fuck am I going to pretend with her?

After a frozen, awkward moment, I somehow find the ability to move again and take a step back.

"Hi," I say.

"Hi," she replies, her heart racing. She's flustered by my unexpected kiss, and so am I.

She quickly slides into the booth and grabs a menu. She stares down at it like she doesn't know it by heart after working here for over a decade.

Clive walks over to us with a storm brewing behind his eyes. "April, Finn," he says, his jaw barely moving. "What can I get you?"

I give him a grin. "Can I get a slice of pie?"

"What *kind* of pie?" he grunts.

"Well, what kind do you have?"

He rolls his eyes at me. "It's on the board."

"Oh, sorry, I can't read it from here," I lie. Of course I can read it. I could read it even if I didn't have perfect vampire vision.

"Apple, cherry, key lime or peach," Clive says, making a fist by his side.

"I think I'll go for cherry," I say. I turn to April and slide my hand over hers, and I can hear the blood rushing through Clive's veins. "What are you having, baby?"

Yeah, okay. I know I'm being a dick, but he's the one who's been harassing April. She doesn't want him. She wants *me*.

Well, she wants me for two months and a hundred thousand dollars.

April pulls her hand away. "Apple, thanks, Clive." She gives him a smile like she's really sorry about all this, and then Clive fills her cup, and fills mine about halfway.

Jerk.

When he's gone to get the pie, April frowns at me across the table. "Did you have to rub his nose in it?"

It's only then that I realize there is a dry streak of a tear on her cheek.

"Hey, are you okay?" I ask.

"Yeah."

"You're not okay."

"I am."

"What did we say about being honest?" The words burn as I realize that I have not been honest with her. I had a chance earlier to tell her, and I didn't. But how can I? How can I tell her what I am? There is no way she'd come back to LA with me if she knew the truth.

I should put her safety first, not my own sick desire to play house with her, pretending that we're dating, that I'm human, living in some fantasy world where I can make April mine for real.

But I'm not that good. I'm a vampire. I'm inherently *bad*. I live off other people's blood. I hurt people. I've almost *killed* people.

She's a good Christian girl, and I'm an unholy abomination.

It's hilarious to me now that Natalie ever expected me to tell April what I am. She should have known from the moment she suggested this whole *arrangement* that I was never going to tell April the truth.

Clive places April's pie in front of her, and then practically drops mine onto the table. "Enjoy," he says, giving me another glare as he stomps away.

I just let out a laugh, and I can see out of the corner of my eye that Natalie is already taking photos of us sitting here with pie. I'm laughing at Clive, but it will look like me and April are having some kind of moment, even if she's not laughing with me.

I should be grateful for this moment that I never thought I would get. I thought I would be driving back to LA right now, April and this town well and truly in my rearview mirror. But here I am, an arm's reach away from the one woman I've never been able to get over.

But it feels all wrong. Clive is glaring at us from behind the counter, April has been crying and now is not the time for photos. I shoot Natalie a look and hope she gets the hint that we need a moment here.

"It's my dad," April says, stabbing a fork into her pie. "He said if I left with you, I wouldn't be welcome back in his house."

"He really said that?" I run a hand over my face and try to resist calling the town's preacher an asshole.

"I knew he'd be upset, but I didn't expect him to say that. Especially after everything I've done for him since Mom…"

"So, you're not coming," I say.

She shakes her head. "No."

"I understand," I say, as a rock hits me in the chest.

She's not coming.

But maybe we can still have tonight.

"I can't let you choose between me and your dad," I say. "It was insane to even ask this of you."

"I meant no, I'm not staying. I told my dad no." She blinks up at me, her deep blue eyes clear and certain.

She is coming. April is coming with me to LA.

I shake my head in confusion. "You would still do this? Even if it meant hurting your dad?"

"It's not even about that," she says, digging her fork into her pie like she's stabbing it to death. "I've done everything he ever expected of me. My whole life, I've always been the good girl."

"Not your whole life," I say. "When you started sneaking around with me, you weren't being the good girl."

She looks up at me. "In all my life, that's the only time I ever went against his wishes."

And look where it got her. Abandoning her father for a fucking monster.

"There's something inside of me," she almost whispers. "Something — kind of dark." She stares at the pie on the end of her fork. "That must sound so crazy."

I let out a laugh. "Not at all. I think we all have something darker within us. Some people are just better at hiding it."

"It's not dark like *bad*. Just—"

"I get it. You have—"

"Desires," she finishes.

As she chews, a little piece of apple sticks to the corner of her mouth. I have to stop myself from reaching out and running my thumb over it and over those perfect rosebud lips.

"We all have desires," I say. "But you can't let this — you can't let *me* — ruin the relationship you have with your dad."

"If he is willing to shut me out over the one thing I've ever wanted to do for myself, is the relationship even worth saving?"

I just shrug. This is a decision she has to make. As much as I want to talk shit about her dad and convince her coming with me is the right thing, she has to decide this on her own.

I finally take a bite of my own pie, which is as delicious as I remember. It tastes like baseball and April, high school and homework. So many vampires don't even bother to eat food, we don't need to eat it, but if I get to spend eternity eating pie, maybe being undead won't be so bad after all.

"Did you see your dad?" she asks. "Is that why you came back?"

I shake my head. "Not yet. I did plan to see him, try to clear the air. But now… I don't know. Is there any point?"

"If you do want to see him, I can come with you. Be your buffer." She shrugs. "We could go on the way to the picnic."

Natalie walks past the window outside and starts taking photos.

"I nearly forgot about the picnic," I say, trying to ignore Natalie outside and Clive glaring at me from the other side of the diner and just enjoy the pie.

"I've never been on a picnic," she says. "It'll be my first."

"Wait, are you kidding me?"

She shakes her head. "Nope."

My lips quirk at the corners. "Well, I'd be delighted to give you another first."

CHAPTER TWENTY-EIGHT

inn

"This was your dream car," April says, running a finger across my interior. After we finished our pie, I changed my t-shirt and April changed into a pretty pink dress covered in butterflies. It's quite a bit shorter than the blue one, and as she shifts in my passenger seat, I get an incredible view of her gorgeous pale thighs.

I tear my eyes away and focus on the road. "I bought it as a present for myself when I got my contract for *Double Agency 2*."

"Oh, you're doing another *Double Agency* movie?"

"Yeah. What did you think of the first one?"

"Oh, I haven't seen it."

My eyes flash over to her face and then down to her legs again for a second before I remember I'm supposed to be driving. "You haven't even seen it?"

"No."

"Oh." It's not like April owes me anything, but I'm kind of surprised she hasn't seen the blockbuster I was in that's been out for weeks now.

"I actually haven't seen any of your movies," she says with a shrug.

"Not even *Hound of the Bakervilles*?"

"Nope."

"*Fallen for Love*?"

"What's that?"

"A fall romance. It's been out on Flixie for months, it was in the top ten!"

"I don't have Flixie."

I give her a look. "You've never seen any of my movies?"

"Nope."

"Can I ask why?"

She sighs. "Why would I want to torture myself?"

"Oh, sorry. I didn't realize my movies were that bad. I mean, *Hound of the Bakervilles* wasn't great, but I think you'd really like *Fallen for Love*. You always liked those kinds of romance movies. Maverick said doing a Flixie film would destroy my career. It didn't. If anything, I think I have even more fans now. But knowing you liked them was a big part of the reason I said yes to doing it."

Her eyes flash over at me, and I look back at her for a second before taking the turn towards my dad's house.

As soon as the house comes into view, the ball of iron that used to live inside of me instantly returns to my chest. I really don't know what I'm trying to achieve or what good coming here will do.

But maybe facing this demon can help me face the rest of them.

I park the car in the driveway and look up at the old house. The paint is peeling on the chipboard, the front porch is littered with old furniture and piles of junk, but it's the man sitting on the porch that has changed the most.

My father is skinny, *too* skinny. And he looks… unwell.

"Nice ride," he says as I make my way towards the front porch steps, April following just behind me. "Ford Mustang."

"Yeah."

"What are you doing here? Thought you were too good for us all now?"

I stop at the bottom of the steps, waiting for an invitation to come up, but he doesn't offer one. He just stands there looking down at me, like he always did.

Well, coming here was a big mistake.

"Just wanted to see you," I say.

He lets out a laugh. "Sure. After over a decade of silence, my son just drops by to see me."

"I thought maybe we could talk."

"I 'aint got nothing to say to you." He glares at me now, and I notice how weathered and gaunt his face has become. He takes off his cap, and he's completely bald underneath. The thick dark hair he once had is all gone.

"Shit, Dad, are you okay?"

"You're too early for your inheritance. I'll go kicking and screaming!"

"I don't need an inheritance."

"Then why are you here?"

"I told you. I just wanted to talk. Clear the air. Say what needs to be said. I don't know, Dad," I say, running a hand through my own thick, dark hair. "I was in town, and I just thought—"

"What did you think? That you could just walk up here like you and your mother didn't take everything from me?"

"Dad—"

"I have nothing to say to you."

"I just—"

I just what? I don't know. Shit.

Actually, I do know. I just wanted him to say sorry, to admit his mistakes. I wanted him to say that he's fucking proud of me.

But it's too late for any of that.

This isn't a fall romance movie for Flixie, and there aren't going to be any hugs or forgiveness between me and my dad. No reconciliation. No sitting at the table for a family dinner.

Not for me.

He turns his back on me, walks up the porch steps and heads back into the house without even looking back at me. The door closes behind him, and I realize — that's it. That's the closest to closure I'm ever going to get with my father.

I feel April's hand on my shoulder. "I'm so sorry," she whispers.

"Asshole," I mumble up at the house. "I don't know why I expected anything else! Idiot!" I kick dirt towards the house and then turn in a circle, clutching my head. "Fuck him. Fuck it!"

April gives me a moment, and then when I turn to her, all I see are her dark blue eyes full of concern for me when her father just told her she was no longer welcome in his house.

"You tried," she says. "You did what you could."

"He looks sick. Do you know what's wrong with him?"

She shakes her head. "I never see him around. I think he's mostly living as a recluse out here these days." She squeezes my shoulder and then drops her hand. "But yeah, he doesn't look well."

"Let's get out of here," I say.

And never, ever, come back.

CHAPTER TWENTY-NINE

inn

NATALIE HAS the picnic all prepared for us for when we arrive at the park in the middle of town. It's not much — just a bit of grass, a pond and a few trees, but it's nice enough. It's a popular spot. There are kids running around while their parents try to chase them, and a few other couples enjoying the slightly longer evenings, and that's obviously why Natalie chose it. She wants us to be seen together.

I take April's hand in mine, and holy shit it feels so good, so right, to have her soft hand in mine. It feels so comforting and safe after everything that just happened with my dad. Having her there today was the first time in ten years that I've felt like I wasn't dealing with my dad stuff alone.

We take our seats on the red and white blanket Natalie has laid out, on either side of the huge basket she's left for us in the middle.

"I wonder what Natalie packed for us." I start pulling out

containers of salads, three types of bread, cold pizza, there's enough food here for twenty people.

"Red wine?" April says, pulling out a bottle of that disgusting synthetic blood.

I take the bottle from her. "That's the non-alcoholic wine I had Natalie bring for me since I'm driving," I say. "But you can have the real stuff." I hold up a bottle of white.

"Thanks," she says, as I pour our drinks into plastic wine glasses.

I don't want to drink the synthetic junk, but I also need to be on my best behavior tonight, so I force some down.

We spend half an hour just eating, trying everything and talking about anything except our dads.

April gets tipsy on the wine, and god she's adorable when she's like this. I've never seen her this way before. I drank a bit when we were in high school, but I never saw her with a drink. She didn't go to parties, and she never came to the bar either. I can only imagine what her dad would've done if he'd found out she was hanging out at the bar with the likes of me and the other boys from the baseball team who were drinking underage.

The wine is making her face all red and blotchy, and she's less inhibited, even more... *April.*

She leans towards me, and I take in an extra long inhale of her scent of apples and daisies. "What happened with you and your dad?" she asks, finally breaking the ice that's been hanging in the air between us since we left my dad's place.

I swallow another sip of Sybline. "You know he was always a piece of work."

"Yeah, I remember he was always giving you hell. But something happened, didn't it? Something he couldn't get over. Something you never told me about."

I pause and top up her glass and then fill mine with shitty fake blood.

"Sorry," she says, flailing her hand around, nearly dropping a slice of pizza. "It's none of my business. Don't tell me."

"No, it's okay," I say. "I never told you about it before because… well, I don't know. I was right in the middle of it, I guess."

"You don't have to tell me now if you don't want to. No pressure."

"It's okay," I say, giving her a thin smile. "I want to."

She moves a little closer to me and puts her glass down, resting it on her knee as she gives me her full attention. God, she's so fucking beautiful. Her cheeks flushed, her lips slightly parted, her dress riding up a little on one side, showing even more of her thigh.

Fuck.

I shake my head and bring myself back to her question. "I have to admit, it hurt to have him act like I was the one who turned my back on him," I say. "When his back was turned on me from the day I was born."

April leans back on her hand and looks at me with a gentle, understanding gaze. It makes me feel like I can tell her anything, and she'll hold it in her soft embrace. She'll kiss me better, take all my pain away.

"It was the day of prom," I start, finally feeling the courage to tell her the whole truth about that night. "I got the call that I'd gotten the part in the movie. Mom was thrilled for me. She was ecstatic. She was dancing around the kitchen and hugging me, jumping us both up and down." I smile as I remember that moment, the joy before the storm. "Dad walked in and saw us like that. He hated thinking people were keeping things from him. He was so jealous, so fucking insecure. He asked Mom what was going on, and she didn't answer him straight away. She was too busy hugging me. Then my dad just… lost it. He went crazy. Started throwing shit."

"Oh, Finn," April says.

"She told him to stop. She told him it was about the movie, that I'd gotten a part. It only made him angrier." I stare into my plastic wine glass. "He grabbed her, pushed her into a wall."

April gasps and puts a hand to her chest.

"There was blood. Everywhere." It still hurts like hell to think about it. I can still see it so vividly, I can still hear my mom's sobs. "I didn't even think, I just went for my dad. I punched him in the face." I rub a hand over the back of my neck. "Sorry. You don't need to hear all the details."

"You were protecting your mom," she says.

"That's not how he saw it. He was furious. Said if I didn't call the studio and say no to the movie, if I went to LA, that he'd call the cops, tell them I hurt my mom. He was friends with Sheriff Hobson. I would have been fucked. Mom was so scared. As soon as Dad's back was turned, she ran. I ran after her. We both got in my truck, and I just drove."

April's eyes water up. "That's why you didn't come to prom. It wasn't just because of the movie."

"It was one of the reasons," I tell her. "But I also knew I couldn't be with you that night, not how we talked about, and then leave you the next day. I couldn't do that to you."

"Oh my god, Finn. I'm so sorry. I thought you just didn't care about me."

"I never stopped caring about you." I shake my head. "I could have done things differently. I could have taken Mom somewhere safe, dropped her at the motel. I could still have taken you to prom. I could have at least come to talk to you in person. Tell you what happened. I could have driven through the night to get to filming the next day. I had options. I could have done it all differently."

So differently.

I could have called her, I could have told her I wanted

her to come out and be with me in LA. I could have suggested long distance. I could have done so many things I didn't do.

"No. Finn. Prom wasn't that important."

"It was important to you." I take another sip of Sybline. "And I'm so fucking sorry, April. I'm sorry I handled it all so badly. I'm sorry that—"

"Stop, Finn. Don't be sorry. You were in a horrible situation. You did what you needed to do."

"I should have called you. Written you a letter. Anything."

She gives me a sad smile, and I know she wishes I'd done those things.

"Shit. That was heavy. Way too heavy for a picnic date. Natalie's going to get a bunch of photos of us looking like we're breaking up or something."

She lets out a soft laugh. "I'm glad you told me, Finn."

"I should have told you that night. But I was scared. Scared dad was going to get me arrested, scared of what would happen to Mom. He was always an asshole, but he never touched her before that day."

"He never hurt you?"

"He was emotionally and verbally abusive," I say. "I didn't know that was what it was called at the time. I just thought he was an asshole. Now I know what it was."

"Have you been to therapy?"

I laugh. *A vampire in therapy?!*

"No," I say. "I haven't been to therapy."

"It might help," she says. "I might even go myself when I get my money."

"Yeah?"

She nods. "Yeah." She finishes her wine and toys with the stem of the plastic glass for a few moments. "How is your mom?" she asks.

"She's doing well. She met a guy a few years ago, Lorenzo.

She lives with him in Mexico now. He's good to her. She's happy. We talk a lot, but I don't see her much."

"I'm glad she's happy."

"Sorry, I'm making all this about me," I say. The sun is setting, and so I start packing up all our picnic stuff. "How are you feeling about things with your dad?"

"Honestly? I'm just really missing my mom right now." She puts a hand on the silver cross she's been wearing since her mom passed. Her mom used to wear it all the time, never took it off. I'm guessing April doesn't take it off now either. "It's been so long since she passed away, but the grief still feels so raw sometimes. Like it just happened. And today when my dad—" A tear rolls down her cheek, and I open my arms.

"Come here." I pull her in close, and she relaxes her body into me like we were made to fit together, and fuck my relationship with my dad, fuck this town, it's being so close to *her* that feels like home. I lower my face to the top of her head, breathing in her scent of baked apples and summer cornfields. "It's okay," I tell her. "You're okay."

I place a gentle kiss on the top of her head, and she lets out a sigh, looking up at me with those big, bright blue eyes.

"We should probably get to the drive-in, so we get a good spot for the movie," I say.

We leave all the stuff from the picnic where it is, knowing Natalie will come and tidy it all away for us, and I drive us out of town towards the drive-in.

CHAPTER THIRTY

pril

DEAR DIARY,

I met Finn in the cornfield again tonight. When we're together, I feel complete. I know, it sounds pathetic. I don't want a man to complete me, but when I'm with Finn, I don't feel so lost, sad or alone anymore.

When Mom passed away, Dad became even more distant than before. He didn't want to talk about her, he didn't want to talk to me.

But I can talk to Finn about anything. I told him tonight that I still talk to my mom at the cemetery. He just squeezed my hand and told me I can talk to him too if I want.

And so I did. I told him I wanted my first time to be with him. He got all nervous and flustered, it was so adorable! Then told me it would be his first time too. I had no idea! I thought he'd had sex with Jemma at least!

I know I should stay "pure" for my future husband, but I just can't understand how there's anything impure about this feeling in my body and in my soul that makes me want Finn in every way.

There's nothing impure about the way I want Finn. It's too beautiful and magical to be wrong!

April xox

WE CHANGE OUTFITS AGAIN — I get into my comfiest jeans and baby blue tee, and Finn changes into a white t-shirt that hugs his broad shoulders even more than the last two shirts did. We swap cars outside the diner and take my car to the drive-in. It's my idea to swap, I don't want to ruin the upholstery of his car with popcorn and fries.

The Lucky drive-in is an institution in this town. It's only open on Saturday nights, and they play a different movie every week. Sometimes new movies, but mostly old classics.

It's only when I drive up to the entrance and see the poster that I realize what movie is on tonight.

Double Agency.

"I guess I'm going to have to see it after all," I say.

Finn lets out a groan. "This is so embarrassing. I don't want to sit here all night watching my own fucking movie, and you don't want to see it either. Fucking Natalie. Let's just go."

"Nope," I say. "I'm not doing anything to jeopardize my contract."

Finn gives me a sideways glance as Larry, who's been working here for a hundred years, hands two tickets and an ancient looking speaker through my window.

"Already paid for," he says with a wink when I try to hand him my card.

I look at Finn, but he just shrugs like he's so used to getting things for free he doesn't even notice.

I drive through the entrance and then park near the middle with the rear of the car facing the screen.

"You're facing the wrong way," Finn says.

I give him a grin. "Nope!" I pop the trunk, grab some blankets and then fold down the back seats. I place the blankets down in the back and the back of my little hatchback car becomes a very cozy place for us to watch our movie.

Almost *too* cozy now that I think about it.

"I'll go get us some snacks," Finn says.

I give him a nod while I set up the speaker that's at least fifty years old. They've had the same speakers here since I used to come here with my mom as a kid. Dad was never really into movies. He said he preferred to stay home and read the classics. The speakers crackle and sometimes stop working altogether, but it's all part of the experience.

Finn is gone for a very long time, and the movie is about to begin by the time he finally comes back with a huge tray of snacks and two massive drinks.

"Did you get lost?" I ask, moving over to give him some more space in the back.

"Oh, sorry. I bumped into some of the guys from the team. Got to talking." He hands me the snacks and squeezes into the back, bumping my knee in the process. "Shit, sorry," he mumbles.

"You okay?"

"Yeah?"

"You're acting kind of weird."

"I'm fine." He wriggles around, and it's clear he's trying to work out how to sit as far away from me as possible.

"Oh, you're bleeding," I say, pointing to a spot of blood on his t-shirt.

His eyes go wide as he looks down at the spot.

"Finn?"

"Uh. Yeah. I had a nosebleed."

"What? Just then? When you were talking to the guys from the team?"

"Uh, yeah."

I grab a tissue out of my purse and hand it to him. "In case you need it."

"Thanks."

I look over at him trying to squeeze into the back of my car, the light from the big screen illuminating his perfect cheekbones. I'm hit with the scent of popcorn, fries, dirt and gasoline and I can't help but think that this is exactly the kind of date we'd have gone on back in high school. That's if we weren't sneaking around because we both knew my dad would never approve.

Well, I don't need his approval now.

The movie starts, and I try to settle into my spot, but Finn is so close, and it's super awkward. I quickly regret my plan and wish we were just sitting in our seats up front. Our hands bump as we both go for a snack at the same time, and he pulls back like I've shocked him.

"What's gotten into you?" I ask him.

"What? Nothing."

"You're definitely acting weird," I say, as Maverick Stone appears on the screen, walking into a coffee shop.

"Am I?"

"Yeah, you are."

"Shit, sorry. This is all — it's a lot. Everything with my dad, this whole *arrangement*." He makes air quotes around the word. "And now I have to watch myself on screen. I'm just feeling a little tense, I guess."

"If you want to go, we can go."

"No, you're right. Natalie will go nuts." He gestures to a truck nearby, and I can just about make out Natalie kneeling behind it taking photos of us.

"Okay, that's weird."

"It's only going to get weirder when you come to LA. Are you sure you're ready for it?"

"Ready as I'll ever be."

Finn's pocket bleeps, and he elbows me trying to get to his phone. "Sorry, shit."

"It's okay," I say, rubbing my arm.

"She wants us to cuddle," Finn says, frowning down at me.

"And you don't want to?"

"Of course I want to, just — ah, shit." He runs a hand over his face.

"Finn." I put my hand on his knee, and I notice Natalie in my periphery getting a photo of us. That one will be good. "What is going on with you?"

"Nothing. I'm fine. I'm good. Come here." He puts an arm around me and pulls me into him, just like Natalie told him to. "Is this okay?" he asks into my hair. "I just really don't want you to feel uncomfortable."

"It's fine." But even though his body is tense and tight, it's more than *fine*. It's *Finn*. "I'm comfortable doing this. I wouldn't have said yes to this if I wasn't."

"Oh god," he groans as his own face appears on screen.

I knew it would be weird to see him up there, but I don't think I was quite prepared for just *how* weird it would be. Finn is huge up there. He's dressed in a black suit and tie, and he looks absolutely fucking *gorgeous*. I mean, he *always* looks gorgeous, but up there, at that size, in that designer suit, he looks like a *god.*

His arm squeezes around me, and even though I'm warm here in this car, under a blanket and in Finn's arms, shivers run up my arms.

Of course, I knew he was in movies. I knew he was

becoming the next big thing. But seeing him up there like this? I think I've just realized that Finn is so much more than what he was when he was mine. He's so much more than Hardball Huxley. Finn is so much more than the boy I used to make out with in cornfields.

Finn is a fucking movie star.

CHAPTER THIRTY-ONE

inn

DOUBLE AGENCY, *four and a half stars*

Double Agency *is one of the best action movies made in the
last couple of years. The* Road Rage *movies were great, but
Double Agency takes it to the next level. Maverick Stone excels,
newcomer Trix Delaney is beautiful and insanely talented, but
Finn Huxley, another newcomer, is the real standout. They are
calling him the next Maverick Stone, but Maverick is a classic
Hollywood action hero — blonde, buff, basic. Finn's darker and
deeper and fully tortured. My wife has already put him on her free
pass list, and I'm already looking forward to part two, which starts
filming soon!*

@Filmmmbufff3456

THE MOVIE CAN'T FINISH SOON ENOUGH. Watching her watch
me on screen was stressing me out. I was constantly

checking her facial expressions to see what she was thinking. Did she like the movie? Did she think my acting was good? What was she thinking about her first Finn Huxley movie?!

But the worst part was that cuddling April in the back of her car because someone told us to, just felt so awful to me. I wanted this to be a real date. I wanted to put my arm around her because it was my idea. I wanted April to *want* me to pull her in close because that's what she wanted, not because Natalie sent me a text and demanded that she did or she wouldn't get her money.

This all feels so cheap.

But that's not the worst part. I'd drunk so much Sybline at the picnic that I really needed the bathroom before I got the snacks, but when I was walking around the back of the snack stand, I bumped into Clive. He glared at me the wrong way and my stomach rumbled. That fucking Sybline doesn't do shit for me, and knowing I was going to spend the night with April — well, I couldn't risk putting her in danger, could I?

I glamoured him, took him into the bathroom, bit him, took what I needed from him and then glamoured him again. I glamoured him to forget the whole thing and also told him he would leave April the fuck alone, planting a belief in his mind that he was over her and ready to move on. I also told him that he'd learn how to make his next girlfriend come and do it to her as much as she could handle.

But it was for the best, right? She's not going to want him back… is she?

I'd always tried to avoid those kinds of situations. Most vampires do it. They find a human, glamour them, drink from them, glamour them again and disappear, the human being none the wiser. But while I hate the idea of taking anyone's free will, and would absolutely avoid it if possible, keeping April safe from me has to be my priority. And if I can get Clive off her back in the process? Great.

I was able to make the bite clean and stopped before his heart rate lowered at all. Maybe it was because it was Clive. After all, I had no real desire for *his* blood, just *someone's* blood.

I let him go and tried to convince myself it was for the greater good, but still, I walked back to the car feeling disgusted with myself, like a fucking monster. All through the movie I was sitting in my own self-pity and wishing I could just be fucking *human* again. That I could have been here with April tonight on a *real* date. No Natalie, no photos, no fake dating, no drinking her ex's blood in the bathroom. Just me and her, like it always should have been.

I saw how she looked at me up there. It changed things for her. She's never going to see me the same way now. I'm not boy next door Finn who fixes her faucet anymore. I'm Finn the movie star, and Finn the monster.

The credits roll, April slowly moves out of my embrace, and her wide eyes take me in in a whole new way. "Finn, that was incredible."

"Yeah? You think?"

"You were amazing."

I give her a forced smile. "I'm glad you think so."

She looks down at the mess we've made with our snacks. Her snacks. I hardly touched them. I plant a kiss on the top of her head. Not for Natalie and her fucking photos, but because I want to. "I should get you home."

"I don't have a home," she reminds me.

"Oh yeah. Shit. Well, I'll get you a room at the motel."

"It's okay. I was just planning to sleep in my car, get an early start on the drive tomorrow."

"I'm not going to let you sleep in your car. I'm getting you a room."

. . .

BUT WHEN WE get back to the motel, a lacrosse team from Prescott has booked all the rooms.

I lean against my car and look thoughtfully and hopefully up at my motel room.

But the last thing I should do right now is invite April to stay in my room. That is the worst idea I've ever had.

"I'm good." She nods her head towards her car now parked next to mine outside the motel. "The car is fine."

I shake my head. "You can have my room. I'll sleep in my car."

"I couldn't let you do that."

"You know what? You can have the room, and I'll just drive back to LA tonight. Get some sleep when I get home."

"That's crazy. You can't drive all night. You'll be exhausted."

I won't be, but I can see why she would think that.

Finn, don't do it—

"We could share," I suggest. "I can take the couch."

She bites her lip, and holy hell, I want to thumb that lip. I want to *bite* that lip, a little drip of her blood as a taster. I want to feel her blood rushing into my mouth, down my throat and into my soul.

I squeeze my eyes shut. It's the first time I've had such an intense feeling about drinking from her. Of course I've thought about it. I think about drinking *everyone's* blood. But me and April have always been about so much more than that. That day in the church all I wanted was to *touch* her... but now I want more. So much fucking more.

When I'm having these thoughts is really the worst time for me to invite her inside.

If I get her in my room, what will I do to her? Will I be able to control myself?

Get in your car and drive home, you idiot!

"I'll take the couch," she says, strolling towards the door.

Her ass looks amazing in those jeans, and the way her hips sway toward *my* room makes my fangs pulse. There is no way in hell she'll be safe with me in my motel room tonight.

Finn, you fucking prick!

I don't stop her. I don't tell her to sleep in her car. I don't drive back to LA. I just follow her to my room, stick my key in the lock and open the door.

CHAPTER THIRTY-TWO

pril

MY HEART RACES as I step into his motel room. *Our* motel room.

This should have happened years ago. We should have been here that night. He shouldn't have been driving his mom across state lines to keep her safe. We should have had one more night together. We should have done what we said we would. Been each other's firsts and then parted ways.

I would have been okay with him driving through the night to get to LA for filming the next morning. It would have been torture to let him go, but so romantic and special to know that we had our one night together before he had to leave to follow his dreams.

Then at least my first time would have been with someone I loved.

Finn closes the door behind him and leans against it. His

eyes smolder, and his biceps flex, and I wonder if he's thinking the same thing I am.

I don't know where the line is between our past, our history, the orgasm in the church and our new *arrangement.*

Am I here in his room because he wants me here? Because he wants us to have one special night here? Or am I just here because I have nowhere else to go?

But something within me *knows* what this is.

This is our moment.

"Can I use the bathroom?" I ask.

He nods towards the door on the other side of the room. I head inside and take a deep breath. I rinse my mouth and try my best to tidy up my hair and makeup.

I look a little older than I did all those years ago, but for a moment I can still imagine that it's that night. That I'm in the bathroom having a little freak-out and psyching myself up before I go out there and have sex for the first time.

It may not be my first time tonight, but I'm just as nervous about my first time with Finn. That orgasm in the church has haunted me these last few days in the best way possible. But it wasn't enough. It wasn't enough Finn. It was like taking a sip from a well that I wanted to dive into. Completely naked.

I step out of the bathroom and Finn's lying on the couch, sneakers kicked off, one hand under his head making his arm look huge. He's flicking channels, and as I watch his thumb pressing the arrows up and down, all I can think of is how he pressed that thumb against my clit and gave me my first non-solo orgasm.

He looks up at me, and it's suddenly so intimate. He's not untouchable movie star Finn, he's boy from Lucky Finn, channel surfing and looking way too relaxed and sexy for his own good.

"Get off the couch. You're taking the bed," I tell him.

"No." The deep, gruff way he says *no* makes me stop arguing with him. He keeps channel surfing, his eyes glued to the TV that looks like it's about to fall off the wall, and it's pretty clear now that we are not on the same page. This isn't our moment at all. This is just me having some only one bed fantasy about my ex, who genuinely just wants to watch a game and crash on the couch.

"I don't have anything to wear to bed," I tell him. "I only have what I grabbed before I left my dad's house." Not my house anymore. Just his.

Finn stands, dropping the remote on the couch and leaving the TV on some sports channel. He leans over his bag in the corner, grabs a clean white t-shirt and tosses it over at me.

"That okay?"

I nod. "Yeah. Thanks."

"No problem."

We both just pause there for a second. Me looking up at him with his shirt in my hands, him looking down at me like he's — what? Waiting for me to take off my dress and put it on?

"Are you done in the bathroom?" he asks.

I just nod.

"I'm going to take a shower." He disappears into the bathroom, leaving me to freak out about what is going on here. Does he want me? Is anything going to happen between us tonight? Or is he just going to watch sports and then fall asleep?

My heart thumps as I take off my dress and bra, leaving me practically naked in Finn's room. I lay them across a chair, and then I slip into Finn's t-shirt. The feel of the white cotton of *his* shirt on my bare breasts makes me feel so sexy, so ready for whatever he wants to do tonight. If he even wants to do anything.

Of course he wants to! He probably just needs you to make the first move!

I remove the blanket from the bed and try to find a seductive way to sit that will have him begging for it the moment he walks out of the bathroom. I lean against the pillows and stretch my legs out, bending one up in a way that shows *a lot* of leg. It's not subtle. As soon as he takes one look at me, he'll know what I want.

When he walks out of the bathroom in nothing but a towel around his waist, his hair all damp and falling in his eyes, my heart almost leaps out of my chest. Finn is so fucking *ripped*! My mouth drops open as I stare at his bare chest, at the dusting of dark hair that runs over his pecs and down, down, down to what's underneath his towel.

"Forgot my clothes," he says, grabbing some stuff out of his bag and heading back into the bathroom.

When he returns this time, he's in a white t-shirt exactly like the one I'm wearing, and a pair of sleep shorts.

Why is he wearing clothes?!

His eyes flicker to my bare legs, and I swear he feels it too. He wants me. He wants this.

I look up at him and bite my lip.

But he just scowls at me. "Jesus, April. What are you doing?" He looks away, moving cushions off the couch.

Okay, this was not the reaction I was hoping for.

"I'm just sitting here," I say.

"You're sitting there looking like a sex goddess, and I'm —" A pained expression crosses his face.

"You're what?"

"Not strong enough to deal with it."

I'm taken back by his words. I'm something he has to *deal* with? "What's that supposed to mean?"

He turns to me and runs a hand through his damp hair. "This isn't ten years ago."

"Yeah. I know."

"We can't just pretend that this is fucking prom night."

"Wow. Okay. That's not what I was trying to—"

"You're sitting there, tempting me, you want me to fuck you and I—"

"And you don't want to."

"Jesus, shit! No!"

I grab the sheet and blanket and pull them over me. The sting of his rejection has me spitting out words I don't mean. "Go fuck yourself then!"

"That would be safer," he grumbles to himself. "But that's not what I meant. Of course I want to fuck you!"

"Then why don't you just do it?" I throw the blanket off and sit up on my knees, glaring at him, practically begging him for it.

"It would complicate everything. People could get hurt."

"Me. I'd get hurt." I look up at the stained ceiling. "I get it, Finn. You're a big star now. You don't want a relationship with me. I understand that. I just thought maybe we could—"

"Wait, I never said—"

"Don't you feel like we still have unfinished business?"

He takes a step towards me. "Yes. I do."

"So, let's finish it."

He draws a strong, large hand over his face, and *oh god*, I want that hand on me!

"Just tonight. Just here in Lucky," I say. "We finish what we started."

He thinks for a moment, his eyes trailing my thighs. "And then what?"

"From tomorrow, our relationship will be strictly professional. We do what Natalie tells us. After two months, I'll be out of your life for good. I'll have the money I need, and you can have your freedom back. Date whoever you want. Move on. I'll just be an ex you had a one-night stand with ten years later and a girl you fake dated for publicity reasons."

He stands frozen, his dark eyebrows knit in worry, and I'm terrified he's going to say no.

"You look so fucking sexy like that," he says, taking a step towards. "In nothing but my t-shirt."

My heart hammers in my chest, heat moves between my legs, and I don't think I've ever felt my pulse run this high.

"Well, I am still wearing my panties," I half whisper.

Very *damp* panties.

He sits on the bed, taking my face in his hands, and I feel so safe, so held, so protected. "Are you sure you want this?" he asks.

I nod. "I want this."

"And you're okay with it just being for tonight?"

"Yes."

No.

He leans closer, the scent of his woodsy soap and his warm skin amplifying everything, and he presses his lips to mine. The heat it creates runs through me like an injection, pulsing through every vein, filling my body with *him*. His thumb runs over the mole on my bottom lip and his breath hitches. Then he parts my lips, slowly claiming my mouth with his tongue. He tastes like red wine, pizza and popcorn and something slightly metallic I can't quite place. I open my mouth wider to let him explore me, excited at the knowing that this is just the start of all the ways he's going to explore me tonight.

He pulls back and gives me that mischievous smirk that I know so well, and then he starts placing warm kisses down my neck. His hands move down my back and find the hem of his t-shirt. He runs his hands up and under the shirt, tracing patterns of ecstasy up and down my back. My back arches at the touch, and my breasts push into him.

"Fuck, you're so gorgeous," he murmurs into my neck. "I want so badly to—"

He leaves his sentence unfinished, but I'm pretty sure I can figure out what he was going to say.

"I want you," he says.

"Have me."

He holds my back with one hand and slides the other around to the front hem of the t-shirt, running his fingers up over my belly and to my breast. His warm hand there, cupping and caressing, sends sparks straight to my clit, and when he finds my nipple, flicking it gently, I let out a squeal of pleasure.

He lays me down on the bed and pushes the t-shirt up over my breasts, and his eyes glaze over as he takes me in.

This is so new for us. We never did this kind of thing before, at least not until the church. We kissed in the corn-fields, and we touched each other over our clothes, but this is the first time he's seen both my breasts completely naked, and I'm pretty sure by the way he's looking at me, like he's never even seen breasts before, that he likes how they look.

"Your tits are spectacular," he says, pushing the t-shirt up in a way that holds it there, so his hands are free to explore.

I let out a laugh as he circles his fingers around both my nipples.

"This isn't fair," I say, running my fingers over the bottom edge of his shirt. "I want to play with yours too."

He stands up, grabs the back of his shirt and throws it to the floor, once again revealing that ripped body that I can't wait to have pressed against me.

He blinks down at me lying on the bed. "You look so beautiful like that," he says.

I smile up at him and then look down at the bulge in his sleep shorts.

"I want your panties off. Now." He's back on the bed, and

his hands oh so quickly find the sides of my cotton floral panties. "These are so fucking *damp*," he says with approval as he balls them up and throws them on the floor.

"Well, you're turning me on," I tell him.

His eyes widen as he places his hands on my thighs, and opens my legs, revealing another part of me he's never seen before. It feels so damn good to be here like this, breasts on display, his t-shirt bunched up around my shoulders, my legs open wide for him. He sits between my legs and runs his hands up and down my thighs a few times like he's readying himself to touch me.

I arch my back and push my hips towards him.

A smirk, *the* smirk, crosses his lips and I can tell he's enjoying this just as much as I am.

This isn't what I expected from our first time. We were supposed to be nervous, fumbling around with no idea what we were doing. But while I haven't had all that much experience in the last few years, I can tell by his easy grip on my thighs that he certainly has.

I close my eyes and try not to think about how many other women he's been with. I try not to think about that woman I saw walking out of here the day he arrived.

Finn is with *me* tonight. I don't know what will happen tomorrow, but for tonight, Finn is mine, and this is exactly where I want to be. This is what I want, even if it's just for one night. Here in Lucky.

Tomorrow, we go to LA. Tomorrow we play make believe. I pretend to be with movie star Finn. Tonight, I'm with boy next door Finn, the boy I've always known and loved.

He squeezes my thighs and takes a deep breath.

"What are you waiting for?" I ask.

"I don't know," he says with a nervous laugh. "I guess I just — I wasn't expecting this tonight."

"No?"

"No. I wasn't expecting your breasts naked, spilling out of my t-shirt." He reaches his hands up and cups my breasts, squeezing them both with the confidence of a guy who's done this a million times before. "I wasn't expecting your panties on my floor, your legs spread open—"

I open my legs wider and arch my back. "Finn," I beg. "Please touch me, do something!"

"Fuck," he murmurs, as his hands run down my stomach, hips and outer thighs, inner thighs and then *finally* he finds my pulsing, wet, hot center.

He runs a finger up and down my wetness, and I moan with pleasure and surprise at how fucking good it feels. He presses my clit with his thumb, just like he did in the church, and it's almost enough to tip me over the edge.

His thumb makes circles, making me writhe with pleasure, and then he pushes a finger inside me. It takes me by surprise in the best possible way. "Finn! Fuck!" I call out.

He lets out a moan. "Your pussy, Jesus!" My hips buck from the pleasure of his finger inside me, and an insatiable desire for more washes over me.

"More, Finn. Please!"

"You sure?" he asks, sliding his finger out of me.

"Yes!"

This time, two fingers enter me, stretching me, and I feel my eyes practically roll back into my head.

"You're so fucking tight, so fucking beautiful," he says.

And then his thumb on my clit becomes his tongue. I let out a gasp as I realize what he's doing. Something Clive never even attempted. Finn alternates between gentle tongue flicks and a sucking motion that feels so incredible I know I'm going to come any second.

"Oh, fuck!" I moan out.

His fingers speed up, fucking me faster while his tongue

flicks and sucks, and I feel like my hips have bucked so high I must be on the ceiling by now.

He lets out a moan. "I want you to come for me, baby. Come on my mouth. Come around my fingers."

But I'm already coming, falling apart around his tongue and his hand, my legs stiffening and opening even wider for him, my whole body pulsing with pleasure in a way I've *never* experienced before.

He doesn't stop when I come — he keeps sucking and flicking and pumping his fingers and a few seconds later I feel a second wave hit, another orgasm, this one even more powerful, deeper, stronger.

"Fuck!" I call out. "Fuck! Jesus! Oh my god! Fuck! FINN!" I yell as I feel myself squeeze around his fingers, my whole body pulsing with pleasure.

It's the most beautiful thing I've ever experienced in my life.

And then I'm done. My body falls onto the bed, heavy. Spent. I feel relaxed for the first time in my entire life.

"Fuck," I whisper to myself. And then I look up at Finn.

He gives me that dirty smirk of his as he slowly removes his fingers from inside me. He wipes his mouth on the back of his arm and looks at me with those dark, smoldering eyes. And I can't wait for what's next.

Now he's going to fuck me.

CHAPTER THIRTY-THREE

inn

"Fuck me, Finn," she begs, opening her legs for me.

I thought my cock was already rock hard, but hearing those words from her lips makes me even harder.

Fucking hell, she looks like a post-orgasmic vision lying here. My t-shirt all bunched up around her neck, her beautiful and sexy as hell tits, her face all flushed, her pussy glistening, ready for more. She bites her lip and looks up at me like she might die if I don't do this.

But this already went way too fucking far.

If I fuck her right now, there's no way I'll be able to do it without biting her. There's no way that with April I will know when to stop.

I'm only just getting a handle on this. I'm only just figuring out how to bite someone without almost draining them. I can't put April in that kind of danger.

I lie down on my side next to her and run my fingers over

her neck again, avoiding her silver cross. I run my hand over her shoulders, and across the top of her breasts.

"Please, Finn. Please fuck me." She rolls over, pressing her body into mine and throwing a leg over me.

It's too good. Too tempting.

She pushes her pussy into the thin cotton of my sleep shorts, that thank god I'm still wearing. They're the only thing in the way of my cock being inside her right now.

"April," I say. "I can't."

Her face falls. "What do you mean you can't? I thought this was our night? And why could you do *that* but not fuck me? It's a weird line to draw." She looks worried, and I can tell there's a part of her that thinks this is about her.

"There are things you don't know about me. Things I need to tell you before I can—" I take a breath. "It's for your own safety."

"I'm on the pill, but we can use a condom," she says. "If you haven't been tested recently."

"I don't need to use a condom, and I can't get you pregnant."

Her eyebrows knit even harder. "You're sterile?"

"Yeah."

"Oh. Oh my god. Finn, I'm so sorry."

"It's okay," I tell her. "I wasn't always sterile. And I used to sell so much of my sperm to sperm banks when I needed the money that I probably have a thousand kids out there." I let out a light laugh, but she doesn't find it funny.

I gently move a piece of hair from her face and have a weird thought. I want to go back to the sperm bank and get some sperm back, donate it to her. She could still have my baby.

Stop it, you asshole. You can't think shit like that now.

"Have you been tested?" she asks. "Because I have too,

even though I've only been with Clive." She bites her lip and the idea of us skin on skin makes my cock throb.

Her heart rate rises higher at the idea of it, and so would mine if my heart still beat.

"You wouldn't catch anything from me," I say, trailing my fingers down her bare arm.

"I want you, Finn. I want you inside me."

My cock aches, and my jaw tightens. "The reason we can't have sex isn't what you think."

She sits up now, pulling the t-shirt down over her breasts. "Finn, why are you being like this?"

"Sorry. I just — I have no idea how to tell you this. And if you're not okay with it, and you probably won't be, you'll *never* want to have sex with me."

"What if I am okay with it?" she asks. "Then will you fuck me tonight?"

I let out a laugh. "Jesus, April, if you're okay with it, I'd fuck you forever."

Her pulse skips and a flush crosses her chest. "So, just tell me," she says. "You know you can tell me anything, right?"

I take a breath.

Fine. Oh fuck. Okay.

"I'm a vampire."

There's a moment of silence, and then she bursts out laughing. "Finn!"

But I don't laugh. I just glare at her. "I'm serious."

She gives me a playful shove. "Why are you trying to freak me out?"

I grab her hand, somehow already knowing that as soon as I do this, she will rip her hand out of mine, rip it right out of my life, and never want to be near me again.

"It's true," I tell her. "I was turned just over a year ago."

"Is this some method acting thing?" she asks, narrowing her eyes and pulling the blanket over her.

Of course it sounds insane. Totally unhinged.

"No. I'm telling you the truth."

"You're acting like a real dick." A few moments ago, she was clenching around my fingers in the throes of pleasure, now she's looking at me like I'm some asshole she doesn't even know.

But I *am* an asshole she doesn't even know.

"April. I'm not fucking with you."

I let my fangs protrude, offering her a pathetic, sad smile.

And then she screams.

CHAPTER THIRTY-FOUR

pril

I scream and leap out of the bed, trying to get as far away from him as possible.

A vampire?! What the fuck?!

Finn stands up and takes some steps back towards the door, putting as much space as possible between us in this small motel room.

"I can glamour you if you want. Make you forget I ever told you."

"What?! Why? So you can finger fuck me again over and over and I'll never remember or never know the truth about —" I gasp for air. "—whatever the fuck this is!"

He runs a hand through his hair, such a Finn move. But this isn't Finn! This is some fucking monster who's just given me the best orgasm of my life!

Oh, holy fuck, what is happening?!

He takes another step backward and holds his hands up

in surrender. "Uh, okay. I'm just going to go." He takes a tentative step forward to grab his keys and wallet from the table. "I'll get Natalie to come by tomorrow and get the rest of my stuff." His eyes flit over his t-shirt that I'm still wearing.

He turns to go, and I have no idea what is going on here. I don't know how the fuck Finn has *fangs*, but even now I find myself wanting to call out to him. Tell him not to go.

But he's a monster! He has fucking fangs!

I grab at the silver cross around my neck, silently praying for Jesus, my mom, even for my dad to come help me.

But no one comes.

Finn opens the door and turns back to look at me, all huddled and freaking the fuck out against the wall.

"I'm so sorry, April. I'm sorry I didn't tell you sooner. I'm sorry I let things go so far tonight. I'm sorry that this is what I am now." He grips the door frame like he's struggling to leave. "I know this changes everything. Natalie has your details. I'll make sure you still get some of your money. Enough to get out of here. Or whatever you want it for." He taps the door frame with his fingers, those fingers that were just *inside of me.* "Goodbye, April." The sadness in his eyes, the remorse, the pain, it nearly kills me.

But I don't speak. I don't move. I just stay huddled against the wall, trying to process what I've just seen.

The motel door closes behind him, and I run to it, and for a second I'm not sure if I'm going to run after him or put the bolt on. I hesitate, but fear is coursing through my body now. Fear of *Finn.* I bolt the door and peek out the window. He drives away—fast—with no hesitation. Back to LA. Back to his life of fame, money and whatever the fuck vampires do with their time.

I rip off his t-shirt, throwing it on the couch. Then I take a shower, washing him off me while tears fall down my face.

I don't know why I'm crying. Is it because Finn is a vampire? Is it because everything I thought I knew about reality is wrong? Is it because monsters exist, and that means that none of us are truly ever safe? Is it because I was falling in love with him all over again and he left? Again? Or is it because he didn't fuck me before he told me?

Wow. I am such a mess.

I open the bathroom door in nothing but a towel and I flinch, half expecting him to be here, about to rip my throat out. Half *wanting* him to be here, lying on the bed, waiting for me, laughing at this insane joke he's just played on me.

But he's not here. And somehow, I just *know* that this is not a joke.

I could grab one of Finn's clean t-shirts to wear from his bag in the corner, but instead, I take the t-shirt he was wearing earlier, hold it to my face and inhale. It still smells like drive-in popcorn and that raw, warm, woodsy smell that I think is partly soap but also just *him*. I put the shirt on. I don't know why. I don't know what I'm doing. My mind is a fucking mess. I don't understand anything I'm doing or thinking right now.

I'm not going to sleep tonight, so I make some coffee and grab my phone while I wait for it to percolate.

"Do vampires exist?" I type into a search engine. I wade through pages and pages of fictional vampires, regular humans who like to drink blood which sounds *way* creepier than actual vampires who *have* to feed from people, and then I eventually find my way onto a weird looking website called www.babyvampires.com. It's full of blog posts about what to do when you've just been turned.

And holy shit, it is *weird.*

At first, it seems like a joke or satire or something, but it's so *specific.*

As I drink my coffee, I dive deep into decades old blog

posts and eventually come across a post linking to a page called "The Donna Sisterhood". Their website says that all fans of The Bite are welcome to join. For a fee, of course.

It's expensive, and now that I'm *not* going to be getting *a hundred thousand dollars*, I really shouldn't even think about paying for it. But I do.

Once I pay, I get a notification saying that before I can have full access to the community, I will need an interview with one of the Donnas. The last thing I want to do is give my phone number to these crazy people, but I've gone so far down the rabbit hole that I figure what the hell.

"You will be matched with a Donna in your area soon," pops up a message on the site.

I let out a sigh. Maybe I can just request a refund.

I flick on the TV and channel surf for a while. I pause on the sports channel Finn was watching for a few minutes and then flick away and find that a vampire movie that was popular years ago is on.

My heart lurches. I've never been that into vampire stories. I much prefer both reading and writing cozy contemporary romance. Stories about *real* people, doing normal everyday things with a touch of spice.

I watch with horror and fascination at the way in which the human girl accepts the vampire boy for who he is. The way she's clearly terrified of him, even though she says she's not.

Is it terror or excitement?

Am I really terrified of Finn? Or is part of me curious, excited even, about what he is?

A vampire brought me to orgasm in a *church*.

Huh.

That should feel terrifying now. But it doesn't. Part of me thinks it somehow makes it feel even hotter.

Okay, I have problems.

I really do need therapy.

I was scared shitless when I saw his fangs, because they were fucking *fangs,* and I had never seen fangs before! I didn't even know vampires existed!

But as I watch the way that Bella looks at Edward, how she lusts after him, even *more* now that she knows what he is, I find myself biting my lip at the realization that I may still want Finn. I may want Finn even more because of what he is.

Okay. I am *seriously* fucked up.

Maybe this is just what happens when you deny the sexual parts of yourself for so long, you end up horny for monsters.

My phone pings.

"A Donna is in your area now and available to meet."

I get a second message telling me to go to Lucky's bar.

Heart pounding, I put my dress and bra back on. My panties are too far gone to wear again, so I grab a pair of boxer briefs from Finn's bag. They're a little tight, but they're better than going to the bar commando.

It's only now that I realize I really can't go back home for anything. Not to see my dad, not to get my clothes, pictures of my mom, not even fresh underwear.

When Finn came back to town, I really had no idea how much my whole world was about to change.

Finn

I STOP for gas and a bite, but when I get inside to pay and find someone to drink from, I feel sick at the thought of it. Usually, I'm so desperate for blood that it's an effort *not* to want to rip someone's throat out for a drink. But tonight, I don't want it. Not like this. Not from some trucker at a gas station in the middle of nowhere.

Not when I think of the look on April's face, her piercing scream, the way she tried to get as close to the motel room wall as possible, as far away from me as she could. The way she clutched the silver cross around her neck like it could keep me away.

I don't know what I was thinking, telling her we could share the room. I should have just given her the key and left. Not given her a choice. No discussion. No opportunity for me to be such a dickhead.

And then when I had her naked in my bed—

No, it was the right thing to do — telling her. I just wish this wasn't happening. I wish I'd had the balls to come back here and see her while I was still human.

I grab some of the Sybline from the trunk and force myself to drink. It still tastes disgusting to me, but if I'm no longer going to feed from humans, I guess I'm going to need to get used to it.

Fuck, am I no longer going to feed on humans?

I shove the bottle in the drink holder and head off back towards LA, calling Maverick from the dash panel.

"Hey, kid, what's up?" he asks sleepily.

"Something happened."

He sighs. "Okay. Hang on." I hear sheets rustling, a door opening and closing. "Did you do what I told you? Close the wounds, call an ambulance?"

"It's not that. I didn't hurt anyone."

"Did someone hurt you?" His voice is curt. While we have our differences, I know that as my maker, he would do anything to protect me.

I don't even know where to start, what to say.

"I told April."

"Told her what?"

"What I am."

"Why the fuck did you do that?"

"I didn't think I could — you know, *do it* with her until I told her."

"Wait, you put yourself in that situation with a woman you actually *care* about?"

"Yeah."

"Well, that's your first mistake. Telling her was your second. How did she react?"

"Not well."

"But you glamoured her to forget."

I pause.

"Finn. You glamoured her. Right?"

"No. I couldn't do it. I didn't want to do that to her."

"It's for her own good. If she's not okay with it, she needs to be glamoured. We can't have people out there terrified of us."

God, is she *terrified* of me?

Well, she should be.

"I didn't know what to do, so I just left."

"Where is she now?"

"Still in Lucky."

"Okay. Take a breath. We can fix this."

"How?"

"You need to go back. Glamour her."

"I can't."

"Finn. You're going to have to get better at glamouring and get used to doing it to people whether you want to or not. It's not an ethical dilemma. It's just what's best for everyone. It will keep her safe. Stop her from being scared. You don't want her to live in fear, do you?"

"No! Jesus, of course not."

"Then you need to drive back. Glamour her."

"I'm nearly back in LA already."

He lets out a loud sigh. "Fine. Okay. Go home. Get some rest. I'll send a couple of Donnas to your place. We'll fix this tomorrow."

"I don't want any Donnas."

There's silence on the line.

"What do you mean you don't want any Donnas?"

"I don't want them. I'm getting off the blood."

Maverick laughs. "Yeah. Good luck with that. I'll send the Donnas."

CHAPTER THIRTY-SIX

pril

I WALK INTO THE BAR, and I immediately know who the Donna is — the gorgeous blonde who was leaving Finn's room the night I drove to his motel. She sits at the bar dressed in jean shorts and a tight t-shirt that says, "Bite Me".

She takes one look at me quivering in my sundress and knows exactly who I am.

"Hey!" She gives me a big grin, jumps off her barstool and pulls me in for a hug. "It's you, right? The one I'm meant to meet here?"

"Yeah," I say into her mass of blonde hair. "I think so."

"I'm Danni," she says, finally letting me free from the hug.

"April."

"That's such a pretty name!" She beams at me, and I hate that I like her.

She was with Finn. She was in his room.

"Can I get you a drink?" she asks.

"Yeah. Sure. Just a beer."

"Poppy, you're here late!" Ed leans over the bar and looks at me like I've been possessed. It makes sense. I don't think I've been out to the bar this late in years. I may never have been out at the bar this late.

I just shrug at him.

"On the house," he says, placing two beers on the bar.

Danni grins at Ed and then guides me to a quiet table at the back of the bar.

"You and that guy?" she asks, nodding towards the bar. "He's cute."

I shake my head. "Oh, no. Well. We kind of had a thing years ago, but no."

Our thing was me losing my virginity to him in the back of his car after prom. We both knew what it was. We didn't have feelings for each other. I was mad at Finn. Not just mad, heartbroken. Ed wanted to get it done so that when he finally met someone he cared about, he wouldn't be a virgin.

"Oh, shit," she says, nearly spitting her drink out. "You're the girl Finn told me about!"

"What?"

"The girl he's been hung up on since high school."

"He told you about me?" I ask, taking a sip of my beer.

"Yeah. He did. And that's why you're here. Because you're involved with Finn?"

"Well, kind of. Yes. No," I shake my head. "I'm just looking for... *information*."

"About what specifically?"

"I don't know. Anything. All of this. I'm—" She looks at me, eyes wide, waiting for me to finish. "This is all new to me," I say.

"Did he bite you yet?"

I shake my head.

Not yet.

"You want to know about The Bite?"

I wipe my sweaty hands on my dress. "I only just found out about this whole world, and I'm—"

She reaches over and squeezes my hand. "Confused as fuck?"

"Yeah."

"Okay, let me give you the nutshell version. You already know what Finn is. There are lots of people out there like him. They might seem kind of scary at first, which I'm guessing is where you are right now. But it's part of the reason us Donnas like them. The *excitement* of the whole thing. The idea that they could kill you in a second if they wanted to, but they don't. That's kind of hot, right?"

The idea that Finn could kill me in a second is terrifying.

"But the *really* good part is The Bite. It's like nothing you'll ever experience in your life. Fucking one of them is amazing, just without The Bite. Some of them are ancient." She looks around to make sure no one is listening. "Some have hundreds of years of sexual experience. You'd think they would get bored with it, but for some of them, it just makes them even more insatiable for sex, and when you have a guy with experience like that—" She exhales like she's orgasming. "It's so fucking good."

"But they're not all that old?"

"No, Finn is a new vampire. Just over a year old, I think. They call them babies at his age. So cute." She laughs. "But—" Her smile fades. "They can also be the most dangerous."

"How so?"

"Their thirst is usually so insatiable that they can't control it. But Finn is different. The way he was with me and my sister was nothing like I ever experienced before with someone so new."

My stomach flips. "I don't need details."

"Yeah, April, you do."

I really don't, but she continues anyway.

"Finn is a good guy. The way he drank from me and my sister Deena was nothing like what you'd normally experience with one that young. He was gentle with us."

My lower belly flames. Somehow, knowing he was gentle with them makes me even more jealous.

She grips my hand over the table. "And that bite, holy shit. It's like being bitten by a *god.* It feels like pure bliss. It's like having thousands of orgasms at the same time."

Okay, color me curious.

"And when they fuck you and bite you at the same time —!" Her eyes roll back into her head as her eyelids flutter. "There are no words to describe it, you just have to *try* it."

"Did you and Finn—" I shake my head and take a huge gulp of beer. "Forget it, I don't want to know."

"Don't worry. Neither of us fucked him. He just drank from us."

"Is that better?" I ask, my face burning.

She smiles at me. "Yeah, April. It is. It's *very* fucking rare for a vampire *not* to fuck a Donna while he's drinking from them. For him, it was just food with us. Just like that beer you're drinking now, that's all he felt for us. Like how you feel about that beer." She takes a sip of her own drink. "He was very sweet about it all."

I stay silent for a few moments while I stare down at the scratches in the table.

"But it's dangerous," I say eventually. "To be with one of them."

She laughs. "Yeah, of course it's fucking dangerous!" She grins and grabs my hand again. "But honey, so is life. You want to live a quiet little life here in this town, and try to stay out of danger, you go for it. That's your choice. But there's a whole world out there. A whole *underworld* full of dark shit... but also incredible pleasure like you've never known."

CHAPTER THIRTY-SEVEN

pril

THE FALLEN STAR *by Evie Everhart*

A sharp pain in my neck made me gasp, and then the most delicious feeling I've ever felt coursed through me. He was drinking my blood, and it felt divine. I didn't know there was pleasure like this. My world had kept this from me. They told me to stay safe, stay away from boys, stay pure, save myself for marriage. But they weren't protecting me, they were only preventing me from experiencing the beautiful agony of lust and the absolute bliss of being touched by a man. There is nothing sinful about sharing your body with a man who loves you, a monster who loves you.

"Baby, I want you. All of you," he growled.

I'd already decided I didn't want to wait. I didn't want to stay pure. What for? Who for? Some imaginary man I may not meet for years? Decades? Someone who may not even exist?

"Then have me," I replied. "I'm already all yours."

. . .

THE NEXT MORNING, I pack the few items I have and Finn's bag in my car, but I need to make one stop before I leave.

"Hey Mom," I say, taking my usual seat by her grave. I lightly touch the cross around my neck and take a breath. "I'm leaving town. You probably already know. You probably saw what happened between me and Dad. I don't want to leave things like this with him, but I know if I go back to that house, I won't go. He'll say something to convince me to stay." I get a little more comfortable on the grass beside her. "And I don't want to stay. Of course, I'll miss everyone. I'll miss singing at church, I'll miss Loretta. I'll miss her pie. I'll miss the library and playing baseball. Badly." I let out a laugh. "But I'll miss you the most."

A breeze picks up, and I swallow back my tears.

"I know, Mom. I know you're always with me."

Okay, now the tears come.

"Is it the right thing to do? LA is dangerous. The crime wave has been all over the news. Maybe it's not the right time. Maybe I should wait. Maybe—"

A little bird lands on Mom's headstone and glares at me, like *really* looks into my soul, and then flies away.

I choose to think it's a sign, from my mom, from God, from someone, something.

It's time for me to fly.

And I know that if I don't go now, I never will.

"I was going to say goodbye, but it's not goodbye, is it? Never goodbye, just talk again soon."

I kiss my fingers and place them on her headstone, and then I walk back to my car with no idea of when I'll see this place again.

. . .

I HIT the outskirts of LA at around 2:00 p.m. and I'm truly shocked by the amount of traffic. It's more traffic than I've ever seen in my life. Of course I've been to cities before, but nothing like this. Being here, surrounded by endless lanes of traffic, both freaks me out and excites me.

I'm really doing this!

When I see Finn's face on a billboard over my exit, a laugh bursts from my lips as tingles rush up my spine. That's *Finn* up there! Sure, he's standing a little behind Maverick Stone and Trix Delaney, but he's *there.* He's made it. Every single person driving on this road is going to see his face. And everyone who doesn't know him yet soon will.

It's only when I stop for gas and type the directions to the hotel into my phone that I really allow myself to accept that this is happening.

I'm going to LA. I'm going to fake date Finn. I'm going to go through with the arrangement.

I'm going to make *a hundred thousand dollars.*

As I get back in my car and drive. I can't get my conversation with Danni out of my head. The way she talked about The Bite, and the way she said Finn was *gentle. God.* I can't stop thinking about Finn being gentle with me.

And when I think about what we did last night — his fingers inside me, the way that orgasm hit, the way I felt so *safe* with him... I didn't feel scared at all.

And I don't feel scared now. I'm just buzzing with excitement and anticipation at what the future holds.

I don't know if I've ever been excited about my future until now.

When I finally get into my hotel room right on the beach in Santa Monica, my mouth hits the floor. It's a gorgeous suite with a lounge room, kitchen and separate bedroom, and the best part? It looks out over the beach.

The beach.

I stand staring out the window like someone who's seeing the beach for the first time.

Because I am.

And I know in this moment that I did the right thing coming here. No doubts. No regrets. Just the sun setting over the California coast.

I throw Finn's bag on the enormous bed, and I practically run out of the hotel and down to the beach.

I yank my shoes off and run into the ocean.

The water is so cold, and the waves hit me hard, and it's all so *vast*! I didn't know the ocean was so big! I close my eyes, letting the waves hit my bare legs, tasting the salt spray on my lips.

This is one of those rare happy moments in life. Nothing else matters. Just me and the water, the lowering sun, and the endless expanse of potential and possibilities in front of me.

I take a deep breath and then I dive right in, still in my sundress.

CHAPTER THIRTY-EIGHT

Finn

Claiming 101

Claiming is super easy! Just activate your influence and then say out loud that you claim the person, and they are yours. If they've spent a bit of time with you, especially sexually, your scent will be on them and another vampire should be able to pick that up, but your verbal claim also kind of creates a field of your energy around the person and most vampires will acknowledge it. If they don't, and some other vamp drinks from someone you've claimed, you are perfectly within your rights to stake that vampire. Most vampires don't actually kill each other over drinking their human because it can create a lot of drama in the community, but in theory you're totally allowed to!

www.babyvampire.com

. . .

I DRIVE through the night and spend the entire day lying in bed staring at the daylight moving across the ceiling until I'm too thirsty to stay there any longer. Then I make myself comfortable on my balcony with a bottle of Sybline, which still tastes gross. I sit, questioning every single one of my life choices as I watch a cotton candy sky of pinks and oranges melt into the LA sky as the sun sets against the beach. The vision is so iconically LA and makes me both glad as fuck to be out of Lucky, and miserable as hell that I'm not still there with April.

My phone rings, and I roll my eyes, expecting it to be Maverick, but it's not. It's Natalie.

"She's here."

I sit upright in the chair and grip my phone. "What do you mean, *she's here?*"

I texted Natalie when I got back into town with a brief update about what happened. She assured me she would fix it, but I couldn't see how. Not when April looked at me like I was going to murder her.

"She just checked into the hotel." Natalie says.

My heart leaps. Okay, so this is unexpected.

I take a swig of the Sybline that's doing fucking nothing to quench my thirst. "You sure?"

"Of course I'm sure. I'm going over there soon with some clothes and other things she might need."

I immediately want to run over to the hotel. It's not far from here, just a couple of blocks. I could be there in minutes.

She's not here for you, asshole. She's doing it for the money.

"She's still okay with the arrangement?"

"I guess so."

"What did you say to her?"

"Nothing."

"Nothing?"

"No, I've been busy all day. I was going to call her later with a better offer, but I guess I don't need to. She decided this on her own."

"Huh."

"I have lunch booked for you at Blank State tomorrow. Don't be late. And don't be awkward like you were at the drive-in. Be confident with her. Act like you're in love."

Blank State is one of those awful LA places that tries so hard to be cool it's just sad. With its grey and white interior, I can hardly even imagine April there.

But she will be there.

"Sure, no problem," I tell her.

But there's going to be one hell of a problem if April is still terrified of me.

I think of the way she screamed when she saw my fangs, how she clutched at the cross around her neck.

Fuck.

I DON'T WANT to drink from a human, but I also don't want to risk being thirsty around April. I can't be around her if my throat is going to be on fucking fire the whole time. The Sybline is kind of doing something, I think, but it's not enough.

I tried to message my blood supplier but just got a generic message saying there were very busy at this time and would get back to me soon.

So as the sky darkens, I get in my car and drive down to Vincent's.

The line to get into the club is longer than I've ever seen it. Usually it's busy with girls looking for The Bite or humans coming here for the weird Gatsby goes goth vibes, but tonight the line is around the block.

I pull my hood up to avoid being recognized by anyone in

the line and walk straight in. The security guys know me, and I'm never charged by the girl on the desk.

The place is heaving tonight. The band is playing a twenties version of a Blink 182 song, and the dance floor is full of sweaty humans and vampires who are eyeing up their next meal.

I make my way upstairs to the VIP section. A pretty redhead I've been with a few times gives me a smile and a nod as she opens the velvet rope for me. The VIP area is only for Vincent's most exclusive members, of which I am one. It's fairly empty tonight, though. A couple canoodle in a booth at the back, and a famous actor I recognize from some eighties movies and who hasn't aged a day, sits with a Donna at the VIP bar.

I take a seat in a velvet booth and within seconds a beautiful black woman comes to take my order.

"I'm Diana, and I'll be your server this evening," she tells me with a smile. "Can I get you a Donna?"

I shake my head. "Just a glass of A positive, thanks,"

"Sorry, sir, but we're out."

"B negative, then. Or whatever you have."

"We're out of all blood types."

"What?"

"It's a supply chain issue. But we have plenty of Donnas here tonight." She gives me a flirtatious smile. "I'd be more than happy to be your Donna for the evening if you wish."

I run a hand through my hair. "Just a bourbon and coke. Thanks."

"Certainly, sir."

I take a deep breath. I'm going to have to feed on someone. Shit. There's no other choice.

The couple who's been going for it in the corner come up for air. The guy gives me a nod. A wave of fear and disgust hits me as I recognize who it is. The woman he's with just stares blankly ahead. He's glamoured her good.

My stomach churns. It's common for vampires to glamour girls into doing whatever they want, but it makes me feel fucking sick, and it's clear from the look on this girl's face that she's completely under his control.

Diana brings my drink, and a second later, he slides into the booth opposite me, dragging the glamoured woman with him. She slumps against his shoulder, her eyes rolled up to the ceiling.

"Coke? Are you fucking serious, Finn?" he asks with a laugh, running a hand over his reddish-brown buzz cut. He's dressed to impressed in a grey suit and white shirt, but the gold chains around his neck make him look like he's trying too hard. "What kind of vampire are you?" He fingers his chains, and I notice that there's one that looks like silver, but for obvious reasons, isn't. It's a weird pendant with some markings and a dent on it. Must be some exclusive designer piece.

"One who's not into glamouring the shit out of girls, I guess." My eyes take her in. She's young. Pretty. She doesn't deserve any of this. She should be out with her friends, studying at college, dating some jerk human guy, anything but this. I fucking hate this guy, but he's tight with the owner, so I try to backpedal. "I guess I'm still learning how to be a proper monster." Okay, maybe that didn't help.

His eyes turn even darker, which I didn't think was possible, and he just glares menacingly at me over the table. "I'm not that much older than you," he says, grabbing the girl's wrist and biting into it without breaking eye contact with me. He sucks on her veins until I hear her already weak pulse slow down. Too slow.

"Stop it, Aiden," I say through gritted teeth. "You're killing her."

He pulls his teeth out of her wrist, but I know it's not because I told him to, and she flops against him. "You think you're better than me, baby vampire? You're going to kill so many people you haven't even met yet."

I shake my head. "What the fuck happened to you? What made you like this?"

He lets out a howl of laughter. "What made me like this? Okay. Well—" he holds up a hand and counts off on his fingers. "First, Mommy dearest left us, then Daddy disowned me when he found me going for it with a boy in my bedroom. I came to LA with nothing, and the only job I could get was turning tricks for vampires. Some of the depraved shit those vamps are into, you wouldn't want to hear about it let alone be a part of it." He looks at the girl beside him with disgust. "I was hooked on blood, a fucking addict. I had no purpose in life but to be bitten and fucked by vampires. I had no one and nothing. I was ready to fucking end it all. Tragic backstory, huh?"

I shrug. It sounded awful, classic case of the abused becoming the abuser, but I don't think he really wants me to tell him that.

He keeps talking. "I was on my way out. When I went to vampire parties, I didn't fucking care who drank from me or what they did to me, I just wanted the pain to go away. I wanted the escape. I didn't care if I was fucking drained… and then I met the most amazing woman. Beautiful, strong, powerful, and she chose me as her companion." He grips the edge of the table and leans forward. "She. Chose. Me. She didn't just want me for my blood, she wanted me for *me*. She turned me and it was like the whole world switched on. We were in love. I never thought I would get to love someone. I never thought anyone would love me like that. And then she was murdered by your friends in the fucking Fraternity of the Everlasting Rose. Your exclusive club full of rich, influential, murderous vamps, in case you forgot. Staked in the heart, *twice.* And so, excuse me if I'm a little… on edge."

We all know the story. Aiden's maker was Lottie Luelle. She was the head of the Fraternity for decades. She was staked to Certain Death twice. The first time, she didn't die. It's the only time in history that a vampire has been staked without dying, so she's kind of become a legend of vampire folklore.

But to me, she'll always be the vampire responsible for chaining me up in a basement and feeding off me with her friends until I was so close to death the only thing that would save my life was Maverick turning me.

And Aiden? He was one of her friends who nearly drained me to death.

I still hate Vincent. Whenever I see him around the club, I have flashbacks to that night, but at least he apologized, even if it was just for his own benefit. But Aiden? The guy is a fucking psychopath. And yeah, sure, a lot of vampires are, but there are many of us who are at least *trying* not to murder people. Then there are guys like him who get off on it.

"Can you look after Lulu for a second while I go talk to Vince about something?" His whole demeanor changes in a second, like we're just bros hanging out at the bar.

"Yeah, sure."

"I've claimed her, so no biting," he says with a dark smirk.

"Aidey, where are you going?" Lulu murmurs as he practically picks her up and drops her back into the booth.

"Gotta go see the boss, babe," he says.

She can barely even sit up by herself. "Don't leave me," she begs.

His expression darkens, and he looks at her like he suddenly can't fucking stand her. "I release my claim on you," he tells her and then his eyes flick to mine. "Do what you want with her. She's just a pathetic piece of human trash."

He turns and leaves the VIP area, and I want to go and break his fucking face, but at least he released her, I guess.

I call Diana over and order three large Cokes for Lulu.

"Drink up, Lulu," I tell her. "You'll feel better."

Coke helps the glamoured sober up a little.

She slowly makes her way through the drinks, but she's still in a bad way, and I know I can't leave her here like this, so I decide to do the gentlemanly thing and take her home.

But first, I need to drink.

"Diana," I ask, calling her over again. "Does your previous offer still stand?"

She grins like she's just won the lottery. "Of course. Follow me." I lift Lulu up by the armpits, drape one of her arms around my shoulder and take her with us.

CHAPTER THIRTY-NINE

pril

THE FALLEN STAR *by Evie Everhart*

"I never stopped caring about you. Not even for one second." He reached out for a piece of my hair and looked at me with such tenderness.

"I did more than just care about you," I told him. "I was in love with you. I'm still in love with you."

"Even now? Even now that you know what I am?"

"Even now. Especially now."

He just looks at me, stunned into silence, and my heart pounds as I wait for his response.

Does he still love me too?

A CAR IS BOOKED to pick me up at midday, but I don't want to sit around my hotel room all morning when the sun is shining and there's a whole new world to explore outside.

Natalie dropped off some clothes for me last night, and I have to admit, she did a good job. Most of it is my style. I grab a dark green dress and try it on. It's pretty, but it's lower cut and shorter than I would normally wear. If I bend over too far Finn's briefs will be on show. Natalie didn't send any underwear up with the clothes. I guess she assumed I would have my own. I use the few bits of makeup I have in my purse — some lipstick and mascara and then shrug at my reflection. It will have to do for now. Hopefully, the paparazzi won't get too up in my face.

I find a bakery and order a coffee to take down to the beach. It's a perfect morning. There's not a cloud in the sky, and I sit and watch the waves coming and going with a dumb grin on my face. I will never get tired of this. I consider getting my laptop out so I can do some writing, but I don't think it would survive the sand.

When my bladder can no longer hold all the coffee, I go in search of a bathroom and end up finding a lingerie shop with some good deals.

I run my fingers over a bra and panty set in light blue. It's sweet but sexy, and I can't stop myself from thinking of Finn's fingers running over the edges, his hands peeling it off me.

My face heats as I throw the set into my basket with some basics.

My phone rings as I'm standing at the counter to pay.

"Hello?"

"It's Natalie. I need to talk to you about your lunch date."

"Uh, sure," I say, handing my card over to the cashier.

"There's been a slight complication."

"Oh?"

"You haven't seen it?"

"Seen what?"

"Finn was photographed with another woman last night."

My heart sinks. Okay, well now I feel fucking stupid for buying underwear I think he might like.

"Don't do anything too couple-y at lunch. We're going to go the friends to lovers route."

The cashier hands me my bag with a smile, and I walk out of the store. "What do you mean?"

"Don't look or act like you're in love just yet. Keep it casual, friendly. Like two old friends catching up over lunch. That's all. A hug would be good, but no kissing, hand-holding, nothing like that. Once this recent scandal is behind us, in a week or so, we'll go all in."

My heart races as I think about what going all in will entail. "Okay. Sure. Got it."

"Great. Good luck."

I ARRIVE at Blank State nervous and way too early. It's one of those exclusive places with stark white and grey décor — stark white and grey people.

I approach the woman standing at the podium by the door, feeling like I very much don't belong in this restaurant or with any of the people who do.

She gives my hair a look like she can tell I haven't been to a salon in years. "Can I help you?"

"I'm meeting someone here at twelve, but is it okay if I come in now?"

She raises an eyebrow at me. "I'll have to check. We are very busy."

I look around at the almost empty restaurant. "Sure."

"What's the name?"

"I'm April. I'm here to meet Finn Huxley."

A rush of goosebumps spread over my arms as I say his full name out loud. As I tell her I'm here to meet him. As I realize that in an hour he will be here. Fangs and all.

Her eyes widen, and her whole demeanor changes.

"Yes, of course, April. Right this way."

I roll my eyes at the back of her head as she leads me out onto an outside deck area that looks out over the beach. It's so much nicer out here than it is inside. She gestures to a table in the very center of the deck, which is a prime spot for being seen by anyone in the restaurant or on the beach below. Of course Natalie booked us this table.

"Can I get you a drink? Something to eat?" The woman says with a smile.

"Just a coffee," I tell her. Then I remember Natalie is paying the bill. "Oh, actually, do you have any pie?"

She makes a scoffing sound. "Sorry, no. We don't *do* pie. But we have a pancake stack."

"Sounds great. Thanks."

She wanders off, and I open my laptop, heading straight to Hollywood Daily to find out what happened last night. There's a picture of Finn and a girl who looks catatonic hanging off him.

Hot stuff Huxley at it again, reads the headline.

I stare at the picture of them together for way too long and then eventually click away. It doesn't matter. I'm not here for Finn. I'm here for the money. I'm here for me.

But as I try to put it out of my mind and concentrate on writing, I just can't. I'm about to have my first fake date with Finn.

I guess technically our last night in Lucky was our first fake date, but that didn't feel fake. Especially with how it ended — me getting finger banged and then screaming up against a wall. And not in a good way.

When my coffee and teeny-tiny pancakes arrive, I take a pause from staring at a blank screen and check the comments on my latest chapter on Scritpy. Most are positive, one from Katrina already begging for more. Since we met at the library, she has read and commented on everything I write. She always loves it.

But there are a few people who really hated the church scene. Of course it was inspired by Finn. In my story, they just make out in church and then take it to his truck, but a few people still thought it was disrespectful.

Maybe they're right, maybe I went too far with that scene, but my encounter in the church with Finn felt so fucking holy. I have absolutely zero shame about feeling that good in the house of God.

Even if the person who made me feel like that was with some other woman last night.

Get over it, April. You're not here for Finn, you're here for the money!

I grimace as I think of the matching lace underwear in the bag at my feet. What a fool I was to think that anything was going to happen between us again. What a complete idiot to even want it!

I finish the pancake stack, which pales in comparison to Loretta's, order another coffee and get back to writing.

I sense his presence before I see him. The sudden race of my heart, the flames in my veins. I turn around and look behind me, and there he is — walking towards our table in those dark blue jeans that hang off his hips like a dream. A black t-shirt, just like the one I wore to bed last night, stretches out over his ripped shoulders and biceps. His hair is a tangled mess, like always, and his eyes are hidden behind a pair of dark sunglasses.

I quickly close the laptop before he can see the spicy words on my screen. Words inspired by him.

He pauses behind the chair opposite me, his expression pained. "I didn't think you'd come."

I shrug. "Neither did I, at first."

He grips the back of the chair but still doesn't sit.

"Do you want to sit down?" I ask.

"Is that okay?"

He thinks I'm still terrified of him. He thinks I'm going to jump over the railing and run down the beach screaming. Maybe I should.

"That's the whole point of this, right? You can't just stand there, or I won't get my money." I slide my laptop into my purse and take a deep breath.

He looks a little hurt by my comment, but he's the one who was with some other woman last night.

He runs a hand through his hair, messing it up even more. "Shit. This is just so weird, after — uh, well. You know. I just wasn't expecting you to be here. In LA."

"I'm sorry if I overreacted to your... *news*," I tell him. "But it was kind of a shock."

"I should have tried to explain it better. I never should have shown you my—" His fingers grip the back of the chair he still hasn't sat down in yet. "You reacted appropriately. It was crazy of me to think you would react any other way."

"Can I get you something, Mr. Huxley?" A young guy appears at our table and looks at Finn with wide eyes.

"Just a coffee, thanks."

"Certainly. If you need anything at all, just let us know."

Finn nods at him, and he disappears.

"Can you even drink coffee?" I ask. "Or do you only drink blood?"

"Jesus, April." He takes a deep inhale. "We can't talk about any of this in public. It's not safe." He looks over to where a number of other rich-looking guests are taking their seats. He finally pulls out the chair and sits down. "Let's just do what we're supposed to do here. Act like two old friends at lunch."

"Yeah. Sure. Of course."

Although I have no idea how we're going to convince

anyone that we're friends when we have a whole *lot* to talk about, especially who the fuck was that woman last night?!

April! Leave it alone!

We sit in awkward silence for way too long until Finn's phone pings in his pocket. He pulls it out and checks his messages.

"Natalie."

"What's she say?"

"She says we look too awkward." He frowns down at the beach like he knows she's down there somewhere taking photos of us. Who needs the paparazzi when we have Natalie?

I take a deep breath, think of the money, put my elbow on the table and lean my head into my hand. I give him a smile. "Do you think this is better?"

He rubs his hand over the back of his neck. "Who knew you'd be better at acting than me?"

"Just play your part, Huxley," I say with a forced smile. "Make some small talk or something."

He shoots me a grin, but it doesn't make it to his eyes. "Okay. So, what do you think of LA?"

I don't have to fake the smile that tugs at my lips. "I absolutely love it."

APRIL LOOKS DIFFERENT HERE. As she looks out over the water, the sun shining down on her chestnut hair, the ocean air in her breath, more flush in her cheeks, she looks lighter, happier. But when her eyes return to mine, I can see that while she may love being here, she doesn't love being here with me.

"How's your hotel?" I ask, continuing on the safety of small talk. We have a lot to discuss, but not here. Not right now. Not while the tables next to us are filling up and Natalie is wandering the beach below getting photos of us together. The paparazzi will be following us around soon enough. As soon as word is out that I've been seen with a mystery woman, they'll be everywhere.

"Amazing," she says. "I've never stayed anywhere so nice. The view of the beach is incredible." She grabs a menu and stares down at it. "I have your bag at the hotel. I didn't know what to do with it."

"I can have someone pick it up. Get it out of your way." I take a menu as well.

"I already had some very small and disappointing pancakes, but since Natalie is paying, I might get something else. What are you getting?" She looks up, and her lips twist. "Oh. I guess you don't eat lunch."

I shake my head. "And neither do you."

"Excuse me?"

"Want the Hollywood Daily to share a picture of you with your mouth full of food?"

"I couldn't care less what Hollywood Daily thinks of my eating habits."

"You say that now, but this industry isn't nice, April. They'll take any opportunity to make something look bad. Like what happened last night." He puts his elbows on the table and leans in a little. "With that girl at the club."

Her face hardens. She's clearly pissed about the girl from the club. I don't blame her. It did look bad. But what was I meant to do? Leave Lulu half drained in a vampire club that had sold out of blood?

"So I'm supposed to sit here and eat *nothing*?"

"I'll get you a burrito after. We can eat back at my place."

I suddenly remember what happened last time I bought a girl a burrito.

"Or a burger. Pizza. Whatever you want."

She shakes her head. "I'm good. I probably don't need anything else, really. I did just have pancakes."

"I'm not going to hurt you," I tell her, my voice low so that no one around us can hear. "I may be… *what I am*, but I can control myself if you come back to my place to eat."

"Did you control yourself the night you got arrested?"

I run a hand over the back of my neck. "We should talk about that later."

"You weren't saving her. You were drinking from her. And what about the girl from last night?"

"April, please," I say through gritted teeth. "We can have this conversation. I will tell you anything you want to know. But just *not here.*"

"Fine." She grabs her own sunglasses from the table, puts them on and stares out at the beach.

My phone buzzes in my pocket.

"Natalie, again," I say. "She's not happy with how this is going."

April stands up and, holy shit, her dress is *short.* She walks around the table, puts a hand on my shoulder and whispers into my ear. "Is this what she wants?"

Fuck that's nice.

She's trying to act confident and tough, but her heart rate is so high, her breath shallow. I just can't quite figure out if it's because she's terrified of me, or because she still wants me.

I want to grab her, pull her into my lap, kiss her to an inch of her life.

Get that idea out of your stupid fucking head right now!

She takes a step back and then starts walking away.

I reach out and grab her hand before I know what the hell I'm doing. She looks down at my hand on hers, but she doesn't pull away.

"Where are you going?"

"Bathroom."

I let go of her hand and then watch her walk away in that dress that's so short every guy in this place is staring at her gorgeous milky thighs. A little breeze kicks up and the hem of her dress lifts slightly, revealing that she's wearing a pair of my boxer briefs.

That probably shouldn't excite me in the way that it does. Maybe she's just out of clean underwear. Or maybe she likes the feeling of my underwear rubbing against her pussy.

Fuck, fuck, fuck.

"What the actual *fuck*?!"

I look up to see Maverick Stone glaring down at me.

"Hey, Maverick."

"What the fuck are you doing?"

"Having lunch."

He takes April's seat and scowls over the table.

"That's her, isn't it?"

"Who?"

"The girl whose hand you were just squeezing. I can tell she's a country girl from a fucking mile away."

"What? How?"

"I can just *tell*. You were supposed to glamour her and forget the whole thing, not bring her to fucking LA and parade her around on the beach!"

I still don't know why I can't tell Maverick about the arrangement, but I did sign a contract stating that if I shared this information with anyone, April wouldn't get her money, and so I don't tell him shit.

"Well, I guess I didn't."

"Did you glamour her into forgetting and then bring her out here, anyway? Or did she suddenly get real cool about everything overnight?"

"I didn't glamour her," I say. "And can we please not do this here?"

"Jesus, Finn. If you hurt her, you'll never forgive yourself."

"Yeah. I'm well aware of that fact."

"And what does she think of your escapades from last night? You and that Donna at Vincent's? Jesus, Finn, why can't you keep your fangs in your fucking mouth?"

"Nothing happened with that girl. I was just getting her home."

"Bullshit."

"It's the truth. She was there with Aiden, and he left her in a real sorry state. I was just trying to help."

"Well, next time. Don't."

What a fucking asshole.

"Yeah? And leave a Donna to drain out on the floor of the VIP section? Nice."

He just shakes his head like I'm a fucking moron and understand nothing.

"You know what? Fuck you," I tell him.

He opens his mouth to respond when April returns. Her mouth hangs open when she sees Maverick Stone in her seat.

He smiles up at her. "You must be April." He stands and offers her the chair back. "I was just inviting Finn over for a drink at my place later. We have some work stuff to talk about, but you're more than welcome to join us. I'm sure Trix would love to entertain you while we talk shop."

"Uh, yeah! I would love to!"

Okay, I really don't like how she's looking at him.

"See you both in about an hour?" He claps my shoulder and then walks back out of the restaurant.

"You guys are close?" she asks, looking impressed.

"Not exactly."

My phone pings again in my pocket. "Natalie says she has enough and we can leave."

"Good." April grabs her purse containing the laptop I saw her writing on when I arrived, and I reach down and grab her bags of shopping.

"We have some time before we need to be at Maverick's. Do you want to come to my place so we can talk?"

She presses her gorgeous pink lips together. She doesn't

need to say anything, it's written all over her face. She doesn't want to be alone with me.

"Or how about we put your stuff in my car and then take a short walk? The beach isn't too busy."

She nods, and I follow her gorgeous ass out of the restaurant.

CHAPTER FORTY-ONE

$\mathcal{A}$pril

"I can tell how uncomfortable you are," Finn says, walking beside me along the sand, but keeping his distance. "I don't want to force you to spend time with me just for money. I know we had an arrangement. I know it was only ever supposed to *be* about the money, but it's going to be kind of difficult if you're... terrified of me."

I sink my bare feet into the sand as I walk. I should say something, but I don't know what. Between him being a vampire, being out with some girl last night and all the feelings I still have for him, it's just... *a lot.*

"That girl last night," Finn starts, "she was really drunk, weak from a vampire taking too much of her blood, and she'd been glamoured one too many times. The guy who did it to her was the same guy who nearly drank me to death when I was still human."

His words startle me. I've been so focused on my own

feelings about it all that this is the first time I think of what Finn must have gone through to become what he is now.

"I couldn't leave her at the club like that. I took her back to her place, got her inside and then I left. Honestly. That's all that happened with her."

"You don't need to explain yourself to me," I remind him. "What you do in your personal life is your business."

"No, it's not. Not for the next two months, it's not. If you decide to stay, I won't be with anyone else. Not even in private. And not just because I could get caught, but because I wouldn't do that to you. Even if this is just an arrangement."

We walk for a few moments in silence.

"I don't know how we're going to do this, how we're going to be believably in love when you're afraid of me." A pained expression crosses his face.

I stop walking and turn to face him. "I was afraid, Finn. It came out of nowhere. I didn't even know that people like you existed. And there you were, two seconds after making me come like I've never come before, with your fangs out. It was — it was too much."

"I'm sorry for telling you like that. But is there ever a right way to tell someone you're a vampire?"

"Probably not. But if there is, it's probably before you do that with someone."

"You're right."

"You made me come in my dad's *church,* and then you… the way you…" I shake my head thinking of his shirt up around my neck, his fingers inside of me. "You did all that to me without telling me."

"I wanted to tell you. But I was scared you'd react exactly the way you did."

"What happened to that girl? When you were arrested? Did you bite her? Did you nearly kill her?" The questions are just tumbling out now.

He runs a hand down the side of his face. "Yeah, I bit her. And yeah, I was messy about it. But she was okay. She *wanted* it."

"Was she a Donna?"

His dark eyebrows knit together. "How do you know about Donnas?"

"I did my research. And I talked to Danni."

"I never fucked her. Or her sister."

Relief floods through me at his confirmation of what Danni said. "She told me, and she told me about The Bite, about how it… feels."

His eyes find mine, smoldering around the edges, a silent question in them.

Yes. I want to know how it feels. Yes, I want you to bite me.

"Yeah. The girl in the back alley was a Donna. She wanted it. I was very hungry. Too hungry." He puts some more distance between us and starts walking again. I do my best to keep up with his long strides. "You have to think of The Bite like sex. Have you ever felt so crazy about someone that you would just fuck them anywhere?"

"No." It's a lie. That day he touched me in church? I would have fucked him right then and there if he'd wanted to.

He raises an eyebrow. "You and Clive never—?"

I shake my head. "It wasn't like that between me and Clive."

He doesn't comment on that.

"The Bite is very pleasant for humans. It makes some of them so crazy for it they'll do anything to get it."

"So those girls are just your food supply? And you're their drug?"

"I know it sounds bad. But they want it. It's mutually beneficial. And what's the alternative? Feeding from people who *don't* want it?" He takes a pause. "There are Dons too. Guys who are into it."

I stop walking again, and a second later he does too. He turns, and his face is so full of anguish and regret.

"April, I am so fucking sorry. For everything. For what I did to you in the church. For how far things went in the motel room. I'm sorry for how I told you. I'm sorry I didn't come back for you sooner when I was still human. But most of all, I'm sorry that I didn't fucking die that night."

My heart breaks at his words.

"Finn. No." I step towards him, but he steps away, turns around and picks up his pace. "We should get back to the car. Maverick will give me a fucking lecture if we're late."

FINN LEADS me around the side of Maverick Stone's Malibu mansion and up a set of stairs that lead from the beach onto an enormous deck with a view to die for. Maverick is sitting on a couch in a t-shirt and shorts, his legs stretched out in front of him on an ottoman, and Trix Delaney is in a short hot pink dress with her bare legs sprawled out over his lap. It's so strange seeing them here like this after watching them in *Double Agency* just a few nights ago. It's like seeing the great and powerful Oz behind the curtain, except they're even better looking in real life. The two of them have been plastered over social media and in the tabloids recently, everyone speculating on their relationship and last year's shotgun wedding. But from the way she looks up at Maverick and the way he brushes some green hair off her forehead, it's clear they are very much in love.

"Finn, April," Maverick gives us a nod.

"Finn!" Trix jumps up and wraps her arms around him. She's so beautiful, and even though it's clear she's happily married, I'm still jealous of the way her body so easily presses into Finn's, and the way his arms wrap around her squeezing tightly.

"It's good to see you, Trix," he says. "I want you to meet April."

And suddenly Trix's arms are around me, hugging me like she's known me all my life. "Hi, April," she says, pulling back and giving me a smile. "You must be hungry."

"How did you know?"

"They always forget to feed us. Come on." She grabs my hand and leads me into the house.

The main lounge area is open and bright, with movie posters on the walls and plants and flowers on every available surface. Trix pulls me into the large wood and marble kitchen, and I'm hit with the delicious smell of cake.

She pulls a cloth off a cake that's been cooling by an open window. "If you give me a few minutes to put the frosting on, we can eat this. Or I can make you a late lunch? I'm guessing you didn't eat much on your date?"

"Not really. I had some pancakes earlier, but they were—"

"The pancakes from Blank State? Ew! They're like eating cardboard! How about I make you lunch, and then we eat the cake?" She starts rummaging through the fridge. "How do you feel about banana blossom fish?" she asks, holding up a bowl.

"I don't understand any of those words, but I'm so hungry I'll eat anything."

She busies herself with slathering mayo on the chunkiest bread I've ever seen, and my stomach rumbles.

"You're the girl from Lucky, right?" she asks. "The one Finn's hung up on?"

There's something about Trix that makes me want to tell her everything, but I take a beat and try to keep my story straight. We're not even supposed to be officially dating yet.

"Oh, we're just good friends, but we did have a thing in high school."

She gives me a look like she knows this is complete bullshit.

"It's new," I tell her.

"High school sweethearts, that's so romantic."

"Yeah. Kind of."

She hands me a sandwich, grabs hers and sits at the table where I join her.

"Oh god, this is delicious," I say through a mouthful of the amazing sandwich.

"It's in the book." She gets up, grabs a cookbook with her smiling face on the cover, and hands it to me.

"Wow, this is so cool," I say, trying to take a look without getting mayo all over it. "I've seen it on your social media, but I don't have a copy yet."

"Take it."

"Oh, really?"

"Yeah. I have loads of them."

I'm not exactly sure what I was expecting, but Trix seems so normal, so down to earth, so *nice*.

"Maverick never used to eat anything at all before he met me. It was my key lime bars that turned him onto human food."

"Wait, what?"

She pauses for a second and then slaps a hand over her mouth. "Oh, shit. You don't know about Maverick?!"

The pieces fall into place. What she said about them forgetting to feed us, the fact that she's not making a sandwich for Maverick right now.

Maverick Stone is a vampire?!

"Oh, fuck! But you know what Finn is? Right? Oh my god! Shit!" She puts her face in her hands.

I let out a laugh. "It's okay. I know about Finn. But I didn't know *Maverick—*"

"Well, I guess if you can keep Finn's secret, you can keep

ours too." She gives me a smile and takes a huge bite of her sandwich.

Ours. It's not just Maverick's secret, it's hers too.

I think of Finn's words from earlier. *I'm sorry that I didn't fucking die that night.* And then I think about my reaction to him, to what he is. How hurt he must have been when I reacted that way.

"I'm new to all this," I tell her. "I have no idea what I'm doing."

"Well, if you ever need to talk about anything, I'm always here. You should meet Poppy too."

"Poppy?"

"She dates a vampire too."

The way she says it like it's no big deal — just something that happens, somehow puts me at ease. There are humans dating vampires. This is a thing that happens.

"What are you doing tonight?" she asks, leaning over the table.

"I don't think I have any plans."

"Okay, we're having a girl's night. There's a bar in Santa Monica that is kind of exclusive but super low-key. No one ever hassles me there. We can get drunk and messy and share stories about how hot it is to fuck our vampire boyfriends."

I let out a laugh. "Oh, me and Finn haven't—"

Her mouth drops open. "What?!"

"It's new."

"I thought you've been into each other since high school?"

"Yeah, but in high school we didn't… and now it's kind of new again."

"Hang on, are you telling me he hasn't even—" she stabs two fingers into her neck like she's making bite marks.

I shake my head.

"Oh, girl, you have *so* much to look forward to!"

"Honestly? I'm a little scared."

But mostly just really excited.

"Scared he'll hurt you while you're doing the deed?"

I just shrug.

"There are things you can do. Make sure someone else is around when it happens for the first time. Maverick could be there."

"Okay, I don't need Maverick Stone watching me get bitten by my boyfriend."

She laughs. "I could do it for you. Have some silver chains nearby just in case. Beat him with them if he gets too rough."

"Okay, I'm not sure any of this is helping," I laugh nervously.

"You'll find your way through it. And when you do? It will be *so* worth it."

She puts our plates in the dishwasher and then grabs a bowl of frosting from the fridge and starts lathering it over the cake.

"Right now, all you have to worry about is what you're going to wear tonight."

CHAPTER FORTY-TWO

inn

"You're too unpredictable to be dating," Maverick says, pouring us both another glass of blood bank blood. Fucker still has some bottles left.

"You sound like my father," I groan.

"I'm your maker. That makes me your vampire daddy."

I roll my eyes. "Okay, *Daddy*, what do you advise I do? Never date again? You're married. You're proof that it can be done. Max and Poppy are making it work. Why is it okay for you two but not for me?"

"Because you're still a baby," he says. "We all have an insatiable thirst for blood, but right now, yours is a thousand times worse than ours. Do I need to remind you of what happened the night you got arrested?"

"No. You don't need to remind me of that," I say. "I'm constantly reminded of that. I never stop being fucking reminded of it."

"Good."

"But it's different with April. I don't want to hurt her, I want to *protect* her."

"Okay, so you don't kill her, but what if some guy looks at her wrong in a bar? Then what? You rip his fucking throat out in a rage? He bleeds out in front of fifty people? That's what happens. Trust me, I've seen it happen too many fucking times."

"I'm not going to do that!"

Fuck, I hope I'm not going to do that.

"What made her come around to the idea of being with you, anyway?"

"She talked to a Donna."

"So she just wants you for The Bite?"

"No! She doesn't even want The Bite! Fuck! I haven't even bitten her!"

"You had sex with her and didn't bite her? Okay, that shows you have some ability for self-control."

"I didn't fuck her either! Jesus, Maverick! Do you have to be so fucking crass?"

"So you were alone with her, doing *stuff* I guess, but you didn't fuck or bite her?"

"No!"

"What stuff did you do?"

"Does it matter?"

"Yeah, it does."

"Oh my fucking god." I run my hands down my face. "Fine. I went down on her, and I used my — fuck. No. I'm not giving you any more details."

"You went down on her, and you didn't bite her inner thigh?"

Okay. This conversation is truly mortifying. Is this how teenagers feel when their fathers try to talk to them about sex?

"No. I didn't. It wasn't about me. It was about her. I just wanted to make her feel good."

He takes a sip of blood. "That suggests you may not be quite as dangerous as I thought."

I take a sip of my own drink, and it goes down so easy. It's *so* much better than that synthetic stuff.

"But you're still dangerous, Finn. You could go into a baby vamp rage at any time. Hurt the people around you whether you mean to or not. I did it a lot when I was first made."

"Yeah? Well, I'm not you. I'm not a murderer. I haven't killed anyone."

"But you will. It's inevitable."

"Thanks for your faith in me. Really."

"My job isn't to have faith in you, it's to keep you and everyone around you safe. And that's why you need to break up with April right now. Glamour her into forgetting all about this, all about you. Glamour her into thinking she was just here on a short trip and tell her to go back to Lucky."

"What the fuck, Maverick?!" Trix stands at the door holding a chocolate cake. April stands behind her, cake forks tumbling out of her hand onto the ground.

Maverick holds up his arms, looking at the girls like he's both sorry and somehow not at all sorry. "You have to understand, girls. Finn is a baby. He's not ready for a relationship."

"Wow," April says. "I expected this shit from our real fathers, but not from Maverick Stone."

April has known Maverick for all of two seconds and she's already putting him in his place. Fuck, I want her so badly.

"Maverick, apologize to April," Trix demands.

"I won't apologize. I'm not wrong. April, I'm sure you understand how dangerous this is. How dangerous Finn is. I'm just trying to keep you safe."

"I'm so done with people wanting to keep me safe," she fumes. "My own father tried to keep me safe for twenty-eight years and all he did was turn me into some twisted version of myself who tried to make everyone else happy. No one ever cared about *my* happiness, not until Finn came back into my life."

My cheeks and heart heat at her words. I know there's a huge cavern between us right now, but I also know that evening we had together in Lucky was one of the happiest of my life. At least it was, before I showed her my fangs.

"He could hurt you," Maverick says.

"Anyone could hurt me!"

"He could *kill* you."

"Maverick! Fucking hell!" Trix glares at him. "*You* could kill *me* in a second! But you love me, so you choose not to!"

"I'm older! I was made decades ago!"

Trix puts the cake down on the table in front of me. "You and me. Inside. Now."

"Are you kidding me?"

She gives him that look married women have — the one that puts their men in place in seconds.

Maverick gets up and follows her inside, leaving April standing there staring down at the cake.

"God. I'm so sorry about him," I say.

She picks up the forks and then sits, puts the plates down and cuts two massive pieces of cake, handing one to me.

"Oh, sorry," she says, pulling the slice back towards her. "I forgot you don't eat."

"I don't have to eat, but I can eat. And I still kind of like cake." I pick up the plate and take a bite. "And I would never say no to one of Trix's cakes."

We sit there and eat our cake in silence, listening to Maverick and Trix shouting at each other from inside the house.

"He had no right to say any of that," I say. "He's kind of a dick."

"He's not wrong though," she says.

"Yeah, he is. I would never glamour you and send you back to Lucky. I would never take your memories or your free will. Not ever."

"Maybe. But he's right about you being a baby."

"I really fucking wish people would stop calling me that."

"You're new. You could hurt me."

"April," I say, looking into her deep blue eyes that draw me in like a demon moth to an angelic flame. "I could. But I would never."

We're suddenly treated to the sounds of Maverick grunting and Trix screaming his name.

"Jesus." I roll my eyes. "Those two are fucking insatiable."

"She's a human," April says. "And he's a vampire."

My eyes find hers. "Yeah."

She looks down and cuts another slice of cake.

And all I can think of is a life where our fights end with my cock in her as she screams my name.

CHAPTER FORTY-THREE

pril

"I WAITED a while before I let Max bite me," Poppy says, running her fingers through her reddish-brown hair. "We did other stuff, but when it came to The Bite, it really felt like I was losing my virginity again." She takes a sip of the cherry cocktail with matching dark red umbrella in front of her.

Hanging out with Trix and Poppy is like being with the sisters I never knew I had, especially after a few drinks. The retro tiki themed bar is busy, but our little table by the window overlooking the starlit ocean feels cozy and no one has looked at us twice. Although Trix is wearing a blonde wig that looks really natural and practically makes her unrecognizable.

"Okay, tell me more about this Max guy," I say, taking a sip of my own very strong pineapple-y cocktail. "He seems very swoon worthy."

Poppy's eyes widen. "Oh, I thought you knew!"

Trix shakes her head. "She didn't know about Maverick either."

"Max Montrose," Poppy says, looking into her cocktail with a blush.

"Wait, what?!"

She nods. "Yeah. Max Montrose is my boyfriend."

"Max Montrose? *The Letterbox, A Knight to Remember* Max Montrose?!" I squeal, rattling off some of my favorite Max Montrose movies.

"Uh huh."

"And he's—?

They both nod.

I take a gulp of the syrupy sweet cocktail like it's going to help. Everything I know about the world is wrong.

"Are *all* movie stars… *you know*?" I ask.

Trix laughs. "No!"

"But a lot of them are," Poppy adds.

"Woah."

Trix takes a sip of her huge cocktail. "But you know, it's okay if you *don't* want to wait to do the deed with Finn," she says, bringing us back to our original conversation about sex with our vampire boyfriends.

"But Finn's a baby," Poppy reminds her. "So waiting is probably a good idea."

"Everyone is so fixated on the idea that he's going to kill me," I say, toying with the umbrella in my drink. "But he's had plenty of chances. Well, a couple. If he was going to kill me, wouldn't he have done it by now?"

"Depends how heated things get in the bedroom," Poppy says. "It wouldn't take much for one of them to—you know."

"Maverick is just worried about you," Trix says, draining her huge fishbowl shaped glass. "I'm sorry about what he said before. He can be such an ass, but his heart is in the right place, even if it doesn't beat anymore. He just wants to keep you safe. Also, we need more drinks."

Trix leaps up to go to the bar, but I grab her wrist and stop her. "I'll go," I tell her.

"Good idea," Poppy says. "We don't need a photo of Trix this drunk making it onto Hollywood Daily in the morning."

"I'm not that drunk," Trix pouts.

Poppy hands me a platinum credit card. "I'll stay with her."

It's only when I'm leaning over the bar to order another round of crazy cocktails that I realize just how short the dark blue romper Trix lent me for tonight is. I'm bigger than her, and while she offered me the outfit because she'd ordered it online in the wrong, larger size by mistake, it's still a little too snug for me and I can practically feel the breeze on my butt cheeks.

I'm not the only one who notices.

A guy slides up next to me, a little too close for comfort, and I immediately get the ick.

"Can I get those for you and your friends?" he asks.

I shake my head. "No thanks. I've got it."

"It's no problem." He pulls out a gold credit card and tries to hand it to the woman behind the bar.

I hold up the platinum one. "I said, I've got it."

Another guy slides up too close on my other side. "What's with women these days? Just let him pay."

"She said no." The bartender takes Poppy's card and runs it through the machine.

"Where's your boyfriend tonight?" the second guy asks.

My heart pounds, and not in a good way. "He'll be here soon," I tell them. "He's meeting me here."

"Liar," the first guy spits. "If you had a boyfriend, he would never let you out in those tiny shorts. Not unless he liked sharing."

"He would never share me," I say. "He'd kill you both first."

"Okay, time for you two to go," the bartender says, waving to a guy from security. "I'll bring your drinks over, honey," she says to me.

I rush back to the table, still aware of the gaze of those guys on my ass.

"Everything okay?" Trix asks as I quickly take my seat.

"Yeah, just some guys at the bar being jerks."

"Oh, I fucking hate that! Where are they? I'll go give them a piece of my mind!"

"Trix, no," says Poppy. "It's not worth it. They might recognize you, and right now with all the violent crime reports, you don't know who you're messing with."

"They're getting kicked out," I say.

"Are you sure you're okay?" Poppy asks me.

I nod. "Yeah." But I'm not okay. I'm kind of freaked out. They were scary, and suddenly I'm thinking of all the news reports about LA's crime wave.

The bartender places our drinks down at our table. "Sorry about those guys, they're gone now. You ever have any trouble here, you just tell me."

We thank her and take our drinks, and just a few short minutes later we're all *very* drunk.

"I'm going to get him to turn me soon," Poppy slurs. "Then we can be together forever."

"You'd want to become one of them?" I ask.

"Yeah! Wouldn't you?"

"I haven't even thought about it," I say, "But the idea of eternity with Finn is not awful."

"She hasn't even been *bitten* yet, why would she want to be turned?" Trix asks. "I want Maverick to turn me one day, but I also just really like how it feels when he bites me, and if

I'm a vampire, he won't bite me anymore. He'll bite someone else."

"Oh Trix! But he won't *love* anyone else," Poppy tells her. "They will just be food for him. You'll be the one he spends eternity with."

"Yeah. But blood and sex is so linked for us. I worry that he'll fall for some other human girl if I'm a vampire."

"This conversation is so fucking weird," I laugh.

"It kind of is!" Trix agrees with a laugh. "But our guys are older than us, so we have time to decide. Finn's the same age as you. If you wait too long, you'll be older than him."

"There's nothing wrong with a woman being older," I say. "Haven't you seen *Highlander*?" I ask.

"No."

"Nope."

"That movie should be required watching for girls who fall in love with vampires," I tell them. "We could do a movie night at my hotel!"

"I'm definitely up for that!" Poppy grins.

"Yes!" Trix squeals! "PJ party!"

"What would you do with all that time?" Poppy muses. "I guess I could read all the books on my list. No wonder Max has such a huge library."

"I could figure out how to end world hunger," Trix says.

"I'd write," I say, without thinking. "I'd write so many novels. Hundreds of them. *Thousands!* I'd be the most prolific writer that's ever lived!"

"You write novels? What kind?" Trix asks.

"Spicy romance."

They both squeal with excitement. "Ok, where can I buy your books?" Trix asks, already getting her phone out to make a purchase.

"I don't have any for sale yet. I just write on Scripty."

"God, I love that app," says Trix. "What's your name on there?"

I'm too drunk and happy to have some new friends that I just tell them. "Evie Everhart."

They both start trying to find me on their apps and I get up to go to the bathroom. The whole bar is spinning and I know I should probably drink some water, but first I need to pee. I try to steady myself, but stumble, nearly falling over.

Trix laughs. "Might be time to go!"

"Yeah. Time to get back to our hot vampires," Poppy says with a giggle.

"Not me," I say sadly, trying to remember how to be upright. "I'm just going back to my hotel."

"You're not staying at Finn's place?" Trix gasps.

I shake my head.

"Oh, that's to keep you safe?" Poppy asks.

"I guess. But I really want to see him right now."

"You should call him," Trix says. "No, wait. Don't call him. It is dangerous!"

"She *should* call him!" Poppy says. "He loves her, he won't hurt her!"

I'm so drunk and confused. Is Finn even mine? Is he my boyfriend? Does he love me? Do I love him? Or is all this just pretend?

"I don't even have his number," I say.

They both just look at me confused.

"I mean, I don't know how to dial," I say, trying to make it less weird. "I'm too drunk."

Trix grabs her phone and starts dialing. "Finn?" she asks. "April wants to speak to you!"

"Oh my god! No! Stop!" I laugh, trying to grab the phone off her. Why do I suddenly feel like I'm thirteen years old prank calling boys?

Trix shoves the phone in my face.

"April?" Finn's low, gravelly voice does me in.

"Hi," I giggle.

"Why are you calling? Are you okay? Where are you?"

"We're at some tiki bar."

"Is everything okay?"

"Yeah, everything is fine! Well, except for a couple of jerks who hassled me, but I'm okay." I follow the girls out through the bar and onto the street. "We're just leaving. Going home. But I was thinking maybe I could come to your place?"

"That's not a good idea," he says.

But I don't want to be good girl, good idea April. I want to be crazy in love with a vampire bad girl April!

"There's my ride," Poppy says pointing to a black town car parked outside. "Be safe April!" She gives me a warm, sloppy, drunk hug. "Trix!" She hugs Trix so tight that Trix lets out a gasping sound.

"April?" Finn's voice rings out.

Shit, I'd almost forgotten he was still on the phone.

"Tell him I'll come to his place with you," Trix says. "But only if he orders pizza. He never has any fucking food at his house."

"You girls need a ride?" The creepy guys from the bar suddenly appear out of a shadow.

Shit.

The bar is tucked away in a back street and it's kind of dark and secluded out here and I don't like this at all.

"No, thanks," I tell them.

"April, what's going on?" Finn asks. "Who's there?"

"Just some guys," I tell him.

"You can come party with us," one of the guys says. "We know a great club that you'd both love. It's called Vincent's."

"We're not coming out with you, we're going home," Trix says. "To our *boyfriends*."

"If you two had boyfriends, they wouldn't leave you alone for a second. You're too tempting."

"Oh, just fuck off," I tell them.

"Oooh, this one is fiery!" one of the guys says.

"I'll take her," the other guy says. "I like a challenge."

"I fucking hate this shit," Trix says, glaring at the guy who's got his eye on her. "I'm wearing a fucking wedding ring!" She waves her hand in front of his face.

"Fake, I bet," the guy says.

"Um, Finn," I say into the phone.

But it's too late. The call's ended.

CHAPTER FORTY-FOUR

 inn

I DON'T HESITATE. I shove my feet into my Vans and I blur down the beach. I don't give a shit who sees me moving that fast, they're all too drunk or high to think anything of it anyway, and within less than a minute I'm outside the bar.

One guy has his arm around Trix's shoulder, the other has his hands gripped around April's waist and the fire in my veins fucking burns.

What everyone warned me about — the baby vampire rage within me — is now truly stoked, and I'm ready to rip both these assholes into pieces, to hell with the fucking consequences.

I grab the guy who's on April, and my hands slip easily —*too* fucking easily—around his neck.

April screams, but I don't care if she's scared of me, I just need to make sure that anyone who would want to hurt her is fucking *dead*.

"You piece of shit," I growl at him. "I should break your fucking neck."

"Finn! Stop!" April's voice calls out to me, but I'm too far gone. I can't stop the rage this time.

I throw the guy into a car on the other side of the street, the force of it smashing him into the windshield. Blood splatters, a car alarm starts blaring, but shit, even that blaring noise can't stop me.

I yank the other guy off Trix and hold him up against the wall by his neck. He gasps, struggling to breathe.

Oh, fuck. This is how I do it. This is how I make my first kill.

"I should fucking kill you both," I snarl.

"Finn!" It's Trix trying to stop me now. "Don't kill them!"

But it's too late. Everyone is right. I am a fucking monster. I can't be tamed. I can't be cured. In this moment I can't do anything but kill these motherfuckers.

I break the guy's arm like it's a twig and throw him over to his friend. He lands in a bloody heap by the back wheel of the car that's dripping with blood and glass.

"Okay, you scared them, Finn. Let's go," Trix says, her voice shaking.

"I'm not done," I say, stalking slowly towards the car, my eyes on the guy who had his fucking hands on April.

I should be excited by the blood sprayed all over the place, but I wouldn't want this guy's blood on my lips. I just want them both eradicated from this earth so that they don't hurt anyone again, *ever*.

Visions of his fucking hands on her dance in my mind, driving me towards him. I bare my teeth, and the guy fucking flips, crying, yelling for help.

"You should be fucking scared," I tell him. "These fangs are the last thing you're going to fucking see."

He brings his hands up to his face. Those fucking hands.

All I can see is the way they gripped April's waist against her will.

I grab one of his hands and I snap it, breaking the bones in every single one of his fingers in one go. The sound is chilling, but holy fuck it feels so good. The guy screams, high pitched, pathetic.

I grin my fangs at him and grab his other hand. "You'll never touch another woman as long as you fucking live," I tell him, as I snap the bones in his other hand. He screams again.

"Finn! Please! Finn! No!" April is crying and screaming for me to stop… but how can I stop until he's *dead*?

"We weren't going to hurt them!" the other guy by my feet pleads. "We were only supposed to take them to the club!"

"What club?" I growl, already knowing the answer.

"Vincent's," the guy says.

"Who told you to take them?"

But I already know the answer to that too. Vincent. Aiden. Doesn't matter which one.

Motherfuckers.

But this guy, this one right here, *he* was the one who was going to take April there against her will, to let her be drained and fucked by some other vampire.

My vision is all black, and my hands are on the guy's neck, and I'm about to do it. I'm about to squeeze the life out of him. There's no fucking doubt in my mind that I will kill him.

But then I hear the sirens.

The only thing within me louder than my rage is survival.

I glare at the guy, waiting for him to fall under my glamour. "You will not remember any of this. Your hands will never fully heal. Whenever you look at your hands, you'll know it's what you fucking deserve. You'll never touch another woman. Ever."

He nods dumbly through his tears of pain.

I stare at the other guy. "You'll give all your money to a women's charity. You'll never touch another woman again either."

He nods dumbly.

"Finn," Trix yells to me. "You need to go. *Now.*"

I step back and look at the carnage — the blood, the glass, the two pathetic pieces of shit lying there.

My eyes find April's. She looks so fucking scared. *Terrified.*

I know this will be it for us. She's just watched me nearly kill two guys. She just watched me break a guy's fucking hands. She'll go back to Lucky tomorrow, and I'll never see her again.

But it's okay. Because at least there she'll be safe.

And then I turn and run.

CHAPTER FORTY-FIVE

pril

He broke that guy's fucking hands.

Because he touched me.

I stand in the shower at the hotel, letting the hot water wash away the night, my fear, my confusion, my sins, while I try to process what just happened.

What the fuck was I thinking following a vampire to LA to fake date him for a hundred thousand dollars?! Especially when there is a crime wave!?

When I finally get out of the shower, I take the last of Finn's clean t-shirts and put it on, enjoying the feel of him on my skin like I always do when I wear his shirts. The soft fabric rubs on my nipples and gently caresses my ass and makes me feel so cozy and safe.

After everything that has just happened, I don't really understand why wearing his shirt over my naked body still makes me so excited, so hot for him.

I shouldn't be having these feelings. Not for someone who is not even *human*. Not for someone who could kill me if he got too excited during sex with me.

It really shouldn't turn me on that he broke that guy's hands. I shouldn't be replaying that moment in my mind like it's a *turn-on*. I should be shocked and horrified. I shouldn't be *glad* he broke that guy's hands.

I should be on the interstate back to Lucky, not lying on a bed in a hotel in Santa Monica thinking about touching myself, getting off on how fucking powerful Finn is, on how deep his rage was when he saw that guy touching me.

I run my hands over my breasts, squeezing my nipples through the softness of his shirt. One hand moves down to my clit and starts making slow, gentle circles, while the other hand grips his shirt, like I'm gripping his shirt still on his body.

I imagine him here with me. I imagine he's just broken that guy's hands.

"I'll never let anyone hurt you," he growls into my neck. "I'll kill any motherfucker who tries. I hope I proved that to you tonight."

His hand finds my clit, and it's not me making these circles, it's him, and then he slides a finger inside me, one powerful finger working my clit while another fucks me. His hands are strong enough to snap bones, but right now, they're caressing me, fucking me, making heat pulse through my whole body.

Then his fangs protrude, and he looks at me like he can't wait to taste my blood—like he can't wait to give me The Bite.

I come, loud and fast, thinking of Finn's fingers and his fangs.

For a few moments, I just rest in the post-orgasm glow,

smiling to myself and thinking of Finn. Wishing he was lying here next to me.

It's only when the glow wears off that I go back to wondering what the fuck is wrong with me.

inn

THE NEXT MORNING, I wake up to Maverick and Natalie knocking on my door.

"What the fuck? It's only seven," I complain, letting them into the light filled living area.

"We need to talk about last night," Maverick says, immediately making himself at home on my couch, kicking his feet up onto my coffee table.

Natalie's mouth is in a thin line, but she doesn't speak, just sits next to Maverick on the couch so that I have to take the armchair opposite.

I feel like I'm in an audition, one that I already know I won't get a callback for.

"Trix told you," I say.

"Of course she fucking told me! She's my *wife!*"

"I glamoured them. I got out of there in time."

"According to Trix, it wasn't even *blood* related," Maverick says. "It's one thing to go crazy for blood, but now you're just killing people for *fun?*"

Maverick is doing that disappointed father act, and I'm not in the fucking mood for it.

"I didn't kill anyone!"

"You could have. If that car alarm hadn't gone off, and if someone hadn't alerted the police—"

"Exactly. Someone alerted the police," Natalie says. "Someone knew there was a problem."

"You're lucky you're not in jail again," Maverick says. "And you'd better pray no one comes forward with information."

"I glamoured the guys into forgetting everything. I'll just glamour anyone else who knows anything."

He gives me a stern look. "You couldn't glamour them last time you were arrested, remember?"

"And what if multiple people saw you?" Natalie asks.

"Oh, give me a break," I sigh. "No one saw me. No one else was there." I look to Maverick. "And where the fuck were you? Why was it *me* who was pulling that guy off Trix? You know what was happening, right? You know what would have happened if I hadn't got there in time. You're not that fucking dense, are you? They were taking the girls to Vincent's. You know what would have happened to them there."

Maverick's face burns. "I got there as fast as I could."

"Daddy Maverick," I say, leaning forward in my seat now. "If you had seen that guy's arm around Trix's shoulder, trying to lure her into a car to get bitten and fucked by vampires all night, what would you have done?"

"If it was me, I would've fucking killed them both and any potential witnesses. But this isn't about me. This is about you."

I sit back and laugh. "You would have killed them, all I did was break the guy's hands!"

"You need to drink more blood," he says, as if that would've changed anything from last night. If I'd had more blood, I would only have been stronger.

"There is no blood," I tell him. "The shortage, remember?"

"I know. Brandon has some guys looking into it. But it's — concerning. The less blood available for vampires, the more murders in the city. This is why I need you to be extra careful right now."

"Wait, you think this is all connected? Vampires are responsible for the crime wave?"

"Yeah. And you've just made yourself part of it."

"There are no blood deliveries, so vampires are killing more than usual," Natalie explains. "They're getting too thirsty and there's not enough Donnas."

"When the blood bank supply gets low, our kind does what they do best. We hunt," says Maverick.

"I don't need to remind you of the seriousness of all this," Natalie chimes in. "If anyone can identify you from the event last night, I have no idea how I'll spin it. There's only so many times we can say you were there to help."

"You're not fucking Superman," Maverick says. "You can't just keep showing up where crimes are being committed and not have the police coming around asking questions."

"If the police come around, I'll just glamour them. It's no big deal," I shrug. "Those motherfuckers deserved what they got, and more."

Maverick leans forward now. "We don't *torture* people. That's what you did last night to those guys. That one guy is never going to be able to use his hands again."

"Good."

"You're talking like a real asshole. You sound like one of

those vampire fuckers who forget their humanity, if they ever had any. They do what they want, take what they want, giving no fucks about anyone else. But that's not who you are."

"Maybe it is who I am," I say, glaring at him. "Maybe I am a bad vampire."

"You're a dick vampire, that's what you are."

"You think you can just come into my place and talk to me like this? This is *my* place, and I don't have to take your shit. I have zero fucking regrets about last night. I would do it again. I'd go further. I'd break the other guy's hands too. And maybe if you were half the man you pretend to be, you'd have done it yourself—"

In a split second, my chair topples and I'm on the ground, Maverick above me, seething, fangs out, ready to what? Kill me?

I just laugh. "The words you're looking for are thank you."

He shoves me and then gets off. "Fuck you, Finn. I've tried to help. I was there for you when you were first turned. I helped you get out of some really fucking stupid situations, but I'm done. Do what you want."

"Maverick," Natalie says. "Take a breath."

He raises his hands in the air. "I'm fucking done. Do what you want. Be a *bad vampire*," he says with air quotes. "I don't care."

It's only when he storms out that I realize he's right. He has been a pain in my ass, but he has also been there for me. And even though I wish I'd never been turned, he did only do it to save me.

"Don't worry about him," Natalie says. "He'll come around."

I shake it off. "Yeah. Whatever."

"But we do need to talk about you and April."

"It's done," I tell her. "I am too fucking dangerous to be

near her. I'll pay back whatever the studio has paid her already. Just let her go."

She just shakes her head. "No can do. Your contract is binding."

"You and April are the only ones who know about that contract," I tell her. "Just rip it up, pretend it never happened."

"No."

"You're still going to hold us to it, even after last night. Even after you said you were worried about me killing April?"

"Yes, Finn. What I wanted to talk about was how I want you to act on your next date."

Wow, my whole life is full of people who are just the fucking worst.

CHAPTER FORTY-SEVEN

pril

Katrina: April/Evie! I LOVE your new vampire story! It's so different from what you usually write but I AM HOOKED!

Evie: I'm so glad you like it! How are you? How is baby Dylan?

Katrina: We are all fine here. But I do have some news. I've started my own literary agency. I know I have my hands full with the baby, but I think I may go crazy if I don't do this. I need something for me. And I'm sure I'll be okay to handle one client, and I'd love for it to be you, if you are interested! I still have a lot of contacts in the industry, and I know this new vampire book will get picked up in a heartbeat!

Evie: OMG YES!!!

Katrina: Okay, do me a favor. Take your vampire book down from Scripty so we don't get in any trouble with them. Send me your chapters, and I'll pass them on to my amazing editor, and we will get you a publishing deal!

. . .

IT'S BEEN DAYS, and I haven't seen Finn since the night outside the bar. He's been busy promoting his new movie, and I've been using my fucked up fantasies in my writing. At first, I had no plans to share it with my readers on Scripty. While my stories have always been spicy, they have never been violent.

Until now.

But when I took a chance two nights ago and uploaded a new chapter where my character Flynn, who turns out to be a vampire, beats the shit out of a guy after he barely touches my female main character, my views, likes and shares went crazy!

My heart races, and I bite my lip as I re-read Katrina's message over and over again.

I should probably see this as an opportunity to reach out to some established agents and publishers, but I like Katrina, and I know she'd do everything within her power to get me the book deal of my dreams.

I'm getting paid so much just from being here in LA, a literary agent wants to represent me, Finn is back in my life.

Everything is working out. Better than working out.

All my dreams are coming true!

I close my laptop. No, I can't get too excited. It's just as likely that Katrina won't have time, being a new mother and all. It wouldn't take much for Natalie to break my contract, especially if she finds out I'm still posting on Scripty, and Finn? Well, last time I saw him, he was breaking a guy's hands.

Because that guy touched me.

I grab the remote and turn on the TV for a distraction. But when Finn's face appears on screen, it's nothing like a distraction. He's laughing at something someone just said.

I drop onto the bed and stare at the screen.

He looks gorgeous, dressed in a dark blue shirt rolled up his forearms—*fucking yum*—and black pants. That's Finn. My Finn. Finn, who broke that guy's hands. Finn, who's a fucking vampire. My first love, Finn. On national TV.

"Juliette," says the host, Dirk Derrick, a blonde man with huge white teeth. "Can you tell us a bit about the new movie?"

"Sure, so I play a single mom with a super cute little kid…" Everyone awwwws. Juliette Cortez is beautiful with her long dark hair and light brown skin. I mean, of course, she's a movie star, she has to be beautiful, but she's next level attractive. Her face is like glass, there's not a blemish or wrinkle on her, and her body is all skinny in the middle and filled out in all the right places.

"Finn plays my boyfriend," she says, giving him a flirta-tious look that hits me like a punch to the gut. "My kid gets sucked into this book he's really into, called *Jungle Story*. We both get sucked into the book too, and then we go on an action packed adventure to save him and the world."

"I love the premise of this," says Dirk, giving them a big grin. "Now, you both have amazing chemistry on screen. Is there anything going on between you two?"

Finn laughs a little too forcefully, and Juliette puts a hand on his leg. "Oh, no," she says. "We're just friends."

"Just really good friends," says Finn with a nod.

"Well, everyone was convinced you were an item until this photo started doing the rounds a few days ago."

Suddenly, a photo of me and Finn walking on the beach fills the screen.

Oh fuck!

We look deep in conversation, which we were. It's not exactly screaming "relationship," but it's clear that we're more than *just really good friends*. I didn't even know anyone was following us, and at first, I'm pissed. I feel so violated that this private moment we were having was photographed for the whole world to see.

But this is exactly what I signed up for. This is exactly why I'm here. To convince the world that me and Finn are dating.

"Okay, Finn. Who's the new girl?"

He chuckles and fidgets in his seat for a moment. "Let's just say she's not someone new."

"I think our viewers are going to need a little more than that."

The audience whoops and claps like they *really* want to know more.

Finn lets out a nervous laugh. Is it real? Or is he just acting? "She's actually someone I used to have a huge crush on in high school."

The audience ooohs and aaaaahs and I do too.

"Oh, I see," Dirk says. "Now that you're famous, she's come back into your life. Suddenly she's interested?"

The audience boos.

Wait, what?

Finn shakes his head. "No, that's not—"

"I bet that happens a lot," Dirk says. "People from the past wanting something from you now that you've hit the big time?"

"Uh, no, not really, if anything—"

"How does this new woman feel about some of your previous escapades?"

Finn's mouth forms a hard line, and flashes of fire rage in his deep green eyes. "None of my—"

"You were spotted just a couple of nights ago leaving a club with an unknown woman."

"I was just—"

"And you've been linked with an adult film star," Dirk

continues.

The audience gasps.

"Look—" Finn begins.

But he's cut off *again.* "And what about your recent arrest?"

"All charges were dropped," Finn says, his expression like steel now.

"Doesn't explain why you were hanging out in back alleys in a particularly seedy part of Hollywood."

"I—"

"Juliette," Dirk says, as if he hasn't just completely destroyed Finn in front of the entire country. "Is there a significant other in your life? Or are you as single as the single mom in the movie?"

Her expression hardens. "Dirk, with all due respect, we're not here to talk about our private lives. We're here to talk about the movie."

The host laughs. "I'm going to take that as a yes and ask you to meet me for a drink after the show."

The audience laughs, and then the screen is filled with Dirk's face. "And now to the newsroom."

Woah, what the hell was that interview?!

"Thanks Dirk. In this morning's news, the violet attacks across LA continue to increase. Two men in Santa Monica were taken to hospital just a few nights ago with serious injuries. One man had both his hands broken in the attack."

Ohhhh fuuuuck.

"The following may upset some viewers. In West Hollywood last night, a man was murdered in a very horrifying way." The news reporter looks unsettled. "The victim's throat was ripped out and found on the ground some feet away from his body. Police are concerned about this new wave of violent crime, which brings the crime rate up thirty percent from this time last year."

I can't listen to any more. I turn off the TV and busy myself with making more coffee just to have something to do. I had planned to go hiking in the Hollywood Hills today while Finn was busy with his appearances, but I'm too scared to go by myself now.

But while there is clearly some unhinged killer on the loose, it's also nice to know that there is a very powerful vampire out there who would do anything to keep me safe.

My phone buzzes and makes me jump.

NATALIE: we're going to need to do damage control after that interview. Lie low today. Now that your photo is out there, it's best if you don't leave the hotel. A car will pick you up at seven, and I'll send something for you to wear.

I GUESS NOW at least I have more time to work on my unhinged novel.

CHAPTER FORTY-EIGHT

Enraged doesn't begin to describe how I feel as I walk off set and follow Juliette back to the green room after the interview.

She closes the door behind us and thank fuck we're the only two in the room because my fangs protrude and I have to grab onto the back of an armchair to steady myself—to stop me from speeding back out there and ripping Dirk's blonde fucking head off in front of the live audience and cameras.

"Finn," Juliette says, taking a step back to give me room to rage. "We'll get him back for this. We'll glamour him, make him apologize."

I glare at her. "Apologize?! The damage is already done! I can't glamour everyone who's seen that interview!"

"It wasn't so bad. Everyone knows Dirk is an asshole."

I grip the chair harder. "It *was* bad. Very fucking bad. For both of us. If this movie tanks because of me, it will affect your career too."

"People are still going to see the movie. You'll still get work. Trust me. I know what it's like to piss off a movie studio."

"I'm so fucked," I say, gripping the chair so tight I rip through the fabric.

"You should call your publicist."

"My publicist?! She's the one that organized this interview. She put me on this show—"

Did Natalie fucking set me up?

I try to shake it off. Why would Natalie want me to look like a hot mess on TV when she's the one who's been trying so hard to make me look like a good guy? Why set me up with April to fix my reputation if she was just going to fuck me over?

But the thought has been planted now, and I can't get it out of my mind. Dirk Derrick and Natalie conspiring against me.

"If I don't get a drink *right now*—" I growl.

Juliette looks at me like she knows that feeling, like she knows she has to get me out of here now. Before I kill him. Sure, I haven't killed anyone *yet*, but Dirk Derrick could easily be my first kill. I wouldn't even regret it. Not for a second.

Juliette nods. "Let's get you to Vincent's. Now."

Oh, Vincent's, fuck no. But where else can we go?

We bump into Dirk in the hallway, and he just grins at me like he owns the fucking world, like nothing could topple him off his perch.

I shove him against the wall, and I hear plaster crack.

A framed picture of him and some shitty president smashes to the ground, and he flinches.

I stare into his eyes, waiting for the moment when his mind opens.

"Security will be here any second," he says, trying to push me away.

For a second I wonder why I can't glamour him. What is he? Fae? Wolf? Warlock?

When that look of total stupidity eventually crosses his face, I relax. Dirk Derrick isn't paranormal. He's just a fucking asshole.

"When you get back on air, you will quit your job. You will give a public apology to me and anyone else you've ever grilled on your show. You'll tell everyone that you have not been in integrity, that I am a great stand up guy and that you were dragging me just because you thought it would make good TV, and that you're sorry for being such an asshole."

He nods dumbly.

"You will also stop acting like such an asshole and start treating everyone you meet with respect."

"Finn, we have to go." Juliette calls to me.

"And you'll never remember any of this conversation."

"Okay," he says, nodding his head up and down like it's on a string.

I let him go, and he drops to the floor, looking around like *what the fuck just happened,* while me and Juliette run down the hallway to the exit.

VINCENT'S VAMPIRE club is open 24 hours in order to serve nocturnals and daywalkers alike. The daylight hours are usually quiet, but this morning the club is jumping.

"I'll order you a Donna," Juliette says as we walk towards the bar.

My veins feel like they're on fucking fire, and my throat feels so dry I think I might die, but I still don't want a Donna.

I just want April. Not because I want to drink from her, but because I just want her to hold me and tell me it's all going to be fucking okay.

Okay, no. I do want to drink from her, of course I do, but when I think of sinking my teeth into her neck, it's only ever with the intention for us both to experience pleasure from it, not just for me to *drink.*

What I feel right now is pure fucking *thirst.*

I don't want April to quench this thirst. But I need something or someone or else I'm going to be in big fucking trouble, and so will any human that gets in my way.

"Finn." I turn at the voice that still haunts my dreams. Vincent Blake. The guy who owns this place, the guy who was partly responsible for draining me to an inch of my fucking life. The guy who tried to take April and Trix and force them to be Donnas.

I hate this guy more than anyone, well, maybe he's tied with Dirk Derrick today. But right now, I need to pretend I don't hate him as much as I do before I become another vampire responsible for this crime wave.

Vincent Blake is powerful. Some say he's more powerful than the Fraternity, which he was never invited into, because even for a vampire, this guy is bad news. His dark wavy hair hangs to his shoulders, and I want to punch him so bad in his medieval, angular looking face.

"I hear you're interested in a Donna," he says, that sly grin crossing his face like he knows he holds all the cards, as always.

"Why the fuck else would I be here?" I say, struggling to keep my emotions in check. I need blood, and I need it *now.*

"Hmmmm. I need to think. You nearly caused me a big problem when you bit one of my girls down the back alley by the burrito place, and then I heard you took a girl home that my good friend Aiden had already claimed."

"He no longer claims her, and this time, I'm not going to go for a fucking burrito first."

He lets out a low chuckle. "Fine. But just so you know. The price has gone up."

"Fine."

"What with the blood shortage and all."

"Surge pricing, great," says Juliette, rolling her eyes.

"I can pay," I tell him.

"Of course you can. It's ten thousand per bite."

"What the fuck?" Juliette explodes. "That's ten times the price!"

"Like you said, surge pricing," Vincent says, grinning at her, fangs out.

"Fuck this shit," she says. "Finn, let's go do this the old fashioned way."

"What if I do you both a deal?" Vincent suggests. "Because I appreciate your custom, I'll throw in two boxes of blood with each Bite."

Juliette lets out an angry breath. "Four."

He laughs. "There aren't that many boxes left. I'm not sure I can push it to four each—"

"Then we're fucking leaving." Juliette grabs my hand and starts pulling me through the crowd.

"I need that blood," I tell her through gritted teeth. "I can't risk—"

She turns, facing me and puts her hands on my shoulders. "Finn. Everyone keeps telling you that you're this baby vampire who's out of control. That you're dangerous. That you can't be trusted. But fuck those people. You know, you get to decide what kind of vampire you are. You can find your own willing victims, your own Donnas. There are girls *everywhere* who would be up for The Bite with you. You told me yourself that you drank from those girls in Lucky."

I shake my head. "They were Donnas."

"But you didn't know that at the time."

I run a hand over my face. "I *am* dangerous. I keep proving it over and over."

"Finn. I'm telling you this because you're my friend. Take your fucking power back. Stop listening to what everyone else is telling you about *you*. Decide for yourself what you are. You're a good guy. You've never even killed anyone. That's fucking unheard of. You've made a couple of mistakes, but you've learned from them. Stop letting them tell you that you're weak minded. Stop letting everyone call you a fucking baby."

"But I am a baby."

"No, you're fucking not. You're over a year old now. Everyone is just *babying* you. It's time to decide what kind of vampire you want to be and just fuck everyone else." She pulls me in and gives me a huge hug, and then she clomps out of the club in her massive heels.

Everything she's just said is right.

And that's why I make the decision to buy a Donna and some of Vincent's blood bank blood. Because it will help keep April safe, and that's the most important thing to me. To hell with the cost or the fact that my money is going to one of the people I hate most on this earth.

CHAPTER FORTY-NINE

pril

NATALIE: This is your first real date. Keep it classy. Romantic. Family friendly. Hold hands, no kissing. We need to put all the rumors to rest and show the world that Finn is kind, serious, family oriented. SHOW TIME!

I TRY on the dress Natalie sent for our date. It's navy blue, low-cut and hugs my curves, but at least this one goes down to my knees. She also sent some black heels that I am still practicing walking in before the car arrives.

"Finn Huxley was grilled on the Dirk Derrick show this morning." My head immediately turns to where Hollywood Daily is playing on TV. "But in a bizarre turn of events, instead of signing off for the episode as he usually does, Dirk gave his resignation and an apology to Mr. Huxley and all the celebrities he had treated so badly over the years. He said that Finn Huxley was one of the best guys he'd ever known, that he took situations out of context to make him look bad, and that he was sorry he'd acted like such a BLEEP."

Laughter bursts out of me. Finn did that. He glamoured that asshole and made him quit!

He said he'd never take my free will, and while I don't agree with vampires taking anyone's free will in theory, this feels like something that the whole world will benefit from.

My phone buzzes, letting me know my car has arrived. I grab the tiny purse Natalie sent, which is just big enough for my phone and the dark red lipstick I bought earlier today while exploring some high-end stores I would never normally have the nerve to enter. Natalie had ten thousand dollars transferred to my account this morning. I bought three expensive lipsticks, some new jeans, a couple of new dresses at a vintage shop on the boardwalk and some more very expensive and very sexy lacy underwear like the blue set that I'm wearing tonight.

I find the car outside the hotel and slide into the back seat. "Where are we going?" I ask the driver. I know we're going for dinner but still have no idea where.

"Stratosphere."

I quickly Google it and discover that it's not all that far away, but it's very expensive and exclusive. "Where the elite meet," says the tagline on the website.

When we arrive and I step out into the warm evening air, I look up at the restaurant and bar that sits on the top of a cliff overlooking the beach below, I can just tell I'm not going to feel comfortable here at all.

Blank State wasn't my style, but sitting out on the deck was nice. Stratosphere, with its steel and concrete design, just looks even more sterile. Like a big concrete blemish on the landscape.

I walk in slowly, trying not to stumble in my heels, and

I'm taken through the soulless space to a table where Finn is already sitting. His hair is a mess, as always, he's dressed in a navy shirt rolled up to his forearms, and he's frowning down at his phone.

God, will I ever get used to how beautiful he is?

He looks up at me, his expression softens and then his eyes widen at the amount of cleavage I'm showing.

"Hey," he says, standing up. It's such an old-school move, but it makes my heart leap when he does it. Finn's still got a little country charm in him after all.

"Hi," I say, taking a very uncomfortable seat opposite him.

"Can I get you some drinks?" asks the woman who seated me and is still hovering around.

"White wine for me please," I tell her.

"What kind of white?" She starts speaking in French or Italian, either way, I can't understand any of it.

"Actually, I might just have a beer."

"Certainly, what kind of beer?" She rattles off a list, but at least I can recognize some of them.

"Budweiser," I say.

"And for you, sir?"

"The same, thank you."

She nods and wanders off, and then we sit in silence for a few moments, just looking at each other.

"You showed," he says. "Even after that thing with those guys—"

"I'm contractually obliged," I say. I don't tell him that the thing with the guys only made me want to be here even more, and that I'm wearing expensive lacy underwear just for him. Just in case.

"Yeah. Of course. Fuck. I really wish you weren't. I wish you didn't have to sit here with…"

"With what?"

"With what I am." He tugs at his collar and gives me a sad smile.

Another moment passes, the two of us just looking at each other. Me not saying what I should say, that I still want him. That I want him even more than ever before.

I break our eye contact and look around the white space. "So, this place is—"

"Exclusive? Expensive? Pretentious as fuck?"

I let out a laugh, and suddenly we're both completely at ease. Not in this restaurant, but here. With each other.

"Does Natalie always decide where you go?"

His eyebrows knit. "Yeah. It's stupid, isn't it?"

I shrug. "Well, I guess she's your publicist for a reason. She knows where you're meant to be seen or whatever."

"I told her to let us both out of the contract. To pay you anyway but let you go." He looks down at his hands and tenses them on the table. "After what happened."

The beers arrive, and Finn takes a large gulp. I do the same, and the alcohol buzz hits me fast. I was too nervous about this date to eat much today, but now that I'm here, even though I'm in this sterile place where a Budweiser costs twenty bucks, Finn feels like a piece of home in this big crazy city.

"First of all, you know I need the money," I tell him. "I don't want to get out of the contract. Stop trying to get me out of it."

He sighs. "I can give you some money."

"I don't want your money. I want Natalie's money. Where is that money coming from, anyway?"

"Starlight Studios." He takes another gulp of beer. "From their publicity department."

"So instead of putting money into billboards or whatever, they're paying *me* to fake date you?"

"Fucked up, isn't it?"

"Should I feel bad?"

"No."

A bowl of olives appears in the middle of the table, and I dig into them, suddenly famished.

"And second?" he asks.

"What?"

"You said, first of all—"

"Oh! Well, second, that guy fucking deserved it."

Relief crosses Finn's face, and then his lips turn up into a smirk. "You think so?"

"Yeah. Fuck those guys. If you hadn't come along, who knows what they would have done to us."

"I know what they would have done. That's why I did it."

"I'm glad you did it."

"You liked it."

A flush hits my cheek. Yeah. I did like it. I went back to my hotel room and masturbated about it like the freak that I am.

"I don't *like* violence," I say.

"Oh, sure. No one *likes* violence. But sometimes it's necessary. And when some guy has his fucking hands on you, April, it's absolutely necessary." His eyes turn dark, and I know he'd do it again in an instant. I know he'd *kill* for me.

I take another huge gulp of beer, and I'm surprised when I suddenly reach the bottom of the glass.

"Another?" asks a server seconds after I put my empty glass down.

"Sure. Thanks."

"Are you ready to order?" the server asks.

"Sorry, I haven't even looked," I say, picking up a menu.

"Take your time," he smiles before drifting away.

I frown down at the options. "I don't understand half of these words."

"Want me to translate?"

I nod.

He reaches over the table and taps the first option with his finger, and all I can think about is his fingers inside me, his hands snapping that guy's hands…

"This one means tiny plate of nothing that will make you hungrier than you were when you walked in." He points to the next one down. "This one is a tiny carrot and a teaspoon of green sauce."

I let out a laugh.

"What I really want is some fucking *pie*," he says. "Why don't any of these places have pie?"

"Oh god. Me too. It's the only thing I'll miss about Lucky."

"You don't miss your dad?"

"Not really. I wonder if that's bad, that I don't miss him?"

"What he said to you when you were leaving was awful, April. It's okay to feel however you feel about that."

"Maybe I only have space in my heart to miss one parent." I thumb the necklace around my neck. "I think my mom would be really proud of me for finally making it out of Lucky, even if it is under some pretty strange circumstances. "You ever miss your dad?"

He lets out a scoff. "No. Never."

"Sorry, I didn't mean—"

"It's just complicated," he says. "He's still my dad, and part of me misses him. But I think I miss a version of him that never existed. I miss the dad I wish I'd had." Finn finishes his beer, and another is immediately placed in front of him.

"Can you still get drunk?" I ask.

He shakes his head. "No. But I still enjoy the taste of it. I'd need to drink a whole keg just to get a buzz."

"I'm feeling pretty buzzed already," I say, sipping some more of my second drink. "I should probably slow down, especially after what happened the other night. I was so drunk."

"That wasn't on you. None of that was your fault. I'm just glad I got there before—" He doesn't finish his sentence. He doesn't have to.

"So, I caught your interview this morning," I say, trying to change the subject.

Smoke billows in his eyes, and I think this is an even worse topic.

"I was hoping you'd missed that whole thing," he says.

"Well, it was kind of everywhere."

"I fucking hate that guy."

"Did you hear he quit?"

A smug smile tugs at his mouth. "Oh, yeah? Did he?"

"He also gave a very extensive apology, especially to you."

"How about that?" Finn leans over the table, and his eyes flick to my cleavage again.

"Should we order something?" I ask, blushing down at the menu. "What should I get?"

"It doesn't matter. People don't come here for the food, they're just here to be seen eating the food."

"Is it always like this? Is this where you spend your time? Places like this?"

"This is where I'm *supposed* to be spending my time. Be seen in the right places. Do the right things. Fit in with Hollywood's elite. Suck up to everyone who has my balls and my career in their hands."

"That sounds tough."

"Yeah. Kind of. But it's not so bad. It's just the price I pay for doing what I do."

One of his hands creeps forward, and I remember what Natalie said about us holding hands tonight. I let one of my hands move towards his, and as soon as I do, he grabs it, pushing his fingers into mine. It's desperate and sexy as hell. My heart swells, and I have complete faith that Finn will never hurt me.

He will always protect me.

He's my own personal superhero.

"Is this okay?" he asks, his eyes on our hands.

I swallow and nod. I know, I know, it's just acting. It's what Natalie told us to do, but it feels so damn real and so good I don't even care if it's not real.

"Hollywood is wild," he says, his thumb rubbing the back of mine and sending sexy tingles up my arm and into my belly. "There are so many things about it I honestly really fucking hate. The lies and manipulation, the way you have to suck up to assholes to get what you want. But there are a lot of good things here too. The opportunities I've had are beyond my wildest dreams."

"I remember when you made that video for *Hound of the Bakervilles*."

He rolls his eyes, and I take a sip of beer with my free hand.

"It was so adorable with all those puppies you borrowed from the shelter." I smile as I remember the way his face lit up with all those puppies running around him. "But it wasn't just the puppies that got you the job. You were *good*."

"Ever since I did that play in junior year, I was hooked on acting. But I never thought I'd end up here." His eyes dance, and I can see just how much he loves this, how he's willing to sacrifice some parts of himself to do what he loves most in the world.

"Your mom was so supportive, she was at every show," I say.

Neither of us mention that his dad didn't come to a single one.

"So were you."

"What can I say? I was transfixed by you long before you were a Hollywood star."

His hand gently squeezes mine. "Transfixed, huh?"

"Have you decided what you'd like to eat?" The server appears above us again, his eyes dropping to our hands. I pull away, not wanting anyone to be part of our private moment. Our private *staged* moment. I take my menu in both hands and look down.

"Give us a minute?" Finn asks.

"Of course, Mr. Huxley."

I let out a giggle at the way this guy talks to Finn like he's such a big deal.

But he is a big deal.

He's always been a big deal.

"You like how he called me Mr. Huxley?" Finn asks, leaning over the table, that flirtatious smirk on his sexy lips.

I cover my mouth, trying to stop my buzzed giggles.

"What a suck-up," he says with a grin. "But you can call me Mr. Huxley anytime you like."

I purse my lips, trying to stop myself from laughing. "Sorry, but I just can't think of you as anything other than Hardball Huxley."

He places the menu down on the table and looks straight at me, his eyes lighter and clearer than they were when I first walked in here.

"You want to get out of here?" he asks, that familiar mischievous smirk letting me know he's up for getting into some trouble tonight.

"What about Natalie? What about us being seen here?"

"We've been seen," he shrugs. "Now let's go."

He throws some cash on the table, slides his chair out and extends his hand to me.

I take it, and when his warm fingers grip mine, I know that I'd follow him anywhere.

inn

A WAVE of nervous confusion hits me as we stand on the corner outside Stratosphere waiting for our Uber. This isn't supposed to be real. This is a fake date orchestrated by my publicist to help my image. I'm not supposed to be thinking of places I can take April to impress her, or places with hidden corners where I could steal a kiss.

I look over at her, and she's so beautiful, so perfect, so pure. What the fuck am I thinking stealing kisses from her?

"What?" she asks.

"I was just wondering if you wanted to go back to your hotel—" her pretty blue eyes widen. "To get changed, I mean." I quickly add. "In case you'd be more comfortable. I mean, that dress is…" I can't help the way my eyes fall over her curves, "Really nice, and those shoes are hot, but you don't have self-healing bones like I do, and I don't want you to break your neck in those things."

The Uber pulls up, and I open the door, gesturing for her to get in.

Wow, okay. I didn't know I was that guy.

She gives me a weird look and then slides into the back while I get in the other side.

"You don't like this dress?" she asks once we're on the way back to Santa Monica.

"I love the dress. You look sexy as fuck in that dress." I run a hand over the back of my neck. "Ah, fuck. I just mean that I—"

She gives me a little amused smirk. "Sexy as fuck, huh?"

"I just want you to be comfortable. I want you to look like yourself, not some character Natalie is forcing you to play."

She smooths out the dress under her hands.

"But if you want to keep it on, that's okay too."

"No, I want to take it off," she says, giving me a look that tells me everything.

This is not fake. None of this is fake. We've both just been playing pretend at playing pretend.

A blush crosses her cheeks as she realizes what she's just said, and my fangs tingle at the idea of that dress on my bedroom floor, her naked body on my bed, my mouth at her neck.

No, you are not going to bite her. Not even if she asks for it.

Suddenly all I can think of is April asking for it, begging for my bite, and I have to adjust myself in my seat.

If she asked for The Bite, and I had fed beforehand, maybe I could… but no. It would take a miracle for her to want me to bite her. First, she freaked in the hotel, then she saw me break that guy's hands. I'm too far gone in her eyes.

But while I don't usually believe in miracles, April is still here. She didn't take the money I offered her. She didn't cut and run. She isn't completely disgusted by the fact that I broke that guy's hands.

In fact, I think she fucking liked it.

Holy shit.

"I mean, yes, I want to get changed," she says.

I tell the driver to take us to her hotel, and we're there in a couple of minutes.

"I'll wait down here for you," I tell her, as I hover in the lobby.

"You can come up," she says awkwardly, fumbling with her tiny purse. "You know, in case you need the invitation. I don't know how it works."

Her pulse is crazy high, and for a moment I wonder what would happen if I went up there with her. Would she let me kiss her? Could we finish off what we started back in Lucky?

I shake my head.

No.

This is the new Finn. The Finn who's taking his power back and not putting himself in insane situations.

"That whole needing an invitation to cross thresholds? It's bullshit. But it's a bad idea."

"You think you'll hurt me."

"I would never hurt you."

"Then why don't you come up?"

"I would never hurt you—*on purpose*," I add.

She gives me a shrug and disappears into the elevator.

I sit on a couch and look at my phone. I turned off notifications when I was at Stratosphere, but I can see now I have a long string of missed calls and texts from Natalie wanting to know why we left the restaurant.

I sigh and hit the call button.

"What is going on, Finn?" she demands. "Why did you leave? You weren't there long enough for people to start talking!"

"We're going somewhere else."

"Where?"

"I don't know yet."

"Finn! Your reputation is already in so much trouble after the stunt you pulled this morning!"

"The stunt I pulled? You were the one who booked that show and let me get slammed!"

"I didn't know he would do that."

"Isn't that your fucking job? To stop shit like that happening?"

"Finn. We need you to use the playbook for this. Don't go anywhere without my approval."

"Approval? You think I need to ask for your approval to leave a fucking restaurant?"

I'm aware that people waiting in the lobby are starting to pay attention to me, but I don't care. I am not going to live my life asking for *approval*. Not from random strangers who are staring at me, and definitely not from Natalie.

"I should let you go," I tell her.

"What do you mean, *let me go*?"

"Fire you."

She laughs. "You can't fire me!"

"I can do what I want."

"First of all, *Finn—*" the way she says my name pisses me off. Like she's a high school principal sitting me down in her office. "—You can't fire me, because I work for the studio, not for you. And even if you could, you wouldn't, because what other publicist would be willing to pay April the rest of the money she was promised?"

Next time I see Natalie, I'm going to glamour her. Tell her to give April the rest of the money, get her to tell me if she's been working against me the whole time and either way, then fire her. Easy. Wait, can the fae even be glamoured?

"You don't own me," I tell her.

She takes a breath, and it sounds like she's gathering herself. "Okay, fine. Look. I don't want to upset you."

"Bit late."

"At least tell me where you'll be tonight so I can make sure we get some photos of you together."

"I'll do you one better," I say.

"Finn, what do you mean?"

"You'll see."

I hang up just in time to see April walking back out of the elevator wearing a white dress covered in blue flowers. Lace trim details accentuate her shoulders and gorgeous cleavage. On her feet are a pair of old, beat-up white Vans. She's carrying a cream-colored cardigan and her hair is down, falling casually and kind of messy around her shoulders. She hardly ever wears her hair down, or at least, she didn't before. She always used to wear it pulled back. But right now, even though she's got that country girl charm going on, she's walking with the confidence of a city girl, and she looks more like herself than I've ever seen her.

She looks gorgeous, and fucking free.

"Now this dress, I *love*," I tell her.

"Me too," she says with a smile. "Vintage, seventies." She does a happy spin, and it makes my heart flutter.

"Okay, so now what do you want to do?" I ask with a huge grin on my face.

"You know what I really want?"

"What? Anything. I'm all yours."

"I want to go on the Ferris wheel."

I take her hand. I don't do it for Natalie or for my fucking reputation. I do it because I want to. Because there's nothing I want more than just to hold this girl's hand.

Well, maybe one thing I want more. Okay, two.

But right now, this is enough. This is more than enough. *This* is a fucking miracle.

When her fingers slide into mine, easy and firm, I know that she's not pretending either. Maybe she doesn't want me to bite her, or fuck her, or kiss her, but right now, April definitely wants to hold my hand.

I'm not an idiot. I know that any kind of relationship with April is totally out of the question. I won't even consider that right now. I can't. I am the new Finn. I'm not a baby vampire. I'm a grown-ass man, and I'm going to fucking act like it.

Sex and The Bite with April is off limits.

But that doesn't mean I'm not going to enjoy the hell out of the little time we have together first.

CHAPTER FIFTY-ONE

pril

I TAKE Finn's hand in mine and pull him through the hotel foyer, out onto the street and down the beach towards the pier and the Ferris wheel. The evening is getting cooler, but there's still a hint of warmth in the air that smells like salt, popcorn, candy floss and happiness.

Sex with Finn would most likely be a religious experience, but holding his *hand* — him holding *my* hand — is making my heart warm in a way I hadn't expected.

This is proving to the world that I am his, that he is mine, that we belong together.

Don't get carried away. This is just pretend, remember?

But nothing about the way Finn's fingers press into mine, the way he grips my hand firmly and certainly, feels pretend.

We don't speak, we just hold each other's hands as we navigate through the crowds towards the end of the pier and the Ferris wheel.

"Finn!" I hear someone call his name and turn around to see who it is. "Finn! Finn!" It's a group of girls around sixteen years old, and they're all jumping up and down and giggling.

Finn turns and smiles at them, but he doesn't drop my hand, and he's telling these girls, these *fans*, that he's off limits.

"I want a selfie!" One of them yells.

"I'll just be a second," he tells me, before sliding his hand out of mine and walking over to them.

He's so fucking charming, and I can see why they are acting crazy, jumping around, gushing, each one of them trying to squeeze in closer to him than the others for the selfie.

"Get your girlfriend to take one!" one of the girls demands.

My heart leaps at the way she just assumes I'm his girlfriend.

"April," he asks. "Would you?"

I hate the idea of these random girls all over *my boyfriend*, but I plaster a smile on my face. "Of course."

He's not your boyfriend!

I take the phone and snap a couple of photos of them all at different angles.

"Thanks," the girl says to me, yanking the phone out of my hands like she thinks I'm about to go through her personal stuff.

"Enjoy your night, ladies," Finn says with a big sparkly grin.

They all squeal as he walks back towards me.

"I love you, Finn!" the girl with the phone screams.

He looks back and gives a wave while I seriously consider going over there and breaking her phone. Smashing it to pieces so she can't have any reminder of him!

I try to shake off my jealousy. Finn is a movie star. This is his life. But that doesn't mean I have to like it.

He tries to grab my hand again, but I step away, moving out of his reach.

"You okay?"

"Yep."

"April." He knows me too well for me to pull the "I'm fine" bullshit.

"That was just — weird."

"It takes some getting used to."

"It was like they felt… *entitled* to you."

"Everyone thinks they're entitled to me," he says. "It's part of the job."

"You don't mind it?"

"Yeah. I do. I fucking hate it sometimes. But then I remember girls like them are the ones who can make or break my career. If they like me, they go see my movies, share about me on socials. That's how I stay popular, stay in work, stay on top." He shrugs. "And besides, it takes a few minutes to take some photos. It's not like I don't have the time, right?"

Something in his expression changes, and then I realize what he means. Things have felt so easy between us tonight, so normal and just like old times, that I haven't been thinking all that much about his fangs or the fact that he's immortal.

He turns to me and places his hands on my shoulders. His hands feel so warm, and I love the way they feel on me. He runs his hands down my arms towards my fingers as goose-bumps spring up all over me. When he takes both my hands in his, it feels like we're one of those science experiments where you put the wires into the potato in the right way and it makes electricity. The energy running between us is… *everything*.

"Wait… are you *jealous*?" he smirks.

"What? No!"

He raises a dark eyebrow. "What did I just say about not lying to me?"

"Fine! Yes! I was jealous! Here I am, finally getting to go on a real date with you, and I have to compete with a bunch of girls ready to throw themselves at you."

Oh god, why did I just call it a real date?!

"April. You have no competition. Not tonight, not ever. The way I felt about you—" He squeezes my hands. "I've never felt that way since. Not about anybody."

Felt. Past tense.

"Will cotton candy fix this?" he asks.

I shrug. "Maybe."

He pulls me towards the cotton candy stand. "Blue or pink?"

"Pink."

He takes the cotton candy with his free hand, and I take a piece and place it on my tongue. I'm instantly reminded of my childhood, days at the county fair with my mom. The familiar lump forms in my throat, and I touch my necklace with my sticky fingers.

Finn is about to put his mouth on the fluffy ball of cotton candy, and I stop him with a squeal. "You can't do it like that! The whole thing will melt!"

"But I don't want to let go of your hand," he says.

My insides warm, and a huge smile spreads over my face.

God, I wish it could always be like this.

I take a piece of cotton candy, put it in his mouth and watch as his face melts into pure joy at the taste of it.

A vampire who loves cotton candy? I throw my head back in a howl of laughter.

"What?"

"Just you. Here. Eating cotton candy. With me."

His green eyes twinkle in the carnival lights. "More, please," he says, opening his mouth.

I stuff a huge chunk into his mouth. He laughs, and when my finger touches his lips, he gently licks it, and I'm pretty sure I feel a tingle in my womb.

I take another bite and grin at him. "Ferris wheel?"

He nods, and we make our way over to the ride, where there's a very long line.

"You're Finn Huxley, right? From that movie?" the ride operator calls out to him.

Finn gives him a wave. "Yeah."

"My daughter loves you! We've watched *Double Agency* a hundred times in our house. Hop in!" He gestures to the booth in front of us.

Finn gives the guy a thumbs up and a grin, and we slide into our seats and then start our ascent.

"Is this okay?" Finn asks, still holding my hand in his even though up here, no one can tell. It's not for show. It's because he wants to.

"Huh?" I ask.

"You're not afraid to be in here alone with me?"

"We're hardly alone."

We slowly rise over the lights of the pier, above the Pacific Ocean, and I let out a gasp. "It's so beautiful!"

"It sure is," he says, without taking his eyes off me.

"Corny much?" I laugh.

"April," he breathes, leaning in close. "I want to kiss you so fucking bad right now."

I turn to face him, heart pounding. "Then why don't you just do it already?"

"Can you hold this?" He passes what's left of the stick of cotton candy to me, and I take it.

He settles into his seat and rubs his hands on his jeans.

"What are you doing?"

"I want this to be perfect. A perfect fucking moment. We've had so many imperfect ones lately."

"All my moments with you in them have been perfect," I tell him.

"Yeah? Even the one where I showed you what I was? Or the one where you watched me break that guy's hands?"

My belly flips at the memory. His fangs, his strength, his violent tendencies.

"Yeah," I tell him as we rise higher over the pier and the ocean, the people down below us suddenly feeling so far away.

"What about the one where you got jealous as hell at those girls who just wanted a selfie?"

"Okay, maybe not that one," I say. "I don't know that I could ever get used to—" I shake my head. I won't ever need to get used to that. Whatever is happening with me and Finn, it's nothing I need to get used to.

Finn brings his hands up to my face and cradles my cheeks. It feels so good, and my eyelids flutter closed. I don't need to see him, I can *feel* him. His firm, large hands on me, his thumb rubbing my cheek. I can feel his green eyes on me.

"Fuck, you're so beautiful," he says, and my heart dances in my chest.

His warm lips find mine, soft and gentle. I let out a sigh as all the tension I've been holding, all my fears, fears of what he is, that he could hurt me, that he could break my heart again, it all vanishes in his cotton candy kiss.

I push myself into him, and my hand that's not holding the cotton candy begins to slide up his thigh.

He lets out a groan.

I grin into his lips, thrilled that I'm having such an effect on him. He could be here with anyone, but he's here with me, and I'm the one whose mouth he's groaning into.

"That's him! And that's the girl from Hollywood Daily!" someone shouts, waking me up from this fever dream.

"Get a pic!"

"It's them!"

"They're kissing!"

Finn pulls back. "Fuck, I'm sorry."

But I'm not sorry. I'm just sorry we're not already back at my hotel room.

"Alright, you two, this is a family venue!" The ride operator berates us with a chuckle. He opens the door to let us out, and Finn takes my hand, pulling me through the crowd that's gathered, all of them gawking at us, taking photos, trying to grab him.

But he's not mad about it, he's laughing, loving every second, and I'm laughing at the absurdity of it all.

We run down the pier, past the lights, the games, the rides, the cotton candy stand, and when we reach the end of the pier, he pulls me down towards the beach.

By the time we get to the sand, I'm laughing so hard I'm almost crying.

I stumble, and he grips my hand tighter. He slows down to a fast walk, grinning at me as we walk underneath the pier.

He pushes me up against one of the stumps, my back arching at the force of his touch, his body pressing into mine completely. My breath hitches, and his eyes turn smoky, wanting.

"Is this still pretend?" I ask.

"April, when are you going to get it? None of this has ever been pretend. Not for me."

And then his lips are on mine again, but this time his kiss is hard, heavy, desperate. It's a secret stolen kiss in a cornfield, a teenage wanting as his tongue desperately finds my own while he pushes his firm, muscular body into me. The firmness in his pants forces a moan out of my lips as he grinds against me.

"Fuck, April. I want you. *Fuck!*"

A breathy giggle escapes from me, but he stops the sound with his mouth, kissing me like he has to get everything he can from it before my dad walks in and catches us.

"There they are! Down on the beach!"

"Finn! April!"

He pulls back with a laugh. "Ah, fuck. They're everywhere!"

"They're not in my hotel room," I say.

His eyes turn dark, considering. We both know it's a really bad idea for an abundance of reasons, but right now, neither of us care. We're too high on cotton candy and Ferris wheel kisses.

And then the thunder cracks, and the rain starts to fall.

Finn wastes no time. He grabs my hand, and we run up the beach getting soaked, laughing like two teenagers, with him pulling me along like if he doesn't get me alone in the next five minutes he'll self-destruct.

And I know exactly how he feels.

CHAPTER FIFTY-TWO

inn

I'M PRACTICALLY QUIVERING as I stand outside April's hotel room, and it has nothing to do with the fact that we're both soaked.

This is the moment of truth. This is when I decide what kind of vampire I want to be — what kind of man I want to be. Will I give in to my desires? Am I going to go inside? Am I going to trust myself to have sex with April Abernathy? Is it going to be as amazing as I'd always dreamed it would be?

No, it's going to be even better.

She leans up against the door to her room, her eyes heavy with lust *for me.*

She knows what I am, and she still wants this.

But does she really know what she wants? Does she know what it would be like with me?

Does she really understand the risks?

I run a hand through my hair. "I've had the night of my fucking life," I tell her.

She bites her lip through a smile. "It's not over yet."

I take a breath, a beat, and a step back, putting a little distance between us for just a second. Just so I can get my lust-filled thoughts in order.

"I want this," she says. "I want you. Tonight."

"April. Gorgeous, April. There is nothing I want more than to join you in your room, to explore every inch of your sexy, beautiful body with my fingers, my lips, my tongue. There is nothing I want more than to be inside you. Completely."

I feel my cock hardening as I step forward, placing my hands on the wall on either side of her.

She gasps and looks up at me with huge, dilated pupils.

I grimace as I prepare for what I'm about to do. I make a fist against the wall. "But I'm trying this new thing called self-control."

"You think denying yourself what you want, what I want, is the right thing to do?"

"In this instance, yes."

She blinks up at me. "Finn. I've spent my whole life denying myself, and for what? So my father will be proud of me? So that the town will see me as good little Christian girl April who's always there to help when they need it?"

I run the back of two fingers down her soft, pale face, moving some of that wild hair out of the way so I can see her fucking gorgeous features more clearly.

She takes a breath and continues, "But when you deny yourself by saying no to me, you're also denying *me* of what I want."

Fuck.

"I never want to deny you anything. But I am dangerous,

April. I need to keep you safe, and that means that I can't put myself in a position that will—"

Her mouth is on mine, and it's clear we're both fucking ravenous for each other. This hallway may be a public place, but there's no one around, and so I don't stop myself from letting my hand move down over her cleavage, gently squeezing her breast over the cotton of her dress and the blue lace I can now see through her drenched dress. I feel her nipple harden through the material, and it sends a powerful message to my cock as it twitches against her.

I pull her strap down but stop myself before she's naked in the hallway. Instead, I play with the bud of her nipple through her wet dress, getting her nipple and my cock harder with each circle I make, each tweak. I move my mouth down and bite her nipple. She lets out a tiny scream. Not because she's scared of me, but because she's so fucking turned on.

While I make her dress even wetter with my tongue, I'm dying to know what's happening below. My hand moves down to her hip and then her thigh, and then I'm shoving my hand up under her dress.

So much for self-control, asshole.

"Matching panties?" I ask her as I lightly touch the damp scrap of lace between her legs.

"Yes. I thought you'd like them."

Oh god, she's wearing matching lace underwear for me.

I groan as my fingers reach the edge of her panties, ready to shove them to the side so I can get my fingers inside of her. "Fucking hell, April. What are you doing to me?" I groan.

The elevator dings, and we jump apart.

An older couple walks past us. The woman tuts, but the man takes one look at April's dress — one strap down, rumbled skirt, and gives me a smile.

I want to murder him for looking at her like that.

Self-control, Finn.

"We can't stop now," April says, biting her lip. "You can't just leave me like this."

I turn in a circle, very aware that I'm not even attempting to hide my erection at this point.

"Please, Finn," she practically begs.

I grab her shoulders. "You don't know what you're asking. I'm—"

"Dangerous. Yeah. I got that memo enough times already."

I pray to God I don't regret the reckless decision I'm about to make. The decision self-control Finn would be really mad about. "Fine," I grunt. "I'll come in, but on conditions."

"What conditions?"

"I'll come in, but no sex."

She laughs. "What?! Why?"

"We can fool around like we did in Lucky, but that's it."

"Finn!"

I lean into her, one hand splayed on the door behind her, the other running roughly over her neck and shoulders. "I'll rub your clit all fucking night until you come a hundred times over. I'll fuck you with my fingers and my tongue until you can't see straight. I know I can control myself doing that. I don't know what would happen if I fucked you. I could lose total control."

She looks at me like she can't decide if this is the best or worst deal she's ever heard.

"I'll pleasure you with every inch of my soul, but I can't give myself to you like that. Not yet. Not until I know—"

"How are you going to know if you never try?"

"April," I say through gritted teeth. "It's this or nothing."

Holy fuck, I hope she doesn't choose nothing!

"Okay."

I smack the door with my fist. "Get your door open. *Now.*"

She rummages in her purse. "I can't find the key!"

"What do you mean you can't find the key?"

"It's not here!"

"Jesus, April! What did you do with it?"

"Oh, shit!" She pulls out her phone and her lipstick and hands them to me while she checks the bottom of her purse. "Oh, it's okay! Here it is."

"April! Fuck!"

She lets out a laugh. "Sorry!"

A notification comes up on her phone while I'm still holding it.

CLIVE: Been thinking about you. Hope it's going okay down there.

MY DICK GOES soft at the sight of it. I guess I didn't glamour the asshole hard enough.

"You're talking to Clive?" I demand, like I have any stake on her.

"What? No!"

"Why is he messaging you?"

"Why are you acting like a jealous boyfriend?"

She opens the door to her room, and I follow her in, closing the door behind us.

"I just want to know. If you still have a thing for him, I'll leave you alone."

"Finn. I don't have a thing for him! We broke up ages ago. He just… doesn't always remember that."

I can feel the anger pulsing through me, and I'm five seconds away from getting in my car, driving to Lucky and punching him in the dick.

"Did you love him?" I demand, heat coursing through me. "Are you going back to him after all this is over?"

"What? No!" She grabs the phone out of my hands. "This message is just friendly. That's all. And if you want evidence that there's nothing between us, scroll up."

I hate being this guy, but I can't stop. I scroll up and look at the messages. There's only a handful from the last year. A couple where he's tried to booty call her, and she's said no each time.

That's it. That's all it is.

"And no, I don't love him. I never loved him," she tells me.

"You went out for years, but you didn't love him?"

She looks up at me, a tired expression on her face. "I wanted to love him. I tried to love him. There were moments I thought maybe it was love, but I realized in the end that it wasn't."

"What made you realize?"

"You want the truth?"

"Yeah. Always."

"There were so many reasons, but the one that kept me up at night, when I was lying in bed next to him thinking about our future together, was that I could never imagine having his kids."

"What?"

"I could never imagine giving birth to his children. I just… couldn't see it. And when I thought about myself pregnant with his kids, it made me feel… *wrong*."

"April. I can't have children."

She lets out a sigh and shakes her head. "Yeah, but Finn. I can *imagine* having your children. Even if I can't."

Oh, fuck, is she going to cry?

"You don't need to be jealous of him," she says, taking her phone back and throwing it on the couch.

"Yeah, well, I am fucking jealous," I say, stepping towards

her now and taking a tendril of her hair in my fingers. "He got all those years with you. I only got five minutes."

"Well, you have me now, and all you want to do is talk about Clive."

"Fuck Clive."

"I don't want to fuck Clive." She looks up at me and blinks those huge, dark blue eyes. "I want to fuck you."

"I told you, that's not happening. Not tonight." I pull her straps down until her dress is just covering her nipples. She gasps, and my cock hardens again, all thoughts of Clive dissolving from my mind. He's hundreds of miles away, and I'm here, pulling April's straps down.

"What is happening?" she asks.

"This." I pull her straps down further now, her breasts tumble free over her dress, and she looks like a goddamn goddess. I want to immortalize her like this. Make a statue, put it on display for future generations of men to admire, because she was the most beautiful woman who ever lived.

I roll one of her nipples between my fingers, and she sighs. Her body relaxes into my touch, and her nipple hardens in my grip, a peak of nerve endings firing, wanting more. More of *me*.

Her heart is hammering. I can hear every beat, every rush of blood in her veins. I can tell she's not scared. She's excited.

My fingers move to her back and the top of the zip of her dress. I pause for a second, knowing that even if we don't have sex tonight, there is still a chance I could hurt her.

You won't hurt her. You love her.

I slide the zip down and then slide the dress over her freckled shoulders, letting it tumble to the floor until she's standing before me in nothing but a drenched, light blue lace bra shoved down under her tits and matching lace panties.

"Fuck, April," I say, cupping my hands over her bare shoulders, just inches from her naked breasts.

She gives me a sexy grin, and I have a very bad feeling that I'm not going to be able to control myself at all. That I'm going to give in. That I'm going to give her what she needs and what I so desperately want.

"Turn around, baby," I say.

She turns and I admire her ass in her barely there panties. I unhook her bra, letting it fall to the floor.

She turns and gives me a smile and then she starts walking away from me.

"Where are you going?" I ask.

"To bed. Are you coming?"

As I watch her perfect, almost naked body sway in the most delicious way towards the bedroom, there is only one answer.

"Yes, baby. I'm coming."

CHAPTER FIFTY-THREE

pril

Are you sure this is a good idea, April?

Good girl April suddenly shows up in my head and for a second, I wonder if she's right. If I should stop this before it goes any further.

But right now, all I want is Finn. His hands on my body, his lips on mine, his body pressed against me.

Sex or not, I don't care. Right now, I just want him in whatever way I can have him.

I have loved him nearly my whole life and I don't care what he is now. Because underneath the fangs and the super strength and speed, underneath it all, he's still the same Finn I fell in love with all those years ago. The Finn I never stopped loving, even when he was living his dreams and I was desperately trying to convince myself I could love someone else.

But I couldn't.

And I know now that I never will. I'll never love anyone the way I loved Finn.

The way I still love him.

I walk towards the crisp, freshly made bed in the center of the room. My pulse skyrockets as I turn around and see him smoldering in the doorway, at the threshold between everything that's happened before now, and what could happen next.

Hesitation flickers in his eyes. He's not sure this is a good idea either.

"What if I just watch?" he asks. "From here."

"Watch what?"

His eyes blaze with lust as they take in my almost naked body. "Watch you touch yourself."

Okay, why does that suddenly feel way more intimate than him just coming over here and touching me?

"What will you do?" I ask him.

"I'll touch myself too, but here. I won't go past this point."

"I thought you said that vampires didn't need permission to enter?"

His jaw clenches. "We usually don't. But tonight, I won't go past here. If I give myself this boundary, it will keep you safe. We can both get what we want."

"Finn, what I want is your cock inside me."

If his jaw was clenched before, now it's positively clamped.

"April, baby. I want that too. More than you'll ever fucking know. But let me do it like this tonight. So I can prove to myself I'm safe to be around you. So I can prove it to you."

"You don't have to prove it to me. I already know."

"April," he growls. "Please."

I step towards him, pushing my bare breasts against his shirt as my lips find his like we've done this a hundred times before. And we have, but not like this. His kiss quickly turns hot and fast, his tongue thrusting into my mouth, claiming me, and I know he wants me with every inch of his being. I can feel that this is hell for him, that he's torturing himself with this idea that we can't have sex.

But I would do anything for this man, and if he needs it like this, then I will give him what he needs.

His hands slide over my shoulders and then he palms my breasts, taking their weight in his hands.

"Holy fuck, April," he whispers. "You are the most beautiful woman in the world. Do you know that?"

"We said no lies, remember?"

He shakes his head. "It's not a lie. To me, you are the most beautiful thing in this world. And one day, I will prove it to you by making love to you in the most perfect way I know how."

"But not tonight," I say.

"Not tonight. But we can do other stuff." His smoldering gaze rests longingly on my breasts as he continues to cup and knead them in a way that makes me think I could orgasm from this alone. His lips find my nipple, and he flicks it with his tongue before giving it a gentle bite.

My whole body shudders. "Finn!" I gasp.

"Go lie on the bed. Now," he demands.

I do as he says, pulling off the covers and lying down on the sheet, my body angled so that he can see me from the side. I roll over, leaning up on my hand and watch as he rips off his shirt, his chest and shoulders broad and rippling in the most delicious way as he throws the shirt to the floor. Then he's working on his belt and I'm getting even wetter, wishing he was taking off his belt because he's about to fuck me.

His pants drop to the ground revealing a pair of the black boxer briefs I'm so very familiar with. His cock strains against his briefs and I realize now, that in all our time together, I've never seen his cock.

"Take off your panties," he commands.

"You first," I tell him.

"April." He gives me that smoldering look that suggests he might burst into flames at any second. "Let me be in charge here." He takes a deep breath. "I *need* to know I'm in charge."

"Okay, you're in charge," I tell him, a wave of excitement running through my body at the idea that *he's in charge.*

"Now, take off your fucking panties."

Oh my god.

I move onto my back, slide my fingers into the lace and pull them down over my legs, throwing them across the room onto the floor in front of him.

"Fuck!" he growls, looking down. He grabs them, brings them to his face and inhales. "Sweet fucking April," he moans as he drops them to the floor, his hands gripping the sides of the door frame like they're the only thing stopping him from fucking me right now.

"Touch your tits," he says. "How you like it. Show me. Teach me."

"I don't have to teach you anything," I tell him, running my hands over my breasts, enjoying knowing I'm doing exactly what he wants and needs.

I close my eyes for a moment, enjoying myself and this feeling of him watching me. When I open my eyes, his briefs are on the ground and his cock is in his hand, throbbing and glistening, and *holy fuck* the thing is huge!

The way he grips it with such power, such *desperate need* and knowing it's all for me, makes me only want to fuck him even more.

Okay, now I know why he wants to watch me, watching is sexy as fuck.

"Touch your pussy," he tells me. "Think about me when you do it."

"It's a bit hard not to think about you," I tell him with a giggle.

"You know what I mean," he grunts as he continues to pump the huge cock in his hand. "Think about me touching you. Think about my fingers inside you. Think about my cock inside you."

Oh my god.

"Finn," I moan, as I start making firm circles over my clit. "I always think of you when I do this."

"Fucking hell, April," he says. "I don't know if I can control myself—"

I look over at him and bite my lip. "You can. I know you can. You can control yourself like this with me. Because if you can prove it to yourself tonight, like this, you know you can trust yourself to fuck me. And Finn—" I gasp as I hit my clit in just the right spot "—I really need you to trust yourself to fuck me."

He lets out a moan as he grasps himself tighter. "Think of me fucking you right now. My cock sliding in and out, as hard and fast as you want it. As hard and fast as you can fucking take it."

I swap from circles to rubbing side to side, faster and harder. My whole pussy is pulsating, juices flowing. I'm so fucking wet and it seems like a damn shame to waste it.

"Open your legs wider," he demands. "Show me."

I shift so that my legs are open to him, my pussy on full display now.

"Oh, fuck. Oh, holy shit! April, you're so fucking beautiful. So sexy. You're incredible!"

His words spur me on, and I run my fingers over my wetness and slide two inside myself, wishing it was his fingers, no, wishing it was his enormous cock entering me.

"I need you to come," he gasps. "I need to see it."

I finally look away from his glistening cock and the way he's looking at me with those warm green but oh so fucking dark eyes, the way he jerks himself hard and fast, the wet tip that I suddenly want so fucking badly in my mouth.

That thought tips me over and I hit my peak, coming hard, coming *for him*. My legs jerk and my pussy pulsates, and I think about him inside me, like I always do when I make myself come.

I let out a moan and call his name as my hips jerk into the air, searching for his cock, his hands, any part of him to slam into me, but he's not there.

I want more, so much fucking more!

"Yeah, baby, ride that wave," he says. "Watching you come is so fucking amazing!"

His words are like food that feeds my orgasm. It hits another level, and I moan out, arching my back, feeling the sweet, sweet release while he watches me.

He lets out a loud moan, and I know he's getting close.

Fuck this. Fuck the rules!

I'm off the bed before I can think twice, before clarity finds me, and I'm on my knees in front of him.

"April, what are you—"

I grab his cock and take it in my mouth.

"Oh, fucking Jesus! Fucking hell! April! Fuck—!"

I couldn't help myself, I just needed him *inside* me, and his beautiful, hard, glistening cock tastes so fucking good. I take him as deep as I can and then I find a rhythm, sucking his cock, fucking him with my mouth. He hardens in my mouth, quivering, and his body starts shaking.

One of his hands grips the door frame, the other finds its way to the back of my head, and he grips my hair with a groan as he thrusts into my mouth.

"Baby, I'm going to come in your mouth. Holy fuck!"

I keep going, sucking him the way his hand on my head tells me he wants it. I need him to come inside me. *Now.*

He grips my hair, and I feel the tension rise, and suddenly he's powering inside me, his seed spilling in my mouth, his hand gripping my hair like he's never going to let me go.

I hear a loud sudden *crack* like something is breaking, but I just ignore it, letting him ride his own wave into my mouth until he's done.

A piece of wood from the door frame drops to the floor, and he releases his grip on my head, steading himself with both hands on the now broken door frame.

I wipe my mouth on the back of my arm and look down at the piece of wood. A joyful laugh bursts from my mouth. "You broke the door frame," I say, looking up at him.

He looks down at me, his eyes full of gratitude. He pushes a piece of very sticky hair behind my ear and gives me a relaxed smile. I haven't seen him like this since before. Since we were kids. Well, except for the fangs that are protruding from his mouth. They don't scare me now though, they somehow only make me love him even more.

"That was like nothing I've ever fucking experienced," he sighs, his fangs retracting back into his mouth.

"Me neither."

I blink up at him and grin. "You didn't lose control."

"April, I broke the fucking doorframe."

"But you didn't break me."

He runs his fingers down over my cheek, wiping away some of his residue. "You didn't stick to the rules. You were supposed to stay in the bedroom."

I turn my head and kiss his hand. "I did stay in the bedroom."

"What you did was really dangerous."

"I think I just proved to us both that it wasn't. Maybe

you're not ready to fuck me yet, but at least now we know that I'll survive a blow job."

His head tips back and a low, dirty laugh rattles against what's left of the doorframe.

"Good to know." He smiles down at me. "Now let's get you cleaned up." He wipes a little more of him off my mouth. "And are you hungry?"

"I'm always hungry."

CHAPTER FIFTY-FOUR

inn

I'M STILL RECOVERING from the best fucking blow job of my life when room service arrives. April is in the shower and so I set everything up on the dining table in the main room of the suite. I'm still reeling and trying to comprehend what just happened. What April just did, the way she took me in her mouth, her desperate need to have me inside her.

Fucking hell.

Just the thought of it makes me want to destroy another door frame.

We never did that kind of stuff in high school. Sure, we fooled around a little. We made out and touched each other over our clothes. She let me put my hand up her shirt but over her bra, but that was as far as we ever went. Back then she was still thinking about waiting for marriage. I remember one night in the cornfield where I told her I'd marry her. She thought I was just saying it so we could have sex, but I wasn't.

I already knew I wanted her to be my forever before I even knew what it was like to have her lips around my cock.

Now I have no idea how I'll ever let her go again.

You're a fucking monster. You have no right to her.

"Hey." April appears in a fuzzy white robe which I assume is the *only* thing she's wearing. I don't know if I can cope with that, because all I can think of is grabbing the belt, untying it and opening it up to reveal her gorgeous naked body. I'd carry her back into the bedroom, throw her down on the bed, and this time I wouldn't hide in the door frame.

I nearly tell her to put some real clothes on, but what does it matter? Whatever she wears, I'm fucked.

"What should we do with this?" She holds up the piece of wood I broke off.

"I think I'm going to keep it as a souvenir," I say, placing the cutlery around the plates on the table.

"And how do we explain it to housekeeping?"

"I'll glamour them in the hallway. Tell them the room was already like that."

She sits, and I take a seat opposite. "Glamouring must come in handy."

"Yeah. Kind of." A memory of biting Clive and glamouring him afterwards comes to mind. But no good will come from telling her about that, so I don't.

She looks at the table of silver dish covers, a bottle of champagne and two full glasses. I'm second guessing the champagne now. Was that just a dick rich guy move?

"Ooh, champagne!" she says, taking a glass. "Fancy." She holds up her glass, and I clink it and drink. I'm surprised to find that my heightened senses make the bubbles taste so... *fun?*

"What did you order?" she asks, eagerly looking over the table.

"Some of your favorites." I lift the silver covers to reveal burgers, fries, waffles and ice-cream.

She leans over to grab some fries and her robe gapes open, giving me a perfect view of one of her breasts. My cock is twitching again already. Jesus, I will never get enough of this woman.

I had wondered if I just jerked off ten times before I saw her if I could make love to her without doing something stupid, but now that I'm already hard for round two, I know that won't help at all. I could fuck her twenty times in a row and still want more.

She puts a bunch of fries in her mouth and all I can think of is her mouth on me.

I grab some food and put it on my own plate, just to focus my attention elsewhere.

"You're going to eat?"

"Well, I'm not going to let you eat alone."

A silence hangs in the air between us as we eat. It's not uncomfortable, but I can feel there are words hanging in the air that we're not saying.

"Are you staying over?" she asks, eventually.

"Are you asking me to?"

"Do you think you can control yourself if we just sleep next to each other?"

"Depends. Will you be sleeping naked?"

She grins. "If you want?"

I shoot a smile back at her. "I don't really sleep now, but I can stay with you if you want me to."

"Only if you want."

"I do want."

"Okay. Good."

"I need to head off early tomorrow though. I'm just telling

you that now, so you don't think I've run off like this is some booty call. Just in case I'm gone before you wake up."

Her face falls. "Was this a booty call?"

"Fuck no. Are you kidding?"

"What was this?" she asks.

I run a hand through my hair.

Fuck, I don't know.

"Does it need a label?" I ask, feeling like a prize fucking jerk as soon as the words leave my mouth. It's not what I wanted to say at all. But it doesn't seem like the right time for a confession of undying love from the undead.

"What's on tomorrow?" she asks, swiftly changing the subject.

"An interview with Stacey and Bob."

"Oh, I love their show. What time will you be on?"

"Seven forty-five."

"I'll be listening."

"They're probably going to ask about you."

"I guessed as much."

"Is it okay if I talk about you? Talk about us?"

"Well, that was kind of the whole point of all this, right? To convince the whole world that we're together?"

"Yeah, it was. When we were just faking it. Or pretending to fake it."

She takes another bite of her burger.

"You know I'm not faking it now, right?" I tell her. "There was nothing fake about what we just did. There was nothing fake about anything from tonight. None of this has been fake for me. From the moment that Natalie suggested we pretend to date, I wanted it to be real."

She puts her burger down and takes another sip of champagne. "Okay, but we're not really dating. You said you didn't want to put a label on it. So technically we're still fake dating."

I lean back in my chair and look at the ceiling. "Baby, I don't know what to tell you. We can't really date, can we? Not when I am what I am."

"Why not?"

Those two words hang in the air.

Why not?

"Because of what I am."

"It makes no difference to me."

"It might when you realize a big part of a relationship with a vampire is that they will want to bite you all the fucking time."

"I want you to bite me."

Fuuuuuck.

"Not to mention I'm fucking immortal. I'm never going to die."

"Unless you get staked," she says.

I don't know why, but a laugh rips through me.

"Well, it's true! I don't know why you guys are always acting like immortality means you can never die. How old is the oldest vampire alive?"

"About a thousand years old," I say. "Allegedly."

"Ha, see? That's not even that old."

"It's a lot older than you'll ever be."

"You know what?" she says, piling a plate with waffles. "We could just date. We don't have to plan out the next one thousand years. We could just be together now."

"You make it sound so simple."

"Maybe it is."

I slather some ice cream in caramel sauce while I consider her words.

"Yeah. Okay."

Her eyebrows shoot up into her damp hair. "Okay?"

"Yeah. Let's date. For real. Be my real girlfriend."

She lets out a laugh. "Okay."

Okay.

And just like that I'm officially, *really* dating April Abernathy.

"Is there anything you don't want me to tell them on the radio tomorrow?" I ask.

"Like what?"

"I don't know. I mean, I'm obviously not going to share any of your secrets or personal stuff. I definitely won't tell them about the door frame."

She laughs, and then her face relaxes into a soft smile. "I trust you to tell them whatever you think is appropriate. I know people are going to know about us. I know what I signed up for."

"Yeah, but now it's real."

"It was always real." She takes another sip of champagne. "I wanted you the whole time too. You know I did."

"You were so scared of me when you first found out," I say. "You didn't have those feelings for me then."

"I was scared because I didn't understand. You were… different."

"I am different."

"How I reacted must have been awful for you. It must have been really hurtful thinking I was so scared of you. I'm sorry."

"I'm the one who's sorry."

"It was just kind of a shock. And yeah, if I'm honest, I was scared of what you were. But even when I was scared, I never stopped—"

Loving me? Is that what she was going to say?

"I don't know what we do now," I tell her.

"Finish our dinner? Finish this bottle of champagne? Watch a movie and go to sleep?"

I smile at the normalcy of it. "But then what?

"Then you do your interview in the morning, and isn't it the premiere of *Jungle Story* tomorrow night too?"

"Oh, shit. I almost forgot."

"So then we go to that. On a date. And maybe, if you're feeling confident about it, we could come back here and try—"

"April, we're going to need to take this slow."

"Well, I'm more than happy to repeat tonight's events anytime." She gives me a sweet, but oh so dangerous look.

"How do you even exist?" I ask her.

She grins at me, and it lights up the space in my heart where there's been so much fucking darkness.

"But then what?" I ask.

"Then we just figure it out as we go."

Her words take a load off. We don't have to have it all figured out. We don't have to have a plan. We don't need to have the next one thousand years all figured out.

We can just take one day at a time.

It's just that I have a lot more days than she does and I want to spend them all with her.

CHAPTER FIFTY-FIVE

pril

FINN'S BLOOD curdling scream wakes me.

My heart pounds as I realize something is very wrong.

"Finn!" I reach across the bed for him, and he jolts awake.

He was screaming in his sleep.

I turn on the lamp next to me and sit up.

Finn sits upright, looking like he's seen a ghost. No, something much worse than a ghost.

"Finn." I place my hand lightly on his shoulder. "What is it?"

He looks at me and blinks. It takes him a second to realize where he is.

"You're safe. You're with me. In the hotel," I reassure him.

His body relaxes slightly, and he runs his hands down over his face.

"What happened?"

"A dream," he says. "That's all."

"Vampires dream?"

"Yeah. It's part of why I try not to sleep too much. When I sleep, I dream, and when I do—" He shakes his head and places a hand on mine. "I didn't mean to sleep. I didn't mean to upset you. It's nothing. Go back to sleep, baby."

"Finn. Please. Tell me what it was."

"I can't."

"If you want me to feel safe with you, you need to tell me what's going on."

He gives me a nod and then stares at the wall. "It's a recurring nightmare where I'm reliving everything that happened… from before I was turned."

"What happened to you?"

"It's too dark. Too much. I don't want you to carry the burden, the weight of it."

"If I can help you carry it, I will. I want to. Isn't that what being with someone is all about?"

He pulls his knees up into his chest, gripping his arms around his legs. "I'm not just a monster. I'm a traumatized monster." He looks over at me, so much pain and suffering in his gorgeous green eyes. "Why would you want to be with someone like me?"

"Because I just do. And if I can help you carry this, I want to do that for you."

He takes a breath, and a pause, and then he speaks. "I was hanging out at this vampire club in West Hollywood. Vincent's. I didn't know it was a vampire club at the time. It was just a cool place where lots of movie types hung out. It was a good place to network. I had a bit too much to drink. I was trying to let off a little steam, and I was wasted. I don't even know how it happened. The next thing I knew I was in the back of an SUV, tied up and gagged."

I let out a gasp. "Who did that to you? And *why*?"

"Vampires," he says. "They took me to a basement in a ranch house not far from Lucky."

"Lucky? Why would vampires be in Lucky?"

"I told them about it."

"What?"

He runs a hand over the back of his neck. "I'd been hanging out at that club for a while. I don't know why I was so drawn to it. Maybe it was the dark gothic vibe of the place, it felt comfortable somehow. I met this guy at the bar one night. His name was Aiden. We got to talking about our shitty lives back in our hometowns and how we'd both moved out to LA in search of more. We kind of bonded. I told him about Lucky. I told him—" he takes a breath, "—that if he ever wanted to hide a body, Lucky would be the best place for it because it's so off the map. I had no idea that he was going to take me so fucking literally. Or that one of the bodies would be mine."

"Oh, Finn."

"I was in that basement for days. Aiden bit me first. He fed off me. He wasn't the only one. There were more of them. It's all a blur. At first The Bite felt good. I liked it. Fuck, at one point I even wanted it. I desperately waited for one of them to come and do it to me. But after each come down, I started to feel worse than I had before. They didn't feed us, we were getting so weak."

I slide my fingers into his and squeeze.

"I was fucking terrified. I knew one day they would take so much blood that they'd kill me. I knew I was dying. I knew because… I watched it happen to some of the others who were down there with me."

"You watched them die?"

He nods. "I knew my time was coming. No one knew where I was. No one was coming to save me. I was trapped. Even if by some miracle the door was left open, I was too weak to even get up the stairs, let alone run through the desert to escape."

"How did you get out of there?"

"Maverick. He found me about to die, and he turned me."

"He saved your life."

"No. He took my life." There is so much pain in his eyes, and I just wish I could take it away. "He took my human life, and he gave me this one."

"But you're still here. You're still alive."

"I'm not alive," he says, pulling out of my grip and running his hands through his hair. "I'm undead, April." He lets out a long breath. "What I am — it's dark. Fucked up. I'm one of them now. One of those monsters who did that to me. That's what I'm capable of. I'm a monster who feeds off blood. I'm undead, unholy, I'm evil."

"Never say that again," I tell him, wrapping my arms around him. "You might be undead Finn, but you are definitely not evil. You don't have an evil bone in your body."

"Yes. I do." He shakes his head. "I bit Clive."

"What?"

"I bit him. At the drive-in. He was pissing me off, and I was thirsty, and I didn't want to bite you, so I bit him and then glamoured him into leaving you the hell alone."

Finn has been baring his soul to me, sharing his darkest, deepest memories with me, but the idea of him biting Clive because he was *jealous* just makes me laugh.

He looks up at me through his dark lashes. "You find this amusing?"

"Just the part where you bit Clive."

"You don't mind that I did it? You don't hate me for it? You don't think I'm—"

I shake my head. "No. You didn't kill him. And you did it to keep me safe."

"I'm so fucked up from all this," he says.

"Is there someone you can talk to?" I ask, running my hands down his arms until his hands are in mine.

"I'm supposed to talk to Maverick, but he's pissed at me, and also, he's kind of a dick."

"You must know some other vampires. What about Max?"

"Max?"

"Yeah, Poppy's boyfriend. She told me that when they met, he was trying to regain his humanity. He wasn't even drinking human blood."

"Oh god, I don't know that I could live off that synthetic stuff forever."

I shrug. "Maybe you could. You might not be human anymore, but you still have your humanity."

He grips my hands, squeezing them like he's never going to let me go. "How are you okay with all of this?" he asks.

After everything that's happened between us, everything he's just shared, saying the words suddenly feels so easy.

"Because I love you."

CHAPTER FIFTY-SIX

inn

APRIL DROPS THE L-BOMB, and I don't know what to say.

Just say it back!

But I can't. Something is gripping my throat, stopping me from saying those three words.

It's just three words.

But if I said them, I would mean each and every one of them, but me and April *in love?*

April *in love* with a vampire?

April still wanting to be with me after all of this?

It's too much to hope for. It's a miracle I can't conceive of.

Saying it back would make it too real and hurt too fucking much when we inevitably get ripped apart by something I do, when my thirst rages so hard I drink from a not so willing victim, when I make my first inevitable kill.

I can't hope for this.

Tomorrow she'll come out of this orgasm-induced haze

and realize that it's not love she feels for me. It's friendship and lust at best.

I pull her in close to me. Her face in my chest, her beautiful chestnut hair that still smells like apple and cinnamon, cotton candy and... *home*, resting under my chin. I drop a kiss on her head but like a coward, I don't say the words. I just hold her like that for what feels like hours but is still nowhere near long enough.

Her body eventually relaxes into me as she gets sleepy in my arms. I lay her down, watching her sleep for far too long.

April is a miracle. She is so good. She is so pure. She is such a beautiful human.

She's like an angel. So full of light. Everything about her is holy.

But I am a devil. I am the darkness. I am unholy.

And yet there is something about her — the way she sees something in me that's more than what I've become. She still sees good in me, and that gives me hope. Maybe I still have some goodness in me after all.

Maybe if I had her, if she was really mine, then maybe I could be good. I could be more.

Her breathing deepens, and she lets out a tiny, gorgeous little snore.

After what feels like just a few minutes, the first stirrings of dawn light break through the curtains. I don't want to leave her. I want to stay here and watch her sleep. I want to rest next to her and just pretend we're the young naïve couple we used to be. Just a couple of teenagers running away to LA together so that we can chase our dreams.

But it's nearly light, and I have a big day ahead. My interview this morning, the premiere tonight, and between the two, I'm going to pop in on Max Montrose to talk about my issues.

I kiss April gently on the cheek. She smiles and makes a little moaning sound.

God, I could get used to that smile. I could get used to that sound.

And I could definitely get used to breaking more door frames with her.

CHAPTER FIFTY-SEVEN

pril

FINN IS GONE when I wake up, just like he said he would be. And while I'm disappointed that his sexy, ripped body isn't beside me, I can't stop smiling as I look over at the wrecked door frame and remember our incredible night together — the cotton candy, the Ferris wheel, the heated kiss under the pier, our messy make-out session outside my door... and then everything that happened when we went inside. Even being able to be there for him after he had that nightmare felt like a blessing in a way. What he went through was so traumatic, but I'm so glad that he was here—that he didn't have to wake from that alone, and that he felt he could share it with me.

I grab one of the t-shirts that I didn't give back to Finn and put it on, wrapping my arms around myself like he's giving me a hug.

I practically skip around the hotel suite, humming to

myself as I pile up dishes from last night. It's only when I'm staring at the coffee machine, watching it drip the coffee through, that I remember he's going to be on the radio any second. I turn on the TV and quickly flip through to the radio stations.

"This morning on the show we have Finn Huxley, star of *Double Agency* and a new movie, *Jungle Story* that's premiering tonight," says Bob, one of the hosts of the show. "But none of that is what we want to talk to Finn about, is it Stacey?"

"That's right Bob," Stacey says. "What we *really* want to know, Finn, is who is this mystery woman that you were spotted with down in Santa Monica last night?"

"Uh, well," Finn begins.

"There are pictures of the two of you plastered all over social media right now," Bob says. "Stacey, have you seen the photos?"

"I have, and *wow* you two really went for it on the Ferris Wheel!"

Finn laughs nervously. I bite my lip, pour my coffee and then head straight to social media to find these photos.

"It was just a kiss," Finn says.

"A kiss on the Ferris wheel!" Stacey swoons. "That's so romantic! And then you were seen making out under the pier!"

"I guess we thought no one could see us down there," Finn says. "It certainly wasn't our intention to put on a show."

"But you must be glad you did, because you can't buy publicity like this, or can you?" laughs Bob. "Come on bud, give us the exclusive. Who is this woman? Where did you meet? How long has this been going on for? And is it *love*?"

"Oh, uh, okay. Her name is April. We met in high school—"

"High school sweethearts!" Stacey squeals. "This is just getting better!"

"She lived across the road from me. We didn't really date in school," he says. "But I always had a thing for her."

"Oh yeah, we saw the way you got bagged on Dirk's show," says Stacey. "That was rough. But you're with friends here. Tell us the truth, is she just after you for the money?"

I can almost hear him swallow. "I already spent most of the money from my first few movies on hot cars and a beach house I could hardly afford, so if she is just with me for the money, she's going to have a bit of a surprise."

Bob and Stacey both howl with laughter.

"Looking at those photos of you from last night, you both look crazy about each other," Stacey says.

"Yeah, we are."

"Will she be your date for the premiere of your new movie tonight?" Bob asks.

"She will. We're really proud of this movie," Finn says, desperately trying to get a word in about the actual film.

"What does April do for a job?" Bob asks. "Is she in the entertainment business also?"

"Yeah," Finn says. My finger pauses from where I'm still trying to figure out how to find the photos of us on my phone. "She's a writer."

Wait, what?

"What does she write?" Stacey asks.

"She writes romance."

What? How does Finn know this?!

"Romantasy?" Stacey asks. "Billionaire romance? Mafia?"

"Is she writing a rom com screenplay for you?" Bob asks.

Oh god, is he going to out me on national radio? Is he going to tell everyone I'm Evie Everhart? I clutch my phone and wait.

If he outs me, everyone in the whole world — including

my father — will know that I write steamy romance on Scripty.

"Oh, I don't know if I can say. But she writes romance on a popular writing app," Finn says.

"Okay, you have to give me her details after the interview." Stacey gushes.

"Sure. If she's okay with it."

"I promise I won't tell anyone!" Stacey says.

"She'll tell everyone, she can't keep her mouth shut," Bob laughs.

"Sorry, Finn," Stacey says. "This interview was supposed to be about you and the movie, I just got really excited when you said romance!"

"Stacey, this interview was never going to be about the movie," Bob says. "All anyone wants to know right now is who is the mysterious April and when is the wedding?"

Finn laughs. "Dating someone when you're in the spotlight is never easy, so we're taking things slow."

"There was nothing slow about the way you kissed her under that pier!" Stacey giggles.

Bob laughs. "Stacey, if you want me to kiss you under a pier like that, you just ask."

"Bob!" she giggles some more.

"After the show we'll go down there and do our own photo shoot."

"Oh, Bob! Stop! You're ridiculous."

"I'm not joking. Finn's hot moves last night have given me the courage to finally ask you out."

Stacey's giggle just keeps getting even more high pitched.

"Finn," Bob asks, "what's your secret with the ladies? Because it's not just April you've been busy wooing, you've been linked with a whole bunch of women who can't seem to resist your charms, including Summer Sanders and Juliette Cortez. How do you do it?"

"Okay, first of all, the fact that people are outraged over me and Summer Sanders feels so... outdated. There's nothing wrong with what she does for a living."

"Totally agree," says Stacey. "People should stop making it an issue."

"Right, Stacey," Bob agrees.

"But honestly, I didn't have any idea that Summer Sanders was an adult film star until everyone was talking about it the next day."

"Seriously?" laughs Stacey.

"I swear to god. I had no idea," Finn says. "She noticed my Diamondbacks baseball cap at the club and asked me how I could wear that thing in LA. We just talked sports."

"That's not how I'd spend my time with Summer Sanders, but okay," Bob says.

"I think that's sweet," says Stacey.

"Okay, so what about another famous woman you've been linked to — Juliette Cortez?" Bob asks.

"We're just really good friends."

"Don't take this the wrong way," says Bob. "But you don't seem to be as much of a womanizer as the media is making you out to be.

"I'm not," Finn says.

I let out a breath. The plan is working.

"I'm no saint," Finn adds. "I've made some mistakes, done things I'm not proud of. But honestly? My whole life, there's only been one girl who's had my heart."

Stacey makes a whooshing OooOooOOoh sound.

"Okay, come on," says Bob. "Give me something. Some tips. What should I do to impress Stacey?"

Stacey giggles again.

"I think that women just want you to be yourself," Finn says. "Let them see all the parts of you, even the parts that are hard to share with someone else. The right woman will love all of you."

"Be yourself? Well, I have no hope then," Bob laughs.

"I wouldn't be so sure about that," Stacey giggles.

"Finn, tell us a bit more about the movie that's coming out tonight," Bob says.

Finn finally gets to talk about the movie and goes into a rehearsed spiel, and I finally find the photos under the hashtag #Finpril which I guess is a mash-up of our names. It sounds like some kind of new depression drug, but okay.

I scroll through them, heart thumping. It's so weird to see myself like this — in grainy images taken from a distance. In most you can barely tell it's us, but there are a few clearer ones of us on the Ferris wheel which must have been taken by a professional camera. Paparazzi? Natalie? I don't know. There's one of us kissing, me holding the cotton candy, Finn's hands on the side of my face, me leaning into him like I've never wanted anything more.

Okay, I really don't hate these photos, in fact it's kind of nice to see such a special moment immortalized.

I do hate some of the comments though.

He's out of her league.

Summer Sanders would be a better choice than this virgin.

I hate everything about her.

She's soooo uggggly!

She's just after him for his money, everyone knows!

Wow, okay, people are mean. And even though Dirk Derrick apologized for what he said on his show the other day, he can't take away what he said, that seed that's been planted in everyone's minds that I'm nothing but a gold digger.

Then I remember that I'm getting paid to be with Finn and realize they're not exactly wrong about me.

Just as I'm about to go into a comment doom scroll that

would no doubt be horrific for my mental health, there's a knock at the door.

I answer and a guy hands over a huge box. It's my dress for the premiere tonight!

I thank him and rush the dress inside, but when I open it, it's the most *not me* thing I've ever seen. It's short, tight, low cut and covered in glittery diamonds.

I shoot Natalie a text telling her I can't wear this and she replies that it's perfect.

But there is no way I can wear this in public.

I send a text to Trix and ask her if she's free to take me shopping.

She texts back straight away and gives me an address where I can meet her.

CHAPTER FIFTY-EIGHT

inn

NATALIE: Great interview today, Finn.

Finn: Thanks.

Natalie: See what happens when you just trust me to do my job?

Natalie: Best behavior tonight at the premiere, okay? No going off script.

Natalie: Finn?

Natalie: Finn. Please acknowledge my message. Tell me you're not going to do something stupid at the premiere tonight!

Finn: Sorry. I was driving. Yeah. Got it. Best behavior.

THE RADIO INTERVIEW goes so much better than I expect, especially after the shit show with Dirk, and after my perfect night with April last night, I'm feeling positive about life... or whatever this existence is, for the first time in a long time as I drive through the Hollywood Hills on my way to see Max Montrose.

I have been to Max's mansion a few times for Fraternity meetings, but every time I walk from the parking area up to the front door I'm still blown away by the sheer size of the place. With its whitewashed with pillars, huge arched windows, a fucking fountain out front and a view down into the valley to die for, the whole thing makes my place on the beach look like a shack.

A butler lets me in, an actual *butler*, and Max greets me in the parlor—a large open space filled with ornate chandeliers, rugs, plush couches and a massive cat tower with about six cats climbing all over it.

"Finn." Max greets me with a firm handshake. He looks like he's heading off to a business meeting in suit pants and a crisp white shirt, his dark hair slicked back like he still thinks it's the nineteen hundreds. "It's such a nice day, I thought we'd be most comfortable on the patio," he says, leading me through the parlor and out onto a back patio overlooking the pool, huge garden and the city far down below.

My house in Santa Monica is cool, but this place is definitely goals.

The butler appears and pours two wine glasses with blood.

"Thank you, Clifford," says Max.

The butler, Clifford, does a little bow, places the bottle on the table and leaves.

"You still have some of the real stuff?" I ask, taking a sniff like I'm some wine connoisseur.

The metallic scent hits my nostrils, wakes up my inner sleeping demons and my vampiric thirst and suddenly I've drained the whole glass.

Max doesn't blink. He just pours me another. "I know it's

been difficult to get with the supply chain issues." Max says. "I'll give you a case of this vintage to take with you."

Max and I barely know each other so this feels like a kind gesture, one that makes me feel like I can trust him with my problems. I don't tell him I got two cases from Vincent's the other night. Besides, I don't know how long they are going to last me, and I just can't risk going thirsty.

"That'd be great, thank you," I say.

"It's quite concerning, this whole thing," he begins, taking a sip of his own drink. He's so refined. So casual. He's not chugging it down like a frat boy on a beer keg like I just did.

"Any idea on what's going on?" I take a sip of my second glass, it's easier now that the first glass took the edge off. I feel a little more connected to my humanity and less like I'm going to drain the next human that walks past.

Max shakes his head. "My usual contacts are… un-contactable. Of course, we suspect Vincent has something to do with it, since he's making a lot of money out of the situation, but until we can find out exactly what's going on, Brandon and I are working on a solution."

"Yeah?"

"It's not quite ready for distribution yet, but soon, I hope. I own a lab in The Valley. I have had a team working on synthetic blood for many years."

"Wait, *you* are the one who created Sybline?"

"Not really. I just funded the scientists who came up with it."

"It's kind of disgusting," I say.

"Ah. Well. Not everyone wanted the blood to taste like wine. It's useful in some social situations with humans present, but it turns out, many vampires want their synthetic blood to still taste like blood."

"Well, you kind of get a taste for it," I say, swishing the blood in my glass.

"We're working on a new version. Something that's a little more satisfying. We're in the final test stages now and hope to release it within a month or so. Of course I'm not delusional enough to expect that it will completely end the recent spate of murder and violence across the city, but I hope it will perhaps satiate our community somewhat." He nods to my glass. "What do you think of it?"

I look at the bottle between us. "Wait, this is *synthetic?*"

He smiles. "It's not a bad drop, is it?"

"You don't need more testing. Get it out there immediately. Don't even tell the vampires it's not real blood. No one would ever know."

"The main issue is getting our product to the suppliers. As I said, they are un-contactable. I've started a shipping company, but it's taking a bit of work to get all the parts moving as they should."

Wow, okay, this guy is a fucking genius. Why couldn't Max be my maker instead of Maverick?

"Now, what was it you wanted to talk to me about?" Max takes his glass to his lips again.

"Sex."

A little blood spurts from his lips. "Oh," he says, wiping the blood from his mouth. "I see."

"April suggested I talk to you. She said that Poppy told her you didn't want to—"

He raises a dark eyebrow at me.

I take a breath and just let it out. "I've been having some… issues in the bedroom."

"I see. What kind of issues?"

Shit. Could this be any more fucking awkward?

"I want to be able to—" I run a hand through my hair. "*Do it.* But I'm… scared of hurting her."

"Ah." Max takes a longer drink this time. "It is a conundrum. The desire we have is very strong. For both blood and for sex."

No shit.

"And with a human, it's difficult at times to control both of these instincts — the carnal desire of the man, and the bloodlust of the vampire."

"Yeah. That."

"And you're a very new vampire."

"Not that new."

"But you've had sex with women? Since you've been turned?"

"Yeah."

He gives me a look like he's waiting for me to finish.

"But only with women I didn't really… care about."

"Donnas?"

"Yeah."

"It's different when you're in love."

My heart jumps at the word. *Love.*

"Honestly, I'd suggest avoiding relationships with human women completely. It's really the best way for most of us. It often gets messy."

I don't need to ask him what he means by that.

"You're only a year old. I was nearly one hundred when I met Poppy, and I still struggled with it."

Clifford appears with a plate of cakes and then disappears again. Max helps himself to something that looks like a tiny chocolate cake.

"But you're not me," he continues. "Your generation is different. And correct me if I'm wrong, but you haven't even made your first kill?"

"No. And I don't intend to."

"But you were involved in breaking a man's hands."

"He had his hands on April. He was trying to — *hurt* her.

Sell her to Vincent." The memory of that guy's fucking hands on her is enough to make me want to do it again.

"I understand completely."

"You do?"

"Yes. I would do the same if a man was to touch Poppy. Honestly, I'm surprised you left him alive."

"Maverick gave me so much shit for it."

"Maverick would obliterate anyone who even dared to breathe in Trix's direction. The fact that you only broke his hands shows what kind of vampire you are."

"What kind of vampire am I?" I ask him.

"A good one."

We sit in silence for a moment, sipping our blood, eating cakes and enjoying the view.

"So, what do I do? How do I have a — *sexual* relationship with a human without hurting her?"

"Please excuse me for asking this, Finn, but why aren't you speaking with Maverick about this?"

"He's pissed at me."

"What for?"

"Because I wouldn't listen to him. He told me to stay away from April. But she's my everything. How can I stay away?"

"You crave her blood like nothing you've ever craved before? You have an insatiable hunger for what's running in her veins?"

"No."

He startles, places his glass on the table and stares at me. "No?"

"No. I don't know that I really even crave her blood. I think about blood a lot, obviously, but when I think of April, I don't think about her like that. I just crave... *her.*"

"But in craving every part of her, her blood must—or at least—*will* come into it, and that is where the danger lies. If you don't stop in time—"

"I know. If I don't stop in time, I could kill her. But we've done stuff. Fooled around." I don't give him details. I don't tell him about the broken door frame. About how she had her perfect lips around my cock. "And I've been able to handle it."

He runs a hand over the very light shadow on his jaw. "The best thing to do then, in my humble opinion, is to continue to practice. Drink a lot of blood before you see her. Never be hungry around her."

I nod. "I already do that."

"Drink even more than you think you need. Just try to avoid getting high, that causes its own problems. And then spend time with her… *sexually*, and just practice controlling yourself."

"I feel like I'm already doing all this."

"Don't make love to her until you feel you can one-hundred percent trust yourself. This is the key. You must trust yourself. If there is any doubt in your mind whatsoever that you would hurt her, you must keep your distance."

"Right."

Shit.

This isn't what I wanted to hear. I wanted him to give me some magic cure. Some tincture or serum, some special blood, some secret code that would help me keep myself in check.

But the secret is just that I have to trust myself.

Great.

"But it can be done," he says. "I found my way with Poppy. Now we have a very satisfying sex life."

Oh god, I don't need to hear the details about this horny old vamp's sex life.

"We don't always do it with The Bite. Sometimes we just do The Bite. Sometimes we just have sex. Mostly we do both. You could try just giving her The Bite. Perhaps have some other vampires around while you do it, just in case. But you will probably find if you give her The Bite, you will want to immediately have sex with her. It can be difficult to separate the two."

"Right."

"If you think you can have sex without The Bite, that may be a good place to start."

"Okay."

Now he's off I can't stop him talking and it's getting way too fucking weird, like I'm getting sex tips from my grandpa. "Poppy enjoys The Bite immensely," he continues. "All human women do, but when they *love* you, there is something about The Bite that doesn't feel so dark or monstrous. It feels like an extension of making love, like making love with your teeth and her flesh."

Oh Jesus.

"Uh, okay."

"Perhaps it can help you to think about The Bite in that way. That it's not something bad, it's not a weapon. It's a gift." He takes another sip of blood. "That idea has helped me, anyway. We may be vampires, but we still get to choose if we're going to use our abilities to harm or to bring pleasure."

He gives me a look. "Has any of this helped?"

"Uh. Yeah, kind of."

"Another thing you can try is to get her to tie you up with silver rope. Have her tie you to the bedpost and have her go on top. Then, if she needs to get away from you, she is able."

Okay, what the fuck?

Wait, that could actually be a good idea.

"It means you have to endure the pain of the burning silver of course, but that can also stop you from going too far with her. It's rather unpleasant, but there's no way you can harm her when you're in that situation. You may also not be able to enjoy the experience at all with your flesh burning, but it's something to consider. Or a pair of silver handcuffs, perhaps."

"Uh, thanks for the tips," I tell him. "I should be getting back. It's the premiere tonight."

"Poppy and I will be there rooting for you," he says with a smile. "I'll have Clifford take the cases of blood to your car."

"Must be nice to have a butler," I say.

"Ah, yes. It is. Clifford is wonderful, but I must admit that I miss my old butler James terribly. He was with me for seventy years."

"Seventy *years?*"

Max nods. "He was bound to me after some trouble between the fae and the vampires."

"The uprising," I say. "I've heard the stories. Something about the Fraternity's old leader ripping people off and a fae who told everyone about his dirty dealings?"

"Exactly," Max says. "James was the one who alerted us to what was happening with our president Renauld Luelle. He was only helping, but Lottie, his daughter, didn't see it that way. She became president when Renauld was given the Certain Death, and she decided that James' punishment would be a lifetime of servitude."

"Well, shit."

"Indeed. But James has his freedom now, and from what I've heard, he's doing very well for himself."

I scrape my chair back. "Thank you, Max. For the blood and all your… advice."

Your super fucking weird advice that may just work.

"Anytime, Finn." He stands and claps my back. "If there's anything else you need, just let me know. I'm always happy to help. I have known Maverick for many years. I know he can be a real pain in the ass. But he is one of the good ones. You could have done a lot worse for a maker."

"Yeah?"

He nods. "My maker was a woman who made my life a living hell for nearly a hundred years. And Maverick's maker —well, I'm sure you know."

I shake my head. "I don't."

"He didn't tell you?"

"No."

"It's not my story to tell, but as his progeny you should probably know about your lineage." He walks me inside and we pause by the cat tower. "He was turned by an evil general who wanted to create a vampire army."

"Oh, fuck." It's only now that I realize that I'd been so immersed in my own trauma, my own horrific experience of being turned, that I hadn't really considered Maverick's pain and suffering. I'd always just thought of him as a pain in my fucking ass who'd forgotten what it was like to be young. Now I know that he runs a hell of a lot deeper. A vampire army? That's some fucked up shit.

Maverick was right. I have been acting like a teenager. Self-absorbed, not even considering that my own maker may have his own shit to deal with.

I think of him sitting on his deck, Trix's legs over him, a huge dumb grin on his face as he stares at her and I feel... kind of bad.

"Maverick doesn't like to talk about it. It might be best if you don't tell him I told you."

"Got it."

I make my way out of the Montrose estate with a car full of blood, a buttload of guilt at how I've been treating Maverick but also a bundle of excitement burning inside me. There is a way to be with April.

It may not be comfortable to let her tie me up in silver rope, but I'll do anything it takes to keep her safe.

I'll do anything it takes to be able to make love to her.

CHAPTER FIFTY-NINE

pril

NATALIE: Best behavior tonight, April. This premiere is a really big deal for Finn.

April: Of course.

Natalie: How does the dress fit? Can you send me a pic?

April: Um, yeah, it's fine!

Natalie: Do you understand the assignment tonight?

April: Hold his hand, get out of the way when he's interviewed or when someone wants a photo. Be seen but be invisible.

Natalie: Good. Now don't let Finn talk you into going off script this time!

A BLACK CAR stops at the curb outside the hotel, and I slide into the back where Finn is already sitting. He's dressed in a black suit, his hair is tidier than usual, slicked back behind his ears and curling up around his neck. He's wearing a gold watch that I think may be a Rolex, and he looks like a Hollywood dream.

He grins at me and his whole face lights up. "Holy shit, April, you look sensational," he says, leaning over to give me a gentle kiss on my cheek. I'm not wearing the short sparkling dress. Instead, I'm dressed in a midnight blue vintage chiffon gown. It's gorgeous but slightly understated. I spent the afternoon with Trix at her favorite vintage boutique. The owner lent me the dress, a pair of pewter heels and a matching purse. Natalie sent hair and make-up to my hotel to hide every blemish and stray hair, and I feel like the most glamorous version of myself ever. I grin back at him, reach over and grab his hand.

"You don't look so bad yourself." I suddenly remember last night, the way he felt in my mouth, how he gripped the back of my head, how he gripped the doorframe. I want this man more than I've ever wanted anyone, more than I've ever wanted *anything*, and all I want right now is to be making love in the back of this car. Finn could always glamour the driver afterwards, right?

"New watch?" I ask him, sliding my hand over the gold band around his wrist.

"Newish," he says. "It was a gift. Felt like I should wear it tonight, get it in some photos."

"It's nice," I say.

"Nice?" he lets out a laugh. "Maybe Rolex can use that in their next marketing campaign."

"I heard you on the radio this morning," I tell him.

"It was a great interview. I really like Bob and Stacey. They're actually decent people. Rare in this industry."

"And you nearly outed me to them," I say, raising my eyebrows at him.

"Ah, but I didn't."

"How did you know?"

"I saw you writing that spicy scene on your laptop that day at Blank State." He gives me a smirk. "My vision is excellent, you know. I could see it from the other side of the restaurant."

"Oh," I say, as I try to remember exactly what it was that I was writing.

"But it was Trix who told me about Scripty."

"That was supposed to be a secret!" But then I remember how drunk I was when I told Trix and Poppy, and now I'm not sure I actually told them that.

"Even from me?"

I just shrug.

"I've read every line. Every word of every story you've written there."

My face heats as I think about all the spicy scenes, the characters I've written who are all *so* clearly based on Finn. "Yeah?"

"You're incredibly talented. You should be doing more than writing on Scripty."

"Actually, I think I may have just gotten a literary agent."

"Baby, that's fantastic! I'm so proud of you. You deserve so much success, and if I can help in any way, I will." He smiles and squeezes my hand, and then cupping my face with his other hand, he leans in and kisses me softly on the lips.

"Thank you," I say, breathless.

"Tonight is going to be crazy," he tells me, letting his hand fall from my face and down to my hand. "Cameras everywhere. Reporters. Everyone will want a piece of you. Are you sure you're ready for this?"

"Yeah, I'm ready."

But it turns out, I'm not ready. When we slide out of the car outside the theater, it's like walking into a blazing sun. Bulbs flash, fans scream, reporters are right in our faces before we can even get out of the car. It's completely over-whelming and absolutely bat shit crazy.

Finn smiles at the crowd, waving at everyone like he's been doing this for decades already.

I walk a little behind him, trying to do my best to smile and wave too. Finn is grabbed by a reporter and I'm all alone in the sea of noise and light, feeling like a complete idiot. But it's okay, no one is really looking at me. I'm a nobody. I just stand and listen to his interview and the cool, calm, rehearsed way he talks about the movie just like he did on the radio earlier.

"You look amazing!" Juliette Cortez appears by my side and links her arm in mine. She looks amazing in a long satin red dress with a huge slit up the side. "Where did you get your dress?" Oh my god, Juliette Cortez is talking to *me*! I'm aware of cameras around us, flashes of light catching this moment, Juliette talking to a total nobody.

"Betsy's Boutique," I tell her.

"Is that the vintage place on Rodeo Drive?"

"Uh huh. Yeah."

"It's stunning." She leans in conspiratorially. "You're the best dressed here."

"Oh? Me? No! No, no. You are!"

"You're so cute. I can see why Finn's so crazy about you."

"I'm pretty crazy about him too," I say, looking over to where he's getting interviewed by someone else now.

"He deserves some good in his life," Juliette says. "I'm glad he found you."

Juliette gets pulled away and then a reporter suddenly gets in my face with a microphone, camera, boom and a massive light in my eyes.

"April Abernathy!" the woman says. "You're here tonight with Finn Huxley."

"Yes, I am."

"The two of you have gone viral the last twenty-four hours after your sexy date on Santa Monica pier. Do you have anything to tell us about your relationship with Finn?"

"Uh, it's still kind of new."

"But he brought you here tonight."

"Yeah."

"So, it must be kind of serious?"

"Oh, I don't know. Yeah. I guess? Like I said, it's still pretty new."

Wow, I am murdering this!

"Who are you wearing?"

"Betsy's Boutique on Rodeo," I tell her. "It's vintage Chanel."

The reporter slices her neck in a cutting motion to let the camera know to stop filming. "Well, at least we got something about the dress," she says, walking off without even saying bye.

Finn finds me and takes my hand. "Don't leave me," he whispers. "I kind of hate these things."

"Finn, you're loving every second of this," I tell him.

"I'm loving it more when I have your hand in mine." He gives my hand a squeeze and doesn't let go again as we navigate the sea of reporters and photographers.

I stand next to Finn with a dumb grin on my face, only talking about the dress and the boutique, but I don't mind. I'm with Finn and he's in his element, even if I'm so out of mine.

We have some photos taken together and I try to pose how Trix and the boutique owner showed me — always at an angle, with one hand on my hip. Finn gets his photo taken with just about everyone, and a whole heap on his own. He stands there smoldering and grinning and all I can do is watch and melt under the lights and the knowing that Finn is *mine.*

After what feels like hours, we are finally ushered into the theater where we take our seats and watch *Jungle Story.*

It was definitely very weird watching him on screen when we were at the drive-in back in Lucky, but now that we're in Hollywood, at the premiere of his new movie, sitting here holding hands, watching this movie with hundreds of other big name stars and their dates, it feels even more crazy, completely unreal.

Every time Finn's face comes on screen, I have to turn to him and check that this is the same person. That he's really up there, that he's really down here, that his hand is really in mine.

It couldn't be a more perfect evening. The reception for the movie is amazing. Everyone claps and cheers and as we're walking back through the foyer, Finn is congratulated by so many famous and important people in the industry.

"Let's do something together," a big time producer says.

"Finn, I have the perfect part for you," says another.

"I would love to work with you on a project," says someone else who's clearly a big deal.

And the whole time, he never lets my hand go.

Everything is perfect.

Finn is here, he's living his dreams, and I'm by his side, working on my own dreams too.

It feels like the stars have finally aligned for us both.

Finn pauses just before we reach the door to leave. He squeezes my hand and turns towards me. "Thank you for this perfect night." He kisses me gently on the lips. My eyes close and I let myself have this perfect moment.

And then I hear the sirens. At first, I think it's just the police going past. I've almost been getting used to that sound being here in LA, but this time it keeps getting louder and louder until it sounds like it's right outside the theater.

Finn pulls back from me and furrows his dark brow. "What is that?"

"I don't know."

He tugs me towards the door so we can find out.

"Finley Huxley," a voice booms through a megaphone.

All the producers and stars who were congratulating him just moments ago are now gasping, shocked, confused and looking around for Finn.

The megaphone voice cuts through the noise. "Finley Huxley, you are under arrest for murder. Drop your weapons and come out with your hands in the air."

CHAPTER SIXTY

April's hand slides out of mine and I raise my hands and walk out of the theater. It's not like I have a fucking choice. I can't run. I'll look guilty.

But as the cameras go crazy and reporters start screaming and yelling my name, asking me who I murdered, I realize I already look fucking guilty.

A cop grabs me, handcuffs me and starts reading me my rights. I look up at April who's staring at me from the steps of the theater.

She's a vision. A fucking angel.

This night had been going so damn well. Everything was fucking perfect. It was like the prom night we never got to have, but with designer clothing and expensive champagne instead of spiked punch. On the way home from Max's place earlier, I picked up some silver rope. It's in a box back at my place ready for her to tie me up with so we could end this night the way we were supposed to on the night of prom.

"Finn!" she calls out to me, tears running down her perfectly made-up face.

A cop shoves me into a police car and before I can even call back to her that I fucking love her, because my stupid ass couldn't do it before, we're driving downtown.

It's okay, I try to reassure myself. *I have abilities. I can glamour my way out of this.*

As soon as I can catch the eye of the cops, I can get them to let me go.

But I can't glamour all the reporters, the photographers, everyone in the whole world who's about to see the footage of me getting arrested at my own movie premiere.

And getting arrested *twice*? Even if all the charges are dropped?

Well, this definitely isn't good for my reputation.

When we arrive outside the station, one of the cops turns to look at me and I stare into his eyes, waiting for the shift, when I know his mind is open to my glamour, my influence.

But he just glares at me and says, "You're in big fucking trouble this time, buddy."

CHAPTER SIXTY-ONE

pril

I JUST STAND THERE, unable to move, unable to do anything at all, as I watch Finn and the six cop cars squeal away.

And then a second later, *I'm* the one suddenly everyone is interested in. I'm no longer the girl trying to get out of the way of Finn's shot, I'm front and center.

"April, who did Finn murder?"

"April, did you know you were dating a murderer?"

"Were you in on it?"

"What does it feel like to be part of a modern Bonnie and Clyde love story?"

Maverick suddenly appears, pushing through the crowd and places his arm around me.

"No comment!" he shouts as he drags me back down the red carpet. Just hours ago this was a dream coming true, now it's a fucking nightmare.

It's only when I'm in the back of a limo with Maverick

and Trix that I can speak again. "What's happening?" I ask, my voice wavering.

Maverick presses a button, and a screen goes up between the three of us and the driver.

Trix grabs my hand. "He wouldn't do this. Not Finn. I know he wouldn't."

"I taught Finn everything I know," Maverick says. "Even if he did it, he knew how to cover his tracks. This has to be a setup."

A set up.

Of course I know Finn wouldn't do this, but relief still floods through me at Maverick's words.

"I'll call the Fraternity," Maverick says. "We'll get him out."

Tears suddenly stream down my face, and Trix puts her arm around me.

"April, honey, we'll get him out. It's all going to be okay."

"No vampire has ever spent more than 24 hours in jail. It just doesn't happen," Maverick tries to reassure me. "We're too good at getting what we want. As soon as Finn gets there, he should be able to start glamouring and influencing the cops who arrested him. Convince them that this was all a big mistake." He squeezes my hand. "This is not the big deal that it appears to be right now. We have our ways, we have influence, power, glamour. Everything will be okay. I think."

"You *think?*" Trix demands, glaring at him.

Maverick shakes his head. "This is… well, something isn't quite right."

"What? What isn't right?" I ask.

"It's just that last time he was arrested… he couldn't glamour the cops."

"What? Why not?" Trix ask.

"I don't know. We thought maybe it was because he was weak, hadn't had enough blood. Or that because he was still a baby he just messed up, forgot how to glamour, couldn't focus."

"And what do you think now?" Trix asks, her eyes narrowing.

"I think maybe someone's had it in for Finn this whole time."

Trix shoves him in the arm. "And you've been such a dick to him! The way you cut him off!"

"I was pissed! I just needed to calm down. I wasn't really going to cut him out of my life for all eternity."

Trix folds her arms over her chest. "You better fix this!"

Our limo stops a block away from the police station which is crawling with reporters and cameras. "I'll see you back at home, Trix. April, just sit tight."

"I'm not going anywhere," I tell him. "I'm coming with you."

"This whole thing is a publicity nightmare, but you turning up to the police station in that dress right after Finn is arrested? It won't be good for either of you."

"Oh, but it'll look okay if Maverick Stone arrives to bail him out?" I ask.

"I know a back way in."

"Why the fuck do you know a back way into the police station?" Trix asks.

He just gives her a little smile and a kiss. "Take April back to our place. I'll be there as soon as I can get Finn out."

But when Maverick finally arrives back at his place in Malibu a few hours later, Finn is not with him.

"What happened?" Trix asks.

Maverick takes a seat on the couch next to Trix. "Same thing as last time. It was strange. He couldn't glamour anyone. It was like he was... under some kind of spell. I glamoured the cops into letting him go. Turns out they didn't even have any evidence anyway, just an anonymous tip."

"They sent all those cop cars to a movie premiere on an *anonymous tip*?" Trix asks.

"What's going on?" I ask, gripping the rainbow knitted throw I've been hugging since I got here.

"Publicity stunt?" Maverick suggests. "Someone wants Finn to look bad. Real bad."

"This isn't good," says Trix.

"What do you mean he couldn't glamour anyone?" I ask. "What would cause that?"

"Not sure," Maverick says. "Magic is the only thing I can think of."

"Wait, magic is real?" I gasp.

Trix nods. "At some point you just stop being surprised," she says.

"I should call his publicist," Maverick says. "Although I doubt there's much she can do about this. It might be over for Finn now."

"Over?" I ask.

"The studio can't work with an actor who's been arrested *twice*, once for murder at his own fucking premiere."

"Where is he?" I demand.

"He's at his place."

It's only when I grab my phone and start booking an Uber that I realize I don't even know where he lives.

"What's his address?"

"April, no," Maverick says. "He's angry. He's not himself. You're not safe around him tonight."

"Finn needs me."

"No. He needs to be alone right now."

I stand up and fold my arms. "Was that his choice? Or yours?"

"Mine."

"Then, fuck that," I say. "You need to stop acting like his dad, thinking you know what's best for him, telling him what he should and shouldn't do. His real dad is a fucking asshole, he doesn't need you acting like one too."

Maverick blinks. "I didn't know that. About his dad."

"Well, now you do. His dad was an abusive piece of shit who tried to control Finn his whole life."

Maverick's jaw tenses. "I'm just trying to keep you both safe. That's all."

Trix puts a hand on Maverick's very large bicep. "Baby, maybe it's better if he's around friends."

Maverick looks up at the ceiling and sighs. "Jesus. Fine. But we all go."

CHAPTER SIXTY-TWO

inn

AFTER HOURS of sitting in a cell with no ability to glamour anyone, Maverick finally comes to my rescue. And for once, I'm not mad about him getting involved in my life.

It was just like the first time I got arrested. When I tried to glamour the cops, it had no impact on them at all. No matter how long I stared into their eyes, their minds never opened. When I tried to use my influence, they just ignored me, told me to shut the fuck up. One of them even shoved me into a wall. It didn't hurt, I haven't lost my strength. But still, what the fuck?!

I've never heard of a vampire losing their abilities, but maybe it's happening to me. I'd happily let go of my super strength and speed, even my immortality if it meant I was human again.

Maybe I'm having a mental breakdown.

Maybe this whole vampire thing is just some kind of paranoid delusion, maybe I was never undead at all.

But my thirst is still very present. My desire to rip out the throat of the cop who smashed me into a wall was at an all time high, but delusion or not, I knew that wouldn't go down too well, especially if my ability to glamour my way out of any mess I made was gone.

The Uber stops outside my place, and Maverick gives me a nod. "Get some rest. We'll talk tomorrow with Brandon and Natalie and see what we can do to clean up this mess." He puts a firm hand on my shoulder and gives it a squeeze. The whole thing makes me want to cry. Maybe Maverick isn't such a bad vampire daddy after all.

I don't say anything, just nod, get out of the car and watch him drive away.

But then, when I walk into my house, I'm greeted by Vincent and Aiden sitting on my couch drinking from a couple of Donnas, getting fucking blood everywhere.

Of fucking course.

"You," I say, as all the pieces suddenly click into place. "You did this to me."

Vincent pushes his Donna off him without closing the wounds on her neck. She falls onto the floor, blood dribbling from her neck onto my rug.

Fucking piece of shit vampire.

She's high on The Bite and writhes around the floor like she's mud wrestling an invisible demon.

"Isn't it obvious?" Vincent asks, licking blood from his fingers as he gives me a dark grin. "You're our low hanging fruit."

Aiden just ignores me, sinking his teeth into his own Donna, drinking until her pulse falls dangerously low.

"Fucking stop! You're going to drain her!" I yell, like he's going to listen to me.

He just laughs, and thank god he does, because it gets his fangs out of her. She slides to the floor, not from the ecstasy of The Bite, but from nearly being fucking dead. "But that's the plan," he says. "To drain them."

"You think you're free?" Vincent asks. "You think it's over?" He lets out an evil laugh, tossing his dark wavy hair back. "Oh, Finn. We're only just getting started."

"Took you long enough to get out of jail tonight," Aiden says. "How come?"

I get the feeling they know exactly how come.

"How'd you do it?" I demand.

Aiden opens his mouth to tell me.

"Don't fucking tell him!" Vincent berates.

Aiden shoots him a look. "Why not? In a few minutes, the cops will be here, and they'll find Finn standing over two dead hookers. Then they'll have all the evidence they need."

Oh shit. No. No, no, no.

"What do you want?" I ask.

"We don't want anything," Vincent laughs.

"We're just here to send a message," Aiden adds.

"What message? To who?!"

Vincent licks some blood from the back of his hand. "A message to Brandon, Maverick, Max and all you other Fraternity fuckers about what we are capable of."

"This is about the *Fraternity?*"

Aiden rolls his eyes. "It's always about the fucking Fraternity."

"What? Why? Who cares? It's just a club for boring old vampires who like to sit around and reminisce about old Hollywood."

"We're taking over LA," Vincent says. "And to do that, first the Fraternity needs to go down."

"One at a time," Aiden adds.

"And we decided to start with you, because you're the little baby," Vincent laughs.

If one more person calls me a fucking baby!

But now is not the time to fight. I would never win against Vincent and Aiden, who've been drinking blood all night while I was out drinking expensive champagne.

Vincent stands, looking down over his Donna like she's a piece of trash on the boardwalk. "You made it so easy. You were already known to the police. And then there was the premiere. I mean, you can't buy publicity like that... *or can you?*"

"And tomorrow you'll be in prison for double homicide," Aiden adds, kicking the leg of the Donna who's slumped on the floor next to him.

"Maverick will get me out," I say. "The Fraternity will stop you."

"Not this time," Vincent says. "Maverick won't be able to save you when he's too busy trying to save Trix."

I run a hand through my hair. "What are you assholes planning? How are you doing this? How are you blocking my glamour?"

Aiden smiles a bloody smile. "We have ways. Ways that will take each and every one of you down until we're the Vampire Kings of LA."

"Vampire *kings*?" I let out a horrified laugh. This is truly unhinged.

"We're taking back LA," Vincent says. "The Fraternity thinks they walk on water, that no one can touch them. But we're in charge now. We're the ones running things."

"You can't do this," I say.

"But we *are* doing it," says Vincent.

"I will get out of this. I'm not going to prison."

Aiden walks over to me, and I can see something in his eyes that wasn't even there the night they took me. It's something… *evil*. These two vampires have completely lost all their humanity. There is no light behind those eyes, only darkness.

It's only now, staring into his pitch black eyes, that I realize — I am not like them.

I am not a monster. I may be undead, I may constantly crave human blood, but I am not evil.

I still have light within me. And it's that light that's going to get me through this and guide me back to April.

Aiden gets even closer now. He's so up in my face, and everything within me wants to break his fucking neck, but with Vincent here, and it being hours since I last had a drink, I know my chances are slim. Not slim. Zero.

"Finn," he whispers into my ear, "We will get away with it. You will go to prison. We will plant more evidence." He looks down at the Donnas, one who's getting closer to death with every second that passes. "There will be no way out of this for you this time. And even if you did by some *miracle* find a way out, we would come for you again, over and over and over again." He grabs the back of my hair and pulls my head back. "And you know what else? If you don't go along with our plan, we'll take April."

I pull out of his grip, grab his shirt and run him into the wall, holding him up by the throat. "If you fucking touch her," I tell him. "I swear to God, I will stake you to fucking Certain Death."

"And how are you going to do that?" Aiden laughs. "You're weak, and you've lost your ability to glamour. And April's all alone in her hotel room. Room 223, isn't that right?"

"Don't you fucking touch her!" I growl.

Vincent pulls me off Aiden. He's strong. Hundreds of years old strong. He throws me onto the floor next to the Donnas like I'm half a pound of flour.

"We will leave her alone," Vincent says, glaring at Aiden.

"As long as you do what we say." He gives me a kick. It doesn't hurt, but it does assert his dominance over me.

"Fine," I say, looking up at him. "Leave her alone. I'll… I'll do whatever you want."

"Atta boy," says Aiden.

The phrase turns my stomach. Something my dad used to say when I won a baseball game. It was the only time he wasn't telling me I was a worthless piece of shit.

Vincent nods to Aiden. "Let's get out of here." He looks back at me. "Let these girls die. Let the cops find them here. Plead guilty and go to prison where you'll rot away in there for all eternity, or we will kill April, after we've had a little fun with her first, of course."

The door slams behind them, and rage like I've never felt in all my life or afterlife takes over.

And then I make a promise to myself that I will not rest until they are both staked.

CHAPTER SIXTY-THREE

pril

MAVERICK KNOCKS on Finn's door, and when there's no answer, he lets himself in with a key. Me, Trix, Max and Poppy follow him in.

And then, there's Finn. Sitting on the floor with two bloody girls, his own wrist open and bleeding over one of them.

I don't know what I'm seeing. I can't comprehend the scene in front of me. There is *so much* blood!

My legs go weak, I stumble and Trix grabs my arm.

"Oh, fuck!" Maverick rushes over to him.

Max turns to me, Trix and Poppy and tries to push us back out of the house. "You girls shouldn't see this, go wait in the car."

"It's too late, I've already seen it," I say, my voice shaking as I stare at the carnage in front of me. This is what they all warned me would happen.

Finn. Dangerous.

"Girls, please, leave," Max pleads once more before rushing over to the bloody mess.

"She's okay. I gave her a little of my blood," Finn says, holding up his bleeding, shaking, wrist. His face is covered in blood and tears and *agony.*

"Finn! How could you? With everything that—" Maverick starts yelling, and Finn flinches, an ingrained response after what he went through with his dad.

Then something crosses Finn's expression. A realization that he doesn't have to take this from Maverick. "I didn't do this!" Finn yells back.

"Finn! Two girls are bleeding out on your floor!"

"It wasn't me!"

"Finn, Jesus! Didn't you listen to anything I tried to teach you? Just tell me what happened!"

"I'm fucking trying to!"

"Finn," Max says, gently lifting up the other girl, who's covered in blood. She looks drunk, but not dead, and Max makes quick work of picking her up and placing her on the couch, which is already so covered in blood a little more won't matter. Max bites his own wrist and pushes it into the woman's mouth.

What the fuck?

"I didn't do this," Finn says, rocking back and forth as he tries to put his wrist back into the mouth of the girl on the floor with him. "It wasn't me."

Maverick ignores him and pulls on the eyelids of the girl in Finn's arms. "Jesus, you're lucky these girls aren't dead."

"It wasn't me," Finn says. "You have to believe me."

"Finn, this is not the behavior of a member of the Fraternity," Max says. The woman he's holding sucks on his wrist, her eyes rolling back in her head.

Finn looks up, and for the first time, realizes that I'm here.

"I didn't do it—" he whispers, and I can see in his eyes he's telling the truth.

I rush towards him, finally unfrozen, and grab his hand. "Finn. Who did this?"

He looks up at me like I'm his lifeline. The only person here willing to believe him. And it feels insane to believe him. He's *covered in blood,* and two women are here, also covered in blood. If I wasn't so in love with him, if I didn't know him before this, maybe I would be able to do the math. But I just can't believe that Finn would nearly kill two women, especially just hours after being arrested for murder.

None of this makes any sense.

Just last night he wanted me so desperately but was able to keep himself at a distance to keep me safe. He was doing everything in his power not to hurt me, so why would he hurt two girls like this that he didn't even know?

Because he's a vampire. He's dangerous. Maybe he can't always control himself.

Finn blinks up at me, tears streaming from his eyes. "April, please believe me. I didn't do this."

Max licks his finger and runs it over the woman on the couch's neck, closing the holes. "Finn, what happened here?" he asks, a little more calmly now that he knows the girls are going to live.

"Vincent. Aiden," Finn says.

Maverick glares at him. "What?"

Poppy lets out a gasp from where she's still standing arm in arm with Trix by the door.

"They were here when I got back. Drinking from these girls. They're going to call the police. Send them here to find me like this. It's all been a fucking setup."

Max looks into the eyes of the girl on the couch. "You had

a big night out, but you're fine now," he tells her. "You don't know anything about Finn Huxley. You don't believe in vampires. You will never go to Vincent's again."

She nods at him and jumps to her feet. There's no sign at all that she looked like she was about to die just minutes ago.

The girl in Finn's arms suddenly jolts upright. "Oh my god, I've never felt so fucking alive!" She runs her hands over her body like she's in ecstasy. "Oh, wow, this is amazing! What did you do to me? I feel incredible! Where can I get more of what you gave me?"

Finn stares into her eyes.

"Why are you looking at me like that?" she asks with a laugh.

"Fuck! Why isn't it working?" Finn exclaims.

"Give me more!" the woman demands.

"I can't glamour!" Finn runs a bloody hand over his face.

Maverick crouches down next to the woman and looks into her eyes. "You were never here. You never saw any of us. You don't know anything about vampires. You don't even believe they exist."

She nods dumbly.

"You won't remember any of this. Now go for a swim and get all this blood off you."

She nods, reaching for the other girl's hand.

Maverick slides open a glass door that leads down onto the beach, and the two girls leave, giggling like they weren't almost just drained to death by evil vampires. They walk down the beach and don't look back.

"Close your wrist," Maverick berates.

Finn doesn't argue, he just licks his wrist, and the bleeding stops.

"What the fuck is going on?" Finn drops his head, bringing his arms around his knees, and I put my hand on his shoulder.

"Why is this happening?" I demand, glaring at Maverick, who's towering above us all. "What could take away his abilities?"

"Magic," Max says. "It's the only explanation. Rarely used because it's so unpredictable. If a witch or fae was known to be using magic against vampires, we'd be within our rights to kill them. It could start another war between the clans."

"What kind of magic?" I ask.

Max shakes his head. "It could be anything. Something he ate or drank most likely." Max's eyes narrow at Finn's wrist. "You weren't wearing that beautiful timepiece when we met the other day. Where did you get it?"

Maverick glares at Max. "You and Finn met without me?"

"It was a gift," Finn says.

"From who?" both Max and Maverick ask at the same time.

"From Rolex, Natalie sent it to me."

"When?" Maverick asks.

"A couple of weeks ago."

"Were you wearing it the night of your first arrest?" Maverick's eyes narrow. "When you couldn't glamour the cops?"

Finn's eyes widen at the watch. "Uh. Yeah. I was."

"Take it off," Maverick commands.

Finn flicks the clasp and lets it fall into Maverick's hand.

"Try and glamour someone now."

"Who?"

"Me," I say. "Glamour me."

"No," he says, shaking his head.

"Just do it, Finn." I grab his hand tighter and look into his eyes.

"Finn, do it," echoes Maverick. "We need to know if this fucking Rolex is a cursed object."

Finn takes my head in his hands and gazes into my eyes.

Within seconds I feel my mind completely relax and open to him.

"Tell Maverick he's a fucking prick," Finn tells me.

The words echo through my mind, over and over again, and it feels like my brain is being re-wired.

"Maverick," I say, turning to face him. I have no choice. I just *have* to say it. "You're a fucking prick."

Maverick rolls his eyes, and Finn rubs his thumbs over my cheeks. "Sorry, baby," he says.

He breaks eye contact with me, and I can feel his release on my mind. I feel woozy, like I've just had five cocktails at the tiki lounge.

Trix appears at my side and hands me a Coke. "Drink it. You'll feel better."

I take a sip, but still feel really strange.

Max turns the Rolex around in his hands, Poppy looking over his shoulder. "Here, see? It looks to me like a dark fae symbol engraved on the back. You can hardly see it."

"What's a dark fae symbol?" Trix asks.

"It's very rare," Max says. "The last time I saw one of these was during the uprising."

"The what?" I ask.

Maverick shakes his head. "You don't want to know. Death. Destruction. Fae against vampires. It was a dark time."

"They said they wanted to be the vampire kings of LA," Finn says.

Max's eyebrows shoot up.

"Vampire *kings*?" Maverick laughs.

"They called me the low hanging fruit. Their plan is to get to everyone in the Fraternity. Eventually."

Maverick folds his arms over his chest. "They're behind the supply chain issues with the blood."

"Of course," says Max.

"They were charging ten times the amount for a Donna at the club," Finn says. "Last time I was there."

My stomach suddenly flips at the idea of him going to a vampire club to drink from someone. Someone who isn't me.

"Vincent must be making a fortune on Donnas with no blood getting to the vampires," Finn adds. "That's why they wanted to take April and Trix that night. They need more girls."

"What do you mean, *take* April and Trix?" I ask.

"The guys who were there that night, outside the bar, they were going to take you to Vincent's. Sell you to them or something. So Vincent and Aiden could turn you both into Donnas," I tell her.

Poppy gasps.

Trix looks like she's ready to go to war. "What the fuck?!"

"We need to call Brandon," Max says. "We need an emergency Fraternity meeting."

"No," Finn says. "You can't."

Maverick glares at him. "What are you talking about?"

"You have to let them take me," Finn says. "Let the police come and see the blood. Even if the girls aren't here. I can still be charged with murder if I say I did it. Even if they don't find the bodies. I have to go to prison."

We all just stare blankly at him.

"But you didn't do this," I say, reaching for his hand again. He squeezes his fingers into mine like he's desperately trying to hold on to something. Like he's desperately trying to hold on to me.

"I didn't. But if I don't go along with their plan..." He presses his palm into his eyes. "They're coming after everyone. All of us."

"That's why we need to shut this shit down, *now*." Maverick says. "I'll go down there now and fuck them both up. Give them both the Certain Death for messing with my wife and my progeny."

Finn shakes his head. "It's better if I just do what they say."

"They threatened April," Max says through a clenched jaw.

Finn looks up at me, and my stomach sinks as I realize that's exactly what happened. If Finn doesn't go along with this, if he doesn't go to prison, whoever nearly killed those girls is coming for me next.

"We need to get the girls somewhere safe. Now." Maverick says, his eyes dark and blazing as he glares at Trix.

"April's hotel room?" Max suggests, pulling Poppy close to his side.

Finn shakes his head. "They know where she's staying. Her room number. Everything. She's not safe there."

Oh my god, what?

"The estate," Max says. "I have excellent security."

"No," says Maverick. "We need to get them somewhere Vincent and Aiden will never even think to look for them."

"Claudia?" Max suggests.

"Yes," Maverick says. "She may be our best option." He gets out his phone and starts texting.

"Who's Claudia?" I ask.

Poppy purses her lips. "She's a werewolf."

"Wait, what? A *werewolf?*"

The familiar sound of sirens in the distance spark action.

"Finn," says Maverick. "Go take a quick shower. We'll take care of the cops."

"No. I need to go. I need to let them take me!"

Maverick grabs his arm and forces Finn to look him in the eye. "I know things have been complicated between us. But I'm not letting them take you. And I'll never let anything happen to the girls. Not to Trix, Poppy or April. We will protect them. Trust me."

The sirens get louder and closer. "Finn, get upstairs," Maverick says.

Finn shoots me a look, and I give him a nod. He speeds up the stairs while Maverick and Max blur into the kitchen to get cleaning supplies and then blur around the living room cleaning the blood from the floor and placing a throw over the bloodstains on the couch.

One minute later, the three of them are sitting around the living area like nothing has happened. Poppy takes a seat next to Max on the couch, Trix cuddles into Maverick's chest on an armchair, and I sit down next to Finn who's already showered and changed, dressed in black jeans and a black hoodie, smelling like a woodsy, salty, breeze next to me on the couch. I grab his hand and squeeze it tight. A promise I'll never let it go.

The doorbell rings, and Max and Maverick get up to answer it.

Two police officers stand at the door, leaning in to look around.

"Can I help you, officers?" Maverick asks.

"We had a tip-off that there was some trouble here," one of the cops says.

"No trouble here, officer," Max tells them. "Just a couple of friends and their girls spending an evening together."

"Mind if we take a look around?" one of them asks.

"Do you have a warrant?" Maverick asks.

"We don't need a warrant. We were told there's been a double homicide."

Max looks horrified. "There most certainly has been nothing of the sort!"

Suddenly both officers look droopy and dumb. Max and Maverick are glamouring them.

"Finn is innocent. The call you got tonight saying there was a murder here was a prank call," Maverick says.

"Finn Huxley is innocent," says Max. "Nothing happened here tonight. You were on a patrol, got some donuts and went back to the station. No one has been hurt."

The cops nod, turn and walk away.

"Now what?" Trix asks. "The cops are gone, but what are we going to do about Vincent and Aiden?"

Max turns to Poppy. "I'm sorry, my love. But if Aiden is involved in all this…"

Poppy's mouth turns into a hard line. "It's okay," she says. "I lost Aiden years ago. And he's dangerous. If you have to…" She takes a breath. "Well, you have to do what you have to do to keep everyone safe."

"My love," Max says, taking her face in his hands. "Some vampires just go bad, and there's nothing any of us can do about it. While the three of us in this room have tried desperately to cling to our humanity, many don't—can't. I know better than most."

"You knew Aiden?" I ask Poppy.

She nods. "He was my brother."

There's another knock on the door, and this time when Max answers it, two very large burly men in jeans and flannel shirts stand there glaring at us.

"Girls," says Maverick. "Looks like it's your ride."

CHAPTER SIXTY-FOUR

inn

BRANDON ARRIVES FIRST, giving me a solid handshake. "We will get through all this, son," he says. There's something about his firm grip, and the way he calls me son, that makes me believe him.

Juliette arrives and throws her arms around me. "Finn! What the fuck is going on? How the hell is a *vampire* being accused of murder?!"

"I'll explain it all when everyone is here."

But as the other Fraternity members begin to arrive, everyone placing their phones in a box by the door to assure absolute secrecy, it's clear that not all of them are on my side like Brandon and Juliette are. Only Brandon has the key to the box, and while it's killing me not to be able to text April and make sure she's okay, I understand why we have to do it, and I trust Maverick, even if I don't trust the werewolves.

"We should have let Vincent and his brother Cassius into the Fraternity a hundred years ago!" says Vivian Stadler, an old Hollywood vampire with a short dark bob, who narrows her eyes at me. "All of this could have been avoided!"

"You've forgotten *why* we didn't let them in," Maverick says.

"And what do you know about the Fraternity?" Christian Stadler, Vivian's old Hollywood husband with a crazy mustache, asks him. "You've only been in it for a few decades!"

"I implore you," says Brandon. "Let's all stay calm and talk about this rationally."

"The time for rationality is over," says Sloane Paxton, one of the biggest stars from the brat pack movies in the eighties who still doesn't look a day over eighteen.

"She's right, it's time to fight these fuckers to Certain Death," Juliette says. "I killed Lottie, and I have no reservations in staking the others who were involved in *my* kidnapping."

"Killing Lottie isn't the flex you think it is," says Rose Chan, CEO of a huge streaming service. "Not all of us here were unhappy with her leadership." She shoots Brandon, our actual leader, a look of distaste. His expression stays blank, giving nothing away. But he must know that not everyone in the Fraternity wants him as their leader.

"She kidnapped and mind controlled four of us!" Juliet exclaims. "Don't lie to yourself and think she wouldn't have done the same to you. We need to take down Vincent and Aiden *now* or we'll never be free."

"We believe they are working with a fae," Brandon says.

There are gasps of shock and horror, like *this* is the worst thing that a vampire can do.

"Fae magic was used, which is why Finn was unable to glamour the police," he finishes.

"You were unable to glamour? That's unheard of!" Sloane gasps.

"A vampire being arrested is unheard of," Maverick says. "And I can assure you, in all my time on earth, this is the first time I have seen a vampire unable to glamour someone."

Brandon clears his throat. "Finn was told that unless he pleads guilty and goes to prison, his human consort will be killed."

"And clearly, we can't let either of those things happen," Maverick says.

"Let him rot in prison," says Vivian.

Juliette shoots her a dark look.

"May I remind you that when you take an oath to the Fraternity that includes a promise to be protected by *and* to protect all members?" Brandon says. "That's what this community has always been about. I know it may seem like its purpose is for the vampire elite to gather, to work together to keep power in our hands instead of others, but at its core—this is a family."

"Some fucking family," says Rose.

Brandon gives her a disappointed look. "If any one of our members was in this situation, we would be here, having this conversation. We all have each other's backs. And if you don't have Finn's back, you are free to leave. But remember we will not have yours if it's you under dark fae influence next."

My heart warms at his words. I'd never thought about the Fraternity as a family before, but even with the dick-heads here who clearly want me to rot in prison, most of them seem to want to take these assholes down as much as I do.

"Look," I say. "I can't let anything happen to April. I will go to prison if I have to. I don't care. I just need her safe. This isn't about saving *me*, it's about saving yourselves, taking back the blood supply so no more innocent humans are drained out on the streets."

"Wait, this is connected to the blood supply?" Sloane asks.

Brandon nods. "Vincent and Aiden have taken control of the blood supply so that they can charge ten times as much for blood at the club."

"Smart business move," says Christian.

"I believe it is time for the Fraternity to change," Brandon says, looking around at the group gathered. "The Fraternity must move with the times. We can no longer condone this attitude that we do not care about human life. All life must be considered sacred."

Noise erupts from the table, some agreeing, some disagreeing.

"He wants to get rid of Donnas!"

"How are we supposed to live off that synthetic shit?!"

"Accidents happen, man!"

"Humans are inferior, they are our *food*!"

"I'd rather die the Certain Death!"

"Calm down, please!" Brandon calls out. "We are still vampires. We must still feed. But we must not *kill*. We can feed from our victims without killing them."

"But it's our nature!"

"I only kill really bad people though!"

"It's the way it's always been!"

Brandon shakes his head. "Look to Finn as your example. He's been a vampire for over a year, and he's never made a kill."

This is news to many of the members here. Some gasp, some look impressed, others are completely disgusted by me.

"Brandon," says Maverick. "Don't you think this is going a bit far?"

"All I'm saying is that I think this is what we should be working towards."

"This is rich coming from you," says Christian. "Have you forgotten all the blood orgies you used to host back in the fifties?"

"No. I have not forgotten. I still have nightmares about them. Many humans were drained at my parties, but the girl who was drained and thrown into my pool still haunts my dreams."

Silence finally descends.

"We all have those nightmares," Maverick says. "I have them about the war."

"I have them about Lottie," Max says.

"I have them about Vincent and Aiden," I say. "Because it wasn't that long ago that I was a human, being drained by them to an inch of my life. You were all there once. You were all turned at some point." I take a breath. Now that I have their attention, I need to keep talking. "I'll go to prison. I have to keep April safe, but this is just the beginning. They are using me to send a message to the rest of you. If they can put a vampire in prison, what else are they capable of?"

"It's time to end this," Juliette says. "It's time to end *them*."

"It's nearly dawn," says Brandon. "As soon as the sun goes down tonight, we will find them, and we will end them."

"I thought you said no killing?" Rose says, folding her arms over her chest.

"I said no killing humans," Brandon says. "But any vampire who fucks with a member of my fraternity will always be free game."

"And what about the fae who's responsible?" Christian asks.

"We must tread carefully, we don't want another uprising," Brandon says. "But I will not sit back and let the fae use their dark symbols on us. I will protect you all with my life. That is my promise to you as your leader."

"We must feed," says Vivian. "If we are going to kill our enemies tonight, we must be strong."

"Some of us need to rest during daylight," says Sloane.

"If you need to go home and rest, rest," says Brandon. "Anyone who would like to spend the day feeding and gaining strength is welcome to stay."

And that's how the blood orgy at my place begins.

CHAPTER SIXTY-FIVE

pril

T HE THREE OF us get in the back of a *werewolf's* truck, while the two massive guys we don't even know sit in the front.

"I'm Hunter," says one of them, a dark-haired guy with a full beard and more tattoos that I knew could fit on a person's skin.

Of course he's called Hunter. He's a *werewolf.*

"Russ," says the guy next to him, a redhead who looks like he should be chopping wood or carrying water around some mountain hideaway.

"Where are you taking us?" Trix asks.

"Skid Row," Hunter says.

"Isn't Skid Row meant to be one of the most dangerous places in LA?" I ask.

Hunter just laughs. "Not for us. And not for you if you're with us."

The sky is just starting to lighten, and my stomach grumbles. I don't even remember the last time I ate. I think it was Lunch with Trix after we'd been to the boutique. I was too nervous to eat before the premiere, and then everything changed in a heartbeat.

How was that only yesterday?

"Can we stop somewhere for breakfast?" Trix asks after my stomach does a particularly loud rumble.

"Not until we get back on wolf turf. It's not safe for you, and Maverick has asked us to protect you at all costs," says Hunter.

"So, where's good to eat in Skid Row?" Trix asks.

"We'll take you to the bar," Russ says. "No vampire would dare walk in there."

"Apart from Maverick," Trix says.

"Yeah, apart from him." Hunter's jaw tightens.

"Why would Maverick go to a werewolf bar?" I ask.

"Oh, you don't know about the Order of Concordia?" asks Trix.

"The what?"

"It's a secret order of four members — one wolf, one fae, one witch and one vampire. Maverick is the vampire and Claudia is the werewolf," Trix explains.

"Plus, we're in a truce with the werewolves," says Poppy. "Max helps them out financially."

"And in exchange for his money, we don't kill any vampires," Hunter says.

"What are you getting for helping us?" I ask.

"It's a favor," Russ says. "And having powerful vampires owe you one is never a bad thing."

THE BAR IS A DIVE. Our two new werewolf friends gesture for us to take a seat at a booth right in the back, far from the door and window, and then an older woman brings the three of us some slightly burned pancakes and cups of coffee.

A wave of homesickness passes over me. The first one I've had since I got to LA. But looking down at these pancakes just makes me suddenly miss Loretta and a decent plate of waffles. Then I think of my dad, wondering what he's doing, how he's coping without me. And now that I'm sitting here in this werewolf hideout because two bad vampires want to kill us all, I realize he was right. LA really *is* dangerous.

I take a sip of coffee. It tastes bitter, but it's warm, and it's caffeine and I need it.

"I don't like how that woman is looking at us," Poppy says, wringing her hands under the table and speaking for the first time since we left Finn's place.

I look over, and she's right. The older woman who served us is staring over at us in a way that I don't like either.

"Maverick wouldn't have sent us here if he didn't think we'd be completely safe," Trix says. "He trusts them, and that's good enough for me."

It should be good enough for me too, but I don't like any of this. I should be with Finn. Wherever he is.

"Poppy, are you okay?" Trix asks.

She shrugs and then shakes her head. "No. Not really. This is all my fault."

"How is any of this your fault?" I ask her.

"If it wasn't for Aiden—"

"Aiden was always going to go bad," Trix says. "If anything, you're the only person who really tried to help him."

"You can't blame yourself for the choices your brother makes," I say. "That's on him."

"God, these pancakes are awful," says Trix, spitting a bite into a napkin.

They are awful, but I'm too hungry not to eat. I cover them with syrup and tuck in.

Poppy stares into her pancakes. "He's not my brother. Not really. Aiden lost his humanity," she says. "He's not Aiden anymore. He's something else."

"Why do some vampires lose their humanity, and others try to hold on to theirs?" I ask. "Finn is desperately trying to hang on to his."

"Finn *wants* to hold on," Poppy says. "That's the difference. Aiden didn't have the will or the desire to hold on to his." She takes a breath. "When Lottie kidnapped me, he had a chance to let me go, to set me free. He could have saved me, but he didn't. It was then that I knew *my* Aiden was gone."

Trix squeezes Poppy's hand. "I'm so sorry, Poppy. This can't be easy."

"It's not," she says. "But he's framing Finn and threatening to kill April. It will only be a matter of time before he comes after all of us. It's time for this to end. Once and for all."

"You're right," Trix says.

Poppy looks up from her plate, a tear rolling down her face. "I just hope it's not Max who has to do it. You know. To Aiden."

Trix nods. "I'll call Maverick." She grabs her phone out of her purse. "Tell him that when it happens, it needs to be him."

Poppy nods. "Thank you."

Trix walks away to make the call, but when she comes back, her face is pale.

"Trix, what is it?" I ask.

"No answer." She looks around her like she thinks she's being watched.

"Are you worried?" Poppy asks.

"I shouldn't be. If something was wrong, I'd know. The blood bond would tell me."

Poppy's mouth twists. "When Maverick drank that bad blood—"

"Bad blood?" I ask.

Trix nods. "When the vampires were kidnapped by Lottie and Aiden, they were forced to drink some kind of blood that shut down their abilities."

"You don't think—"

Trix plasters a smile on her face. "Our guys will be fine," she says.

But she doesn't sound so sure.

"I'm going to get some more coffee," I tell them, looking at our empty cups. Old diner habit, I guess, filling cups. Also, I just really need something to do.

"Hey, hun, what can I get for you?" asks the older woman who brought our food.

"Just some more coffee, thanks."

She leans over and taps my hand. "Everything will be okay in the end," she tells me with a grandmotherly smile.

Her words comfort me as she goes about making the coffee.

A phone sitting on the bar rings, and she grabs it quickly. "Hello?"

But it's too late. I've already seen the name. I know who she's speaking to.

"Everything is fine," she says. She looks at me and smiles. "Take a seat, honey. I need to go out back and grab some more coffee. I'll bring it out to you." She disappears into a back room, but instead of going back to the table, I follow her, standing outside the room she's just walked into while shivers run down my spine.

Maybe I'm wrong. Maybe it's a different Vincent. I'm sure they have werewolves called Vincent, right?!

"I'll keep them here for now," she says, only just audible

through the door. "The boys don't know anything... No... only me and Claudia are in on it..."

In on what?!

And *Claudia?* Didn't Maverick say she would keep us *safe?*

I try to calm myself. I don't know what I'm hearing. I could have this all wrong.

"Of course I won't kill them, I'll leave that to you."

Okay, what the fuck?

Fuck, fuck, fuck!

I rush back to the table.

"We're not safe here," I whisper to Trix and Poppy. "We need to go. *Now.*"

"What are you talking about?" asks Trix. "I thought you were getting coffee?"

"Claudia's in on it, and that older woman too."

"In on what?" Poppy asks.

"There's no time!" I grab my purse. "Come *on!*" I rush out of the bar, Trix and Poppy on my heels.

Hunter is standing out front with a cigarette in his hand, Russ stands a few feet back, avoiding the smoke.

The boys don't know anything.

"I need your truck," I tell Hunter.

He just laughs and takes a drag of his cigarette. "What the fuck for?"

"We're not safe here," I tell him.

"If you're with us, you're safe. I promise you," he says.

"Claudia is in on it," I tell him.

His eyes narrow. "In on what?"

"I don't know!" I yell. "That older woman in there was talking to Vincent on the phone, making some kind of deal with him about killing us!"

Russ places a hand on my shoulder. "Hey, just take a breath."

I shove him off me. "I don't need a breath! I need a fucking ride!"

I look behind me, and the woman is off the phone, her face in a scowl as she looks around the bar for us. She doesn't see that we're outside, but if we don't go soon, she will.

"Please help us," I plead, hoping the woman in the bar was in fact referring to Hunter and Russ when she said the boys weren't in on it.

Hunter shrugs and nods to the truck. "Fine. Get in, girls."

CHAPTER SIXTY-SIX

pril

APRIL: We weren't safe. They were working with Vincent!
April: Why aren't any of you replying? We are all worried sick!

"ARE you sure you heard what you think you heard?" Russ asks, turning to look at me.

"It was definitely Vincent," I tell him as adrenaline courses through my veins.

"Could be another Vincent," Hunter says, his eyes on the road ahead.

"It is a vampire name," says Russ. "And I can't think of another Vincent Beverly would be talking to."

"Why the fuck would she have him in her phone with his real name?" Russ asks.

"Because she's old. Old people don't think about those things," Trix says.

"What does this mean?" Russ looks over at Hunter as he drives, I don't even know where.

"It means that the truce between vampires and werewolves is null and void. Again." Hunter sighs. "And I've got three vampire girlies in my truck."

"What the hell do we do now?" asks Russ.

"Please don't kill us!" Poppy begs.

"If you hurt us, Maverick will rip your fucking heads off!" Trix exclaims.

Oh fuck! Fuck, fuck, fuck!

"Max gave you all that money!" Poppy says through her sobs. "And now you're going to kill us, anyway!"

"Wait," says Hunter. "You and Max Montrose?"

She nods. "Yes. Max is my boyfriend."

Hunter rubs a hand over his jaw. "He paid for Jayden's treatment."

"Yes, Claudia's son's hospital bills," says Poppy.

"Fuck," says Hunter.

"A vampire saved your kid's life?" Russ says. "What a head fuck."

"You and Claudia?" Poppy asks.

Hunter shakes his head. "It was just a one-night thing that somehow resulted in the most amazing kid in the world."

"So, wait, all that money that's been coming into the community… that's vampire money?" asks Russ.

"Yeah," says Hunter. But that's supposed to be on the down low. I only know because I forced Claudia to tell me where she got the money for Jayden."

"Why would Claudia be in on some plan to kill the vampire girls?" Russ asks. "After everything the vamps did to help her and our pack?"

"Because she's a racist. Has always hated the other supernaturals. Part of the reason I could never be with her. Unless…"

"Unless?" Russ nudges.

"Vincent is offering her more money. In that case, a better deal could be really good for the pack."

The three of us in the back exchange looks. If Hunter decides to side with Claudia, the mother of his child…

"I don't trust any vamps," Russ says. "But Max has made good on his word. Vincent? I don't trust him for shit."

"So, you'll help us?" Poppy asks.

Hunter takes a breath. "It's complicated. If Claudia finds out I helped you, she could try to stop me seeing Jayden. I can't risk that." He grips the wheel. "We can't. I'm sorry."

Russ shakes his head. "But if we let them go and something happens to them, Maverick will rip our fucking throats out."

Trix's phone pings.

"Oh, thank fuck," she says, grabbing her phone out of the pocket of her jeans. But when she looks down at it, she gasps, and all color leaves her face. "No. Not again."

"What? What is it?" Poppy asks.

"They have them. Vincent and Aiden. They have our guys."

"Who has our guys?" I look at Trix's phone and shake my head. "No. No!"

UNKNOWN NUMBER: We have Maverick. Come to Vincent's and say your goodbyes. You have one hour before he's staked to Certain Death.

MY PHONE VIBRATES and Poppy's phone pings. We both have the same message.

They have Finn.

"No," I say again, unable to find any other words. "How would they—? How could—?"

"It can't be," Poppy says, tears rolling down her cheeks. "I would have known, I would have felt it down the blood bond!"

Trix shakes her head. "The blood bond has been blocked before…"

"What do you mean, they have your guys?" Hunter asks. "Who has them?"

"Vincent and Aiden," Trix says, her face turning from blank horror to fierce determination. "And we're going to go get our guys and rid the world of some bad vampires."

"There's nothing I'd love more than to shift and rip apart some vampires," says Russ.

Hunter grunts and lets out a howling sound, and for a second, I wonder if he's going to shift right here in the driver's seat. "We can't come with you, it could end in another war between the clans. But we can get you some weapons."

APRIL

"OH MY GOD," I whisper, taking in the wooden stakes, crossbows, rifles filled with silver bullets, crucifixes and bottles of holy water filling a secret closet in the back of Hunter's apartment.

"Take anything you want," Hunter says.

"This is a bad idea," says Russ. "There's no way you girls can take on Vincent."

Trix picks up a crossbow like she knows exactly what she's doing. "You underestimate the power of three bad bitches on a holy mission."

Poppy grabs a shotgun from the wall. "I shot a vampire once. I can do it again." She looks fucking terrified, but I absolutely believe she'll do it.

Hunter's eyebrow quirks at her, and then he turns to me. "Have *you* taken on a vampire before?"

I shake my head. The closest I've come to taking on a vampire was watching Finn break my doorframe.

Hunter passes me a bottle of holy water. I shake my head. "Holy water doesn't work."

"How do you know?" asks Russ.

I think of Finn's hands in my panties in the church. "Just a hunch."

Hunter looks at me curiously. "Take whatever you think works, and whatever you think you can handle."

I start going through the armory. I stuff wooden stakes down the waistband of my jeans and in my bra, and then I check the weight of the guns like I have any idea how to shoot one.

Ten minutes later, the three of us are waiting for an Uber on a corner, packing some serious heat. Two revolvers with silver bullets are wedged into the back of my jeans and I have a crossbow I can barely lift in my arms.

Our driver arrives and frowns through his window. "You're going to need to put your weapons in the trunk."

Gotta love LA.

CHAPTER SIXTY-SEVEN

pril

"THE ONLY THING *that can kill a vampire is a stake through the heart. Beheading can work as long as the head and the body never find their way back together. There have been instances of a vampire body without a head killing a human, and a head can still bite without a body! There are only three types of wood that can kill a vampire, so chances are pretty good that if you get staked by a chair leg or a piece of banister that it won't kill you. You can pull it out, and you'll be just fine. If it's one of the bad ones, you're fucked, so try to avoid getting staked as much as possible."*
www.babyvampire.com

WE CLIMB out of the Uber a block away from Vincent's club and get our weapons ready.

"Shooting them with silver bullets slows them down,"

says Poppy. "They can pull the bullets out, but it can buy us time to get close enough to stake them."

"I wish we had some silver chains," says Trix. "Then we wouldn't have to stake them. We could just tie them up, free the guys and let them do it."

"Shoot them with the crossbows," Poppy says. "Right in the heart."

"The bolts aren't the right wood to kill them," Trix says. "But they have silver tips so it will slow them down. Don't stop at one, send a whole bunch into them. Pulling them out will keep them busy."

I clutch my crossbow, heart hammering. I'll do anything to get Finn back, but I'm scared shitless. Scared that I'm going to lose Finn again. This time, forever. Scared that the three of us are going to go in there and die too.

Trix nudges me with her shoulder. "You just stand back, April. Just keep shooting at Vincent and Aiden. I'll stake them."

"I think it has to be me who stakes Aiden," Poppy says. "I started all this, and I need to finish it."

Trix squeezes Poppy's arm. "Poppy. No."

"I'll do it," I tell her, with a sudden rush of confidence. "Trix can't do it. You're best friends. It doesn't matter if we can't be friends after this. It doesn't matter if you hate me for killing your brother."

"April," says Trix.

"It's okay. It's just the way it has to be. If killing Aiden means saving Finn, I have to do it. I know I can do it."

I don't know I can do it.

We approach the club, and the security guards' eyes widen as he takes us in — three young women carrying guns and crossbows.

"Trix?" the security guy asks. "What the fuck is this?"

"We're going in," she says, pointing a gun at him. "And you're not going to call for backup."

He holds up his hands. "Trix, seriously, this is a really fucking bad idea."

Trix just nudges the gun at him. "Get out of the way. Go. Disappear."

He looks towards the club and then back at us. "If I don't stop you, they'll kill me."

"How are you going to stop us?" Poppy asks, lifting her crossbow and pointing it at him.

"You girls are fucking crazy!" he yells before turning and running down the street.

When we wave our weapons at the woman inside the door who takes the cover charge, she just runs straight out.

And then the three of us walk into the packed vampire club. The big band stops playing, and shrieks and screams fill the air as everyone starts running.

"The slayers are here!" Poppy yells out, firing silver bullets into the air.

The Donnas run straight out of the club and vampires scatter, and within moments, the club is empty except for a pretty pink-haired bartender who's holding a phone to her ear.

"Beth?" asks Trix, walking towards her.

Beth slides the phone into her pocket. "Trix."

"Where are our guys?" Trix demands.

"What?" Beth asks.

"Maverick. Max. Finn. Where are they?"

She shakes her head. "I don't know!"

Trix points the crossbow at her. "Where's Vincent?"

Beth raises her arms and nods towards an ornate staircase in the middle of the club. "You should get out of here before he—"

But it's too late. The vampire who can only be the infamous Vincent, walks down the staircase like he owns the place. Of course, he *does* own the place.

"Ladies," he says, giving us an amused smile while he takes us and our weapons in. "I see you got my text messages." He steps towards us and all three of us freeze. "And you've emptied my club." He tuts. "Perhaps I should take this afternoon's earnings out of you three. I expect if I sell you as Donnas I could get a few bucks. All three of you are clearly blood whores."

Trix aims her crossbow at his chest. "We're not blood whores!"

"What are you, then? Vampire slayers?" Vincent laughs and looks over at Beth, who gives a chuckle.

"Where are they?" Poppy demands, holding up her shotgun. "Where is Max?"

"Not here," Vincent says with a shrug. "Some of the Fraternity members had to leave the club earlier last night to go to a Fraternity meeting. I can only assume that's where he is."

Oh fuck. We've been set up.

"Maverick isn't here?" Trix growls. "Finn?"

Vincent laughs. "No, my dears. And you've just walked yourself into my club with no vampire boyfriends to protect you."

Trix screams and pulls the trigger, and a wooden bolt tipped with silver flies through the air, hitting Vincent right in the shoulder.

Beth screams, but Vincent just yanks it out, his eyes narrowed.

Trix shoots him with another bolt, but he's impossibly fast. He pulls it out and lunges towards her.

Poppy pulls the trigger of her shotgun, shooting him three times in the back. It doesn't slow him down. He shoves Trix to the floor, and I just stand there with all these fucking weapons, and I can't *do* anything. I'm frozen. Petrified. Completely immobile.

Fuck!

Poppy shoots Vincent another three times in the back before she throws the gun to the ground. "I'm out of bullets!" She scrambles around for the gun she shoved down the back of her pants.

Do something, April!

Vincent has Trix pinned to the ground. She's struggling, but his grip is like a vise. She's not getting free unless I help her.

"What do you think you're doing?" Vincent growls at her. "With these pathetic werewolf weapons. Who gave them to you?"

"We stole them," Trix says.

"You think three little girls could take on one of the oldest and strongest vampires in the city?" He laughs as he presses his face into Trix's neck. "All you've done is brought me my next three meals."

My stomach flips at the idea of what he's insinuating.

He's going to drink from us all. He's going to fucking drain us.

"We're not little girls," says Trix, somehow managing to knee him in the balls. "We're women!"

He flinches, but only for a second before he's leaning over her again. "Let's see how you think my bite compares to my brothers'."

I suddenly remember Trix's story about Cassius biting her. How she told him no, but he bit her anyway, and he didn't close the wounds.

I can't let Trix get bitten without consent for a second time.

"Fuck you, asshole," I say, finally finding the ability to speak and move again.

I hold my crossbow to his temple, my finger shaking, ready to release the arrow.

But as my bolt is about to fly, I'm grabbed from behind. The bolt flies into nothing, and my crossbow clatters to the ground.

"What the fuck do you think you're doing?" growls a voice in my ear.

"Ending this fucking game you're playing with Finn!" I tell him. "With all of us!"

"Aiden," Poppy says, holding her gun at him with shaking hands. "Please. Let her go."

Oh, fuck, this is Aiden!

The vampire with no humanity. The vampire who would have let his own sister die. He won't have any hesitation ending me.

Rope burns my wrist, and within seconds my hands and feet are tied to a bar stool, and I'm gagged.

Vincent does the same to Trix, and Beth grabs Poppy and ties her to a stool.

Our weapons sit at our feet as the three of us sit, tied and gagged at the bar.

"What now?" Beth asks, folding her arms and taking us in. Trix mumble-screams something to her, but Beth just shrugs. "I'm a vampire now, Trix," she says simply, like this explains why she doesn't care if we live or die.

Oh my god. I'm going to die here.

"This couldn't be more perfect," Vincent lets out a sick laugh. "When Beverly told me you were being taken to Skid Row, I couldn't believe how stupid your vampires could be, leaving you in a den of wolves. When I heard you had fled, I was concerned about my plan for a moment, but one text message was all it took to land you in *my* den. You didn't even ask for proof of life, you just walked right in."

Aiden laughs. "And now you're the bait and it's time to lure in your vampires."

"We can wipe out three members of the Fraternity all in one go. When the Fraternity hears what we've done, they'll change their tune. They'll all profess their obedience to me as the Vampire King of LA."

"You mean *us*," Aiden says, shooting Vincent a look. "We're *both* going to be vampire kings."

"Sure," says Vincent. Even I can tell he has no intention of letting Aiden rule alongside him. I have no doubt he'll stake him as soon as he's no longer useful.

"But first," Vincent walks over to me and roughly grabs a tendril of my hair. "Let's see how your precious Finn feels about you being all tied up here with me."

He grabs his phone out of his pocket and raises the camera to me. "Proof of life," he says.

I just glare at him. I won't give him the satisfaction of thinking I'm scared. Even though I've never been so scared in my life.

Suddenly, a boring life in Lucky doesn't look so bad.

CHAPTER SIXTY-EIGHT

inn

VINCENT: *I've got your girl.*

IT'S early afternoon when the last vampires at the party start leaving with Donnas or going home to get some rest, and Brandon decides we can finally have our phones back.

Hours after getting a string of texts from April telling me she's in trouble with the werewolves. My heart races like a freight train as I check my message from Vincent.

There's a photo attached. It's April sitting on a stool at the bar at Vincent's. Rope tied around her wrists and feet and a gag in her mouth. Her eyes are dry, her gaze determined, but they have her.

They have her.

Rage doesn't begin to describe this feeling. This goes beyond rage. This goes beyond baby vampire fury, this is me about to go on a fucking rampage and rip out the throats of everyone in that fucking vampire club. Especially this motherfucker.

There is no part of me that's able to pull myself out of this. No part that thinks this is a bad idea. Not one single cell in my being doesn't want to bring Certain Death down onto the vampires who did this.

Vincent. Aiden. I'm coming for you. Get ready to die, you motherfuckers!

The plan was to wait until nightfall. That was the plan. That was it. We had no fucking idea what we were going to do. Walk into Vincent's on a Friday night and start staking vampires?!

But fuck the plan. However loose it was. Fuck waiting until nightfall. April is in trouble *now*.

I don't wait. I don't call for backup. I don't call Maverick or Max or Juliette.

I just get in my car, and I drive.

Fast.

I weave in and out of traffic like I'm my own stunt driver, and soon I'm squealing to a stop right on the curb outside the club. Fuck finding parking.

I pop the trunk, grab the baseball bat that Ed gave me back in Lucky, and I go in swinging.

There's no security on the door this afternoon, no one collecting a cover charge.

Good. Because tonight I'm not paying to get in.

They are the ones who are going to pay.

I walk into the club, and for a second my confidence falters. It's not just April tied up at the bar. Trix and Poppy are here and tied up too.

I should have called Maverick and not gone rogue, because it's not just Vincent and Aiden, it's Beth too. Beth, who was tied up next to me and also drained to an inch of her life in the basement outside of Lucky.

I thought we were friends. "Beth, you fucking traitor," I spit.

She just shrugs. "Not my fault you're not vampire enough."

Whatever the fuck that means.

As soon as I lock eyes with April, her terrified eyes begging me to save her, to get her out of this, to take her home to Lucky, to wipe her mind of all of this, the baby vampire rage everyone was so fucking down on is now going to be the only thing that saves us all.

"You fucking pieces of shit!" I yell, swinging my bat at Vincent's head.

He ducks out of my way with ease. "Oh, here comes Baby Ruth!" he laughs.

I take another swing, and then another. I don't hit him, and the irritation of missing my shot only intensifies my rage. With every swing I become crazier, more enraged, more desperate to kill this fucking bastard!

Aiden watches, laughing, and since I can't get a hit on Vincent, I swing for him instead, and this time I connect with my target. I crack Aiden in the head, and he growls, clutching his head.

"Aiden, you pathetic excuse for a vampire," Vincent laughs. "It's just a bit of wood."

Beth smiles at me. Fucking Beth. After we were turned together, I thought we were going to be like brother and sister. I never had a sibling, and I thought maybe she could be that for me. Maybe I could be a brother to her. But instead of letting her maker Brandon guide her, she left and ran away to join the very people who had taken her human life.

It was one thing to put it behind me and come to this club

to get my fix of blood when I needed it, but when Beth turned her back on Brandon and chose Vincent to be her surrogate maker, she made the choice to side with the darkness.

"Come on, Finn," Beth says. "Can't you see this is for the best?"

"How is killing my friends for the best?"

"You think any of them are your friends?" Aiden says with a bloody smile. He's fed recently.

Fuck.

I look over at the girls.

Please don't let that be April's blood. Please, God, no!

"The Fraternity doesn't care about you," Beth says. "And these human girls only want you for The Bite. I know. I remember what it was like. Your girl there doesn't want you. She just wants the fang."

"Bullshit!"

"They just used you, Finn." Beth walks in circles around me, running a finger down my arm and across my back. "Maverick doesn't even like you. Max barely knows you. April was only trying to make her boyfriend back home jealous, and now she only wants The Bite."

April tries to scream, struggling against the rope holding her. I know she's calling bullshit.

"Shut up!" Vincent yells in her direction.

Aiden, clearly trying to make Vincent pleased with him, slaps April across the face, and my rage hits eleven, eleven hundred, eleven fucking thousand.

I lunge for Aiden, swinging my bat at his head again. He ducks, but I turn and hit him in the back instead.

He throws his head back and laughs. "You think you have any power here? You're nothing. A nobody."

I swing for him again, and this time I connect with his fucking mouth. That mouth that has ripped into way too many unwilling victims. He pauses for a second, and I take the chance to hit him again.

A tooth flies out of his mouth and hits the floor on the other side of the club.

"My fucking tooth!" Aiden runs over to the tooth and tries to shove it back in his mouth. I'm behind him again in an instant. I hit him again in the back of the head, and he yelps.

Vincent was right about one thing—Aiden is a pathetic vampire.

I swing for him again while he's down, but Vincent catches the bat, snatches it out of my hands and snaps it in half like it's a pencil. He lets go, and the two pieces fall to the floor. He just laughs and walks back to the bar while Aiden lets out a muffled laugh as he holds his tooth in his bloody mouth. At least I know that's his own blood this time.

I look down at the pieces of the bat. The bat that Ed gave me after that game in Lucky. After I watched April play ball for the first time. After I got my first home run in a decade.

It's time for another fucking home run.

I take the two pieces of the bat, one in each hand, and I run like all bases are loaded. Like this whole game is on me. I'm practically flying through the air as I lunge at Vincent.

He's not ready for it. He thinks I'm pathetic. A baby vampire with a baseball bat.

But I'm not a fucking baby.

And in this moment, right now, I know I get to choose my own story.

I'm not a monster. I'm a fucking hero.

I lift one piece of the baseball bat, and the smile on Vincent's mouth suddenly fades. He knows. He knows it's his time. He knows that after hundreds of years of chaos, blood and death, Finn baby vampire fucking Hardball Hero Huxley is about to deliver his Certain Death.

I stab him in the fucking heart, and he goes down.

"Ash wood, motherfucker!" I tell him, watching while his blood turns black and his immortal life leaves his eyes.

But I don't have a chance to celebrate, because Aiden's on my back, clawing my skin and screaming. It takes no effort to throw him to the ground, straddle him and stick the other half of the bat in his heart, or where his heart would be if he still had one.

Poppy screams as the black ooze begins to seep from his heart.

He was her brother.

And then, even as I watch the blackness of his heart ooze out of him, I have a happy thought. Maybe, if she can ever forgive me for this, I can be like a brother to Poppy, and to Trix. Maybe Maverick and Max can be my family too.

Beth's fingernails dig into my shoulders. "Finn!" she sobs. "How could you?" She grabs a small piece of the wood from the floor and comes at me.

I grab her arms and hold her off. She's surprisingly strong. But she is a new vampire, and I've just killed the two vampires she considered her family. "Beth. Stop! Just go! Get out of here! You can do better than this."

She pauses for a moment. Tears in her eyes, confusion all over her face. Was she being drugged? Was she being controlled by these fuckers in some way? Was she just in too deep? Or did she really want this? To run with this bad crew?

She gets the wood a little closer to my heart, and I can hear April's heart beating loud and fast while she sobs and screams through the gag.

"Beth," I say, as calmly as I can. "You don't want any more blood on your hands."

I grip her wrist tighter, and the wood falls to the ground.

"Get out of here while you still can," I threaten.

She blinks, takes one more look at Vincent and Aiden's bodies, lifeless on the ground, and then she runs.

CHAPTER SIXTY-NINE

pril

FINN IS STILL on the floor, staring at Aiden's lifeless body, when Maverick and Max rush through the door.

"My love!" Max exclaims, making his way over to Poppy and immediately pulling off her gag and rope.

Maverick rushes straight towards Trix, pulling the gag out of her mouth and pulling her into his arms before he even gets her untied. "Finn! What the fuck! What the hell happened here? Is that Vincent? How the fuck did you—"

"I… I killed him," Finn says.

"Your first kill… was Vincent fucking Blake?!" Maverick's eyebrows are shooting off his face.

"Yep," says Finn.

"Well. Fuck." Maverick says.

"Impressive," says Max. "Really. Very well done."

"Where the hell were you?" Trix demands, trying to shove

Maverick off her. "Why didn't you pick up my messages down the blood bond and come save us?"

"I had no idea," he says, shaking his head. "Something must have blocked the blood bond." Maverick moves some of Trix's green hair out of her face and blinks down at her. "I only came because I could feel Finn was in trouble. Jesus, fuck! I am so glad you are okay!" He pulls her into him tighter, and she starts to sob.

I scream through my gag, and Finn startles. He rushes towards me and doesn't even take my gag out. He just pulls me into his chest, and it's only now that I know I'm safe, now that Finn is here and everything is okay again, that the tears finally fall.

"Baby," he says, finally pulling out my gag as I gasp for air. "I'm so sorry, oh god!"

"Finn!" What else is there to say but *Finn*?! I say his name over and over again as he holds me in his arms, and I sob into his chest.

"April, it's all okay now. I'm here. I'll never let anyone hurt you baby." He quickly unties the rope around my wrists, and as soon as he does, I grab his head in my hands and pull his face towards mine, kissing him with a teenage intensity worthy of a cornfield in Arizona. Kissing just hits different when you thought you were going to die just a few minutes ago.

We're all tongues and deep breathing, roaming hands, and I can't get enough of him. Can't get close enough to him. I run my hands up the back of his t-shirt, feeling his warm, smooth skin under my fingers. He pulls me closer to him, groaning into my mouth.

Maverick clears his throat and after a moment Finn pulls back, giving me a hint of a mischievous grin that tells me that desperate kiss was just the beginning of something more.

"What could have blocked the blood bond?" Poppy asks, standing now, tucked into Max's arms.

"Something they gave us at Skid Row," Trix says, wiping her own tears from her cheek. "Not the pancakes. I didn't eat any. It must have been something in the coffee?"

"The werewolves?" Max's gaze darkens. "They were in on this?"

"Claudia and Beverly," I tell him. "But not all of them. Two of them helped us."

"What?" Maverick's eyes burn as he clutches Trix even tighter. "You were in danger? I put you in danger! Oh god, Trix, I am so sorry!" A tear runs down his cheek as he grips her so tight I'm not sure she can even breathe.

"It's okay, I'm okay," Trix says, her own eyes soaking his shirt.

"It's not okay. There's nothing okay about this. I put you in danger. It is my *job* to protect you! I will never leave your side, never again. I will never trust anyone to look after you, no one but me."

"No one but you," she says into his chest.

"So much for the supernaturals working together again," Max says.

Maverick glares at him. "We trusted the wrong people, the wolves put our girls in the hands of our enemies, and our girls nearly fucking died!"

"No, Russ and Hunter helped us. They gave us weapons," Trix explains. "We thought the three of you were in trouble and so we came here by ourselves."

"They did *what? You* did *what?*" Maverick's voice booms.

"We came to save you!" Trix tells him.

"You could have *died!*" Max says, holding onto Poppy with dear life. "Never do that again! Let me die before you put your own life in danger!"

A dapper looking man in a suit with slicked dark blonde

hair bursts into the club. "Sweet lord!" he says, his eyes landing on Vincent, who's now lying in a pool of black ooze.

"I could feel Beth's fear and I—" he looks around, confused. "Where is she?"

"You're a little fucking late, Brandon," Maverick grunts.

"Beth ran," Finn tells him. "I let her go. After I killed Vincent and Aiden."

Brandon's eyes practically pop out of his head. "Finn? You did this?" He looks down at Vincent's lifeless form on the floor of his own club.

Maverick puts an arm around Finn. "I'm so fucking proud of you," he says, and I can tell that Finn is choking back his own tears as he finds himself in Maverick's firm embrace. Finn fists the back of his shirt and takes a deep breath.

It's such a father-son moment. All Finn ever wanted was for his own father to hug him and tell him he was proud to have Finn as his son.

Finn steps out of the embrace and grabs my hand again, his eyes glistening a little at the corners.

"Who was wearing the pendant?" Brandon asks.

"What pendant?" asks Finn.

"Where's Aiden's body?" Max looks around suddenly.

But as I look to where Aiden fell when Finn staked him, he's not there.

CHAPTER SEVENTY

"Oh, fucking hell, not again!" Maverick exclaims. "We need to find that asshole, *now.*"

But he doesn't need to find him. Aiden steps forward with a crossbow pointed at Maverick. "You think you can kill me?" he laughs. "I'm fucking immortal!"

"We're all immortal," says Brandon.

"But I survived the Certain Death." Aiden turns the crossbow towards me, and I hear April scream — that blood curdling scream from the night she first saw my fangs. I squeeze my eyes closed, and I remember everything. That night in Lucky, her showing up in that way too short but oh so sexy dress for lunch, our night in Santa Monica, the kiss on the Ferris wheel, under the pier. The way I practically fucked her outside her hotel room, and then everything we did once we were inside. And then I'm back in church, touching her pulsing hot clit, making her come in God's house. And then, finally, I'm in the cornfield, kissing her, holding her, making a teenage promise to her that I would be her everything if she'll just let me. "You're already my everything," she whispers.

Me and God have never been all that tight, but I figure if there's a time to say a prayer, it might be now.

Dear God, get us out of here. Save us. Save me. And if you can't save me, save her.

Aiden pulls back the crossbow, and the bolt flies towards my heart. I don't know if it's a totally harmless type of wood or if it's one of the three that could deliver the Certain Death.

Everything happens in slow motion. Maverick comes flying at me, wooden bolts flying into his back as he throws me to the ground to protect me and then he lands in a heap by my side.

Trix screams, and when I look up, Aiden smiles that bloody smile down at me.

No, not a bloody smile. A black ooze smile.

He seems to realize it at the same time I do. He wipes his mouth, looks at his finger covered in blackness and then falls down in front of me, a stake wedged in his back. April stands behind him, looking down at him like a piece of shit she's just finally gotten off her shoe.

April staked Aiden in the back of his heart.

April fucking staked a vampire.

Poppy sobs in Max's chest, and Trix pulls the bolts out of Maverick's back while she begs for him to be okay.

"It's okay, babe," he tells her. "It's the wrong kind of wood. Just get the silver tips out. I'll be fine." He sits up, and with a grimace she starts pulling out the bolts.

"Oh, thank fuck you're okay!" she says, falling onto him.

And then April, the woman who just fucking saved my life, all covered in black Certain Death ooze, flies towards me and I pull her into my arms.

"I'm so fucking sorry," I tell her, tears falling from my eyes now. "This is all my fault. Everything. I should never have let you come here. I never should have—"

"Shut the fuck up and just kiss me," she says.

And so I do.

CHAPTER SEVENTY-ONE

inn

BRANDON YANKS the strange pendant from Vincent's throat. "I'll take this and return it to the witches," he says.

Witches?!

Then the sound of slow clapping echoes through the club, and we all turn to the staircase to see who's giving us this mocking ovation.

I've never seen this man before. He's built, with light brown hair that covers his ears. He's dressed in a crisp white shirt and gray suit pants, and even from here I can tell he's wearing a very expensive Rolex, more expensive than my cursed one.

"Well played," he tells us, like he was somehow the mastermind behind all of this.

"James," Max gasps. "What are you—?"

"You're fucking kidding me," says Maverick. "*You?*"

"Me," he says, taking a step towards us.

"Why would you—?" Max shakes his head. "James, I thought we were *friends*!"

"Friends?" James laughs. "You thought we were friends? So fucking naïve."

"You orchestrated all of this?" Brandon asks.

"Who is this motherfucker?" I ask. "And why don't we just kill him too?"

Maverick shoots me a look. "No. We don't kill the fae. No matter how much they fucking deserve it."

Wait, this is James? Max's old fae butler?

"Fae?" April gasps. "He's a fairy?"

James glares at her. "Not a *fairy*. I'm the Fae King of LA."

"And you were going to help Vincent and Aiden become the vampire kings," I say.

"Not Aiden," he laughs. "Just Vincent. We were going to rule together. But I can see that I may now need to change my plan."

"Can we not form a truce of some kind?" Max suggests, holding tightly to Poppy. "What is it that you want?"

"What do I want?" James laughs and then his eyes turn to steel as they narrow at Max. "Retribution."

"But you're free now, what more do you want?" Max asks.

"Free? Oh, Max. I was bound to be your servant for seventy fucking years. You think you can just *free* me and I'll forget everything the vampires did to the fae? You think I'll just forget how many of us were murdered at your hands?"

"Not at my hands," Max says. "I never killed a fae."

"You never stopped the others from killing my family and friends either," James says.

"If we had gone against the Fraternity, we would have been killed," Maverick says.

"So you let my fae brothers and sisters be murdered so that you could live? Pathetic." He folds his arms in front of him. "We want retribution. We want all the vampires who were responsible, and all those who stood by and let it happen imprisoned. For seventy years. At least. And their descendants." He looks at me now. "You must pay for the sins of the fathers."

"I wasn't even alive during the uprising!" I say. "That's fucking bullshit."

James glares at me. "Excuse me?"

"I said," stepping in front of April and taking a step towards him. "That's. Fucking. Bullshit. I am in no way responsible for the shit my own father did, and I'm definitely not responsible for the fact that my maker didn't give his life for your people. Because even if he did, what difference would it have made?" I grab a gun from the floor, which I hope still has at least one more silver bullet in it.

"Finn," Maverick warns.

I take another step towards this James asshole. "If Max and Maverick had stood up to the vampires who were killing the fae, do you think it would have stopped them? No, it wouldn't. They'd be dead alongside all the people you loved. And without Maverick, we never would have had the *Road Rage* movies. Without Max, we'd never have that *Angels All Around Us* movie that won all those Oscars."

"You think the fae care about *movies*?" James scoffs.

"James," says Poppy. "You know Max. You know he helps so many people. He has such a big heart. He gives so much money to so many causes. He's saved so many animals, and aren't the fae supposed to care about nature?"

James rolls his eyes. "Of course we care about nature!"

"But you care about money more," says Maverick. "How much do you want?"

"I can make as much as I need in my sleep. I don't want your money. All I want is for my granddaughter to live her life without living in fear of vampires."

"Natalie," I say. "Natalie is your granddaughter?"

"She was working for you?" Brandon asks.

"The watch," I say. "She gave it to me, said it was from Rolex, but it was from you."

James shakes his head. "Natalie is not involved. She knew nothing about the watch. I only intercepted the package. All I want is for Natalie and the other fae to live freely, and the only way to do that is to lock you all away in cages."

I lift the gun and point it towards him. "And how exactly are you going to do that?"

The doors to the club swing open and the entire Fraternity, the most powerful vampires in the city, fill the space.

"Vincent and Aiden are dead," says Brandon, filling them in quickly. "And James Truscott has been pulling the strings this whole time. This is about fae retribution."

"For the uprising?" Christian Stadler asks. "For God's sake, man, get over it! You're free now, why spend your immortality crying over the past?"

"I think you're a little outnumbered," says Juliette, looking around at the club that's full of vampires now, all staring at James. "And while most of the vampires here would be too scared to kill you in case it breaks their souls or whatever, I'm not like most vampires. I don't give a fuck about my soul." She grabs a gun from the ground and points it at him.

"Me neither," says Sloan, grabbing a crossbow and pointing it at him.

"I wouldn't usually kill a fae," says Rose. "But I would do it to protect my family."

My stomach does a little flutter as I realize that *this* is my family. All these fucked-up immortals, with all their quirks and trauma, all their suffering and hurt, they are all here for *me*.

"If you hurt any one of us," I tell James, "I will come for you, and I will kill you. I don't care about my soul either."

A rumble of agreement goes through the room, and James takes a very small step backwards.

"This isn't over," he says. "I will not rest until none of you can cause harm

"Yes it is," I tell him. "This is over. This is where the story ends. This is where we all finally get our happily ever afters, and I will do anything it takes to make sure of that."

His mouth moves into a hard line, and for a moment it looks like he's going to say something else, but he doesn't. He just turns and leaves.

And two seconds later, the room erupts in applause and cheers, and everyone starts grabbing me and hugging me and I have never felt so at home than I do in this moment, surrounded by my vampire family, my vampire daddy Maverick, my vampire uncles Brandon and Max and my beautiful human girl, April.

CHAPTER SEVENTY-TWO

inn

SOMEHOW, me and April killing Vincent and Aiden turns into another blood orgy at the club, which thanks to glamouring Vincent's lawyers over a video call, now belongs to Brandon and the Fraternity, and me and April are the guests of honor. I shouldn't be surprised. Everyone here wants to celebrate, and for most vampires, that means Donnas and Dons, blood and sex.

The New Order of Concordia is disbanded, for now at least. But the Fraternity of the Everlasting Rose is stronger than ever.

We stay for a few drinks. Whiskey for me and coke for April, while the members of the Fraternity all come to congratulate us and wish us well.

But before it starts getting too messy, I know I need to get April home.

"I don't want to go to my place," I tell her, as we stand out the front of Vincent's, sorry, *Brandon's*, waiting for an Uber. "Not after everything that happened there—"

April places two fingers against my lips. The warmth of her hand on me burning in the best way. "We can go back to my hotel. No one is after us now. We'll be safe there."

"I'll get you another room. Just in case they told Beth or someone else."

We slide into the back of the car, and April scoots over, sitting in the middle so there's no space between us. She puts her head on my shoulder and pushes her fingers into mine. Her heart rate is high, and I know she's thinking exactly what I am.

This is our time.

When we arrive at the hotel, I go straight to reception and book the best suite they have available. I also have a quick word with the concierge, who recognizes me immediately. I give him my house key, and he quickly rushes off to get what I need, assuring me it will be delivered to my room within the hour.

I take April's hand, and we ride the elevator to the top floor, and then I pull her into the penthouse suite that overlooks the beach and the Ferris wheel that's dancing with light.

"Wow," April says, taking in the room, which is bigger than both our houses back in Lucky combined. "This is too much," she whispers.

I squeeze her hand and pull her into me. "Nothing is too much for you, April." I place a light kiss on her forehead. "There's no pressure for us to do anything tonight," I tell her.

"Are you kidding?" she asks with a nervous laugh. "We were basically just crowned king and queen of the vampire prom, and now we're in the most beautiful hotel room I've ever seen. This is the most perfect night for us."

"But are you okay? After everything that happened? I

mean, you just killed a vampire. Maybe you just want to sleep, or eat or—"

She shushes me with a kiss. "All I want is you, Finn."

I can't help but grin at her. Sure, we had one hell of a day, but we're safe now. No Vincent, no Aiden, no threats, and no one coming for us. At least not tonight anyway.

"But I think I will take a shower first. There are a few black spots I'd like to remove."

"Me too," I tell her. "But you go first."

"Or we could go in together?" she suggests with a shrug.

I grab her by the waist, throw her over my shoulder and run towards the bathroom. Decorated with shiny white tiles and gold accents, there's a huge tub with gold feet and a rain shower that's definitely big enough for the both of us.

I gently put her down and then I grip the hem of my shirt. April bites her lip as I tear it off, throwing it onto the floor. She reaches out, running her fingers over my chest, and it feels like heaven. Her featherlight touch after all the fighting and killing is like a balm for my weary soul.

I step towards her, pushing her hair behind her ear and taking in her beautiful features. I press my finger to the mole on her bottom lip, and she pushes her tongue out, licking my finger and then opening her mouth to suck on it. The motion goes straight to my cock, and I can feel myself hardening against her. It's the same beautiful way she sucked my cock that night, and I let out a moan as I watch her lips move up and down my finger.

"Fuck, April, what are you doing to me? You know I still need to maintain some control here," I warn. "I still don't know that I'm going to be able to—"

She releases her mouth from my finger. "Yes. You can. Trust yourself, Finn. I do." She pulls her own t-shirt off, revealing a dark blue lacy bra. The lace is thin, and I can see her hard nipples through the fabric.

"Oh god," I murmur, as I bring my mouth to one nipple, cupping and squeezing her other breast with my hand.

She makes a noise like she's so fucking into this, and I have no idea how I'm going to be naked with her in this shower and not have sex with her.

But maybe this can be how I prove it to myself. If I can stand in this shower with her without biting her or fucking her or hurting her, then I can do anything.

"Do you wear your necklace in the shower?" I ask.

She shakes her head.

"I can't touch it," I tell her. "Silver."

Her eyes widen, and then she unclasps the necklace, gives it a little squeeze and then places it on the marble vanity.

I run my fingers down over her neck and then reach to her back and unclasp her bra, letting it fall to the floor. "Fuck, your tits are gorgeous," I say, holding the weight of them in both hands.

"Thanks," she says with a laugh.

I pull her to me, pressing my hard chest to her softness. Goddamn, it feels fucking divine. I kiss her gently on the neck and feel my fangs start to tingle.

Fuck.

"Do you want to bite me?" she asks.

"Yeah."

"I want you to."

"Not yet," I tell her. "First, I want to prove to myself that I can act like a gentleman in this shower with you."

"Okay," is all she says before stepping away and unzipping her jeans. She tugs them down, revealing a matching dark blue scrap of lace.

Fuuuuck.

"Turn around, baby," I say.

She turns, and her ass looks fucking magnificent in this thing. But it will look better on the bathroom floor. I step forward, running my hands over her naked shoulders and down her back. "Fuck, April. Fuck," I say, at a complete loss for words.

"I hope so," she says with a giggle.

I slip my fingers into the waistband of her barely their panties and tug them down until they're on the floor and she's completely naked.

I run a hand over my face and across my jaw as she turns around to face me, and I take all of her in. "This is the closest I've ever been to your completely naked body," I say, unable to take my eyes off her.

"You should get used to it," she says. My eyes meet hers, and, holy fuck, I love this woman.

"I'll never get used to it."

I reach into the shower and turn on the water, making sure it's warm enough. "Get in," I tell her as I unbuckle my belt and let my own jeans fall to the floor.

Her eyes dance over the erection tenting in my boxer briefs. She grins up at me and does as I say, getting into the shower and under the water.

And Jesus, the way she looks as the water falls over her makes my briefs tent even harder.

I slip them off and I join her, standing under the warm water and wondering what I did to deserve this woman.

I grab the liquid soap and squeeze plenty into my hands, and then I go about exploring every inch of her body. Cleaning her, caressing her, loving her.

When I'm done, *I'll never be done*, she washes my chest, shoulders and back, but when her fingers brush my cock, I grunt and pull back. "No." I tell her. "Not yet."

She pouts, but nods and steps back while she watches me run shower gel over my painful erection. I hope the concierge has what I need and *fast*.

I wrap April in a towel, pat her down and then dress her

in a fluffy white robe, hoping that I'm going to be taking it off her again very fucking soon.

I dry myself and dress in a robe also, and then check out the front of the door for my delivery.

"Thank fuck," I say, taking the box in my hands and bringing it back inside. "Bedroom," I tell her. "Before my balls burst into flames."

She laughs at my pain, but does as I ask, bouncing into our huge bedroom for the night. And I thank God the bed has bedposts.

I pass her the package. "This is for you."

An eyebrow quirks. She opens the package and lifts out a roll of silver rope. "What's this?"

"Let me check it's legit." I grab the rope. "Ah, fuck! Yes. It's legit!" I try to shake the stinging, burning sensation from my hand, but I guess I better get used to it if I'm about to be tied up with it.

"What's it for?" she asks.

"I want you to tie me up with it." I lie down on the bed and hold my hands up to the bedpost. "It will keep you safe. If I lose my fucking mind over you while we're having sex, if I bite you and can't stop, you can get away. You'll have total control."

"But it will hurt you."

"Hurting you will hurt me more."

"Are you sure?"

"So fucking sure."

She starts wrapping the rope around my wrists, and I squeeze my eyes shut, trying to ignore the burn.

"No," she says. "I won't do it."

"You have to do it. It's the only way I'm going to trust myself to fuck you. At least the first time. Maybe the first couple of times. First one hundred times probably."

"You think we're going to do it a hundred times?"

"Jesus, I hope so. I hope we do it thousands, tens of thousands, hundreds of thousands of times."

Her lips twist into a smirk.

"April. Just fucking tie me up. It's what I want. Don't question me. Please."

She nods and finishes tying me to the bed. I tug on the ropes, and she's tied me up good. If it was normal rope, I could break it in a second, but the silver weakens my grip, and I can't move. I'm completely at her mercy. And there's nowhere I'd rather be.

She reaches for the tie of my robe, and I feel my own pulse race.

This is it. Fucking finally. I get to give myself to this woman. I get to take her as mine.

This is the happily ever after I never thought I'd be deserving of. But I proved it to myself tonight. By killing the bad vampires, I proved to myself, and everyone else, that I am a good one.

And now I'm going to prove that I can be a good guy for April.

She opens my robe, runs her fingers down over my chest and then grips my cock. Hard.

"Fuck!" I gasp.

"You like that?" she asks, giving it a powerful tug while she grins up at me.

"Yes, of course I fucking like it!"

"Do you like this?" She bends over me and licks the pre-cum off the tip of my cock, and my whole body shudders in response. "Is that a yes?" she asks, not waiting for an answer as she wraps her lips around my cock.

"Fucking hell, April!" I practically yell before finally catching my breath and settling into the delicious movement and the softness of her lips, while I thrust into the wetness of her mouth. "If you keep doing that, I'm going to come," I tell her. "And I'd rather save it for your pussy."

She releases her lips from my cock and looks up at me with a huge, light-filled grin, her deep blue eyes full of want. Her fingers find the tie of her own robe. She opens it and drops it to the floor.

"You're so fucking beautiful," I tell her, itching to touch her, to drag my hands over her tits and belly and down to her pussy. But my hands need to be tied.

"Yeah?"

"So much, yeah."

"If you come inside me, I won't get pregnant?"

I shake my head. "No. I can't have kids. My sperm is dead." Okay, probably not the hottest way I could have put that.

"But you have some in a sperm bank somewhere, right?"

"Yeah."

"How would you feel…" she says, gripping my cock with her hand again, "…if I got some?"

"Wait, what?"

"Well, I know this is new and all. But I think I really want to have your baby."

Okay, why the fuck am I crying?! Jesus!

She leans forward and kisses away the tears. "I guess we can talk about that more later. If it's something you want."

"It's everything I want," I tell her, finding her lips and kissing her as hard as I can without being able to hold her face.

"You okay? Not burning too much?" she asks.

"You're kind of distracting me from the pain."

"Good." She grins as she straddles me, holding my shoulder with one hand and my cock in the other, lining us up.

"You're so fucking wet, warm, fuck!"

She grins at me, places both hands now on my shoulders, and she oh so slowly slides herself down onto my cock and my whole fucking world changes. She slides her tight, wet pussy up and down on my shaft, and I can't believe this is finally happening. It feels so damn good, and I think I'm going to blow my load way too fast. Just like I would have that night after prom.

But she's enjoying it too much for me to blow just yet.

"Oh, Finn," she gasps, lowering herself down and taking a little more of my cock each time she slides up and down on me. "Why did we wait so long to do this again?" She lets out a groan, and I wish I could touch her, kiss her, grab her hips and thrust myself into her harder.

But no. This is the way it has to be this first time. There's plenty of time for that later.

"Touch your clit," I say. "While you ride me."

She moves a hand to the place where her pussy and my cock meet and runs circles with her fingers while she rides my cock, and it's the most beautiful thing I've ever fucking seen. The way her body slides up and down on me, the way her breasts jiggle, the way I think I'm going to come every time she slides down onto my cock as it totally fills her. The way she bites her lip and looks down at me like she's having the time of her fucking life.

Me too, baby. Holy fuck, me too.

Her body starts to tense, and I know she's moments away from the first orgasm she's going to have with my cock inside her. The first of what I know will be so many.

"Give me your neck," I tell her.

She leans forward, pressing her neck into my mouth. My fangs protrude, and, knowing that she can get away at any point if she needs to, I sink my teeth into her.

And holy fucking hell, nothing has ever tasted or felt as good as having this woman ride my cock like it's her own personal sex toy while her blood is pouring into my mouth. Sweet and warm, April's blood tastes like apple pie, waffles with syrup, Arizona sunrises, LA sunsets, cornfields and baseball diamonds and pure fucking happiness.

She's about to reach her climax, and so am I, and suddenly I'm shuddering and grunting her name while she's coming around me, gripping my shoulders and pressing her neck into my fangs like she wants and loves every part of me, my light, my goodness, my dark side too.

We start to come apart together.

"Finn! Fuck! Yes!" she calls out as her pussy begins to tighten around me.

"Oh, April," I moan into her neck.

Her pussy spasms and clenches and then she's panting and moaning and gripping my shoulders, and I'm coming inside of her, filling her like I've always fucking wanted.

Once I stop seeing stars, I release my fangs, proud of myself for not taking any more than I wanted, no more than I needed to give her the ecstasy of The Bite.

"Wow," she says, as she slumps over me. Her beautiful warm soft body settling on my chest. Both our hearts racing.

"April," I say. "I love you."

She looks up and blinks away a tear. "I love you too."

"Okay, now can you please untie me so I can hold you? Maybe order us some room service?"

She laughs and reaches up to untie the ropes. "Maybe you can tie me up next," she says with a wink.

"We'd have to use regular rope though," I tell her, as I lick my fingers and close the wounds on her neck.

Her eyes flutter closed as I rub my saliva into the fang holes, healing them in an instant.

"What if you used this?" She grabs a tie from one of the robes and waves it around.

I just shake my head at her and grin.

I'm not scared anymore. I know I won't hurt her.

"Very fucking tempting," I say. "But I think it's a little soon for that."

She pouts those gorgeous lips at me.

"Baby, I promise. One day I'll take my turn to tie you up. But I'll do it loosely. So you can get away if you want to."

"Finn," she says. "I'm never going to want to get away."

CHAPTER SEVENTY-THREE

pril

Dear Diary,

Finn's only been gone a week, but I know that I'll never be the same. I know I'll never love anyone else but him. I feel like I'm dying. Like I can't breathe. I cry all the time, I'm so fucking sad!! But there's also a part of me that's happy! I know that sounds so dumb! But I'm so happy that I had Finn in my life, even if it was just for such a short time. I'm so grateful for every moment we had together, every kiss in the cornfield, every knowing look we exchanged in class.

It's the same way I feel about Mom. So fucking sad, but also so grateful that I had such an amazing mom, even if it wasn't long enough. I don't think Dad feels the same. I think he only has sadness. That's why I can't leave him. Without me, he'll have nothing left.

April xox

. . .

I KNOCK on my father's door. The door that I've walked through so many times without needing his permission. But things are different now. I no longer live here. I live in LA with Finn, in a gorgeous house in Malibu, just a few blocks away from Trix and Maverick. Finn didn't want to take my money, but it was non-negotiable for me to use the advance on my first book to at least pay for part of it.

"April." My father frowns at me. "And Finn."

"Sir," he says.

I didn't want to do this. It was all Finn's idea. I was happy to stay in LA, never come here again, but Finn's been going to therapy, and he thinks we should try to tie up all our loose ends before we begin our next chapter together.

And so here we are.

"Would you like to come in for some tea?" he asks, as if he didn't just tell me never to come back here only six months ago.

We go inside, and he makes the tea. It's the first time I think he's ever made me tea.

"What's all this about?" he asks, because god forbid, we're just here to see him.

"I'm here to ask for your daughter's hand in marriage," Finn says, taking my hand and giving it a squeeze.

"No," my father says. "Sorry, Finn, but you do not have my blessing."

I don't know whether to laugh or cry. "Dad," I say. "I love him. We're getting married whether or not we have your blessing."

My father just sits there and sulks.

"It's just a formality," Finn says. "I love your daughter, and she loves me. We've been so blessed to have found each other in this world. Love isn't always easy to find, and so when you find it, you have to hold on to it." Finn stands up, and I stand with him. "We are getting married, and we will start a family. And we want you to be a part of our children's lives. But only if you are willing to show a little love, compassion and forgiveness."

Love, compassion and forgiveness. All things my father has been preaching about his whole life, but unable to show to me, his own daughter.

"You're starting a family?" he asks.

I squeeze Finn's hand. "Yes, Dad. And there's nothing I want more than to bring my babies to church now and then and have them listen to their Granddaddy preach about love, compassion and forgiveness."

He lets out a sigh. "You've always been my greatest teacher, April," he says. "Do you know that?"

"No. I didn't."

"Being a father is very humbling." He takes a sip of tea and then looks up at me. "Fine. You have my blessing."

We have a way to go, my father and me. But this feels like a step forward, even if the road ahead is long.

"Are you sure you want to do this?" I ask Finn as we stand at his own father's door.

"Yes."

He places a bottle of bourbon on the mat and then steps back, turns and walks towards the car.

We don't stay and wait for his father to find it. We just trust that he will. We trust that Finn's dad won't question a free bottle of liquor. And we trust that the drops of Finn's blood that he put in the bottle will be enough to cure his dad from whatever his illness is.

And we hope that when he's cured, when he's given the miracle of a second chance, that he'll use it to turn his life around. Maybe he won't. But at least we tried.

"What next?" Finn asks when he's driving us away from

his old house, from our old lives. "Do you want to go see your mom at the churchyard?"

I shake my head and touch the cross at my neck. "I don't need to," I say with a smile. "I know she's always with me."

"Okay, so what do you want now?"

"I only want three things from you, Finn," I tell him.

"Yeah? And what are they?"

"First of all, I want a slice of pie from Lucky's diner."

"You're not worried about running into Clive?"

"No," I laugh. "Loretta told me he's met someone new. The woman who took my shifts when I left. Deena, I think her name is."

Finn huffs a laugh. "Well, I'm glad they found each other, and I hope he expands his sexual repertoire for her. What are the other two things you want?"

"I want to check in and have sex with you back at the motel. Pretend it's prom all over again."

"Sex, okay. Not going to complain about that. And what's the third thing?"

"I want you to know that you're going to be a father."

"Wait, what?" He slams on the brakes right by our old cornfield.

"Well, I found the sperm bank, and luckily for me, they still had some of yours."

His face turns pale, and for a second I worry I did the wrong thing, that I should have talked to him about this first.

"Wait, I don't think they're supposed to give out that information," Finn says. "How did you know it was mine?"

"Maverick came with me. He glamoured them into telling us."

"So, it is mine, and you're—"

"Yes, Finn. I'm pregnant."

Tears spring from Finn's eyes. "You're having my baby?"

I nod. "Yeah. I am."

He wraps his arms around me and sobs.

"But what about what I am?" he asks. "The fact that I'm immortal? I could lose you both, have to watch as you both age and—"

"That's a choice our children can make for themselves when the time comes," I tell him. "But I've already made mine. After I've popped out a whole hoard of kids, I want you to turn me."

He shakes his head. "It's not what you—"

She places a finger on my lips. "I've already decided. Finn, I want to be with you forever."

"April, you have always been my everything, and I'm going to give our children everything. Our children may not have human parents, but they will never question our love."

"Never," I say, wiping a tear from Finn's cheek. "Our kids are going to be so happy to have you as their dad."

Finn grins through his tears and presses his lips into mine. The kiss is salty, happy and hopeful, and just the start of our happily eternally ever after.

 oppy

ON OUR FIRST WEDDING ANNIVERSARY, Max bought me a rescue ranch in the mountains. We spend most of our time here now, looking after our aging horses, our crazy dogs, all our cats, including Callie, and a whole herd of goats that came with the ranch.

I love being here with the animals and with Max, but I also love that we have plenty of space for guests, and this weekend our best friends and found family are here to visit.

Trix hands me a bowl of potato salad and then hands out bowls of various other salads and breads to the three of her adopted boys, who should be old enough now to carry the bowls without breaking them. I hope.

Trix grabs a huge bowl of green salad and grins. "Thanks for having us all over. I know we're a lot."

I follow them out the back door. "A lot to love, and I love

having you all here for the weekend. I love seeing my nephews."

"Oh, Billy!" Trix calls out. "Hold it with both hands, sweetheart!"

We somehow make it outside with all bowls still in one piece. We place them on the long table between the bottles of synthetic blood that Max helped create and are now providing blood to the vampire community without the need to steal from blood banks.

All of our friends are here. Maverick has his youngest boy in his arms, his middle boy resting his head on his dad's shoulder. Heavily pregnant April — I swear that woman is always baking a baby — sits with Finn and their two little girls. Juliette Cortez and Brandon Curtis squeeze into the middle of the chaos, huge grins on their faces.

We've all been through so much together, but it's only made us closer and stronger. No one is out to get us now, and there's peace in that. There's peace in this place, with these people who have become my family. I never really had my own blood family, and now I have so many amazing people in my life that they can barely fit around this table.

"Tuck in!" Trix says, and everyone starts filling their plates.

Callie jumps up onto Max's lap and meows. He gives her a little treat from the table.

"You spoil that kitten," Maverick tells him.

"Callie is my daughter, and I will spoil her as much as I like," Max says, holding Callie in his arms. One of the things I love most about Max is that he feels the same way about the animals that I do. We don't have human children, but we have so many furry and fluffy ones that we love deeply. And all our nephews and nieces wear us out enough!

"So, what's next for us all?" I ask, piling my plate as high as I can with Trix's mushroom burgers, homemade bread and salads.

"I'm doing another movie," Trix says with a big grin.

"Yeah? I thought you were done with movies and just focusing on your TV show and books?" I ask.

"What can I say? I've got a taste for it." She glances at Maverick.

"And there's no way we can make *Double Agency 3* without her," he says. "Or Finn."

The *Double Agency* franchise has been a massive hit for all three of them.

Finn raises a fork in response. "You're just lucky I'm going to manage it with my busy schedule."

Maverick rolls his eyes, but Finn has been busy. The last few years have seen his career catapult. Brandon hired our favorite witch, Henrietta, for some remote work. She worked some magic on Finn's social media, and everyone quickly forgot about his two arrests and all the other drama. And now that he's a dad with two little girls, his fans only swoon after him even more!

"April has some big news," Finn says.

"I think we can see her big news," Maverick laughs.

Finn glares at him over the table. "*More* big news."

"They're going to make *The Fallen Star* into a movie," April says.

Everyone gasps and cheers and congratulates her. "That's incredible!" I say. Me and millions of other readers loved her second chance small town vampire romance.

Maverick's eyes narrow. "Do you really think a movie about vampires is a good idea?" he asks. "We don't really need the publicity."

"It's called art," says Max. "And besides, I'm going to be starring in it."

"Oh, Jesus," Maverick groans. "A vampire playing a

fucking vampire in a romance movie? This is the worst idea ever."

Brandon just laughs. "It's perfect," he says with a grin.

"I suppose you're producing it?" Maverick says.

"Yes. And if you play your cards right, I may consider you for the sequel."

Maverick broods over the table and stabs a piece of plant-loaf with his fork. "You should be so lucky."

"What about you, Poppy?" Trix asks. "What's next for you and Max?"

I look over at Max, Callie purring in his lap while he takes a bite of Trix's macaroni salad. He closes his eyes as he chews, enjoying every second of the bite. I smile at him and look around the table, then look out at the mountains around us. I have everything I've ever wanted. A family, animals to love and care for, and a man who I love in a way that I never even knew was possible. Max finishes chewing, opens his dazzling blue eyes and looks at me in the same way he did all those years ago when I nearly fell into his pool.

I look back at Trix and answer, "Hopefully, just an eternity of this."

~

IT'S NOT OVER YET!
Addicted to The Bite and want more?!
Get free access to a secret steamy scene:
Maverick and Trix fighting and making up at their Malibu mansion
Sign up for your exxxtra scene at:
https://dl.bookfunnel.com/olu24rb9ir

Please share the love!

If you have enjoyed this book, please consider leaving a review on Amazon and/or Goodreads, sharing on socials or telling a friend about it!

Tag me on socials so I can re-share and send you some love!

www.instagram.com/stormy.ohara

www.tiktok.com/@stormy.ohara

ABOUT THE AUTHOR

Stormy O'Hara is the alter ego and pen name of a well-known spiritual author who divides her time between writing stories, reading tarot and exploring ancient monuments in the Peak District of Derbyshire, where she currently lives.

Stormy believes in the magic, power, creativity and connection of the human heart, soul and spirit, and no generative AI is ever used in the creation of her books, covers or marketing materials.

www.stormyohara.com
www.instagram.com/stormy.ohara
www.tiktok.com/@stormy.ohara

ACKNOWLEDGMENTS

First of all, thank *you*, dear reader! Thank you for sticking with me on this journey through the Immortal Hollywood series! And if you've only read this book, guess what? There are two more waiting for you!

If you've read from the beginning and taken this whole wild ride with me, I am so incredibly grateful to have taken this journey with you by my side.

I am also so very grateful for all the love and support my new readers have shown me on socials, via email, by pre-ordering books and even just reaching and saying hi! I'm just an indie out here. It's all me, and I do actually read and reply to all my DMs and emails. Drop me a line anytime! I'd love to connect!

To my amazing beta readers who worked so damn hard on helping me make these books better and spicier! Sonya, Caz and Megan, your feedback on this final book was so helpful, and I am forever grateful!

And of course, a huge thank you to my inspiration, my rock, my first reader and the person who always supports all my crazy ideas! Ian, you are my everything! xxxx